REN'S SONG

G. KOI

This book is a work of fiction. Names, characters, places, and incidents are products of the author's imagination or are used factiously and are not to be construed as real. Any resemblance to actual events, locales, or organizations, or persons, living or dead, is entirely coincidental.

REN'S SONG Copyright ©2022 G. Koi. All rights reserved under International and Pan-American Copyright Conventions. By payment of the required fees, you have been granted the nonexclusive, nontransferable right to access and read the text of this e-book onscreen. No part of this text may be reproduced, transmitted, introduced into any information storage and retrieval system, in any form or by any means, whether electronic or mechanical, now known or hereinafter invented, without the express written permission of G. Koi.

Cover art by Natasha Snow.

Edited and proofed by Flat Earth Editing.

For the man with the apple.

FOREWORD

Congratulations!

You've just jumped into a China-based romance between two sexy actors. If you're new to this world, I have included footnotes and a glossary at the end to help with some of the Chinese and genre terms.

Don't worry, you'll catch on to all of this fast!

I hope you enjoy getting lost in this world with me.

G. Koi

1

WOW. HE'S BEAUTIFUL
REN AN XUE

Fuck. Fuck. Fuck.

How could he be late today? Of all freaking days, not today.

Ren An Xue bounced his leg, willing the car to move just a little bit faster now that they were through the worst of the traffic. How could he be late? He'd been ready to leave on time. No, he'd been ready *early*, but the car his manager had sent was late, and then traffic had been a freaking nightmare.

Not that he could walk into the room with a list of excuses falling off his tongue. He was supposed to be a professional.

His phone buzzed and he saw a text from his manager saying that the director had been notified of his imminent arrival, citing horrible traffic. At least Sun Jing didn't think he'd totally blown off today's introductory meeting as unimportant, but he was still going to make a bad first impression, and that was the one thing he'd not wanted.

Fuck. It wasn't as if he didn't already know he had no business being cast in the first place. When they'd started announcing plans for *Legend of the Lost Night*, word had gotten around fast that Chen Junjie was going to get one of the key roles. The man was endlessly talented, stunning, and one of the most in-demand actors in China right now. When he decided a role interested him, it was his. Done. Complete. Finished.

But as the main casting was closing up, news hit that Chen Junjie was dropped from the show. Ren thought he'd heard that it had something to do with COVID, but he wasn't sure if Chen had tested positive, or if there were new restrictions, or if it was an excuse because his attention had drifted elsewhere.

Whatever the reason, Ren's manager had moved the heavens themselves to get him the audition. He'd practiced for the reading for countless hours with Zhou Yuying, but in the end, it was her closing words to him as she'd sent him into the audition that stuck.

"Don't forget to show off those big puppy eyes!" Zhou Yuying had said with a pat on his shoulder, catching him off guard.

And that was it.

He'd answered their questions, read the part, and was careful to bat his big chestnut-brown puppy eyes, had even added a tiny pout of the bottom lip. The producer had squealed and the director had nodded with a grin. He'd gotten the role because of his fucking eyes.

Whatever. The job was his now, and he was going to prove to everyone that he deserved to have it.

The car pulled up to the front of the production offices, and he leaped from the rear seat before it completely stopped moving. His backpack banged against his spine and his running shoes slapped the concrete as he dodged a few people and plunged into the revolving doors.

He paused inside the dark lobby and blinked his eyes a couple of times to get them to adapt to the shadows after the bright afternoon sunlight that gilded Shanghai. Just as the world of marble floors and silver elevators came into focus, he spotted a woman with a phone pressed to her ear, frantically waving at him. She looked vaguely familiar. Maybe the assistant he'd seen with the director, Sun, the day of the audition?

Didn't matter. He nodded and hurried to her side. The second he moved, she was off at a brisk walk. They caught the elevator and rode it silently up to the tenth floor. When the doors slid open, she started running and Ren followed, his longer legs easily eating up the distance.

Late. Late. Late. He was so fucking late on his first day.

The assistant stopped at a door and pulled it open. Ren burst inside and came to a sharp halt as nearly three dozen sets of eyes snapped on him and stopped.

Oh, God. They were all staring. He was the last to arrive. They knew he had no business being there.

"Ren! You made it!" Sun Jing boomed, shattering the tense silence of the room and snapping Ren from his sudden paralysis.

"I'm so sorry. So very sorry," he blurted out, bowing to Sun Jing and then a second time to the entire room.

Sun Jing laughed, a deep, friendly sound that was almost a hug. A meaty hand slapped him on the shoulder and gently eased him back to standing. "No need for any of that. We're still settling in. Today's nothing formal. I wanted the main crew together so we could all start getting to know each other."

Yes, he knew the schedule. The meeting was supposed to last a few hours as they went over the production timeline and made introductions followed by a table reading of a handful of scenes to give the cast a chance to interact a little. Nothing formal.

Except this was already so big.

Legend of the Lost Night was a wuxia[1] costume drama, and he'd done all contemporary shows up until now. Most of them had been light and fluffy romantic comedies with small casts and crews. This was huge for him, and this was only the principal cast members. There were going to be dozens of supporting actors and hundreds of crew members.

He'd been so lost in that thought that he hadn't realized Sun Jing was leading him to the last open seat until he was standing next to it.

Or rather, he was standing facing his costar, Song Wei Li. The man gazed up at him, his face completely expressionless, and Ren's frazzled brain could cough up one thing alone: *Wow. He's beautiful.*

"And now we have both of our stars," Sun Jing announced proudly as Ren collapsed into the empty chair. The second Sun stepped away, returning to his seat, an assistant rushed over and dropped a stack of papers in front of him along with a bottle of water.

Ren shoved aside chaotic thoughts about his costar's stunning looks and focused on his job as best he could. He listened with half an ear as the director and producer took turns talking about their excitement and expectations for *Legend*. Ren took a couple of seconds to glance through the papers he'd been given that listed times, dates, and locations for a variety of things. Before they could even start filming, there would be fittings and some initial promotional photography as they experimented with the appearance of the main characters. Then it would be at least two weeks of training sessions such as fight training, wire training, elocution lessons, and more. That didn't include the week of table readings they had ahead of them.

Oh, God. He'd agreed to do wire work[2].

Of course he'd known that. Nearly every wuxia had characters who could fly. And he was going to be one of them.

Great, gangly awkward thing that he was.

This was a mistake. They were going to regret ever hiring him. If he didn't break his neck, they were going to fire his ass so fast.

A different voice cut through the room, and Ren's head

snapped up to see someone else speaking. The head cinematographer was introducing himself. He sat and the woman next to him stood, introducing herself as the head of costuming. They were going around the room.

He didn't think it was possible, but his anxiety jumped even higher. He wasn't ready to do this. He'd been hoping to spend a little more time sinking into the quiet, letting everyone forget that he existed before he had to call attention to himself again.

Pressing his sweaty palms into his pants, he rubbed his thighs while wondering if his sweat was already soaking into his shirt to noticeable levels. It was warm for late March, but not nearly warm enough for the amount of sweating he was doing.

The tables were arranged in a huge square, and he was in the dead center with Song Wei Li, directly opposite the director and producers. Too quickly, they made it around the table and Song stood next to him.

"Hello, I'm Song Wei Li, and I'm going to be playing the part of Tian Xiuying. I'm looking forward to working with everyone." The man's voice was surprisingly deep and smooth, like water swiftly flowing over worn boulders in a stream. For just a couple of heartbeats, it was enough to distract Ren from his mini panic attack, and then Song sat and stared expectantly at him.

Shit! Yes, introductions.

Ren shot to his feet and offered a shallow bow to the room. "Hi. I'm Zhao Gang and I'm—" A muffled laugh alerted him to what had come out of his mouth. He could feel the flush burning his cheeks as he cleared his throat to try again. "I mean, I'm Ren An Xue, and I'm going to be playing the part of Zhao Gang. Thank you."

He sat as quickly as he could, praying the floor would open up beneath him and swallow him whole.

It didn't.

Instead, Song smirked at him, one dark eyebrow lifted. "Getting lost in your character already?" he whispered. "A bit early, don't you think?"

Ren couldn't think of anything to say. He didn't know Song. Didn't know if the man was giving him a bit of friendly teasing or genuinely mocking him. All he could do was offer up a crooked smile, then turn his attention to other introductions.

Luckily, the rest of the meeting went easily enough. No one required him to say or do anything for at least an hour, which was enough time to recover from the worst of his mortification and concentrate on the job ahead of him.

Legend of the Lost Night might not have a big budget, but it was clear that the crew was highly experienced. They would know how to get the most from each shot and keep things moving smoothly.

Ren had a lot riding on this role. It wasn't just that *Legend* was wuxia, which were hugely popular right now, but it was that *Legend of the Lost Night* was also based on an insanely popular danmei[3] that had an enormous and ravenous fan base. While they'd never be able to get a tenth of the more romantic moments past the censors, there was still a good chance they could keep the fans happy and potentially launch his career to the next level.

He had to finally get himself out of fluffy hell.

He wanted more serious roles. He wanted to play someone gritty and darker. He wanted something that would force him to stretch his skills.

And Zhao Gang offered that and so much more. It was why he'd worked his ass off to land this role. Fuck it if he got it for his damn puppy eyes. He was making this *his*.

The pep talk helped to restore his sense of balance by the time they got to reading some of the scenes. There was nothing too intense. Zhao Gang was able to playfully tease Tian Xiuying, flustering the man. Ren also had a few pages with the female costar he was going to be playing with. Sun gave some early instructions to help Ren and Song get into the heads of their characters before they moved on to some of the other actors.

The meeting closed up with talk about training that was going to start in a week. The room filled with groans, and Ren sent up a silent prayer of thanks that he religiously went to the gym every day. With any luck, it would give him a tiny advantage over those who didn't, but he wasn't counting on it. He had to be one of the least coordinated people on the planet, and very soon everyone was going to see regular proof of it.

Ren picked up the papers he'd been handed and skimmed over the training schedule. As he'd expected, there was fight training, martial arts training, and wire training. The odder classes were for elocution and posture. They were supposed to teach him how to stand, bow, and talk? Seriously?

Oh, and he had fan training.

Ugh. Yes. Zhao Gang's weapon of choice was a fucking fan.

This guy was supposed to be a badass psycho killer, and he used a freaking fan. How was this supposed to be intimidating?

Of course, Song and many of the other actors got to use swords. They even had sword training.

And while they were in sword training, Ren was going to learn how to use his fan…and flute training? That was new. He was supposed to play the flute? That wasn't in the book. He'd read the book cover to cover, *twice*. There was no flute.

This had to be a misprint. Maybe there was another character, like his female costar Ma Daiyu.

As the meeting broke up, Ren jumped to his feet with the schedule in hand. He exchanged pleasant comments with the other actors and crew as he made his way to Sun's side. He wasn't looking to make waves or complain at all. He only needed to confirm that this wasn't a mistake.

Sun grinned at him when Ren reached him through all the

people slowly leaving the room. "What do you think? Excited to get started?"

"Yes, definitely," Ren replied, and it was the absolute truth. He couldn't wait to jump into work even if he was scared out of his mind. "I have a question about the training schedule. It says I have flute lessons. I don't remember Zhao Gang playing the flute…"

"Oh, that." Sun waved a dismissive hand and chuckled lightly, which didn't seem reassuring in the least. "It's a recent revision to the script. Zhao is going to play the flute a few times. We think it'll help give him a softer side. You know, between all the killing he does."

Yeah, because the fan doesn't make him soft enough.

Not that Ren would dare say that out loud. He just had sword envy. His first wuxia and he didn't even get to use a sword. *What the hell!*

"Okay, but I'm not sure I can relearn that fast," Ren said a bit hesitantly.

"No! No! You don't have to learn how to play. This is to make sure you look convincing." Sun suddenly stopped and blinked at him. "Relearn?"

Ren nodded. "I played some when I was young. I haven't picked up a flute in probably fifteen years."

"Ah. No problem. This will be a quick brush-up for you then. Oh! Before I forget." Sun whipped around and dug through his bag for something. When he turned back, it was to hand Ren a large, white folding fan. "There. From now on, have this with you at all times. I want it to become an extension of your body. This thing is a core piece of your character. It is as much you as Tian Xiuying will be a part of your soul."

Ren stared at the thing in his hand, knowing he wasn't doing a great job of hiding his skepticism. A fan. A symbol of this dangerous, broken hero was a fan.

"Snap it open."

Ren's head jumped up to see Song watching him through

narrowed eyes. The same smirk was pulling up one corner of his mouth. "Snap it open," he repeated. Confused, Ren started to reach over with the hand holding the schedule to open it, but Song shook his head. "No. One-handed. Snap it open."

Pinching one side of the fan, Ren gave it a hard flick with his wrist, opening it in a flash. A crack echoed like a sudden crash of thunder. The room had been filled with a low murmur of conversation, but it was now completely silent.

It was nothing compared to watching Song's smirk morph into a slow, beautiful smile that added a twinkle to those lush, dusky eyes. Ren swore he'd been kicked in the chest. He couldn't breathe. Couldn't even think.

"Just imagine Zhao Gang is irritated with me," Song teased. He gave a shake of his head and then turned to leave. "See you in a week, didi[4]," he called out as a parting shot.

Ren was vaguely aware of Sun Jing jogging after Song as he left the meeting room, but everything around him was white noise. His brain was still lost in that smile that was shorting out his ability to think, to function as a human being.

How in the world was he going to spend the next five months with this man?

He'd known Song was hot, but this…this was so much worse.

He was fucked.

Seriously, hopelessly…fucked.

2

SONG AND SMART ARE NO LONGER ACQUAINTED
SONG WEI LI

HE HAD TO GET OUT OF THAT ROOM.

Oh God, he had to get outside and into some fresh air before he said anything else, proving what an ass he really was.

He definitely blamed Ren An Xue. When the man stopped by the empty chair next to him and Song had looked up, his first thought should *not* have been, *Fuck, you're gorgeous.*

Why couldn't his brain have gone with tall? Ren was ridiculously tall, topping six feet easily. His own height was a relatively average five eleven, which meant he was going to spend the next five months staring up at that face.

But no, his traitorous brain had gone straight to gorgeous, and then started cataloguing all the parts that made him so very exquisite.

Full, pouty lips.

Enormous chestnut-brown eyes.

High cheekbones.

Strong nose.

Adorable round chin.

And every freaking emotion zipping across his extremely expressive features in the blink of an eye for Song to read.

He made one teasing comment and Ren had flashed this

wounded look at him, leaving Song feeling like he'd kicked a puppy.

That should have taught him right there not to talk to Ren An Xue yet. At least not until he had no choice, but no, he couldn't help making one more comment. A smart man would have simply left.

Song and smart were no longer acquainted, thanks to Ren An Xue.

But he couldn't just leave.

The poor guy had been staring at the fan as though someone had handed him a feather duster to fight with. He wasn't thinking about all the things his character would be able to express with that one prop. He'd been handed *a gift*, not a curse. Ren couldn't see that yet.

The second that *snap* had echoed through the suddenly silent room, those wide eyes lifted and Song's freaking heart fluttered in his chest.

Trouble. Ren was trouble.

Song had run. He wasn't proud of it, but he at least recognized that it was the wise thing to do. Retreat and gather reinforcements. Clear his mind. Get focused on the job ahead of him.

With his trusty assistant, Mo Bao Shi, at his side, Song was out of the room and halfway down the hall before he heard the director calling for him.

Inwardly cursing his luck, Song clung to his most easy-going smile as he stopped and turned toward Sun Jing. The portly man with thinning black hair slung an arm around his shoulder and grinned that one grin he used when he wanted something. This was not their first TV series together. It was their third, and Sun was half the reason Song had signed on. They had a good working relationship; they understood what they wanted from each other when it came to different scenes.

"Lao[1] Song, I need a favor," Sun started immediately.

Song lost his smile and rolled his eyes. It had to be a big

favor if Sun was calling him *Lao* Song. "Can I go ahead and say no?"

"No, you can't, because this is going to make your life and my life easier in the long run," Sun argued. They had resumed walking down the hall toward the elevators. Sun's voice was low so they couldn't be overheard, and Song's assistant had moved several feet ahead to give them at least the illusion of privacy.

"What do you want?"

"I want you to take Ren An Xue under your wing for this production. Watch out for him. Be his laoshi[2]."

Song closed his eyes and gathered his strength. He didn't want to be Ren An Xue's teacher because that was going to mean being close to the man for more than just their scenes. Of course, the idea of trying to keep his distance was ridiculous. They were the leads. *Romantic* leads. They needed chemistry, and that came from becoming comfortable with each other.

"Aren't we the same age? Isn't that a little awkward for me to assume the role of laoshi?" he asked, opening his eyes to give Sun a very pointed look.

"You're a year older, but you've also been doing this twice as long as he has." Sun's grin turned into a knowing smirk. "You've done the costume dramas and the wire work. He hasn't. This is a completely new world for him, and I don't want him so overwhelmed that he can't get his head in his character. Zhao Gang is complex enough."

Song quickly glanced over his shoulder to make sure no one was around to hear him. Even when he spoke, his voice was a rough whisper. "Why did you cast him if you were this worried?"

Sun made a dismissive sound. "I'm not worried. He has Zhao Gang nailed, crazy and soft parts. He's going to be perfect opposite you. I want to smooth the way for him some, and you can help with that in a huge way. You know it, Lao Song."

A loud, heavy sigh escaped Song, and Sun cackled because he knew he'd won. But Sun was also right. Ren needed help, or he was going to feel like he was drowning for the next five months. Song didn't wish that on anyone. And no one was going to get the best out of Ren if he was floundering to keep his head above water the entire time.

"I'll keep an eye on him," Song agreed.

"Besides," Sun drawled, giving Song a look that could only be described as evil. "I need chemistry. Hot. Shippable. Chemistry."

Song snorted, trying to ignore the anxious tremble in his stomach while he shrugged off Sun's arm and stepped free of the man. Sun stopped and Song turned to walk backward so he could face the director as he said, "You just worry about getting all this chemistry past the censors."

The director rolled his eyes and waved a hand at Song before heading toward the meeting room.

When Song swung around, it was to find Bao Shi holding the elevator for him. He slipped inside and leaned heavily against the wall. He reached into his pocket and pulled out a black mask that would cover up the lower half of his face. He slipped it into place. The production company was good about keeping the fans at bay, but the added anonymity helped to ease some of the lingering tension in his shoulders.

"You worried?" Song lifted his eyes to his friend, one eyebrow lifted in question. Bao Shi jerked his chin in the direction of the meeting room. "About the new guy."

Song shook his head. "Nah. I'm sure he'll be fine. Sun Jing knows what he's doing."

He closed his eyes and let the soft hum of the elevator soothe his rattled nerves.

They had started the moment he'd let Sun talk him into the role of Tian Xiuying, the broken and dying hero of *Legend of the Lost Night*. He'd liked the idea of playing the dark hero with the troubled past filled with horrible events and bad decisions. It had definitely been his mindset at the time.

At least it wasn't another cold, emotionally distant, and lonely prince. He'd done that role so many times he was terrified of becoming pigeonholed in that same spot for the rest of his life.

Legend being based on a BL[3] novel wasn't a problem either. Several BL-based shows had come out in the past few years and become explosive hits, launching all the leads to astounding heights in the entertainment world. This was a good potential stepping-stone for his career.

It wasn't as if he'd need to kiss his costar. With Chinese censors ready to stomp on anything remotely homosexual, Song was going to be lucky to be standing within a foot of Ren.

Shame, since Ren had what looked to be very kissable lips.

Song's eyes snapped open, and he straightened as that image slithered through his mind. He had *not* thought that. *Nope. No fucking way.*

"You okay?" Bao Shi inquired when he jerked upright.

"Yeah. Just tired," Song said while silently cursing himself. He was tired. Definitely tired. That was all it was. Tired. He'd been keeping a ridiculously busy pace the past year—filming, interviews, recording his album, photo shoots, product promotions, and even a few small singing performances. He honestly couldn't remember the last time he'd simply taken a day off and done nothing but read or watch TV.

"Well, you've got one interview, and you're done for the day."

Bao Shi was trying to be reassuring and supportive, but another interview where he had to plaster a smile on his face and give a bunch of canned answers sounded like hell. He wanted to return to his apartment, crawl under the blankets in a dark room, and stay there until he had to report to the first full day of table reading. Then it was on to training. At least Sun Jing was letting him skip the wire training and the beginner sword training. He'd done enough costume dramas and wuxias at this point to be capable of teaching the courses.

Within a matter of minutes, Bao Shi had him tucked in a car and was whisking him across town to whatever interview he was scheduled for.

Behind the heavily tinted windows, Song removed his mask and pulled out his cell phone. He checked for urgent messages from his team, but there was nothing that needed his immediate attention. He started to open one of the social media apps but closed it again. Instead, he turned the phone over so that the screen was pressed to his thigh.

Leaning his head back, he closed his eyes and tried to relax for a few minutes.

Against his better judgment, he let his mind wander to Ren An Xue.

When Sun told him that Ren had been hired to star opposite him, Song hadn't felt anything. He hadn't heard of the guy, hadn't known anything about him. A quick search online revealed that he'd done a handful of TV shows, been the main lead a couple of times, but nothing like what they were filming now.

And yes, he was good-looking. Weren't they all supposed to be? All his costars—both men and women—had been beautiful. Why would he think Ren would be any different?

Except he was.

He didn't know how or why, but he was.

The moment Song had gazed up into those enormous brown eyes, he'd felt utterly lost. He couldn't speak, couldn't smile, couldn't do anything but stare at him.

And then, Ren had looked away. The eye-contact broken, Song had felt as if Ren had stolen something, part of his soul had left him and he wasn't sure how to get it back.

Even now, in the safety of the car, miles growing between them, Song felt like there was a hole left behind.

What the fuck was happening?

He'd never reacted this way to anyone.

Ren An Xue was no one.

Or at least he had been until today.

Starting in May, they were going to be costars and would spend countless hours together over the next four months, away from the rest of the world, in Hengdian[4]. He couldn't lose any more of himself to this man.

3

WOULD YOU PREFER IF I CALLED YOU AH-XUE?
REN AN XUE

Ren hobbled into the wardrobe department. Everything hurt. Legs, arms, back, stomach. Even his fingernails hurt. How was that even possible?

For the past five days, he'd been in intense training for general fighting, martial arts, and wire work.

All of it was a nightmare.

As he'd always known, he was the most uncoordinated person on the planet. The proof was that the instructor had pulled him aside for additional training because he was progressing so much slower than the other actors. So instead of the usual eight-hour training sessions, he was now putting in ten hours.

The only reason he wasn't drenched in sweat and listening to trainers bark at him was that he was due for a series of costume fittings. His first few outfits were ready along with a wig.

This break was a blessing. He'd get to see exactly how they envisioned his character for the first time. He was one step closer to sinking into the mind and soul of Zhao Gang, and he couldn't wait. He just wished he didn't hurt so bad.

As he entered the room, he immediately stopped when his

gaze landed on Song Wei Li in one of the chairs in front of the mirror. He hadn't expected to see Song here. He'd caught glimpses of him yesterday and earlier in the day, working on his own training, but they hadn't actually spoken. Even when they'd done the days of table readings, they never had what Ren would call a real conversation. Only tense pleasantries about the weather and traffic.

Song was currently staring at his phone, humming softly to himself as a hair stylist worked on arranging his long black wig.

Those dark eyes suddenly looked up and met his in the mirror. They held there for a heartbeat, and Ren completely forgot about the pain coursing through his entire frame. It was as if they were frozen, and he wasn't sure what to do or say. Should he leave? It felt as though he was invading Song's privacy, even if he had been specifically sent to get his fitting.

But then Song smiled, and it was as though Ren's lungs had been given permission to work again.

"Finally escape?" Song inquired.

A soft whimper jumped from Ren's throat before he could catch it. Song laughed, a bright and lively sound that filled the room and left Ren feeling lighter.

"I swear it gets easier," Song promised when he stopped chuckling.

One of the hair-and-makeup artists hurried over and ushered him into the chair next to Song's. He managed to give Song a warning glare, but the man only dissolved into an adorable fit of giggles.

"Really, Song laoshi? You *really* think it's going to get easier?" Ren demanded as he dropped carefully into the chair. "I'm sure you saw me out there. It's not pretty."

Ren watched closely as an interesting variety of emotions crossed Song's face. He tried, but he couldn't completely hide the fact that he had seen Ren struggling with the fight training and the wire work. It was as though Ren couldn't properly control his arms and legs at the same time. The moment he concentrated on moving his arms a certain way, his legs went into business for themselves and tried to wander off.

"I know it doesn't seem like it, but it will," Song replied with surprising gentleness. "You're trying to cram a lot of training and experiences into a short amount of time. When it comes to shooting the actual scenes, it will be a little easier. Plus, we'll have stunt doubles to help in spots."

Ren grunted softly, letting his body relax as the stylist started pinning and arranging his hair so she could pull on the wig he'd be wearing. He'd never had to wear a wig before, let alone one that would give him long, silky black hair that hung down the length of his back. He couldn't begin to guess what he'd look like, but he was curious.

He slowly slid his eyes across the mirror to find Song staring at his phone. With his attention gone, Ren could watch the man in the wig, admiring the way his long bangs framed his face. At the very least, he wanted to be as handsome as Song in his costume.

Ren shifted his eyes to find Song watching him in the mirror, a knowing smile on his lips. *Fuck. He was caught.*

Ren opened his mouth to apologize or say something that didn't sound stupid, but Song spoke first.

"Song laoshi?" he said in a teasing tone.

"Oh. That." Ren dropped his attention to his hands. His fingers were tangled together in his lap and he wished he'd been smart enough to pull his phone out of his pocket so he had something to do rather than stare like an idiot at his costar.

"Sun talk to you?"

Ren jerked his eyes to the mirror, meeting Song's sable gaze. The tips of his ears were starting to burn. "He did. He thought...since you've done all of this before...you'd be a good resource for me. But I don't want to trouble you."

Song chuckled. "I don't mind. It'll make both of our lives easier. Ask me anything you want, didi."

Ren's nose wrinkled. That was the second time Song had called him "didi." He forcefully ignored the way it made his heart flip and aimed for annoyed. "You know I'm only a year younger than you, right?"

Song's smirk returned. "Yes. Would you prefer if I called you Ah-Xue[1]? Or maybe Ren laoshi?"

Ren pressed his lips together. Nothing in this world would make him admit out loud that he actually liked it when Song called him didi. Ah-Xue wasn't much better. There was something about the breathless, lazy way it rolled off Song's tongue that sounded almost intimate.

He directed his gaze straight ahead to his own reflection, refusing to look at Song. But it didn't matter. The man's wild laughter once again filled the room. Only this time it was cut short by the stylist, who was trying to fix his hair without him moving around so much.

Song apologized, sounding partially chastened, with some lingering giggles.

They fell silent for a time and Ren closed his eyes, letting the quiet of the room soak into his soul. Some of the aches and pains were easing at last.

Beside him, the stylist told Song he could change into his first outfit. There was a shift in the seat and an unexpected rattle of what sounded like a bottle of pills.

Ren opened his eyes to see Song holding a white bottle right in front of his nose. "Take two. It'll help with the muscle ache."

Song opened his hand and the pill bottle dropped. Ren just barely managed to catch it before it tumbled to the floor.

"Oh. Thanks."

Song smirked and then disappeared, moving to the next room so he could change. The stylist got Ren a bottle of water, and he swallowed two little pills that looked like nothing more than ibuprofen.

He glanced at the mirror to find that his wig was in place and the change in his reflection was startling. This was Zhao Gang. Harsh, determined, and just maybe...seductive. Was this the man who was a shameless flirt? The man who relentlessly chased Tian Xiuying while slaughtering his enemies on all sides? The man who crossed any and every line?

Anything to keep his Ah-Ying safe.

The stylist gave him a pat and directed him to the next room to change as well.

Ren rose in something of a daze and went where he was told. As he entered, he heard a sweet voice singing behind a curtain.

Was...was that Song?

He didn't get the chance to figure it out. A costumer grabbed his elbow and pulled him behind a different curtain. She handed one item after another, instructing him exactly how to put them on. He wanted to tell her that it wasn't necessary. He might be a complete newbie, but he knew how to put on clothes.

Except they kept coming. Layer after layer.

He'd heard about the layers, but when he was on the third robe and second tie, he was about to cry out that she had to be joking with him. This couldn't be real. So many clothes.

But before he could say anything, she was ordering him to come out so she could check over everything. The costume jiejie[2] fell on him in a heartbeat, tugging at pieces and smoothing others, getting his hanfu[3] to lie exactly how it was supposed to. She moved around to the back, tugging free strands of his wig that had gotten caught under the layers.

Ren barely noticed. His eyes were locked on Song. The man was standing in front of a trio of mirrors, wrapped in robes of varying shades of blue and pale gray. The hanfu was simple in comparison to his own, but the blue complimented Song's pallid complexion, making him stunning.

Song met his eyes in the mirror and then dropped to take in his pure white attire. There was subtle white stitchwork of bamboo stalks and leaves covering it. He didn't know if he was prepared for a funeral or appearing as a vengeful ghost in these robes.

"Not bad, didi," Song murmured in appreciation.

The costumer stepped in front of him and placed a matching white fan into the palm of his hand.

With a slow smile, Ren flicked the fan open and lazily moved it as he crossed to stand beside Song in front of the mirror. Something about the white made him appear even taller next to the man, though there were only two to three inches difference between them.

Ren stared at his own reflection, and he couldn't help noticing that his shoulders were a little straighter, his entire posture more erect. Even his facial expression was different. The robes had helped him take yet another step into the character of Zhao Gang. It was as though he could feel the man's confidence, his innate smugness settling into his frame.

He directed his smile at Song. "You look beautiful, Ah-Ying." Song's eyes widened and snapped to his in the mirror. He swallowed hard, and Ren felt his own smile become a touch more predatory, his gaze sharpening. He thickened the honey in his tone as he continued, "Can I call you Ah-Ying? I have a feeling that we're going to become…*close*…friends over the next several weeks."

Song ripped his eyes away and turned his attention to his own robes, but Ren didn't miss the little shudder than ran through his slender body. "No. No, you can't call me that," he grumbled.

Ren nearly apologized but stopped when he caught the tiniest quirk of Song's lips as if he were fighting a smile. That was Song's character. Tian Xiuying was a gruff and grumpy man of few words. He fought and pushed against Zhao Gang's advances for pages before he finally started to unbend and welcome his friendship.

Well, in the book, he welcomed a lot more than friendship, but they weren't going to be filming those parts.

Ren never got the chance to continue with his teasing. The costumer was quick to shove them out of the room and down the hall for photographs.

Ren released a giggle and twirled ahead of Song, allowing the robe to flare out around him. All the layers were a bit heavy, but there was such an elegant flow, a natural grace, that he couldn't help sinking into Zhao Gang's mind.

"Enjoy it while you can, because you're going to learn to hate these robes," Song's voice cut through his thoughts.

Ren stopped and stared at his companion who was lagging. "What do you mean? They're beautiful."

Song snorted. "They're not bad now. In a building. That's air-conditioned." The shorter man closed the distance between them, an evil look spreading across his face. "But imagine spending hours in them, outside, in the sun, during the height of summer."

Oh, God.

This was going to be bad. So very bad. He was going to melt into a puddle of sweat and grossness. And that was if he didn't faint from becoming overheated.

He was supposed to act in all that?

Song suddenly grabbed his forearm, snapping him from those ugly thoughts. "Do you have a portable hand fan?"

Not thinking, Ren held up the fan that was already in his hand.

Song shook his head. "No, one of those battery-operated ones."

Ren blinked at him, trying to get his brain working when all he could feel was Song's strong hand burning through countless layers of fabric to brand his skin. "I-I think so."

"Get one. No, get *three*! They are the difference between life and death in the Hengdian sun."

Song released him and continued down the hall, leaving Ren to catch up. Acting in the summer sun in all these clothing layers. He was so very screwed.

In the next room, they were photographed together and separate. For now, the threat of the heat and sun was forgotten in the face of teasing. This time, Song started it, making fun of Ren's height, but the man was quickly flustered when Ren slipped into the character of Zhao Gang and shot back with his own flirtatious teasing.

Ren hated to admit that it was easier to interact with Song when he was behind the mask of Zhao Gang. His character could get away with saying outrageous things while Ren would be completely tongue-tied and embarrassed to utter those words. Zhao Gang offered him confidence and indifference to the opinions of others. He was a coat of armor.

With a round of photos completed, they were sent to the costume jiejie for another outfit change and then more photos.

At the end of two hours, Ren felt his energy flagging. He'd spent the first half of his day in training, and while the pills he'd taken earlier had removed the last of his aches and pains, he was still tired. It also didn't help that it felt like his scalp was on fire. He wanted to shift and itch and scrape his nails across his head, but he couldn't risk his perfectly arranged wig.

"You okay, didi?" Song inquired suddenly.

Ren was in the middle of solo photographs. Song had just finished, but it seemed as though he was waiting around for Ren to finish his last ones so they could leave together.

Ren grunted, trying to hold his serious facial expression and tilt his head in the photographer's direction. "I think I'm not used to the wig. It feels like my head is on fire."

Song's face became deathly serious. He crossed in front of Ren, completely ignoring the protests of the photographer. "That's not right." Turning Ren slightly, he tugged and pulled at the back of the wig with nimble fingers. It was only a second before Song was muttering an ugly curse and pulling Ren down the hall toward the hair-and-makeup artists.

"What's wrong?" Ren asked, his stomach twisting up. He'd never seen such an angry expression slashing across Song's face. What had he done to upset his costar? He needed to fix this.

When they hurried into the room, the stylist jumped to her feet from where she'd been seated, waiting for them. Song shoved Ren into the empty chair. "Hurry up and get the wig off him. He's allergic to the glue," Song barked out.

Both Ren and the stylist gasped.

"What?" Ren choked out.

Song's expression instantly softened. He released Ren's arm and patted his hand a couple of times. "You shouldn't have that burning sensation. You've got the start of a pretty bad rash on your head. I've seen it with some other costars. You're allergic to either the material of the wig or the glue. It's probably the glue, though. I'll see about getting you something to help."

And then Song was gone, disappearing through the door.

Ren watched in the mirror as the stylist carefully removed the wig to reveal that the area around his hairline and into his scalp was turning bright red. Fantastic. That looked like shit. He was going to need a ton of makeup to mask it. And that didn't even begin to cover the itching that was kicking in.

The stylist apologized profusely, but Ren easily waved it off. She hadn't known. Hell, he hadn't even known he was allergic. He'd never had to wear a wig for his other productions.

Song breezed into the room a minute later, half out of his last costume and growling orders into his cell phone. He ended the call and flopped into the chair next to Ren, worry filling his eyes.

"Is it that bad, Song laoshi?" Ren asked.

Song sighed. "The jiejies will be able to hide the rash with makeup, but you're going to be miserable. You have to wear the wig, and there aren't a lot of options for the glue. I've got my assistant running down the medic. There's a prescription you can take to help with the allergic reaction. I've heard it can get rid of the worst of the itching and burning."

"Thank you, Song laoshi."

A little smile played on Song's lips. He reached across the short distance between them and patted Ren's hand again. That touch burned his skin, but it was so much more pleasant than the burning of his scalp. No, this was sweeter and so much more intense.

Those slender, nimble fingers were rougher than he'd been expecting, lightly scraping across his flesh.

But before Ren could wonder at that touch, Song was drawing his fingers away, back to his own lap and his phone, as if he'd forgotten about Ren's existence completely.

That was for the best. Their costumes were coming off. They were leaving behind the flirtatious Zhao Gang and the grumpy, ruffled Tian Xiuying. They were once again the awkward Ren An Xue and the teasing, confident Song Wei Li. Two men who had nothing in common.

Yes, that was for the best.

Otherwise, Ren might start to wonder about Song's touch. About the way those dark eyes watched him move. Or about how those perfect lips parted in a delicious sigh when Zhao flirted with him.

That way led to madness and trouble.

4

DRUNK REN IS TROUBLE, TROUBLE, TROUBLE

SONG WEI LI

Song gripped his phone with both hands between his legs, willing the butterflies in his stomach to disappear. This was fucking ridiculous. What was his problem?

Oh, he knew exactly what his problem was. It was Ren An Xue and his adorably flushed face.

Today was their last day in Shanghai before they would travel to Hengdian and start shooting. At Sun Jing's urging, much of the main cast had gone out to dinner to celebrate their last night of "freedom." Tomorrow, they belonged to Sun Jing as well as the assistant directors, makeup artists, costumers, and anyone else who wanted to boss them around to get that perfect shot.

A cast dinner was nothing out of the ordinary. He'd been to plenty and had made pleasant small talk with all of his fellow actors over good food and drinks.

But after the first round, he'd figured out that Liu Haoyu was going to be trouble. The actor had eagerly plopped into the seat next to Ren and proceeded to poke and prod the man into drink after drink. Ma Daiyu wasn't much better, but she didn't seem to have the same level of alcohol tolerance as Liu and had quickly backed down after the third round.

The moment Ren's smile became even the tiniest bit crooked, Liu was all hands. They fluttered about Ren, caressing his shoulders and grabbing his arm. At first, Ren beamed and slipped away, but as more drinks were served, he appeared to notice it less.

Now, at end of the dinner, Song was ready to smash a beer bottle over Liu's head, but that thought evaporated from his mind when Ren turned to him with those big puppy eyes of his and held up his phone.

"Could you help me call a taxi, Song laoshi?"

Oh God, for those eyes he was pretty sure he'd carry Ren's big, gangly body wherever the fuck he wanted to go.

"You don't have a car picking you up?" Song managed to ask when the two brain cells he had left decided to work.

Ren flashed him the dopiest grin and shook his head. Fuck, this man was so freaking drunk.

Liu immediately slung an arm across Ren's slumped shoulders and pulled him in close. "Don't worry, Ren An Xue. I can make sure you get to your hotel safely. You don't want to bother Song."

Something like panic cut through Ren's eyes, and Song jumped to his feet. Yep, those last two brain cells were now gone, and he was working purely on caveman instincts. And those instincts were screaming *His* and *Protect*.

Grabbing Ren's arm, he hauled Ren out of Liu's touch and up to his feet. "I've got him. My car is already waiting. Or did you miss the part where he called me his laoshi?"

He didn't care what anyone else at the table thought. His attention was locked on Ren. Slinging the bigger man's arm across his shoulders, Song wrapped one of his arms around Ren's slender waist. He carefully guided him out of the private room they'd booked and through the nearly empty restaurant toward the entrance. With his free hand, he quickly texted his driver and bodyguard that he was heading out.

Ren lay his head against Song's as they ambled out of the

restaurant. He was steadier on his feet than Song had been expecting, which was a great help, but it didn't mean that Ren's heat wasn't scorching every inch of where their bodies touched. It was as if Ren had become a living flame that was running all along Song's right side.

"Thank you, Song laoshi," Ren whispered in an absurdly loud voice. "I didn't want to go with Liu. He's all handsy." As he said the final word, Ren held both of his big hands out in front of them, opening and closing them as if he were squeezing something large and soft.

"You shouldn't have let him talk you into so many drinks," Song chastised a little harsher than he'd meant to, but he couldn't tear his eyes away from those amazing hands.

Oh God, how had he not noticed Ren's hands until this moment?

Ren An Xue had perfect hands. Long, slender, elegant fingers at the end of enormous palms. There was something so very graceful about those hands, even though the man was so very drunk. The things he could do with those hands…

"I know, but I didn't want to be rude. What if they don't like me? I'm so new and we have four months of working together." Ren lifted his head and once again flashed those puppy eyes that were going to be the fucking death of Song.

"It's not rude to watch out for your own well-being. Fuck them if they don't like you because you don't want to drink."

Ren blinked, the puppy eyes disappearing and the sloppy smile returning. "Thank you, Song laoshi. Thank you for watching out for me."

They made it outside to the fresh air and Song sucked in a deep, cleansing breath like a diver suddenly breaking the surface of the water. It helped to clear his foggy brain but did nothing to help put out the fire licking along his body.

The second he appeared, his driver was at his side, helping to get Ren into the car. It took two tries to get the address of Ren's hotel.

Which put him in the exact position he was in now with

his hands clenching his phone to keep from giving in to the temptation of becoming too "handsy" with the dozing Ren. His costar currently had his head on Song's shoulder, each breath brushing lightly against Song's cheek in a hot caress.

What the fuck was wrong with him?

Yes, Ren was attractive. He'd worked with plenty of attractive actors in the past, and not one of them had stirred this kind of reaction in him.

It was nothing.

Nothing!

There might be only a year in age difference between them, but there was nearly a lifetime of experience separating them. Song knew all the dangers of this business. He'd seen or experienced plenty of them firsthand over the years.

Ren, with his large brown eyes and pouting lips, looked so freaking innocent and vulnerable all the time. The guy was simply triggering Song's need to protect. That was it. Sun had asked him to be his laoshi, and he was going to watch out for him.

And no, it didn't matter that Song had never once felt protective of any of his other costars in the past.

The driver pulled into the parking garage rather than out front where anyone could snap a quick picture of them. When they stopped, Song could have easily handed Ren over to his driver, letting the man tuck the actor into the elevator and send him on his way. That was part of his job. This was where Song's responsibility ended.

But when the door opened, Song knew he wasn't letting Ren go yet.

With a little help and a lot of nudging to wake Ren, Song half carried Ren to the elevator and held him upright as they rode up to the fourteenth floor. A soft giggle lifted from Ren as they stumbled down the corridor, searching for the number Ren had given him.

"Key?" Song asked when they reached the correct door.

Ren blinked slowly, staring at him as though he'd spoken another language.

"Where's the key to your room, didi?"

The sloppy smile returned, and Ren hummed softly. "I love it when you call me didi."

Oh, God. Trouble. Trouble. Trouble. This is all trouble. Stop. Do not say it.

"Didi," Song repeated softer and maybe a touch sweeter. "Where's your room key?"

Fuck, I'm an idiot.

Ren's smile grew even wider and he straightened enough to release Song and dig through his pockets. He rocked backward, his shoulders landing against the wall next to his door to keep him upright. With a flourish, Ren produced the plastic card between two long fingers.

Song snatched it from him and waved it in front of the reader. It took three tries—which was just enough for panic to set in with the belief that Ren had told him the wrong room number—but the light switched from red to green, and the door unlocked.

He reached inside and flipped on the light before helping a stumbling, giggling Ren into his room. The space was neat and tidy, with very few signs that Ren had been living there for the past few weeks. There were no clothes strewn about, no random bits of life. He glimpsed only a few spare toiletries on the bathroom counter and that was it.

But then, they were all heading to Hengdian tomorrow, so Ren might have packed up his things in anticipation of making an easy exit in the morning.

Ren flopped his long body across the bed, his arms and legs spread out like a starfish. His puppy eyes were closed, and a crooked smile lifted his full lips.

Song stood over him for a minute, watching as his breathing slowed and evened out. *Ugh.* Part of him hated how quickly Ren drifted off to sleep. He couldn't remember the last time he'd fallen asleep so easily, even when he was dead tired from work.

Of course, Ren had more likely passed out than fallen asleep.

With a sigh, Song moved to the foot of the bed and carefully pulled off Ren's shoes and socks. He crossed to the bathroom and filled a glass of water. After setting it on the nightstand, within easy reach, Song found himself lingering, staring at Ren in the low light cast by the single small lamp that had popped on when he'd hit the switch by the door.

Shadows settled in the hollows of his face and slipped down around his long neck while the golden light gave his skin an almost pearlescent glow. He was beautiful. Song thought he'd read somewhere that Ren An Xue had started his career as a model and had fallen into acting mostly by accident.

And yes, maybe in the last week, he'd given in to curiosity and pulled up a few videos of his shows. Ren's early stuff was rough and stiff, but then he'd not been helped by clunky writing and bland plots. Song would have been worried, except he saw glimpses of what he was sure Sun had seen in the audition.

There had been moments when they were in their costumes for the first time and Ren was delivering Zhao Gang lines with such ease that it was as if the air had been sucked out of the room. Song hadn't been able to rip his eyes away. Tingles had shimmered and sparked along all his nerve endings, lighting him up. He'd struggled to even come up with answering lines in Tian's character.

Almost against his will, Song beamed at the sleeping man. He reached out to brush some hair from his forehead but stopped himself at the last second. What the hell was he doing? Idiot. He was a freaking idiot.

As he drew his hand away, Ren's shot up, catching him by the wrist. Sleepy eyes peeked open, and a lopsided grin formed across those perfect lips. Song's pulse jumped and he tried to pull his arm free, but Ren was surprisingly strong for being half-asleep.

"Thank you for watching out for me, Song laoshi," Ren mumbled. "I promise I won't cause you any more trouble. Promise."

Song pulled his arm and his wrist broke free while Ren's hand flopped onto the bed. A light snore lifted from the man.

Backpedaling, Song quickly and soundlessly left the hotel room, hurrying to his waiting car. It was only when he was in the car and it was racing down the street to his own place that he felt as though he could draw in a full breath.

He closed his eyes and dropped his head on the seat, willing his speeding heart to slow. Had he ever been that wide-eyed and eager? Had he ever been that innocent?

Song mentally snorted at himself. No. Not possible.

He'd started acting when he was a teenager, but Song was sure he'd been born skeptical of the world. Everyone had an ulterior motive. Everyone wanted something. And if they could use him to get it, why not?

But Ren?

Oh, he definitely wanted something. The man wanted to be a successful actor. There was no question of that. Would he use Song to climb to the top?

That was the question he struggled with. He couldn't bring himself to say yes, and it was pissing him off. With those puppy eyes and that sweet smile, Song felt himself getting sucked into believing Ren was really that soft and innocent. But that was all the act, right? He wasn't that vulnerable and open.

Get your head straight, Song.

Ren might not be playing him, but there was no reason to believe that Ren was truly that innocent. It had to be an act to get people to lower their defenses and trust him.

Whatever. It didn't matter.

The only thing he did know was that Ren had nearly

gotten himself into trouble with Liu tonight, and he needed to be more careful. Not everyone cared about his best interests.

Liu had better watch his fucking step, too. He needed to learn quickly that Ren was *his* didi, and Song was not going to let anyone touch him.

A rough bark of laughter jumped from Song, and he dropped his head to the cold glass of the window. *What the fuck…*

Not going to cause me any more trouble, didi?

They hadn't even started filming yet, and Song was confident that Ren An Xue was going to be nothing but trouble for him.

5

YOU WHISPERED IT RIGHT IN MY EAR
REN AN XUE

Ren lugged his roller bag behind him as he pushed the door open to the room he'd been assigned for the length of his filming in Hengdian. There wasn't much to the place. A tiny kitchen with a bar and a couple of stools, as if he were going to suddenly have a guest for dinner. A narrow single bed was pushed against one boring beige wall while a small TV hung on the opposite wall.

He moved farther into the room, spotting the bathroom and tiny closet for his clothes. About the same size as his last hotel room and not much different from his first apartment.

A snort escaped him at the thought. Not much different from his current apartment.

He'd moved a few months before discovering he'd landed the role in *Legend*, and he'd been working nonstop. He hadn't even had time to completely unpack or decorate the place.

Regardless, this was going to be his home for the next four months. He hadn't brought much to make the place feel more comfortable. Maybe he'd stuffed his favorite blanket into his bag. And he might have brought a gaming console. He knew he wouldn't really have time to play, but sometimes the only way he could relax at the end of the day was to log on for an hour. The repetitive motions of the fighting games helped to shut his brain off.

With a grunt, he tossed his roller bag and backpack onto the bed. He started unpacking and settling his belongings in their new places around the room.

The morning had kicked off with the booting ceremony[1], where he'd been shoved and positioned next to Song and the director while the blessing was given. There were photos and questions from reporters. Then he'd been shuttled off to other places for more pictures and interviews, this time with a different portion of the cast. He hadn't yet had a chance to say anything to Song.

What was he going to say to Song after last night?

Well, obviously he'd apologize. But after that?

Ugh. Ren groaned softly to himself and focused on his bag. It was late afternoon, and he would have preferred to spend a quiet night in prior to the start of filming tomorrow. Unfortunately, Sun's assistant had already cornered him and informed him that he was expected at the large welcome dinner.

Fuck. Definitely not the kind of thing he could skip.

He was halfway through his bag when there was a knock. He glared at the door for a second. If that was Sun's assistant with more news about dinner or other obligations, he was going to scream. Or throw a temper tantrum. *Wouldn't that be lovely? Actor throws temper tantrum before filming can even begin.* His manager, Zhou Yuying, would wring his neck and he'd deserve it.

But it wasn't likely to be the assistant since she'd simply send out a mass text.

Frowning, Ren put down the shirt in his hands and crossed to answer the door. His heart and brain stopped working to see Song Wei Li standing on the other side with his trademark smirk.

"Hey," Song greeted. His hands were stuffed into the pockets of his jeans and he was wearing an ordinary dark-red

T-shirt along with a pair of Nike slides, but somehow the man managed to make it look so damn sexy. It wasn't fair that he could do it so effortlessly.

"Hey," Ren repeated, because really, his brain wasn't capable of original thought just yet.

"I wanted to pop by and say that I've got the room across from you," he said, pointing with his thumb toward the door directly behind him. "Feel free to stop by if you ever need anything."

Ren lifted his eyes to the bland brown door. Song was going to be a couple of dozen steps away. Such a short distance when he was sleeping, eating, or showering…

He quickly ripped his brain away from a wet and naked Song, but that only brought him back to other, uncomfortable thoughts. He let out a huff. "Is this more of Sun Jing making sure you're watching over your didi?"

Song's eyebrows jumped nearly to his hairline, disappearing behind his long bangs. "Does didi need watching?" he asked, his tone growing more playful.

Ren made a grumbling noise and turned into his own room, leaving the door open so Song could either follow him or return to his room. He didn't care. Embarrassment from last night still burned like acid through him. His memories were a bit hazy, but he was pretty sure that he'd acted like an ass and had been hanging all over Song.

Fuck, why did I have to drink so much?

Well, that was easy. Nerves. He'd been nervous and so desperate to fit in with all the other actors who'd done the wuxia dramas and the elaborate shoots at Hengdian. He felt like an outsider, and it was leaving him anxious and unsure of himself.

"Ren?" Song called out. The playfulness was gone, and there was only concern wrapped around his name.

Inwardly cursing himself, Ren turned to find Song had taken a couple of steps forward but was still standing in the doorway, as if he wasn't sure he was welcome in Ren's room.

"I am so very sorry about last night. I swear to you that it will never happen again." He bowed deeply to Song and stayed there, hanging his head in his shame. He was supposed to be a professional, and he'd proved exactly how far from the truth that was last night.

"Hey. No. That's not necessary." The shuffle of footsteps and the soft snick of the door had Ren reluctantly straightening to find that Song had come a little farther into the room, one hand extended toward him as though he meant to touch Ren's shoulder. Song dropped his hand to his side and smiled. "Look. You let loose and got tipsy. It's not a big deal. At one point or another, we're all going to have a rough day here and do that." His smile widened and he tilted his head to the side. "Are you going to be there for me if I have too much to drink one night?"

"Of course!" Ren automatically answered. Then his brain proceeded to melt down as it thought about a smiling, cuddly Song hanging on to him as they stumbled their way to his room. Oh, that seemed like a very bad, very dangerous, very wonderful thing.

Song shrugged. "No big deal. But to answer your other question: No, I don't think we were assigned these rooms because Sun wants me to watch over you." He paused and his smile shifted.

Ren dropped his head and groaned. "Chemistry."

The director had caught him between photograph sessions and very deliberately reminded him that he needed to spend more time getting to know Song so they could develop the chemistry they needed to make their on-screen bromance believable.

Song's choked laugh filled the room. "Yeah, chemistry."

Ren shoved his bag back onto the bed and plopped onto the edge. "How are we supposed to develop chemistry?"

Song shrugged and strolled across the room toward the bar that separated the kitchen from the rest of the living space. "We hang out. Talk. Share meals when we can. Nothing major." He turned his head and narrowed his eyes on Ren. "How did you develop chemistry with your other costars?"

Ren cleared his throat and shrugged. "We didn't worry about it too much. It was all acting. For my other shows, we were together to shoot only a dozen episodes. There wasn't time to worry about things like chemistry. It was shoot a scene, then rush to get ready for the next one while trying to remember your lines and blocking."

"I guess it's a good thing we've got fifty episodes together."

"Except we're not sharing any scenes for the first two days. We're on different teams."

Song nodded. "They're all relatively minor scenes with very experienced cast members. It's to give us a chance to get into the headspace of our characters before we're together." Song's mouth lifted into a smirk that Ren was getting very accustomed to seeing. "Plus, that's two days for us to work on our chemistry."

Ren rolled his eyes and Song chuckled at Ren's grumbled, "Whatever."

His costar turned and started for the door. "We're meeting for dinner in a couple of hours, right? Could you do me a favor and bang on my door in an hour? I'm going to try to grab a quick nap, and I tend to sleep through my alarm."

Ren waved a hand at him. "Sure. I got it. Oh, and I am sorry about last night."

Song turned and walked toward him. "Really, don't worry about it. Not a big deal. You have not done anything to change my opinion about you."

Narrowing his eyes, Ren frowned up at Song. "I don't know if that's a good thing or a bad thing."

Song smiled. "It's fine." But the smile fell away a little too fast, causing Ren's heart to stutter. "Just…if you do drink again and I'm not there to watch your back…be careful, okay?"

"Yeah, of course," Ren slowly agreed. "Was there…something…last night?"

"No, I…" Song began and stopped. A myriad of emotions flickered across Song's face, but Ren was having trouble reading them. None of them seemed good, though. "It's nothing."

"What was it?"

Song's eyes darted away and he suddenly appeared incredibly uncomfortable. "I don't want to start any rumors. I could be totally wrong. I…I got this feeling that Liu didn't have your best interests at heart last night. Have you worked together before?"

Ren shook his head, his heart hammering. "No. Last night was the first time we really talked. We made small talk during training, but that was it."

Song grunted. "Okay. Just…be careful."

"You don't think he…" Ren couldn't even finish that thought. What was he even thinking? That Liu had planned to get him drunk and take advantage of him sexually? No. That couldn't be right.

"What? I…" Song paused and then violently shook his head. "Nah. I mean, no. I'm sure he was going to play a harmless prank on you." Song offered a smile that felt forced and bumped the side of his leg against the side of Ren's knee. "It's okay. I got you back to your room, no harm done."

Why didn't Song sound so convinced about the harmless prank part?

But he was right. Ren needed to let it go. They had to work with Liu over the next few months without things being awkward. Song saved him and had gotten him to his room. No harm was done, and he'd learned his lesson. He wasn't going to make another stupid mistake like that.

"Um…last night…I didn't say or do anything particularly embarrassing after we left the restaurant, did I?" Ren inquired slowly. Song had protected him and gotten him to the room, but he couldn't recall everything he said. In his memories, it was all nonsense and babbling.

A wicked grin spread across Song's lips, and he leaned closer to Ren. "You don't remember last night?"

"It's all a little foggy."

Song smiled at him, not saying a word as he left Ren dangling in uncertainty.

"Song laoshi!" he cried at last, unable to take the suspense.

His companion cackled and shook his head. "No, you were adorable but not embarrassing."

Ren rolled his eyes. He wasn't sure if he'd consider his actions adorable *or* embarrassing, but it could have been a lot worse. The few times he'd gotten drunk, it had been pointed out that he suddenly became the world's most cuddly person. He wanted to hug and latch on to the person he was closest to like a koala bear. He did not want to contemplate forcing Song to put up with that kind of unwanted attention.

"Though…" Song started and then left him hanging.

"What?" Ren inwardly cringed, waiting for the bomb to drop on his head.

Song rubbed his finger along his bottom lip, which worked wonders for distracting Ren from whatever in the world he was supposed to be worried about. Men should not have lips like that. Big and full. Song's bottom lip had been created so it could be bitten. And sucked.

"You did tell me you love when I call you didi," Song practically purred.

Ren sucked in a gasp so hard he nearly choked on it. "*I did not!*"

Song nodded, his smile becoming so very wicked. "You did. You whispered it right in my ear. You love when I call you didi."

Ren's face felt as if it were on fire as he twisted around and grabbed the pillow from the head of the bed. He swung it at Song, but the man laughed and dodged it. He hurried to the door and Ren threw the pillow. It smacked Song in the back as he jerked the door open.

"I'm not waking you up! You can sleep through dinner and then tell Sun Jing why the amazing Song Wei Li was too good to eat dinner with the rest of us!" Ren bellowed at the top of his lungs.

Song's cackles followed him as he darted out of the room, putting the door between them. But before it closed, Song stuck his head into the opening, grinning like a lunatic at him. "But didi, aren't you going to take care of your laoshi?"

Ren shouted and snatched up his last pillow. He hurled it across the room, but it landed on the floor well prior to reaching the door and Song's face. All the same, Song jumped away and closed the door behind him. From the hallway, Ren could still hear Song's wild laughter.

With a groan, Ren twisted his body away from the roller bag and flopped onto the small open space on the mattress, both hands covering his face. It wasn't that he thought Song was making it up. Oh no, as soon as Song had murmured the words, the memory clarified in his brain. He'd said exactly that to Song.

He was never, ever drinking again.

At least what he'd said wasn't too bad.

It could have been so much worse.

It could have been a nightmare.

6

A GOD WITH THE FACE OF A VERY WICKED, VERY TEMPTING DEMON
SONG WEI LI

Song strolled onto the set, wrapped in the same blue robes he'd worn that first day in the photo shoot with Ren. They'd not seen each other for two days. They'd been sent to separate sections of the giant studio set to shoot scenes central to their characters' backstories.

Today was going to be the first time they'd be acting together.

Well, there had been the table read where they'd sat next to each other, playing off their gestures, facial expressions, and vocal tones. They'd also taken a bit of time that morning while sitting in the makeup chairs to go through some of the scenes they'd be filming today.

But now they were in costume, and they were falling into this world together.

It was weird for so many butterflies to be flitting through his stomach, sending nervous energy twitching through his frame. He'd done this dozens of times before. The first day with his costar was not a big deal.

So, why did it feel like such a momentous event with Ren?

He grinned at himself, biting the inside of his cheek to

keep from laughing out loud. Their first scene together, they were going to be separated by an entire street. It was like eyes meeting across a crowded room. And yet, he couldn't deny he was excited.

Ridiculous.

Song was half convinced he was the newbie in this situation rather than Ren.

When he reached where they would begin filming for the morning, he found Ren standing with Sun Jing. A hair stylist was already picking at his wig and working to smooth it into place while a costume jiejie was plucking at his all-white costume, getting everything set just right.

Ren's expression was incredibly intense as he nodded at whatever the director was saying, but the second those enormous brown eyes found his face, happiness broke forth like the sun peeking through a bank of black clouds.

Fuck, that smile.

Song's heart stumbled over itself before racing forward, as if it were trying to reach Ren's side ahead of the rest of him.

"Are we ready to do this?" Song asked as he came to stand beside the director.

Sun laughed and rolled his eyes. "I'm starting you off so easy. You don't even have lines for this first shot. It's all in the eyes."

"It's not like you're relying on Tian Xiuying to say much at all in this show. Mostly just grunt, right?" Ren teased.

"I'm a man of few words. Unlike Zhao Gang, who is determined to talk us all to death," Song countered.

Ren lifted an eyebrow as he snapped open his matching white fan. He lazily waved it in front of his long body. "One of us has to prove he's gained some culture in his lifetime."

Oh, he was getting so very good with that thing. Song had gotten used to seeing the fan over the past few weeks. It had become one of those things that was almost always in Ren's hand. He spent hours opening and closing it, flipping and turning it one way or another while stretched out in a chair. Since the very first day, it seemed Ren had learned countless tricks with it, as if the fan had been made for his long, nimble fingers.

Even more, the man's face could be completely unreadable, his voice dead, but Song could read Ren's emotions from how he handled the fan.

"All right, all right, save it for the camera," Sun said with a slightly exasperated sound, but Song did not miss the excited smile that spread across the director's face as he turned away. Yes, he and Ren were getting into sync and falling into their characters very nicely, and they still had four months of shooting ahead of them.

They were each ushered to their spots and given instructions. Song was to literally be lying in the gutter after a scuffle with some ruffians when he spotted Ren for the first time as he came over the rise of a small bridge on the opposite side of the street.

Song was in place.

Cameras were in place.

Sun's assistant called for action.

Song pushed aside the world, letting Tian Xiuying sink fully into his body and claim his brain. He was breathing heavy from the fight, trying to hide his innate abilities from the world while keeping his head attached to his neck. He looked up, and...

The wind was sucked from his lungs.

The angle of the sun was just right as Zhao Gang crossed the bridge and paused at the apex. The golden light made his white costume with the delicate stitchwork glow. It was like seeing a young god stride across the earth on an early morning stroll among the mortals. Tian lifted his eyes, watching as the fan leisurely moved and then paused near the god's face. No, a god with the face of a very wicked, very tempting demon.

Their eyes locked and held. Tian couldn't even count his heartbeats. His heart had stopped completely.

Those full, peach lips tilted upward in the most delicious smile.

"That's it. Head up a tiny bit. Slow smile. Confident," Sun's voice rang out loud and scratchy through the megaphone, giving direction to Ren. Song's concentration wavered at the unexpected intrusion, but he held Ren's stare. The first round of shots were all on Ren and his reaction to seeing Song. They'd do it again with the focus on Song. "That's it. Little smug. Remember, you're the gong[1] in this relationship. You know it from the first time you see Tian Xiuying."

Song coughed, nearly choking when he heard that from Sun. Yes, he was aware of that interesting bit of information from reading the book, but for some stupid reason he hadn't expected Sun to actually say that. He should have known better.

Ren's only tell, to his credit, was a slight widening of his eyes, as if to say, "I can't believe he just said that!" but he recovered quickly. If they kept all of this shot, watchers would take it as nothing more than Zhao's appreciation of Tian.

Sun called "Cut!" and Ren immediately exploded into laughter, while Song rolled in the dirt, chortling like an idiot.

Everyone seemed to ignore them, getting things ready for the next shot. Song's eyes met Ren's across the street in shared amusement, and Song swore he could feel the warmth of Ren's happiness as if it were an embrace.

After reviewing what they got, the scene was reset so that they could capture Song's reaction to Ren.

Song closed his eyes and shoved his amusement aside, calling back up the feelings he experienced when he first spotted Tian on the bridge.

It wasn't necessary. The same wave of shock and desire swamped him all over again. How could any man be this beautiful?

"Okay, Tian, rein it in some. We can save some of the lustful looks for later in the show," Sun's voice cut through. Song hadn't even realized they'd called for action, he'd been so lost in the moment. He barely stopped himself from sending a glare in Sun's direction, but he hadn't been controlling his expression as much as he should have been.

Shock was good. Definitely not lust. Not yet at least. Tian fell for Zhao slowly, almost against his will. Zhao wore Tian down with a thousand acts of kindness and friendship—things the man hadn't experienced in his long, difficult life.

No, for this first introduction, Tian was lost to Zhao's unexpected beauty, but he was also curious and distrustful. It took only a glance to know there was more to Zhao than a perfect face.

"Cut! Perfect!"

THE MORNING SCENES WENT QUICKLY. THERE WAS NOTHING too intense. No wire work. No fighting. For the most part, it was just Zhao relentlessly flirting and teasing Tian, while Tian grunted and snapped at the man.

Sun really was taking it easy on them, but Song suspected that the director was trying to give Ren a chance to become comfortable with his character and the rhythm of the work before throwing him into the deep end.

It was after the midday lunch break, when they were chatting in the shade of a tree, that Song began teasing Ren. He was still stuck in his white costume and would be for the next few days. That meant he had to be extra careful to avoid dirt and grime. The poor guy refused to even sit in a chair without a towel or some other thing set in place to protect his clothes.

"Poor Zhao Gang. Fallen from the heavens and afraid of a bit of dirt."

"Hey!" Ren cried out and smacked him with the fan he was clutching in one hand.

Song giggled, but it stopped when one of the costume jiejies snapped at Ren.

"Don't you dare break another fan, or I will have your head!"

Ren squeaked and actually tried to duck his longer body behind Song while shouting, "Sorry! Sorry! I won't!"

Song bit his lip and had to try twice to twist around to look at Ren in the face. "Another? Have you broken a fan already?"

Ren released Song and stared at the fan tightly clutched in both hands. "I broke a fan on the first day of shooting. I was supposed to sharply open it, but I didn't realize I was so close to a stone bench. I snapped it in half on the first shot."

"Oh shit," Song gasped and then giggled. He cleared his throat when he saw how miserable Ren was over breaking a prop. "Don't worry about it. I'm sure they ordered extras just for that kind of thing."

"I broke another one on the second day of shooting. I'm not used to these long robes. I was backpedaling quickly in a shot, caught my heel on the edge of my robe, and fell on my fan. Snapped it right in half...again."

"Fuck," Song barely managed, his teeth clenched against the rising laugh.

"This is the last fan," Ren added miserably. "More have been ordered along with some cheap ones for faraway shots. They want to take away the fancy ones since I keep breaking them, saving them for only when they know I'll need them for the close-up shots."

Song couldn't hold it in any longer. He rocked in laughter. When Ren tried to run away in disgust, Song wrapped his arms around the man, holding him close and leaning all his weight on him as he laughed. His poor didi.

"You're an asshole," Ren muttered, but even through the tears, Song could see hints of a smile as Ren pinched his lips together.

He was an asshole. And Ren was uncontrollably adorable.

Their first day of filming together was an insanely long day.

The sun was setting. The crew was finishing setup for the final shot of the day while they still had the light.

Song could feel the sweat saturating his clothes and trickling down his spine. He wanted a shower. No, a long soak in a tub and food. May was being kind to them so far with moderately warm temperatures. The only problem was standing in the sun in all these layers. There was no escaping the heat. They undressed to T-shirts when they had significant breaks between scenes, but those respites never seemed long enough.

Closing the lid on his bottle of water, Song turned, his eyes searching for Ren's tall frame. They'd separated after their last scene so that Ren could get his wig and makeup touched up.

It didn't take him long to locate the elegant, white creature standing in the shade of a tree by himself. His back was to Song, and he appeared to be swaying gently from side to side.

Curious, Song wove his way through the people, closing the distance between them. When he was within a few feet, he could hear the man humming a gentle melody.

With a smile, Song placed a hand on his arm, drawing Ren's gaze to his face. Song reached up and motioned to his ear, wordlessly asking what Ren was listening to.

Ren's answering grin was stunning. To Song's surprise, he pulled the earbud from his ear and offered it to Song.

He took it without question and placed it in his own ear.

The sound of Xue Zhiqian's haunting baritone filled him as he crooned about lost love. Song couldn't help it, he immediately started singing along. It was a song he'd listened to on many occasions when he was feeling down.

In the next verse, he caught the first hint of Ren joining him in song. His voice was hesitant and unsteady but gained in confidence with every line. He had a nice, full voice, if untrained. There were some whispers of them potentially singing a duet of the theme song for *Legend of the Lost Night*, but he had a feeling that Ren was the one who was dragging his feet.

Song's second love behind acting was singing. He'd sung for several soundtracks already and released his first full album a year ago. Maybe he should work with Ren a little bit. It could be fun to sing a duet with him, and it would be a great experience for him to place on his résumé in the long run.

The song ended and another from Xue Zhiqian kicked in. Also a forlorn ballad.

Without a thought, Song plucked Ren's phone from his fingers and started scrolling through the playlist. A smile spread across his lips as he recognized a vast majority of the songs. Clearly, Ren had a thing for sad love songs.

He turned the screen toward Ren. "Which one is your favorite?"

Ren's eyes skipped up to his face, looking a bit unsure, before slipping to the display again. Without taking the phone from Song's hand, he slid the tip of his finger along the glass, scrolling through the lengthy list of songs. He tapped one.

A second later, the first notes from a piano were accompanied by a different, smooth and almost breathy voice filling his ear. Yes, he knew this song too. "Rain in Shanghai" was one of his favorites as well.

They stood together, shoulders brushing lightly as they both swayed to the song. Their voices melded and danced around them as they sang along to the broken-hearted ballad. The rest of the world drifted away.

And for just a heartbeat, Song was sure his soul recognized part of Ren's because it was so like his own. How could he have found such a person like this?

Was he going to be able to let him go after four months?

7

NO LICKING
REN AN XUE

Stuffing his phone into his back pocket, Ren shuffled into the elevator as the doors silently slid open. It had been another long day of work. They were at the end of their second full week of shooting.

Yesterday was his first day of wire work, and he was still trying not to think too much about it. There had been so many takes. So many instructions from the director, the trainer, and the stunt coordinator.

Ugh. Even Song had needed to give him advice on how to hold his body.

They'd gotten what they needed at last, but Ren still wasn't happy about any of it. At the end of the day, Song had bumped him with his hip and reassured him that if Sun was happy, it was good. Sun Jing didn't accept crap.

Today had been better. No wire work. Just a little fighting. Lots of talking on his part.

So much fucking talking.

God, sometimes Zhao Gang wanted to hear his own voice.

There were moments when Ren had to wonder why Tian Xiuying didn't cut Zhao Gang's tongue out to get some peace and quiet.

Except Tian Xiuying was probably lonely, and Zhao Gang had a way of making him feel alive and wanted. Even if Tian refused to admit it to anyone, including himself.

"Hey! Hey! Ren! Hold the doors!"

Ren woke from his thoughts in time to stick his arm between the closing doors, stopping them. They reopened, and Song zipped inside the car. He flashed Ren a questioning look before collapsing against the back wall.

"Sorry. Lost in thought," Ren murmured.

One corner of Song's mouth kicked up in a half smile. "No problem. Long day."

Ren grunted. It was, but that wasn't why he was so lost in his thoughts. He glanced over at Song, a new idea forming. Song had a lot more experience, and he was supposed to be his laoshi.

"What are you doing for dinner?" Ren inquired.

Song was held up by the wall, his eyes closed. He lifted a shoulder in a partial shrug. "I think I've got some leftovers from last night."

Ren nearly groaned. Song's eating habits were abysmal. It was amazing the man could function each day. He put mostly crap into his body, and that was only when he remembered to eat. The one positive was that he was usually seen with an apple in his mouth during the middle of the day.

"You're coming over. I'm cooking tonight," Ren declared.

Song cracked open one eye. "Didi cooks?"

Ren moaned and halfheartedly kicked at him, barely brushing Song's calf. "Yes, Song laoshi, I cook. You're coming over to eat something healthy tonight."

"Shower first, and then I'll be over."

Ren made a noise in agreement. He could use a shower to get the sweat off and to help clear his head.

They walked down the hall together in companionable silence when they reached their floor and separated at their rooms. Ren made quick work of a shower and changed into a pair of loose basketball shorts and a T-shirt.

On his way to the kitchen, he paused long enough to crack open his door, allowing Song to enter without knocking. He pulled out what he needed for dinner. It wasn't anything special, but he could make it fast and the ingredients were fresh. The meal probably also contained more vegetables than Song had likely eaten in a week.

"I brought a couple of beers," Song called out as he entered.

Ren looked up as he was chopping peppers to see Song slide onto one of the stools at the bar, the bottles in front of him.

"Thanks. How spicy do you like your food?"

Song's nose wrinkled. "Not that spicy. Maybe a medium."

Ren grunted and planned to cut out half the chilis he'd pulled for the meal.

"Where'd you learn to cook?" Song inquired, falling into their usual, comfortable chitchat.

"My mom. She started teaching me at a young age whether I wanted to learn or not. I think she's afraid I'll never marry, and she wants to make sure I can take care of myself."

Song snorted. "I bet you've got all kinds of girls making a grab for you. Your mother has nothing to worry about."

Ren bit his tongue. The truth was that he'd not given any thought to the idea of marriage, and he couldn't remember the last time a woman had caught his eye. His life was about work…and right now, the man watching him carefully heat oil in his wok.

"So…you gonna tell me what's been eating at you since you took that phone call at the lunch break?" Song drawled.

A rough bark of laughter surprised Ren when it jumped from his throat. Of course, Song had noticed something was wrong. He didn't think he'd screwed up his last scenes too badly, but he had been distracted.

Ren opened his mouth and then closed it without saying a word.

"Come on. Tell Song laoshi what's wrong, so we can fix it together."

Ren looked over his shoulder at the man with the smug smile. "Song laoshi is an ass."

Song shrugged and took a sip of his beer. "Maybe, but that's not improving your mood. Talk to me."

Ren sighed heavily and tossed the vegetables into the wok. Song was right. He needed to talk it out. Song would be able to tell him if he was being ridiculous.

"My manager called to remind me that I've got an audition in two days," Ren mumbled. That wasn't the unexpected part. Song had already left Hengdian twice for photo shoots and an audition. Some of their schedule was kept open so they could meet other obligations during the long filming period.

"You don't sound excited about it. You worried about the project?" Song asked, all the teasing gone from his voice. It was one of the things Ren appreciated the most about him. Song could make jokes endlessly, but the moment they needed to get serious about work, all the teasing fell away.

"I'm not really that interested in it," he admitted.

"What's the script look like?"

Ren shrugged. "I haven't been sent a script. It's for a supporting role. Ten episodes and I'd need to be around for five days of shooting. It sounds like they want to begin filming by the end of summer, though, which means I'd be bouncing between the new show and *Legend*."

"Ten episodes? Drama?"

Ren hung his head and shook it. "Another romantic comedy. They sent me two pages to read for the audition, but it's clearly the part of the clueless and overly enthusiastic best friend of the male lead." He knew the role well since he'd played it on more than one occasion.

"There's nothing wrong with romantic comedies. They're popular for a reason. Are you interested in this show?" Song demanded, his voice hardening.

Ren shook his head.

"Then why are you auditioning?"

"Because I need to have my next job lined up after this is finished. I still don't have a lot of work under my name, and I need to keep building my résumé so I can move on to better, more complex, bigger budget shows."

A scoffing noise left Song, and his beer bottle hit the counter a little harder this time. "Bullshit. You've got the lead in *Legend of the Lost Night*. That's a fifty-episode wuxia drama."

"It's BL."

"So are *Frozen River* and *The Promise*. They were epically huge last year. *Legend* is going to be huge too. You need to start demanding more."

"Yes, but it's going to be at least six months before the first episode of *Legend* airs after we finish filming in August. That's a long time with no proof to producers and directors that *Legend* is the next hot thing," Ren argued. It wasn't so much that he disagreed with Song. The man was giving voice to his feelings. He felt compelled to give the side his own manager had presented earlier in the day.

"Look at me, Ah-Xue," Song snapped.

"I'm cooking, Song laoshi," Ren needlessly reminded him. He could glance up, but he didn't want to risk anything burning if Song succeeded in distracting him. Yet another thing Song was incredibly good at whether he tried or not.

A scrape of the stool across the floor was his only warning that Song had gotten up. He strode into the kitchen and leaned his shoulder against the refrigerator right next to Ren. Out of the corner of his eye, he could see Song's stern expression and the bulge of his biceps as he crossed his arms over his chest.

"Ren An Xue, you have too much talent to continue snapping up just any job you can get your hands on. You're past that stage in your career."

"But—"

"Listen to your laoshi." Song cut him off in an unyielding voice. "You are good. I've worked with you for weeks now. I've seen it firsthand. Sun Jing has seen it, too. You are good. And if your manager doesn't understand or believe in how good you really are, you need to kick her to the curb."

"I think she does," Ren mumbled. He paused and sighed. "I've been pressing for any job. I need to build my résumé before I can afford to get picky."

"You're there. Let yourself be picky. Make things you know you're going to be proud of later. No more cookie-cutter bullshit."

Ren threw him what he thought was a repressive look, but Song grinned at him like a lunatic. "Thank you, Song laoshi. I'll think about what you said and talk to my manager."

"Are you still going to do the audition?"

"Probably. I agreed to it weeks ago. I don't like breaking my promises when arrangements have already been made."

"Okay. But if you're wanting more dramas to stretch yourself, I can make some calls. I've made a lot of friends—"

"No," Ren said sharply. "I want to do this on my own. No favors."

Song grinned at him again, then broke into a low chuckle as he turned to move to his seat behind the bar. "Trust me, Ah-Xue. I'd be doing them the favor by placing you in their hands."

Ren barely stifled the shiver that ran through him. When Song called him didi, it felt like a warm hug. But there was just something about the way Ah-Xue slowly rolled off his tongue. It felt different. A seductive caress that slipped under his clothes and moved over his heated skin.

Jerking his thoughts back to cooking, Ren turned and pulled down plates and bowls, dishing out the food he'd made.

He put everything on the bar in front of Song, finally grabbing some rice and two sets of chopsticks before settling onto the open stool next to him.

"Oh no," Song cried as he looked over the food.

Panic ripped through Ren. He hovered with his butt inches above his seat. "What's wrong? Should I make you something else?" He was ready to leap into the kitchen and make Song whatever he possibly wanted.

"Everything smells amazing. Apparently, I need to start calling you Ren laoshi. Who knew you were such an amazing cook as well as an amazing actor?"

The tips of Ren's ears burned, and he focused on shoveling some rice into his mouth. He could take Song's teasing with grace. He could not accept his praise with such dignity and aplomb. Zhao Gang could take those words and simply accept them as his due, but Ren was not Zhao Gang on his very best day.

"Shut up and eat, Song laoshi," Ren mumbled around a mouthful of food.

They ate in relative silence for several minutes. The only sounds were happy humming noises rising up from Song. Every once in a while, the man would sway or wiggle on his stool as if some bit of food had particularly pleased him.

Ren couldn't help selecting a few choice pieces of beef or a perfectly cooked vegetable and placing it into Song's bowl.

After the fourth time, Song lifted one of his dark eyebrows and stared at him. "Are you trying to take care of me, Ren laoshi?"

"Someone needs to," Ren replied irritably. He hadn't realized he was doing it until Song called him out. "I've seen how you eat, and it's terrible. I can't believe your manager hasn't assigned another assistant to you to simply feed you."

Song grinned. "Bao Shi usually does, but that's when I'm not filming at Hengdian."

"Why when you're not here?"

Song shrugged. "Hengdian is good at keeping the fans at a distance compared to when I'm traveling for other shoots or interviews. I need Bao Shi to run interference for basics like food. Here, I can manage on my own more."

"But that's just it. You're not managing. You eat crap when you remember to eat at all. I bet you forgot to eat lunch today."

Song lowered his bowl and turned on his stool so that their knees brushed. Ren froze. He probably should move. His bare knee was touching Song's bare knee since they'd both elected to throw on shorts after their showers. But he couldn't move. He was trapped in the wide, slightly wicked smile Song was directing at him.

"You going to take care of me, Ren laoshi?"

Oh God, that tone of voice was like alcohol poured straight into his bloodstream.

Song was so close. Turned like this, Ren was washed in the light scent of his shampoo and soap. Something warm with a hint of coconut that left Ren wanting to lean close and lick his bare neck to see if he tasted as good as he smelled.

Thankfully Song had called him laoshi. If Song had used Ah-Xue, he was pretty sure he would have licked the man.

No! No licking.

What the fuck were they talking about?

"Yes, I'll take care of you, Song laoshi," Ren replied. The words came out lower and rougher than he'd wanted, but Song didn't seem to notice. "I cook lunch for myself most afternoons. If you come to my trailer, I'll make lunch for you, too."

Song stared at him for a second and then suddenly twisted around to face the counter. He cleared his throat, his attention centered on the bowl cradled in one hand. "You don't have to do that for me."

Ren shifted, purposefully bumping his knee against Song's. "I'm already cooking. It's not like it's more trouble. And it would save me from worrying that you're going to fall over in the middle of the shoot."

"Whatever," Song muttered before shoveling rice into his mouth.

Ren smiled and grabbed a piece of meat for himself. Song might grumble, but he fully expected the man to follow him straight to his trailer when the midday break was called.

Yes, he liked this idea of cooking for Song Wei Li very much. Someone needed to take care of the man.

And Ren liked it even more that it was going to be him.

8

ALL REN'S GIGGLES BELONG TO HIM
SONG WEI LI

Ren's giggle was the best sound in the world.

Song was sure if someone could bottle that sound, he would get drunk on it every night.

Except he didn't want to share Ren's giggles with anyone else. All Ren's giggles belonged to him.

That wasn't exactly true since they had been giggling like idiots on the set almost all day where the entire cast and crew could hear them. But Song had caused all of Ren's giggles, and that made them his.

The first month of filming *Legend* had flown by in the blink of an eye. The days had grown unbearably hot, and their portable fans were barely making a dent. Song *had* developed a new appreciation for Ren's prop, though. While Ren tried hard not to make it obvious, Song noticed how Ren held his body and moved the fan so that the breeze hit both of them every time it lazily cut through the air.

He was eating lunch in Ren's trailer nearly every day. He'd actually managed to add on a couple of pounds. Song couldn't remember the last time he'd gained weight.

Sure, plenty of the cast and crew teased him about dutifully trailing after Ren as soon as the lunch break was called. *Screw them.* They were jealous. They didn't have a sexy man with amazing eyes and a devastating smile cooking them delicious food.

Song poked Ren in the ribs again, making him twist and giggle before Ren poked him back. Song dodged the long digit, snickering as he managed to elude Ren.

Around them, the costume and makeup jiejies formed a large circle as if they were trying to corral a pair of wild horses. Luckily, they'd learned—without suffering any significant injuries—not to try to fix their clothes or hair when they were in this mood. They'd only get run down.

Sun Jing's loud and heavy sigh cut through their antics, and they both stopped. "Can I separate you two for just a few minutes? Zhao Gang is needed to deliver a few lines. I promise to return him after he's done."

Song laughed, but Ren's face flushed bright red. His companion managed to give Song's shoulder a quick shove as he walked past. The second he cleared Song, the jiejies descended on him like a flock of locusts, plucking at his dark-navy robes and combing his long wig. Song smiled as he watched Ren. The man moved with confidence now, comfortable in his surroundings as if he'd been doing this for years rather than four short weeks.

Out of the corner of his eye, he saw Ma Daiyu sidle up next to him. She bumped him with her hip, dragging his eyes to her. The tiny young woman barely topped five feet, but she was full of sass and wide grins. Most of her scenes were with Ren, but they'd had a handful together. This morning they'd had one that had been a lot of fun, and they were scheduled to shoot another after Ren finished his current one.

"You and Ren have gotten close," Ma Daiyu observed. She held her hands behind her back and gazed up at him with dark eyes that dominated her delicate face. Her red lips were pinched together as if she was trying to hold in a smile.

"Yep. You'd kind of expect that considering we share nearly every scene together," Song replied in a low voice, trying not to disturb Sun and Ren as they walked through a scene together and discussed the blocking.

"No, I mean close. Like *close*." Ma drew out the last word while lifting her eyebrows. There was a long, heavy pause as she continued to stare at him, waiting for the word to really sink in.

Oh. She meant that kind of close.

Close like more than friends. More than brothers.

Close like lovers.

Song clamped down on all his micro expressions, which was not the easiest thing when his body demanded that he swallow hard or even clench his teeth. Ma was watching him like a hawk for any kind of tells.

Was this what she thought of their interactions?

Ma had filmed a lot of scenes with them in the past month. If she thought this after so few interactions, what did the rest of the crew, who surrounded them day in and day out, think?

Forcing a loose grin, Song shook his head. "You're crazy. We're close because we spend all day together."

"And I hear he's cooking lunch and dinner for you," Ma said in an almost singsong voice.

Song shrugged. "Ren likes to cook."

"And you're both so adorable."

This time, he rolled his eyes. "That's why we got the part. We're too adorable for words. Viewers want pretty. Just like you."

An indelicate snort left Ma, and she bumped her shoulder against his arm. "Yeah, well, if it gets any more adorable around here, I'm going to puke." She paused and then stared up at him, both eyebrows lifted this time. "That's it? I mean, I'm cool…if it's more. You and Ren are so…" She didn't finish with a word so much as a dreamy sigh.

"That's the point, isn't it? This is a BL—"

"Bromance," she corrected. "Thank you, censors," she finished in a growl under her breath.

"Whatever. The point is that Ren and I are supposed to be shippable."

Ma grunted softly. "And the BTS[1] cameras are constantly rolling. I get it."

At the mention of the behind-the-scenes cameras, Song had to fight the urge to glance about for them. Most of the time, he forgot they even existed, though there was some level of awareness in the back of his mind. The one thing the fans lived for were the supposedly "real life" moments that happened while a show or movie was being filmed.

The BTS clips were what helped to build the buzz early on and kept the excitement long after the show had aired.

The whisper going around the set was that the first clips were supposed to be "leaked" this week now that they were more than a quarter of the way through filming. Part of him was anxious to hear how fans reacted to their first glimpse of him and Ren together.

But there was another part that didn't want the BTS videos to go out.

Yes, he was sharing Ren with a few dozen people every day, but currently, they were in their own little world in Hengdian. Their interactions with fans were generally limited to social media and previously scheduled appointments.

At the end of the day, they returned to their rooms.

Or rather, Song rushed through a shower in his room before going to Ren's room, where he stayed until one or both of them were close to passing out.

The second the first BTS video hit the Internet, Song would need to share Ren with the rest of the world. That shouldn't feel like such a horrible thing, but it did.

"I didn't mean to be nosy or anything. I was just curious,"

Ma said. She bumped him one last time, then moseyed off in the opposite direction.

Song wanted to laugh. No, she'd definitely meant to be nosy, but he did believe that it was idle curiosity on her part. They'd performed together briefly on another project. She was a hard worker and didn't make a habit of spreading gossip.

But her questions did prod loose some thoughts that were now chewing on his brain.

Was he spending too much time with Ren? Was he giving the cast and crew—possibly even what was being picked up on the BTS cameras—a very wrong impression?

Was he damaging Ren's image?

It was one thing to grow comfortable with each other so they had the right chemistry in front of the camera, but they could take it too far. The chemistry was already there and set. They were in sync. If they finished each other's sentences one more time while pitching how to tweak a scene, he was sure Sun was going to have a heart attack.

Maybe it would be best if he pulled back a little. Put some breathing space between them. At least during their off-hours.

Ren had to be getting sick of spending his every evening with Song underfoot.

And Song could figure out how to feed himself for a couple of days.

His stomach twisted into a knot at the idea. He turned away from where they were setting up the shot and went to hunt down his phone. He was constantly putting the damn thing aside in the weirdest places. Bao Shi was still shadowing him for a good chunk of the day, constantly picking it up and carrying it until Song went searching for it again.

As if reading his mind, Bao Shi stepped in front of him with a smirk and held up his phone.

Song was seriously starting to wonder about his ability to

function as a normal human being. At this point, the only things he was responsible for were breathing, showering, and acting. Bao Shi and Ren had everything else in his life covered.

Yes, he needed to put some space between him and Ren, if only for his own sanity.

No.

Shit. Shit. Shit.

He couldn't do that to Ren. Not right now. Tomorrow Ren was on the schedule to shoot his big emotional reaction scene. His character had just discovered that Tian Xiuying was dying. Following it was a day of wire work and fighting. It was Zhao Gang's bloody rampage as he dealt with his conflicted emotions over Tian.

Ren had admitted that his nerves were a tangled mess over those two hard days of shoots. It was bad enough that Song was going to be in Hong Kong tomorrow. He was scheduled to give a small concert in a month, and his manager had him meeting with a crew to talk through the venue and meet with a choreographer. As it was, he wouldn't be in Hengdian for at least two days. If Song suddenly pulled away from him, leaving Ren feeling like he had no support, it would crush him.

Nothing in this world could make him hurt Ren.

But wasn't he putting Ren in danger if they continued their closeness in front of the world?

Maybe his hesitation was pure selfishness on his part. He didn't want to pull back. He didn't want to stop spending his evenings with Ren, or stop sharing meals, or stop their silly laughing antics. He was loving every second of their time together. Especially their long conversations about their careers, their families, and their lives in general. He wanted to know everything he possibly could about Ren An Xue.

No, he'd wait until after Ren got through these two bad

days of shooting. His schedule lightened while some of the tougher scenes shifted to Song. They could talk through Song's concerns. Maybe they'd decide that he was making a lot out of nothing. Maybe Ren would agree that they needed space.

Song stared at the blank screen of his phone. He couldn't even remember why he'd gone looking for it in the first place. A queasiness spread across his stomach and his head was throbbing. Or maybe it was his chest.

No, this was probably a sign that he needed to put some distance between him and Ren. For his own sake.

Something crashed into his back, and a pair of long arms wrapped around him from behind. He didn't even need to turn. There was something about those arms, even the familiar scent of sweat, deodorant, and faded cologne that made the tension in his chest ease.

"Ready for our scene?" Ren laughed in his ear.

"Done with your scene already, didi?"

Ren scoffed and released him. "Glad to see you're paying attention to my outstanding performance."

Song turned and placed his phone into Bao Shi's extended hand. "I was so blinded by your skill, I had to turn away. Otherwise, I might never have regained my eyesight."

As expected, Ren chuckled and shook his head. That was the true blinding sight. Ren's joy. It took Song's breath away each time and left him oblivious to the rest of the world.

But he had to gain some perspective. He needed to do what was best for his career and for his didi. *Fuck!* He had to do what was best for Ren.

Time away from Hengdian and Ren were going to be good for both of them. He'd be able to get his head on straight and think clearly.

Tonight, he would enjoy the time he had with Ren. They'd laugh and eat dinner like they always did. His didi would head into two hard days of shooting with confidence that he could tackle them with zero problems. He believed in Ren.

It was just that Song was having trouble believing in himself when it came to Ren.

He wasn't sure what he was doing.

Or what he even wanted anymore.

9

NONE OF THIS IS REAL
REN AN XUE

He was raw.

Not physically. Emotionally.

Most of the day had been spent shouting at a variety of different characters about the impending death of Tian Xiuying.

As the sun was setting, storm clouds rolled across the sky, blocking out the last rays of the sun, and a gentle rain started to fall on Hengdian studios.

Sun Jing jumped on it. People scrambled to take advantage of the change in weather. More lights were brought in. And Ren was shoved into his final scene of the day, where he collapsed on the ground and succumbed to his tears.

Ren had wallowed in the thought of losing the man who'd been his constant companion for over a month. The man who watched out for him. The man who reached out to him in his darkest moments and stood unflinching by him when the world called him evil.

As the tears fell and his crying shifted to sobbing, he realized his mind was blurring together memories of Tian Xiuying and Song Wei Li. His heart struggled to tell them apart.

If Song had been there at the end of the shoot...

If he had just smiled at him and told him he'd done a good job, Ren might have been able to pull himself together.

But Song wasn't watching his scene like he always did.

Song wasn't in Hengdian.

Ren hadn't even heard words like "action" or "cut." He'd gotten lost in the moment, handing all of himself over. When it was done, Ma Daiyu and Sun Jing had kneeled and whispered encouragement to pull him out of it, but it didn't work.

In the end, Ma had stood over him with an umbrella, a silent guardian in the rain as she let him simply cry the feelings away.

Now he was back in his room. He didn't exactly remember how he'd even gotten there. The trip from the lot to the housing area had been a blur with him shuffling along like a zombie. He'd showered, and stood in front of the refrigerator with the door open, but he didn't have any appetite and everything felt like too much work.

Instead, he'd flopped onto the bed, his phone clutched in one hand. It was so tempting to text Song. They'd exchanged contact information weeks ago but rarely texted because they were constantly together.

Song had told him to text if he needed anything.

But he couldn't. He couldn't pull himself together enough to fake being okay.

What he needed was to see Song in the flesh, to reassure himself that Song was safe and healthy. He needed to touch him, hold him. To wrap himself around Song and listen to the steady thump of his heart while Song teased him about being overly dramatic or ridiculous.

His phone buzzed.

Ren lifted it and glanced at the screen.

Song: How'd it go?

His heart skipped, and the lump returned to his raw throat. Of course Song would remember what scene he was slated to shoot today. Of course he would be worried about his didi.

Ren tapped on the window to type out his reply but stopped. What the hell was he supposed to say? He couldn't possibly admit to Song that he was an emotional wreck. He didn't want Song thinking he was this unprofessional. Or worse, he didn't want Song to worry. Not when he was trapped hundreds of miles away.

Before he could wrap his brain around an answer, another message popped up.

Song: Didi, talk to me, please.

Fuck. He saw the read receipt. He knew he was online and not talking.

Ren: It was okay.

He flinched after he hit Send. That was bad. He shouldn't have sent that. It wasn't convincing in the least.

Song didn't reply. A second after his message was marked read, a video call from Song started to ring.

Ren hesitated with his finger over the button to answer the call. He didn't want Song to see him like this, but it wasn't as though the man didn't already know he was a mess. And he was just thinking that all he wanted to do was see Song, to hold him. A video might help to pull him out of this emotional funk.

With a sigh, Ren tapped the screen and it was instantly filled with Song's beautiful face. Ren ignored his own image, but he could guess what Song saw. Red eyes and a slightly sappy smile. He honestly didn't care. He had Song back, even if it was from a distance.

"Oh, didi," Song cooed at him, worry instantly filling his dark eyes. "Talk to me. What happened? Was it that bad?"

Ren shook his head. "No. I think what we got was really good. Sun didn't demand a lot of takes." He paused and huffed out a chuckle. "It rained here, and they changed the scene to take advantage of it."

Song's worry turned into a scowl. "How long did they make you sit in the rain?"

"Not long."

"Ren An Xue," Song growled.

"Really, the scene itself didn't take that long. I...I just..." Ren drifted off as he blinked back a fresh rush of tears. He forced a laugh and shoved his hand through his damp hair. "So stupid."

"It's not stupid. I get it. You got swamped by the emotions of the scene. It's character bleed. None of what you're feeling is real. You're having trouble separating all the emotions. I've been there."

Ren's eyes drifted away from the screen, unable to face Song's intensity.

"Didi, look at me."

Ren couldn't help but follow his command. He lifted his gaze to see a mix of worry and fierce confidence in Song's beautiful eyes. The swell of pain ebbed and he could breathe again.

"Didi, I'm okay. Tian Xiuying is not real. Zhao Gang is not real. Song Wei Li is right here. I'm fine. I'm not going anywhere, okay?"

At long last, Ren sucked in enough air to fill his lungs and nodded. He held it for a couple of seconds and then released it slowly through parted lips. "You're okay. Everything is okay. It's not real," he repeated softly.

"I'm so sorry, Ah-Xue," Song whispered.

Ren flicked his eyes to the screen. He hadn't even realized he'd closed them. "What?"

"I should be there. If I'd known how things were going to line up, I would have demanded they change the order of the shoot or try to reschedule. I'm sorry."

A genuine smile lifted Ren's lips. "Don't, Song laoshi. This was the best time for these scenes, while you're away. We're in most scenes together. If you're not here, I can't work either unless I'm doing the hard solo scenes." He paused and smirked. "Besides, if you were here, I'd probably be attached to you for the rest of the night like a koala hugging a tree."

Song's smile turned into a lazy grin that did dangerous things to Ren's heart. "When I get back, I promise you can hug me all you want."

Ren froze. Song didn't really mean that. And he certainly didn't mean to create a wonderful image of them stretched out together in this bed, arms wrapped around each other, legs tangled up. Ren would slide his fingers into Song's hair, feeling the silky strands slipping along his fingers as he buried his face in Song's throat, chasing after the scent of him.

"How's your trip been? What do you think of the venue?" Ren suddenly demanded, mentally wincing at how his voice jumped in pitch. Yeah, there wasn't anything suspicious about that. Song wouldn't be able to guess where his mind had traveled.

"Good. Good." Song paused. His expression grew warmer and there was a new, excited spark in his eyes when they met Ren's again. "I shouldn't be telling anyone, but I want to share it with you."

"What? What happened?"

"They actually changed the venue to a bigger location."

"What? Seriously?" Ren half shouted.

Song nodded. "I found out today that I'm going to be holding the concert with Zhu Fang."

Ren frowned, searching his mind for why that name sounded familiar. It hit him, and his eyes widened. "He was one of the leads in *Frozen River*, right?"

Song nodded, biting his bottom lip. "No one told me they'd even approached him, but he's willing to do a joint concert with me. He'll sing some songs. I'll sing a few. Then we'll sing a few duets." Song's smile shifted into a more self-deprecating smirk. "His last concert was a sold-out stadium, so

I can't believe he agreed to do this. Even with the bigger setting, it's still less than what he's capable of filling."

"Song laoshi, this is going to be amazing!" Ren shouted at his phone. He gave it a little shake as if he were shaking Song. "I've heard a few of his songs. Your styles are going to mesh very well. This is going to be so wonderful for you and your career. Your fan base is going to explode!"

"And how would you know about my style?" Song asked. His expression turned so sly, so very seductive.

Parts of Ren were starting to heat, but he ignored it as best he could, clinging to a teasing tone. "Song laoshi, you sing all day when we're on set. I know your voice. Besides, do you really think I haven't downloaded your album and added it to my playlist?"

"You didn't have to do that," Song replied, looking unexpectedly shy.

"Yes, I did. You're my laoshi. Plus, we both know I have excellent taste in music. You're going to be fabulous."

"Whatever."

It was on the tip of Ren's tongue to press, but he decided to move them along. Song had already saved him from his wallow. There was nothing to be gained by making Song feel more uncomfortable and self-conscious. "Have you met him yet?" he asked, pushing the conversation along.

Song shook his head. "Not yet. Today was mostly me walking the venue, making some initial plans for what songs I want to sing now that I know I'm going to have Zhu Fang with me. We'll meet tomorrow and talk out some more plans."

"I'm so excited for you! I wish I could go to the concert."

Song's expression turned surprisingly soft and he tilted his head to the side. "Yeah, I wish you could go too."

But that just wasn't possible. They were keeping a very tight shooting schedule. They couldn't afford to lose both of their leads at the same time, or they would fall behind. The director and producer were running a tight ship. Another TV show was scheduled to take over their section of the lot the day after they finished.

Ren flashed him a grin. "I'll be sure to watch all the fan videos that go up that night."

Song laughed, but the sound was cut off by a knock and a muffled voice. Song's happiness fell away and his expression became serious before looking at the camera. "I've got to jump off. Another meeting."

"No problem. I'm okay. I promise."

"Good. Get some sleep, didi. You've got another busy day tomorrow."

"You too."

Song winked at him, and then he was gone.

Ren rolled over and placed his phone on the nightstand. He stayed there, curling up a little. The warmth of Song's smile lingered, but some of his words were surfacing in his mind again.

You got swamped by the emotions of the scene. It's character bleed. None of what you're feeling is real.

Was that all this was? Character bleed?

Was he so lost in the mind of Zhao Gang that he was making the character's pain and emotions his own?

He'd suffered it a bit with some of his other characters, but nothing to this extent. There had been a few long days on the lot when he'd mistakenly called his costar Ah-Ying rather than by his real name. But Song had done the same thing with him. Neither of them thought anything of it.

But if that was it, why did his skin tingle every time Song's hand brushed his arm? Why did his entire body heat wherever Song leaned into him? Why did he spend way too long staring at the man's perfect mouth, imagining what his lips felt like, tasted like?

Why was Song's laughter the best part of his day?

Why was he obsessively worried about whether Song was

eating? Or whether he'd stayed up too late the night before reading?

Ren shivered and curled up into an even tighter ball. Was there any point to these emotions? So what if he was falling for Song Wei Li? A choked bark of bitterness erupted from his lips. Half of China was in love with Song Wei Li. Why should he be any different?

And after *Legend* was released, the rest of China would be completely infatuated with Song.

Why did any of this matter? Song Wei Li was *not* gay. The man's name had been linked to half a dozen different actresses over the years. Sure, they'd all been disproved as trashy gossip, but that didn't mean he wasn't secretly dating some beautiful starlet.

Ren squeezed his eyes shut against the rising pain. Maybe he was falling for Song—not Tian Xiuying, but the real Song Wei Li. That way only led to misery. He needed to let that all go if he was going to survive the rest of this shoot as well as life after the shoot.

None of this was real.

Song Wei Li was not his. And he never would be.

10

DON'T GET ATTACHED
SONG WEI LI

R*en*: H*ave you met him yet*????

Song: *Why does it feel like you're more excited about this meeting than I am?*

Ren: *I'm not more excited than you. I'm excited FOR you.*

Song: *Aren't you supposed to be killing extras right now?*

Ren: *Shut up.*

Ren: *Get a selfie with him.*

Song: *If you wanted my picture, you should have just asked.*

Song: *[image] [image] [image] [image]*

Yes, he'd sent Ren a current selfie as well as three of his cutest, most adorable, and sexiest pictures from his gallery because he was utterly shameless when it came to this man. He also wanted to be sure that Ren was in a better mood compared to last night's near breakdown. Ren seemed happier, but it didn't hurt to be a little silly if it meant Ren was smiling.

Ren: *HA! Like I haven't taken dozens of pictures of you already without you knowing it.*

Song's heart stopped. What? Had Ren really taken his picture for his own collection?

Ren: *Fuck! Song laoshi, I'm joking!!!*

Ren: But seriously, have you been sleeping? You look tired in one of those pics. Bao Shi is supposed to be taking care of you.

Song: I'm fine. I'm sleeping and I'm eating, my sweet laopo[1].

Ren: Get a selfie and I'll send you a selfie of me covered in blood later.

Song: Lunatic. Go kill some extras. I think he's here.

Ren: XDDD

Song had to get off his phone because he could feel himself grinning like an idiot and he couldn't think of how to wipe it off his face. He hadn't expected to get a text from Ren right then. His costar was supposed to be up to his eyeballs in a violent battle filled with dead martial-arts extras. He must have been on a break as they set up the next shot.

God, he needed to get back to Hengdian.

He'd been gone for less than two days, and it felt as though he was missing part of himself. Ren was right. He'd slept like shit last night, unable to shake his worries about Ren. He might have looked better when they jumped off the video call, but Song didn't feel like he'd believe it until he finally saw him in the flesh.

Unable to stop himself, Song scrolled to the top of their conversation and let his eyes linger on each one of Ren's replies. This was the first time they'd truly texted. It was stupid that he felt this giddy over it. He saw Ren almost every day. They talked constantly. Ate most of their meals together. Why did texting feel like such a big deal?

Because it meant even though they were apart, he still had a way to reach out to him, that he didn't feel disconnected and drifting.

Sharp footsteps echoed across the concrete, drawing Song's gaze from his phone at last. Zhu Fang was here, accompanied by a small entourage of assistants, his manager, the manager for the venue, and probably a bodyguard or two.

Song slid his phone into the pocket of his slacks and smoothed away the goofy grin Ren had put on his lips.

Zhu Fang was a handsome man, not that it was surprising. Song had watched *Frozen River* a couple of times to get a feel for what was popular in BL shows. But Zhu Fang's good looks weren't overwhelming. There was something subtle about them.

His appeal seemed to be more in his natural charisma. The man smiled and you just wanted to like him.

It reminded him of Ren. They both had a sweetness and a playfulness. The only difference was that Ren was devastatingly handsome even when he wasn't smiling. When he was in angry Zhao Gang mode, there was a hotness to Ren that threatened to melt Song's few remaining brain cells.

He couldn't see that in Zhu Fang.

They met in the middle of the stage, where Song had been waiting for him with his manager and assistant. They politely shook hands with a bow of their heads. While they were about the same age, Song had been acting longer.

However, *Frozen River* had effectively launched Zhu Fang's career into the stratosphere, and he was holding on to that popularity more than a year after the release, even after suffering through a few fan-generated scandals and gossip.

"Thank you so much for making the time in your schedule to do this concert," Song greeted.

"Not a problem. Happy to," Zhu Fang replied, an easy half smile lifting one corner of his mouth.

If he wanted to say more, there wasn't a chance. Zhu Fang's manager launched into a bunch of excited platitudes, which were then met and topped by his own manager. Of course, the venue manager couldn't be outdone, so he added his two cents.

Song glanced up at Zhu Fang—yes, up, because the man was tall like Ren—and saw him roll his eyes and smirk. At least they shared the same feelings about that.

There was a lot of talking between the various managers and assistants that didn't require any input from him and Zhu

Fang. They were simply the talent. They knew the job: Go where they were told, smile, do what they were supposed to, and don't fuck up.

Close to an hour passed with the various managers and event planners discussing all that needed to be done and how the show would progress. Zhu Fang's growing annoyance became more pronounced as time wore on. He appeared to have reached the end of his patience. Song had heard whispers that he could be a bit temperamental and flighty, but Song got the impression that it was typically directed toward people who wasted his time.

"Go! Go figure all this out. Let me have some time with my new friend." Zhu Fang suddenly exploded. All but his own manager seemed shocked by this outburst. He waved his hands at them, shooing them away.

They moved across the stage under protest like a gaggle of squawking geese, disappearing into the backstage area.

Song hesitated when they were alone. He was no stranger to smoothing over silence with easy chitchat, but something about Zhu Fang made him think his companion had something specific he wanted to discuss with him.

"Thanks again for agreeing to the joint concert," Song repeated after nearly a full minute of silence.

Zhu Fang shrugged one shoulder. "No problem. *Frozen River's* fandom is still going strong even though it's been out for over a year and we have nothing more to give them. It only makes sense to start moving them into the *Legend* fandom."

Song nodded. It was true. People who followed Zhu Fang because of *Frozen River* would now be exposed to Song Wei Li and all the marketing that would come with him related to *Legend*.

"I saw the BTS video that dropped this morning," Zhu Fang suddenly announced, and Song's heart stuttered. Was this what he wanted to talk about?

Of course, that wasn't his primary thought.

"A video was finally leaked?" He'd known it was coming, but they hadn't given him the exact date. He'd also not spent much time on social media recently. He had people who handled that. His main concerns were Ren, filming, and this concert. Everything else sort of fell away.

Zhu Fang's smile widened into something a little more mischievous. "You didn't know? Have you seen it?"

Song shook his head. "Filming has been brisk. I haven't been online much."

There was something in the twist of Zhu Fang's lips that made Song think the man didn't completely believe him. The singer dug into his pocket and pulled out his phone. It took him only a second to pull up the video, as if he'd queued it up for this conversation, and played it with the volume raised to the max.

The first thing he heard was Ren's laugh. Song's heart tightened.

Fuck, he missed didi.

His costar was offscreen, teasing Song about how he was standing.

He remembered this day...

They were a bit more than a week into shooting. The weather had been heating up and Song was running off whenever he could to find slivers of shade in between scenes.

Song replied to Ren, but the words were lost to shouts from the director to some other member of the crew.

It didn't matter because the focus was entirely on Ren as he strode into the shot. He stood next to Song and held out his arms, using his height and the full sleeves of his robes to cast this pocket of shadow for Song. At the same time, he turned the fan he was constantly holding and slowly waved it, creating a breeze for Song. A blissful smile filled Song's face, but it was nothing compared to the expression of concern and joy on Ren's face.

The BTS moment was barely a minute long, but there was

a sweetness to it. It was all completely innocent, but something about it felt invasive. He didn't want anyone else to see that look of happiness on Ren's face.

At the end, some interviews had been tacked on. All the main cast had been pulled aside at random times to answer questions about their characters, working on the show, and other random personal things.

There was a shot of Song talking about Tian Xiuying followed by Ren talking about Zhao Gang. It had to have been taken during the first couple of days, because poor Ren appeared so stiff and uncomfortable. So different from who he was now while on set.

Zhu Fang lowered the phone to his side when the video ended. "It's a good first video. Sweet and enough to tempt the fans into demanding more. Though I think your ship sailed the second they released the first sets of pictures of you both together."

Song lifted an eyebrow at the man. "You think *Legend* has a shot of reaching *Frozen River* status?"

Zhu Fang tossed his head back, his loud laugh dancing around them. "If it were based on chemistry alone, I think it could."

"Any words of advice?"

The man standing opposite him shifted his weight from his left foot to his right while shoving his phone into his pocket. He tilted his head up a bit and stared at the rows of seats that rose in front of the stage. At last, he smiled slowly and turned his head to regard Song. "Enjoy it while you can. Soak in all the madness and try to roll with the chaos. Everything is going to change. Try to make sure that it's for the best."

Song nodded. That made sense. He was expecting, or maybe hoping, for madness and chaos. His career was going well, but he wouldn't turn down a big boost.

He also wanted that for Ren. Each day he spent at his side,

the more he realized how incredibly talented he was. The world needed to see what Song saw when it came to his didi.

"Any words of warning?"

Zhu Fang's expression immediately hardened. The muscles in his hard jaw flexed for a second like he was clenching his teeth. "Don't get attached."

Song gasped. That was not what he'd been expecting to hear from him at all. "What—"

"Don't. You've been filming for how long? A month? Two?"

"One."

He shook his head, his eyes growing darker and his thick eyebrows snapping together over his long, slender nose. "Don't do it. Save both of you the pain and frustration. Don't get attached."

A hundred denials immediately rose in his throat, but he swallowed them. He knew what Zhu Fang was talking about. It was the unspoken rule that everyone knew when it came to BL in China. The government just barely allowed them, but there were rules that had to be followed.

One strict rule was that the two lead stars could never be seen together after the promotional period was done. There were no more random pictures together. No more interviews together. They couldn't even mention each other's names. If they attended the same industry event, their arrivals and departures had to be carefully coordinated so that they didn't accidentally run into each other.

After *Legend of the Lost Night* was released and the promotional junket was done, Song wasn't allowed to ever see Ren in public.

There were arguments they couldn't even meet in private because there was always the chance that a fan could sneak a picture of them.

Song could only stare at nothing in a daze. It was as though Zhu Fang had reached into his chest and ripped away a part of his soul. Never see Ren again. Yes, logically, he'd known from the very beginning that the day would come, but to be slapped with the reality so coldly? He couldn't breathe. Couldn't think.

His hand slipped into his pocket and tightly gripped his phone. The texts were his last connection to Ren. Was that his future? Random texts and secret video phone calls when they could sneak them in between work obligations.

Twisting around, Song looked behind them and then about the concert hall to make sure there was no one close enough to hear them. Zhu Fang did the same thing before meeting Song's gaze.

"I...what if..." Song started and stopped. He didn't even know how to put the panic and pain into words. What was he even trying to ask? He knew the rule, and there was no way of getting past it.

Zhu Fang narrowed his eyes and tilted his head to the side, staring at him. After only a second, he rocked back as loud laughter jumped from him, but this time it sounded like it was also tinged with bitterness. Zhu Fang leaned close, his voice dipped low. "It's already too late, isn't it?" He shook his head, chuckling to himself. "Yeah, it happens that fast."

Song's eyes widened. *Did he mean that he and his costar...?*

"Where's your phone?" Zhu Fang suddenly demanded.

Song pulled his phone out of his pocket and held it out. Zhu Fang hit a button on his phone, then tapped his phone against Song's. There was a *ping* and a notification appeared on Song's screen. They'd swapped contact information.

"In case you need to talk," Zhu Fang said and paused. He smirked as he added, "Preferably *before* you do something that can be categorized as fucking stupid."

"I'll keep that in mind."

As he was about to put his phone away, it vibrated in his hand. Without a thought, he tapped the glass and a picture of Ren in his black Zhao Gang costume popped up. For a second, Song couldn't move a muscle. His brain locked up at that shot. His expression was cold and lethal. Fake blood was splattered across his face, dripping down the edge of his chin. His white fan had been replaced with a red one and was held out in front of him like a blade. He looked like a messenger from Death sent to get revenge for the pain Ren had felt yesterday.

It was hard to believe it was the same man who'd stared at him with tear-streaked eyes and a crooked smile last night. The same man who blinked at him with wide puppy eyes and always got his way.

"Whoa," Zhu Fang breathed beside him, reminding him that he was not alone. His new friend bumped their shoulders together and grinned. "You have certainly got your hands full."

Maybe. It wasn't as though Ren felt anything for him besides friendship, and that was probably all they would ever have. Song would be happy with that. But he couldn't stand the idea of losing all contact with Ren. There had to be a way.

"Can we get a selfie together?" Song found himself saying. "He asked…"

"Sure," Zhu Fang easily agreed.

While Song flipped the camera view and lifted the phone to the proper angle, Zhu Fang stepped closer and draped an arm across his shoulders. Somehow they managed to affect matching smirks. He snapped two quick ones and lowered his phone. But before he could move, Zhu Fang lifted his own and snapped a couple.

As they straightened, Zhu Fang checked the pics. "Gege[2] claims I don't know anyone famous."

Song snorted. In terms of famous, Zhu Fang had him beat. But he was more curious about who "gege" was.

He looked up at Zhu Fang to see him hesitate, his finger hovering just over his screen. His eyes slipped over to Song for a second; then he seemed to have made a decision. He dove into his photo gallery and finally stopped on a picture. He expanded it and tilted the screen so that Song could see it.

"Gege," Zhu Fang simply explained.

"Is that…" Song gasped and then stopped, his eyes jumping up to Zhu Fang's face.

"Yep."

The picture was of Zhu Fang with his arms wrapped around his costar Guo Zi while Zhu Fang pressed a kiss to Guo Zi's cheek. The other man was smiling brightly for the picture and they were both dressed in casual clothes with their own hair. This wasn't a promotional pic. It was something just for the two of them.

"When—"

"I took it two weeks ago in Paris," Zhu Fang replied with a devilish grin as he tucked his phone away.

Two weeks ago…that was well outside their promotional period, and they were finding a way. They were still seeing each other.

Song's heart was racing. He swallowed hard, trying to get his tongue to move so he could speak. "It can work. There is a way…"

The happiness evaporated from Zhu Fang's expression and his face hardened. "There is. It's not easy. It can get fucking ugly. Even from directions you wouldn't expect. I don't recommend it if you can let go now. But if you can't, you've got to be sure about each other, about your feelings." He paused and licked his lips. "We wouldn't have made it if gege hadn't believed in us so completely."

That warning left Song cold. What were Ren's feelings? *Fuck, what were his own?*

He didn't know what he wanted. It was just that something in him had panicked at the thought of never seeing Ren again. His first instinct was to reach for him and never let go. To fight anyone and everyone who dared to get near them.

"Figure that out first," Zhu Fang instructed with a grin.

"The pain isn't worth it if you don't at least have that locked down."

"Thanks," Song murmured. "I've got a lot to think about. I...we...we're friends."

Zhu Fang hummed and nodded. "Yep. Been there. If that changes, call me. I'll get gege to talk you back from the edge." He smirked. "He'd be the first to say that I'd drive you off the cliff or convince you to do something stupid."

Song choked out a laugh. "Thanks for the warning."

"If you want real horror stories, I can give you Yuan Teng Fei's number. Gege and I got off easy in comparison to what he went through." Song's brow furrowed at the name as he tried to place it with where he recalled it from. He was vaguely aware of the actor. "*Path of the Poison*," Zhu Fang supplied before he could ask.

It was like getting hit by lightning. Yuan Teng Fei had been a lead actor in *Path of the Poison*, another BL that had come out at roughly the same time as *Frozen River*. Except it hadn't been a wuxia drama. It had a more contemporary setting and a very tragic ending.

"He and his costar?"

Zhu Fang nodded. "It all worked out in the end, but it was bad for a while. Don't talk to him unless you want nightmares."

"Got it." He smirked up at the man with the broad smile. "Is this some sort of club?"

Zhu Fang's laughter returned big and loud, rocking his long body in a wild sway. When he recovered, they could already hear approaching footsteps. Apparently the various managers had decided Song and Zhu Fang had been allotted all the private time they could afford.

"Next time, I'll show you the secret handshake," Zhu Fang whispered. He winked and then turned to the sharks about to sink their teeth into them.

Song had a hundred more questions, but they would have

to wait. Their privacy was at an end. He wanted to know what had happened between Zhu Fang and Guo Zi. And part of him wanted to know the horrors that Yuan Teng Fei had gone through with his costar, Shen Ruo Xuan.

But that was all idle curiosity.

What he really needed to know was how he truly felt about Ren An Xue. Had he simply found a friend that he was reluctant to lose? Was this the same character bleed he'd told Ren about last night?

Or was there something there worth risking their careers and their lives over?

11

YES, YOU BETTER REMEMBER WHO I AM TO YOU

REN AN XUE

SUMMER SUCKED.

The temperature was soaring, and he was wearing so many layers.

Whenever he had an extended break between scenes, he stripped off as many of the pieces of clothing as he possibly could. He didn't care if the BTS cameras were catching a near-constant strip show. He was hot, sweaty, and miserable.

At least the costume jiejies weren't giving him dirty looks. They just stuck out their hands and caught each robe as it came off. He felt sorry for them because each one was soddened with sweat.

The one nice thing was that Sun or one of his assistants was considerate enough to tell him when the shots were going to be from only waist-high. That allowed him to pull his robes up to let the air get to his legs. Yeah, he'd shifted away from the costume pants and stuck with his basketball shorts as much as possible.

All this unbearable heat was made worse by the fact that Song was still off set. He was supposed to be back sometime that night, but Ren wasn't counting on seeing him. The poor man probably needed to catch up on other work or at least get some sleep before he returned to filming tomorrow.

He hadn't heard from him much since his meeting with Zhu Fang. Just a quick text that the meeting had gone well. A rough song list had been sketched out, and they had some rehearsal dates planned out that wouldn't screw with the *Legend* filming schedule.

Fuck, he wished he could be there.

Yes, he was something of a fan of Zhu Fang, but this was also one of Song's first major concerts. He wanted to be there to cheer him on, to see his excitement when he stepped in front of all his screaming fans, to see the joy on his beautiful face when he lifted his voice in song.

Not going to happen.

As it was, he had a break coming up in a few days where he had to leave for a photo shoot and commercial. It was only twenty-four hours away from Hengdian, and Song was going to be busy filming a solo torture scene.

He scrubbed a hand across his face. Maybe a break away from Hengdian was a good thing. He needed to get out of Zhao Gang's head for a while. Remember what it was like to be Ren An Xue. It was becoming so he didn't know what it was like to walk around in his own skin any longer.

It was probably not a good thing that he felt the need to bite his tongue when Liu Haoyu sank into the open chair next to him. The odd thing that did occur with the disappearance of Song was the reappearance of Liu into his life. He hadn't really seen the man since that first night of dinner and drinks before the start of filming.

Liu played a rather important major character in the TV series, but their characters rarely crossed paths until the end. However, there were a few spots where they shared scenes without the presence of Tian Xiuying. With Song gone, Sun had moved all their scenes up to be filmed now.

After the first day of filming, Ren was inclined to think

that maybe he and Song had misjudged Liu. Sure, he was a little clingy and tried too hard to ingratiate himself, but that didn't necessarily mean he was a bad guy. He was probably trying to find his place within the cast and make new friends. Ren had been there plenty of times.

By the second day, Ren was tired of his teasing and offhand comments about the other actors. He wanted to blame his irritability on the heat, but Liu just rubbed him the wrong way.

Today, he just wanted Song back.

Closing his eyes, Ren tipped his head toward the sky and directed the wind created by his red portable fan at his sweaty neck. They'd returned from their lunch break a few hours ago, and he was so ready to be done. By his count, he had a couple of short scenes to shoot and a few close-ups, and then he was finished at last. A bit earlier than usual, thankfully. Then he was headed to the coldest shower he could find.

"You've got to be so miserable in those black robes," Liu murmured next to him.

Ren grunted, not bothering to open his eyes. He was miserable in clothes, period.

"You know, a group of us are heading out for a late dinner tonight. *After* the sun sets and things cool off," Liu suggested.

Ren chewed on the inside of his lip for a second, trying to decide what to do. The idea of hanging with a bunch of people after spending his day surrounded by people and heat sounded horrible. But the only person he ever spent any time with was Song. He'd not gotten to know the rest of the cast as well as he should have.

He knew he should say yes, but without Song, all he wanted to do was hide in a dark room.

"I don't know. Right now, I'm just tired. Can you or someone in the group send a text when you're planning to go?" he asked. There. That wasn't a hard no. Maybe after he cooled off and rested a bit, he'd feel up for going out with people.

"Sure, but I guess you'd rather catch up with Song Wei Li in private than hang out with the rest of us."

Oh, he did not miss that twist of jealousy in Liu's voice when he mentioned Song.

Ren flicked his eyes open and smiled lazily at Liu. "Song won't be back in town until late tonight. We'll catch up tomorrow, I'm sure." He ignored the whole dig about wanting to hang out "in private." He wasn't going to get sucked into Liu's need to stir the pot.

"Really?" Liu replied, his eyes widening suddenly. "Because I swear I saw him over by the trailers not five minutes ago."

"What?" Ren sat up in his chair, his heart skipping a beat. Did Song return early to surprise him? That had to be it if he came all the way to the set. He had the entire day off. He wasn't scheduled to shoot any scenes. There was no reason to come to the studio unless he maybe wanted to see Ren.

"Yeah, I saw him talking with someone I didn't recognize from the cast." Liu shrugged and closed his eyes as he directed his fan at his sweat-slicked face. "They looked close. Must be an old friend or maybe someone he's filmed with in the past." Liu paused and cracked an eye open as he delivered what he knew was the most devastating piece of information. "They were hanging all over each other."

No.

Liu was exaggerating.

It was nothing.

Then why had his chest constricted? He could barely draw air into his lungs. Each *thunk* of his heart was painful, like a knife sawing through his chest.

Song was back, but he hadn't told him.

Song was talking to someone else. Someone he was close to. Someone he felt comfortable being *physically* close with.

Something dark and ugly poured through Ren. He fought hard to keep his expression blank as Liu's eyes remained locked on his face. Everything in him demanded that he march toward the trailers and locate Song. He wanted to rip that other person—man or woman—off his laoshi.

He *needed* to stake his claim.

Zhao Gang would not tolerate anyone touching *his* Tian Xiuying. He littered the landscape with dead bodies for his Ah-Ying.

Right now, he wanted to leap from his chair, grab Liu by the throat, and demand he tell the truth about Song.

Luckily, one of Sun's assistants and someone from wardrobe rushed over to get him back into costume. They were ready for his final shots of the day.

He left without saying anything else to Liu. He was ushered over to the set with people wrapping him in robes, combing out his hair, and touching up his makeup. The scene was a blur, but it was clear his mind wasn't on his work considering Sun had to tell him twice to stop grinding his teeth. He was supposed to be calm and serene.

He suspected he looked like he wanted to rip someone's head off.

Less than an hour later, the scene was finished and he was free.

Ren stalked off the set. The jiejies made a grab for his hanfu and only got part of it. They just barely managed to get his wig. He shouted over his shoulder that he'd leave the rest of his costume in his trailer as he snatched up his phone and bag. Liu was probably somewhere smirking and laughing at him, but he didn't fucking care. A quick tap on the screen of his phone showed that he didn't have any waiting texts from Song announcing that he was in town.

Did he not want Ren to know?

Had he sneaked onto the lot just to see this "friend"?

What the fuck?

Ren clenched his teeth. It wasn't as though Song belonged to him. Ren didn't have any claim on the man. Didn't have any right to say how he spent his time. Or who he spent it with.

But couldn't he have sent a quick text to say "hey"?

Bullshit.

As he reached the trailers, he spotted Song talking with someone he did recognize. Beautiful and sexy Chen Junjie. The man who was supposed to have his role. What was he doing here?

Oh, and Song most definitely knew him. His costar laughed loudly and grabbed Chen's shoulder as he rocked backward. Chen chuckled as well and leaned closer so that their heads nearly touched.

Too close.

Chen spotted him first and it wasn't hard to read his lips. He froze, eyes going wide while his lips parted in something that looked like "Whoa."

Song must have heard him or noticed the difference in his friend, because he turned his head and his eyes locked on Ren. His eyes also widened, but he didn't say anything as Ren approached. It felt like his gaze ate him up.

Yes, you better fucking remember who I am to you.

But that thought nearly stopped Ren cold.

Who was he to Song?

A costar. Another fellow actor. Maybe a friend, but probably only a temporary one before he moved on to his next project.

Ren faltered a step, his emotions floundering in his chest. He didn't know what the fuck he was doing anymore, and he was just a few yards away from his target. He needed to get his head together.

Desperate, he pulled on the one thing that was natural right now. Zhao Gang.

He wrapped himself in his character's cool confidence and

icy exterior. Nothing could touch Zhao Gang except for his Tian Xiuying. And he wasn't even sure Tian—*no, Song*—wanted him.

"Ren! I was just coming to find you!" Song shouted as he drew near, seeming to recover from his surprise.

"You're back early," Ren replied in a calm tone that he didn't feel. He offered Song a tight smile as he stopped a few feet away from Song and Chen. As if from muscle memory, he snapped out the folding fan in his right hand and started to slowly wave it, stirring a small breeze as he stared at Chen.

"Yeah, I managed to change to an earlier flight," Song said. He dropped his hand from Chen's shoulder as if he suddenly remembered it was there. "Have you met Chen Junjie before?"

Ren could feel his expression growing as brittle as melting ice and bowed his head. "I haven't. A pleasure to meet you at last. Have you and Song worked together in the past?"

"No, not yet," Song murmured slowly. There was something in his voice as if he was confused, but Chen succeeded in catching his attention.

"No, we were on that variety show together."

"*Ugh!* Don't remind me! That one was a nightmare."

And yet, they both dissolved into more boisterous laughter that left Ren's hand tightening on his fan.

Chen recovered first, wiping one corner of his eye. "We've kept in touch over the years." He straightened and gave Ren a rather dazzling smile. "I start filming tomorrow on another set and I heard *Legend of the Lost Night* was shooting over here. I thought I'd pop by and check in with Lao Song."

"He didn't know I'd gone out of town. It was just luck that we ran into each other," Song added, but Ren's brain was still stuck on "Lao Song."

"That is lucky that you found each other," Ren managed to say without grinding his teeth.

"Actually, we were talking about grabbing dinner together. Would you like to join us?" Chen offered.

Ren barely stopped himself from shouting "Yes!" He'd tag along and pin Song to the table in the middle of the restaurant. He'd kiss the man senseless, leave his lips swollen and bitten. He'd mark him so that all the world knew that Song Wei Li belonged to Ren An Xue.

But he couldn't do that.

And he wasn't sure he could control his temper for more than another minute.

With a sigh, he shook his head. "Unfortunately, I've already made plans for this evening with some of the cast."

"Really? Are you sure you can't join us?" Song inquired.

Ren's resolve wavered for a second, but he tightened his grip on his impulses and shook his head again. "Maybe some other time. You two have fun."

Using up the last of his control, Ren strolled away and slipped into his trailer. He did *not* slam the door like he wanted to. He did *not* rip off the last of his robes; he carefully removed them and folded them up for the costumer.

He did *not* cry, even though he wanted to, as he stepped into the tiny shower and turned on the cold water.

The lukewarm wash helped to clear his mind to a couple of very ugly and painful realizations.

One: He was disgustingly, horribly, almost uncontrollably jealous of anyone who got near Song.

Two: He was falling in love with Song Wei Li.

Ren leaned on the cool wall and swallowed against the burn of unshed tears. He was so screwed.

He was falling in love with Song Wei Li, and there was nothing he could do about it. Song wasn't gay. Song didn't see him like that. At best, he would be only a friend to the man.

If he didn't pull his head out of his ass and get control of his emotions, he was going to lose his right to even call Song his friend.

How had this happened?

Yes, he'd always known he was bisexual, but he'd been careful to keep the part that his world deemed undesirable tucked away. A relationship with a man wasn't an option. If anything, attempts to be with a man would ruin his life and the lives of his family.

It wasn't because Song was attractive. He was in the entertainment industry. He was surrounded by beautiful people all day, every day.

No, it was because Song was Song.

There was something so endlessly enticing and intriguing about the man. He was lively, funny, silly, infuriating, sweet, frustrating, and warm. Every time Ren thought he knew all there was to Song's personality, he'd do or say something new that would completely shock him.

Everything within his soul cried out to grab Song and tuck him close, to hold him, protect him, and love him with every fiber of his being.

But Song was not his.

Song would never be his.

And something inside of Ren was dying each day he had to pretend that he was okay with that.

12

SONG DOESN'T WANT TO SHARE
SONG WEI LI

Something had gone horribly wrong.

Since returning to the set, the chemistry between him and Ren was off.

Maybe it was him. Maybe Ren could tell he was disappointed that Ren wouldn't go to dinner with him and Chen. Yes, he would have preferred it to be just the two of them, but he'd thought Ren would be excited to see him after being in Hong Kong. He'd thought he'd be eager to hear about plans for the concert and meeting Zhu Fang.

But he got nothing.

Not even a teasing question about whether he acquired the selfie Ren had practically begged for.

It wasn't as though he had any real right to be pissy. It was a good thing Ren had plans to hang out with other cast members. Song had been dominating a lot of his time. He needed to meet other actors and build his network.

Except Song didn't want to share him.

When he'd landed yesterday afternoon, his mind had been filled with daydreams of stealing Ren away from the set the second he was done with filming. They'd grab some noodles at the little shop on the way back to the residence hall. From there, they'd talk for hours. They'd talk about Ren filming two of his big scenes. Song was dying to know all his thoughts and feelings about them. He wanted to wrap an arm around his shoulders and dispel the last of his lingering fears and worries.

Song would then share his news about the concert and what he thought about meeting the interesting, and slightly strange, Zhu Fang.

But that was where his daydreams tangled up. Everything in him was demanding he also share Zhu Fang's secret relationship with Guo Zi. He wanted to see Ren's face light up with wonder…and maybe hope that they could have…

Have what?

Song wasn't even sure what he wanted from Ren. He didn't want to stop their time together, their talks, their meals. He didn't want to lose their closeness.

The only thing he felt sure of was what he didn't want.

He didn't want to lose Ren.

And he certainly didn't want this sudden cold indifference he was currently faced with.

The morning and afternoon shoots were changed to a night shoot, thanks to a series of showers that moved into the area. The heat was thankfully pushed away, but it was replaced with stifling humidity that made the air thick.

They were less than halfway through the series, and Zhao Gang and Tian Xiuying were supposed to be well on the path to being friends. Tian might be a little stiff, but they were teasing each other more. They were comfortable around each other. There was more banter.

Tonight's scenes were supposed to be easy. They were backstory conversations, brainstorming the tangled mystery they were faced with, and drinking.

Luckily, the wine pots were filled with water, because at this point, they'd both be utterly wasted, thanks to the number of takes they'd been through.

Nearly every line Ren delivered was stiff and haughty rather than light and playful.

And of course, Song couldn't stop himself from reacting to Ren's energy, so he kept replying in the same gruff and reserved manner.

By the fifth take, Sun Jing pulled them both aside away from the rest of the crew and chewed them out, demanding they get their heads out of their asses.

They apologized and it improved by slow measures for the rest of the evening, but Song could still feel the crackle of tension between them.

When the meal break was called at last, Song grabbed Ren by the wrist and practically dragged him to the trailers. He didn't give a shit what it looked like to the rest of the cast and crew. Something was wrong, and the longer they didn't talk about it, the worse it got. They could not go on for another three months like this. They'd kill each other by the end of the shoot, and *no one* would believe they were a loving couple.

Just as they reached the area with the trailers, a sharp crack of thunder cut across the sky. He hesitated, then jerked open the door to Ren's trailer since it was closer than his own. He stepped inside and Ren stomped inside after him.

"What the fuck is going on with you?" Song snapped the second the door closed behind Ren.

"Nothing," Ren snarled, twisting so that not a millimeter of his body brushed Song's as he made his way into the trailer.

"Bullshit. You've been giving me the cold shoulder all day." He nearly mentioned the three texts he'd sent and the silence he'd received in response. He was afraid those words would sound far too pathetic and needy, as if he were desperate for any ounce of attention Ren would direct at him.

"I don't know what you're talking about. We haven't seen each other all day." Ren undid the tie around his outer robe and shrugged it off. He carefully folded it up and placed it aside before moving into the kitchen.

"Exactly. We essentially had an entire day off, and I didn't hear one word from you." *Fuck it.* He'd embrace the pathetic if it got Ren talking to him at last.

"I spent the day working. I'm sure I don't have as many assistants as you do keeping up with things like social media, so I was catching up on that. I've got an audition soon. And I've got some emotional scenes coming up I wanted to run over."

"Why didn't you call me? I would have run lines with you."

Ren grabbed the electric tea kettle and filled it with water. He flipped it on for the water to heat. "It was fine. I didn't want to bother you."

Song opened his mouth to say that it was impossible for Ren to bother him when there was an even louder boom of thunder followed by a torrential downpour hitting the roof of the RV. One moment there was no rain and in the next second, it was as if a monsoon had opened up on their heads.

"Shit," he whispered. "Looks like I'm trapped here now."

Ren's head snapped toward him, his eyes flaring wide for a second and his mouth pinched into a hard thin line. For a heartbeat, Song could very clearly see why Ren had gotten the role of Zhao Gang. When Ren was pissed, he could be fucking scary.

His friend whirled around and marched to the far end of the RV, his stomps almost rising above the sound of the rain. When he returned, he thrust a long, black umbrella into Song's face.

"Here. I'd hate for you to be trapped with me," Ren snarled.

Fuck. Song nearly moaned. He needed to stop talking, because somehow he was making all of this worse.

But he had to keep talking if he was going to save whatever friendship they'd found together.

He snatched the umbrella away from Ren and tossed it onto the couch behind him. "That's not what I meant."

"Whatever," Ren muttered and crossed to the kitchenette. He pulled out a couple of teacups, each one loudly clicking on the counter as it hit. He slammed open another cabinet and pulled down the box of apricot oolong he preferred and the blackberry sage oolong that Song drank every time Ren made tea for him.

Song wanted to laugh. Ren was insanely pissed, but he was still making tea for Song. He doubted the other man was even aware of what he was doing. It was muscle memory at this point.

But Song held the laugh in. He'd already majorly fucked up with the rain comment. If he teased him about the tea, Song was likely to get a face of scalding hot water.

"Didi—" he started again, and the death glare snapped to him.

Yeah, okay. Didi was not allowed to be used right now.

"Ren An Xue," he tried in a tone normally saved for rabid animals. "Please talk to me. Whatever I have done to hurt you or upset you, I'm sorry. I'm sure I didn't mean it intentionally. Please, help me understand what is going on. The last time we talked was two days ago. Just before I met Zhu Fang. I thought everything was okay."

Ren grabbed the edge of the counter with both hands and squeezed his eyes shut. Song remained unmoving, closely watching Ren struggle to bring his emotions under control. Everything in him screamed to close the few feet that separated them. He wanted to wrap his arms around Ren's waist and press his face into the middle of his back. He wanted to hold him and promise that he was going to fix whatever was bothering him.

But Ren was a powder keg looking for a spark. Song had

set him off so many times already, he was sure one more wrong move would destroy the last shreds of friendship they had left.

"Have you been close to Chen Junjie long?" Ren asked. It sounded like he'd tried very hard to keep his tone neutral, but the words still came out sounding like they were being ground up between rocks.

Of all the things he'd expected Ren to say, asking about Chen had never made the list.

His mind raced to pick the question apart. Ren had said "close" rather than friends. *Did he think...*

"We're not all that close," Song replied, trying to stall for time as his mind struggled to guess what was really behind Ren's distress.

Ren shoved away from the counter and walked over to stand in front of Song. Only a couple of inches in height separated them, but when Ren was angry, it felt like he towered. Where was the awkward, shy man he'd first met in Shanghai? There was zero sign of him.

"Not close, but he came to this set to see you," Ren countered, anger filtering into his voice. "You were gone for two days and the first thing you do is hang out with *him*. The first time I see you in almost *three* days, you and he are wrapped up in each other."

Shit...was Ren...was Ren jealous?

For one beautiful, sparkling moment, Song's heart screamed and cried with joy. If Ren could feel jealousy over a little attention from Chen, it meant that just maybe he had some feelings for Song.

Well, feelings other than blind rage.

But he couldn't celebrate. And he definitely couldn't pick apart Ren's wrong comments.

He could reassure him, talk him down. Even though he wanted to shout that there was no one in the world that could possibly compare to Ren. There was no one else that shone brighter in his life than the scary man in front of him.

Without thinking, Song reached out and placed his hand on Ren's slender waist. The undershirt he wore beneath the robe was almost as thin as tissue paper, allowing the intense heat of his skin to scald Song's palm. They both gasped at the contact and froze.

Sure, they'd exchanged a hundred little touches in the course of a day, but those had been countless shoulder bumps, pokes, slaps, and shoves. This…this was intensely intimate.

Song's eyes snapped up to Ren's face, expecting to see rage or even horror and disgust.

What greeted him was shock. The anger was completely gone. Those beautiful, perfect puppy eyes were shining on him again, looking so very lost and scared.

"Song?" Ren whispered, almost like he was begging Song to help him. Save him.

"It's okay." His fingers tightened on Ren's waist. He didn't pull him closer, even though he longed to feel the press of Ren's body against his own. He didn't tip his head up to brush his lips along Ren's even though his soul was crying for it. "There is nothing between Chen and me. I was coming to find you when he found me first. I flew home early to see you."

It was the truth.

Right after he finished his meeting with Zhu Fang and his entourage, he got Bao Shi to reschedule his flight. The earliest he was able to get. He'd wanted that night. He'd wanted to get back to Ren as quickly as possible. Another twelve hours was even too long.

"I—" Ren started and stopped, his voice breaking.

Song slowly moved his thumb along Ren's stomach in a gentle caress. Muscles jumped under his touch, and his breathing became ragged. He watched as Ren's pupils dilated, the blackness nearly consuming his eyes. Song could feel himself falling into that darkness, getting lost in Ren's beauty.

Ren moved, his head tilting forward barely a millimeter. The tip of his tongue slipped out between parted lips and wet the plump bottom one. Song's eyes followed that motion like a hawk, his body coiling to seize it and more.

A sharp whistle cut through the trailer as the water in the tea kettle boiled and steamed. They jumped apart as if they'd been electrocuted. Ren hurried across to the kitchen and shut it off. Song could only watch as he finished making their tea with trembling hands. Song wasn't any better. It felt like his entire body was shaking.

What had almost happened?

He was disappointed that it had stopped, but maybe it was for the best. Maybe.

No. No, it fucking wasn't.

When the water and tea leaves were combined in the cups to steep, Ren grabbed the edge of the counter again. "I'm… I'm so sorry, Song laoshi. I don't know what's wrong with me."

"It's okay, didi," Song murmured. He started to close the distance between them, wanting to see if he could pick up where the tea kettle had interrupted, but Ren's next words stopped him cold.

"Do you think…do you think this is character bleed?"

What? Song's heart screamed.

"I…everything is such a fucking mess inside of me. I just completed two hard days of emotional scenes and then the first time I saw you, the first time I saw Tian Xiuying, you were with this stranger. Maybe…" Ren fell silent, his head hanging with his eyes closed.

Song's heart hammered and cried out as his mind followed along the logical path Ren laid out. It all made too much sense. Zhao Gang was incredibly possessive of his Ah-Ying. He would break into a fit of jealousy if he saw someone even standing too close to *his* man.

Was that all this was? Ren didn't feel anything for him. He'd been channeling Zhao Gang for too long. When Ren saw him, he didn't actually see Song Wei Li, but Tian Xiuying.

Something inside of him howled.

On the outside, he smiled at his didi.

Song closed the short distance between them and he tilted his head to the side so he could see Ren's face. "Didi, I'm serious. It's okay. This filming has been intense, and you have been doing an amazing job. People are going to fall in love with you and your Zhao Gang."

Ren turned tear-filled eyes toward him, and Song fell a little harder for the man. "But I'm making you suffer because I'm crazy."

"You're not crazy, and I'm not suffering." Song's smile trembled on his lips. If this was suffering, he'd gladly spend the rest of his life in this misery. Ren was becoming his heart. "I'm just worried about you. I also feel like I've found a good friend on this shoot, and I really don't want to lose him."

Ren's expression suddenly became fierce. "You won't. I promise."

Song believed him, but there was a deeper ache that echoed through his chest. Was friendship the only thing they'd have?

If this talk had answered anything for Song, it was that he wanted far more from Ren than friendship.

But he didn't say that. He smiled and motioned to the two cups of tea. "Did you make one of those for me?"

Ren jerked upright and nodded. He pulled away the tea leaf diffuser and topped off the drink by adding the perfect amount of honey. *Yes, Ren knew him.*

"Go sit down, Song laoshi. Let me make you something to eat," Ren suddenly ordered in a tone Song knew and loved so very much.

With his cup of tea in hand, Song retreated to the table

and chairs so he could sip his tea and watch Ren work. There was no point in arguing with him. Besides, it allowed them both to slip into familiar ground after walking along the edge of the unknown for so long.

They chatted about a lot of mundane and silly things that didn't matter. Ren asked him hundreds of questions about the concert plans and what Zhu Fang was like. He quickly brushed off Song's questions about the previous day's shoot. Ren wasn't ready to talk about anything related to Zhao Gang.

And Song didn't offer up the selfie with Zhu Fang. It reminded him too much of things he'd started to hope for. They weren't going to happen now.

Song had to find a way to be happy with the friendship he'd found with this precious man.

13

BEHAVE YOURSELF, AH-XUE
REN AN XUE

Mornings were the best time.

The unbearable heat hadn't sunk into the set yet, and while things were busy as the crew set up for the first shot of the day, it wasn't a hectic race. There was still time for sips of coffee and lazy words of greeting.

And yes, maybe his scalp hadn't started to burn and itch yet from the damn wig.

And yes, he wasn't covered in sweat yet.

And yes, his body didn't ache from hours of standing, fighting, and flying awkwardly in the wire harness.

But best of all was seeing Song Wei Li first thing in the morning.

Even after an hour in the makeup chair getting his face and hair just right, the man was still half-asleep and a little grumbly. It was the one time Song was naturally similar to his character, Tian Xiuying.

The normally silly, friendly, outgoing Song Wei Li was not a morning person. He was more like a growling bear who wanted to crawl back into his den and sleep. He didn't want to interact with people or act. Sun Jing even knew better than to try to put Song in a wire harness first thing in the morning. Everyone gave the actor a wide berth for a few hours.

Except for Ren.

He was the only one who could coax that first smile from Song in the morning.

And today was going to be a great day simply because he was expecting everything to be normal. Song had returned and was going to be acting beside him all day. They would be able to slip into their normal banter and nonsense.

It didn't matter that there were dozens of other people around them all day, or that they were scheduled to spend at least a good chunk of the day sharing their scenes with Ma Daiyu. She was friendly and fun. A fabulous actress.

The important thing was that Song had returned and they'd be together. The rest of the world sort of fell away and didn't matter anymore.

As Ren reached the set, he found Song already lounging in a chair, his long wig hanging behind him in an inky black cascade. His eyes were closed and he was holding his blue portable fan to his chest as if it were his teddy bear.

God, what he wouldn't give to be that fan.

Ren faltered a step as that thought crossed his mind. The one thing he refused to worry about was whether their argument from yesterday had changed things between them. Had he ruined what they had because he couldn't get his head on straight?

When they finished their scenes last evening, everything had felt normal. They'd laughed and joked, talked like they always had.

But there was a lingering buzz in the middle of his chest when he thought about their fight.

And how close Ren had come to kissing Song.

They'd been standing inches apart. It would have been so easy to lean in those final few inches and press their lips together. When the need first hit him, his lips had tingled and his breath caught. What would it have been like to feel his warm, soft mouth? To explore his taste? To kiss him again and again until Song was clinging to him and moaning with need?

Or have Song pull away and slug him because he wasn't fucking gay.

No. No more of those thoughts.

Song wasn't like him. Didn't think of him that way.

He needed to let all of that go, or he was going to risk losing what he had with the man forever.

Clenching his teeth, Ren mentally tightened his grip on his happiness and walked over to stand beside Song's chair. Very carefully, he reached down and slipped one finger under a lock of his hair. It was his *real* hair. Song had grown out his hair so that his real bangs could be used in order to protect some of his hairline. Fuck, he wished he'd known about that trick. With Zhao Gang's hairstyle, though, he didn't think it would have worked.

Ren moved the lock of hair away from Song's forehead, keeping it from falling into his eyes.

Song's brow furrowed a little as he cracked open one eye to look up at him. "How can you be so cheerful this early?" Song grumbled, but the hard line of his mouth softened.

"It is a beautiful day, and my Song laoshi is back on the set. How can I not be happy?" Ren teased.

Song closed his eyes, but his lips tilted up into a small smile. "You're so silly, didi."

Ren couldn't help himself. He reached out and moved another piece of hair from Song's forehead even though it didn't really need to be moved. Standing so close, he just wanted to touch the man and right now, Song was so relaxed and still, as if he welcomed Ren's attention.

"Have you eaten yet, Song laoshi?"

Song grunted, which usually meant no. He'd probably sucked down some hot black tea on his ride over to wardrobe and makeup.

Chuckling, Ren reached into his massive sleeve and felt around for the correct hidden pocket. When he found what he was searching for, he plucked the fan from Song's grip. The man's eyes popped open and a whimper escaped his parted lips. As he made a grab for the fan, Ren placed an apple into his outstretched hand.

"Eat."

"But—"

"I'll hold your fan. Eat."

Song's bottom lip jutted out a little in a pout as he stared at the shiny red apple in his hand. "I'd rather save it for later in the day. You know I always need something in the afternoon."

"And I've got another one for you chilling in my trailer for later today. Eat this one now."

A slow smile spread across Song's lips as he lifted his gaze to meet Ren's. The butterflies returned in force to swirl in Ren's stomach and harass his poor heart. Song's smile was his weakness. But then so were his sad eyes, his angry glares, and his worried looks. Yes, everything about Song Wei Li made Ren weak.

"What would I do without my Ren laoshi taking care of me?" Song teased before sinking his teeth into the apple.

Ren opened his mouth to answer, but Liu replied first.

"Most likely starve to death."

The man strolled over and bumped into Ren's shoulder, flashing a wicked grin at Ren. Out of the corner of his eye, Ren could see Song shift to the edge of his chair as if he meant to crowd Liu. His sweet smile was gone and he was actively scowling at their fellow actor, but the man didn't seem to notice.

Liu had one quick scene with them this morning, and then he was moving over to another team actively shooting on the other side of the studio lot to finish his day.

"I found out that I'm not needed on the other set until late in the day. I was hoping to call in that rain check you promised me for lunch," Liu said, this time with a wide smile.

"Oh...umm..." Ren stammered, his brain was completely locked up. He had evaded a couple of lunch invites from Liu while Song had been out of town. The last one he escaped only by offering a rain check for another time.

Liu shifted his gaze to Song, and his smirk sharpened to something jagged like broken glass. "But now that Song laoshi is back, I'm sure you're not available." He gave a sigh and the sweet smile for Ren returned. "Don't worry about it. I'll catch you another time."

The actor strolled away, humming to himself and swinging the sleeves of his robe as though he didn't have a care in the world.

What the fuck was that about?

Ren turned his attention to Song, and his stomach instantly sank. Song looked pissed.

"What—" Song started but was cut off when one of Sun's assistants ran over.

"We're ready for you!"

With a final glare at Ren, Song shoved out of his chair, snatched his fan away from Ren, and marched toward the set, taking a vicious bite out of his apple as he went. Ren trailed after him, not exactly sure why Song was suddenly so mad at him.

They paused on the edge of the street where they would shoot their first scene. The first bit was easy. Just walking down the street and some light banter. The next scene was in a pub where they would encounter Liu's character and exchange some threats.

"What's wrong?" Ren asked in a low voice while they waited for everyone to finish getting ready. The wardrobe and makeup jiejies floated around them like hummingbirds, combing their hair and adjusting their robes. One plucked away Song's apple core and reapplied his rose-colored lipstick.

Okay, he definitely didn't need to watch that while wondering what it would be like to lick that color away to get to the real man.

Song's frown deepened and his eyes darted to the people too close to them. When they disappeared, he started to speak and stopped. He looked over his shoulder and Ren's eyes followed to spot the BTS camera trained on both of them.

Ren had gotten used to ignoring it, but he'd also gotten crafty with his ever-present prop.

With a flick of his wrist, the white folding fan opened and he lifted it so that it blocked both of their faces as he leaned in closer.

"What's wrong?" he repeated in a whisper.

"What the hell are you doing with Liu?" Song snarled in a matching low voice.

Ren jerked his head back, eyes widening. "What do you mean?"

Song reached up and touched his hand, holding the fan in place in front of them. Those warm fingers burned into his flesh, and it took Ren an extra second to focus on the words falling from Song's lips. "I told you to be careful around him."

Ren shrugged. "While you were gone, we had a few scenes together. We chatted. No big deal. He's harmless."

Song glared at him, little lines digging into the flesh between his brows while his lips pressed into a hard line. "If this is what happens when I'm not on set, I'm not leaving you alone again."

A surge of pure joy lit through Ren's veins and bubbled over in his heart. If Song thought this was a threat or punishment, he was insane. Ren wanted nothing more than this: Song always with him.

Carefully schooling his features, Ren nodded, trying so desperately to appear contrite. "I'm sorry for making you worry, Song laoshi," he murmured as he lowered the fan. "How about I cook lunch to apologize for worrying you?"

Song's eyes narrowed on him, and Ren nearly squirmed.

Did he suspect Ren was inches away from throwing his arms around Song's neck and laughing like a lunatic?

"Noodles?" Song asked softly.

Ren smirked. "I made you noodles just the other day. But I have some of those dumplings you like."

"Okay," he mumbled, sounding so very petulant, but Ren didn't miss the hint of a smile that glinted in his dark eyes. At last, he sighed and shook his head. "Put away the puppy eyes, didi. You're killing me."

"Anything for Song laoshi."

And it was the truth. He would do anything for Song. Even give up what his heart wanted most in the world just to keep him as a friend.

The first half of the day went smoothly, with the scenes requiring very few takes. The only bad thing was the temperature steadily climbing with the sun in the clear cerulean sky. When the afternoon break was finally called, both he and Song were quick to start stripping off their many layers. A gaggle of wardrobe jiejies followed after them like a flock of magpies picking up shiny objects for their nest. Outer robes, ties, decorative ribbon with the jade pendant, and undershirt all came off. He had a thin T-shirt below that he wished to shed as well, but he was not willing to let the BTS camera catch him walking around the set shirtless.

Yes, he had a shirtless scene that would be shot in a couple of weeks, but that was enough for the cameras.

When the wardrobe was safely retrieved, the jiejies hurried away, seeming grateful to have their charges free of the careless actors.

"Are you hungry, Song laoshi?"

"I'm melting, didi," Song moaned. "Cool me off, and then I can think about being hungry."

Clapping his hands on Song's slumped and sweaty shoulders, Ren directed Song to the trailers. "Air conditioning and lunch. In a little while, you'll be ready to grump at Zhao Gang."

"Only because Zhao Gang deserves it."

In the relative darkness of the trailer, where the air conditioning was turned up to the max, Song stretched out on the couch, playing with his phone while Ren pulled food out of the fridge for their lunch.

"What are you making me for lunch, didi?" His costar sang, his lovely voice filling the relative quiet of the space.

Ren smiled. He loved when Song serenaded him. He had the most hypnotic voice. Everything felt like a love song.

"Dumplings and…whatever else I can find. I think I need to ask my assistant to restock my fridge."

"You need to train your assistant better," he sang again. He stopped and chuckled.

"Wu Dong Mei is still new," Ren countered. He'd picked up a permanent assistant after his manager saw how horribly he was keeping up with social media and how hot the buzz was for *Legend* already. Yuying had high expectations for his career. Ren was worried about disappointing her.

"And it's her job to make your life easier so you can concentrate on work. Investing some time in her training now will save you so many headaches in the long run," Song admonished.

Ren looked up to see that Song's eyes were still locked on his phone. With a smirk, Ren shook his head as he returned his attention to the food in front of him. "Yes, Song laoshi."

"Don't 'yes' me, didi. Do it."

"You know I hate telling people what to do."

Song snorted. "You have absolutely no problem bossing me around."

Ren glanced over his shoulder at Song. "Only because you're so cute when I boss you around."

Dark eyes lifted to stare at him over the edge of the phone.

A chill ran down Ren's spine and his mouth went dry. *Dear God. No one should be so sexy.*

"Behave yourself, Ah-Xue. Make my lunch." He said it low and deep, those beautiful dulcet tones dousing his brain in alcohol. He was getting drunk on Song's voice.

Swallowing hard, Ren forced his eyes to the dumplings in front of him.

What the fuck am I doing? Oh, that's right. Making lunch.

Song was going to be the death of him.

"Do you believe in soul mates, didi?" Song suddenly inquired.

Ren jerked at the question, all thought screeching to a halt. *Where had that—*

That's right. They had a scene coming up tomorrow where Zhao Gang admitted that he thought Tian Xiuying was his soul mate.

"No," he said simply, continuing to pull together what he needed for their meal.

"Really?"

"Yep. Don't believe in them."

"Who hurt you, didi?" Song asked so very softly.

Laughter burst from Ren and he shook his head. "No one hurt me, Song laoshi. I just don't believe in them." He paused and then shrugged. "I don't think there's some soul mate out there waiting for me. I guess I always thought that I'd be alone, and I'm fine with that."

Song huffed softly. "I'm never going to let that happen."

Ren shifted his body to turn more of his back to Song, hiding the wide grin that spread across his lips. No, he hadn't meant it how Ren's heart wanted him to, but that was okay. If they could have more afternoons like this with lazy conversation and good food, Ren would be happy for the rest of his life.

But if he could have one kiss…

14

IT'S NOT A BL WITHOUT A ROOFTOP DRINKING SCENE!

SONG WEI LI

Nearing the end of the second month of shooting had both good and bad qualities.

Good: They had a long string of night shoots ahead of them, which meant cooler temperatures.

Bad: Most of their night shoots were fight scenes and had lots of wire work.

Good: Night shoots meant darker shadows in which he could spend time with Ren without worrying about exactly what the BTS camera was catching. It meant a few lingering touches and more heads bent together in whispered conversation.

Bad: One less month of working with Ren.

But Song shoved that thought aside as he carefully climbed up to the rooftop where he and Ren would be shooting their drinking and bonding scene.

Ren spotted him and lifted the white jug that held their "liquor" and laughed. "It's not a BL without a rooftop drinking scene!"

Song snorted and carefully crossed to him. The top part of the roof was flat so they could safely walk across, but where they were supposed to be seated for the conversation was sloped and covered in clay tiles. Each of them was wearing a small safety harness to keep them from falling off.

They weren't incredibly high, but a drop from here would likely result in a broken bone or two.

But Ren's smile was worth the risk.

Song lifted his jug into the air in a toast while an assistant crowded close to make sure he didn't suddenly tumble.

"About time you got here," Ren complained when Song lowered himself into position. "I've been stuck up here for an hour listening to Sun grumble at me."

"I heard. You weren't being grumpy enough," Song teased.

"It's so hard to be grumpy." Ren leaned back on one elbow and held his liquor bottle up as if he were toasting the bright full moon above them. The real one. Part of this scene would be shot with a green screen in front of them so that the effects artist would be able to implant an even bigger, more lustrous moon into the scene. "Look at that moon. Even the stars are sparkling for us. How can Zhao Gang be grumpy under such a moon?"

"Because Zhao Gang is naturally an angry bastard when he doesn't get his way," Song mocked.

Ren tilted his head toward Song and turned on his lethal puppy eyes. "Then his Ah-Ying needs to listen to Zhao Gang so he's never grumpy."

"But if Xiuying does whatever Zhao Gang says, won't he lose interest? He's only excited about the chase, right?"

Ren gasped and sat up straight. "Absolutely not! Zhao Gang and Tian Xiuying are soul mates! Zhao Gang might be having fun in the chase, but the second he catches Ah-Ying, he's going to devote his entire existence to his happiness. He's going to save him and they will live happily ever after."

Song chortled. This from the man who'd said not long ago that he didn't believe in soul mates.

"Except Zhao Gang is racing toward his own death,

thanks to all the enemies he's made. How are they going to live happily ever after if he gets himself killed?"

"How can you have so little faith in me? I'm going to escape and take care of you, Ah-Ying. Don't you worry," Ren replied, flowing straight into the honeyed tones he used whenever he was in character.

There was nothing Song could say to that. It was a pretty dream. Escape the world they were in that said they couldn't be together, and take care of each other for the rest of their days.

"This is my favorite scene," Song announced while the lighting and cameramen continued to argue in the background.

"Really?" Ren reached and put his bottle aside so he could pick up his folding fan. He stretched out a bit, lazily creating a breeze that stirred some of his hair. "It's not what I would have guessed you would pick. Why?"

"This is a big moment for Xiuying and Gang. Up until now, Gang has been chasing Xiuying. He's the one constantly going to Xiuying, popping up in weird places, tagging along, and even herding him. This is the first time that *Xiuying* goes to him. It's an important step in their relationship. Gang is hurting and lonely. Xiuying tries to comfort him."

Song's heart swelled to see Ren close his eyes, a smile slowly drawing up the corners of his mouth. The moon kissed his pale skin, making it glow against the night sky.

"I like that." Ren suddenly opened his eyes and narrowed them on Song. "In the book, isn't this scene where they kiss for the first time?" Ren wrinkled his nose and shook his head. "I always thought the kiss was far too early in that spot."

A surprised bark of laughter jumped from Song. That was not the kind of thing he'd expected Ren to have an opinion about.

"Really? Then where do you think they should have kissed for the first time?"

"Waterfall scene," Ren stated without a breath of hesitation.

"What?" Song choked out. He'd thought the man would at least have to think about it.

"The waterfall scene. You know, where they are on the run from the prince's army and they are cornered on the waterfall. They have to jump to escape." Ren turned the fan and pointed it in Song's direction. "Speaking of, I am not looking forward to filming that scene at all."

"Sun Jing is not going to make you jump off a waterfall. There are stunt doubles for those dangerous scenes." Song chuckled.

"Don't be so sure of that!" Sun countered through his megaphone, proving that he was listening to their conversation with at least half an ear.

Ren snapped his fan shut, aimed it at Sun, and then at Song. "That is not funny. You cannot make me jump off a cliff, even if you have me in a harness."

"You're not," Song reassured him in a firm voice. He was going to strangle Sun if he thought terrifying Ren about that scene was a good idea. No one was allowed to scare his didi. "Ignore him. Why is that scene the best place for the first kiss?"

Ren paused and threw one last dark and grouchy look in Sun's direction before reclining on the roof again. "By this time in the story, they've been through danger and betrayal. They've only just started trusting each other, they've been actively flirting. It's a big moment where they could be literally jumping to their deaths and they do it *together*. After dragging each other out of the water and to safety, it's natural they have a big first kiss there."

To Song's shock, Ren tipped his head back and released a long, sappy sigh. "It's a perfect moment."

"Ren An Xue, are you a closet romantic?" he teased.

"Nope. I just understand romance better than *some*," he

disputed, leaving Song speechless. Ren had dipped into his Zhao Gang tone, making him feel like he was speaking in character. But something…the look…or maybe what they'd been talking about…

Was he saying something else?

Did he think Song couldn't be romantic?

Oh, Song had news for his didi. If he knew Ren would be receptive, Song would romance the hell out of this man. Ren would become putty in his hands. He'd melt in an instant.

Smirking at Ren, Song lifted his voice. "Sun, did you put real alcohol in Ren's bottle? I think he's drunk and talking nonsense up here."

"If you both can get this scene done in as few takes as possible, I'll send bottles of wine up to your rooms tonight!" Sun shouted.

Ren narrowed his eyes on Song and flicked his folding fan open. He tilted his head just right so that half his face was hidden behind the fan, leaving only those dark seductive eyes staring at him, heating every part of Song's body.

"You've finally come to me, Ah-Ying. Romance me," Ren purred.

Oh God, he was going to die on this roof.

15

YOU ARE MY SWAN
REN AN XUE

If Song wasn't already injured, Ren would have strangled the man.

He'd known the moment Song got hurt. They were doing wire work that would finish up a fight scene they'd been shooting for two days. Song was being lowered slowly to the ground from a height that had left Ren's stomach turning itself inside out.

Ren reached the ground first, and his job was to walk forward, then turn to face Song so he could chastise the man for taking unnecessary risks. *How ironic.*

His costar was graceful as always, but the ground was uneven with a number of large rocks scattered about. One foot must have hit a rock, because there was the tiniest wobble before Song's other foot caught him. Nothing showed on his face, but Ren had sworn he could see pain flash through Song's dark eyes.

Every instinct had screamed for him to rush to Song's side and check on him, but the cameras were rolling and Song pushed through. The shot looked good, and Ren hadn't wanted to be the reason they had to do another take.

The second Sun shouted "Cut!" Ren was running to Song,

his hand gripping his shoulder, but Song brushed off his concern with a wink and a tight smile.

Song was not okay, but he refused to stop.

They'd continued on for another four hours, finishing up a number of scenes. They walked, ran, and stood.

Ren bit his tongue the entire time, watching as Song's motions grew slower until he was practically limping through the last scene of the day.

When he could tolerate it no longer, Ren marched over to the director rather than Song. He threw a dark look at an assistant who had walked up at the same time, and the poor woman shuffled backward and out of listening range.

"Tell me you're done with Song for the day," Ren practically snarled in Sun's ear.

"Well..." Sun hesitated, glancing at the schedule of shots he had lined up.

"You're done with him," Ren snapped. Sun's wide eyes jumped up to his face. "Song is hurt. He's been hurt for hours. He needs to lie down and rest."

"I know. I know," Sun started with a sigh.

He knew and he kept Song working!

Ren took a step into Sun, and the director threw his hands up. "*Aiyaa!* Relax, Zhao Gang! I asked him two hours ago and he said he didn't want to stop, that he was fine."

Ren grunted. "He's not fine."

Sun sighed. "We got enough for today. Go take care of your laoshi."

Ren bowed his head to the director. "Thank you, Sun Jing."

Sun waved him off, and Ren darted over to Song's side, though he thought he heard Sun mutter something about Ren being scarier than Zhao Gang. Didn't matter.

As he reached Song's side, he grabbed the man's left arm and draped it across his shoulders, taking pressure off his left leg. Song had been favoring it since his bad landing. Song yelped in surprise and immediately tried to pull away, but Ren held tight to his wrist.

"We're going back to my trailer so I can look at your injury," Ren announced.

"No. I'm fine. I just tweaked my ankle and knee a little. It's nothing," Song quickly argued.

Ren leaned close enough that their noses nearly touched. Song's eyes widened and he swore he heard Song gasp. "You are coming with me to my trailer *or* I'm taking you to the hospital. Those are your only two options."

"Okay," Song whispered.

"Which option?"

"First one."

Ren nodded and helped Song hobble to the nearest golf cart. A couple of wardrobe assistants came along to grab their hanfus, but Ren waved them off, promising to drop them off personally later. They didn't appear pleased, but Ren had always been careful with their garments, so they seemed willing to trust him. For now.

"How bad is it? Honestly, Song laoshi," Ren pressed when they were riding across the studio toward their trailers.

Song opened his mouth, and Ren nearly growled at him when it seemed like he was going to brush him off again. His words turned into a sigh, and he nodded. "It's throbbing in time with my heart and probably swollen. Elevation and ice would be so nice."

Ren nodded. He'd take care of Song.

"How did you know?" Song murmured.

"How could I not?" he snapped, his eyes jumping to Song's face. "I saw the landing."

Song winced, and Ren immediately regretted his words. "It couldn't have been that bad since Sun didn't call cut right away."

Ren growled and rolled his eyes, looking away from him because he was afraid Song would see too much. "No, the landing was fine. I-I-I just saw it, okay? I know you. I knew you were hurt and hiding it. You are *never* to do that again. What if you were to make it worse by ignoring it?"

Song chuckled and tapped his chin. "Those big eyes of yours don't miss anything."

Ren let out a huff and turned his attention to the buildings they were passing, trying to ignore the tightness in his chest. How did he know? It didn't matter. He just knew Song. He knew when he was hurting, and he hated it.

The ride to their block of trailers took only a few minutes, and then Ren was helping Song up the three short steps.

A deep sigh of relief fell from Song as the cool air wrapped around them. The day had been sweltering, and they were both soaked with sweat.

While Song was still standing, Ren quickly helped to strip him out of the long outer robe before getting him stretched out on the couch. Ren shucked his own robes much faster and tossed them in a heap to the side. Yes, the jiejies would have a fit, but they were already disgusting with sweat and dirt. They'd have to be cleaned prior to being worn again.

"I just need some ice, didi, and a little rest," Song called out as he disappeared in the back of the trailer.

Ren ignored him. He had some muscle cream he'd used when he'd pulled muscles in all their fight scenes and wire work. It had helped. He grabbed it and returned to snatch a bottle of water out of the fridge.

He handed the bottle to Song and carefully lifted Song's leg so that he could slide under it while the other was stretched out behind Ren.

"What are you doing, didi?" Song demanded. His voice jumped and he tried to pull free, but he was trapped against the arm of the couch. The plastic of the bottle loudly crinkled under Song's hands.

"I have a muscle cream that will help. I was going to massage it in while you relax."

"Really, didi, you don't have to," Song argued.

Ren sat, one hand tightly gripping Song's calf while he glared at the man. "I thought we were friends, Song Wei Li. You're hurt, and I'm trying to help my friend. Are you telling me that I make you uncomfortable?"

"I-what? No! Of course not!"

"Then quit being such a baby. Let me help you."

Song sank back, leaning into the corner of the couch. "Don't hurt me, Zhao Gang."

"Right now, Zhao Gang would give me a wide berth," Ren muttered under his breath as he carefully pulled off Song's shoe.

It reminded him more of a bootie with a rubber sole. There wasn't much in the way of ankle support in the thing. They actually spent a lot of shooting time in their street shoes, using the costume shoes only when there was a chance of them being in the frame.

He tossed the shoe to the floor with a *thump* and peeled off the cotton sock to reveal Song's bare foot. Ren's heart picked up its pace a bit at the idea of undressing Song, but he stomped on the unexpected rush. Song was hurt. Plus, they'd both sat around in T-shirts and shorts plenty of times. Song's bare foot and ankle were nothing to get excited about.

Even if they were cute.

"It doesn't look swollen," Ren murmured as he picked up the tube of ointment he'd set aside.

"That's a bonus, I guess," Song grumbled.

Smearing some on his fingers, Ren hesitated a second. "Tell me if I hurt you or anything doesn't feel comfortable, Song laoshi. I don't want to cause you any more pain."

"I will, I promise, didi." His voice was barely more than a whisper. A gentle caress that got rid of one set of nerves and introduced a brand-new set.

Very carefully, Ren started rubbing in the cream around his ankle, massaging it in along the tendons. His touch remained light and gentle, slowly increasing in pressure as he worked until Song finally released the tiniest sigh of relief. His skin was so warm and soft to the touch. There was a short break between his ankle and the dark hairs on his leg. They weren't too heavy, but they left him wondering if Song had any hair on his chest.

Hadn't he seen Song's bare chest? When they were changing clothes or at least stripping out of their sweaty robes?

Wouldn't he remember something like this?

Ren's eyes suddenly widened as he realized the path his mind had wandered. He did *not* need to be thinking about any parts of Song—bare or otherwise—while he was rubbing his *friend's* ankle.

Screwed. Screwed. Screwed. He was so screwed.

Under his fingers, Song moved his foot, straightening and turning it, stretching the muscles.

"Better?" Ren rasped, trying to get his flustered brain back on track. Or at least rip his thoughts away from his libido's control.

"Much. Thank you."

All right, one part down. One to go.

Leaning forward, he snagged a hand towel off the table and wiped off the remaining ointment from his fingers before working the loose pant leg up above Song's thigh. He tried not to think about how Song had a very nice, muscular calf. They'd discussed their workout routines on numerous occasions. His costar had played soccer for years and had recently switched to jogging to keep in shape. The constant physical activity showed.

But those thoughts were forgotten when he reached his knee.

"This is swollen," Ren announced.

Song huffed. "It's not that bad. That ointment and some ice, it'll be fine." Ren glared at him, and Song glared back.

"I'm serious. I've suffered far worse. Ointment, ice, elevation, and rest. That's all I need."

Ren hummed his disagreement. "You're not as young as you used to be."

Song gasped. "Are you saying I'm getting old, didi?"

"What if I am, gege?" Ren teased as he squeezed more ointment on his fingers.

"Do not call me that. I'm still your laoshi even if you are taking care of me."

Ren smirked and started to gently massage in the cream. He worked slowly, letting the ointment sink into the skin and muscles before applying pressure. Song remained tense at first, but relaxed bit by bit until he was sighing with almost every breath.

"Do I want to know how many times you've had to do this to yourself since filming began?" Song inquired. He sounded relaxed, but there was an undercurrent of worry.

"Probably not," Ren mumbled. "But…this is my second tube of this stuff. It works wonders."

"Ah-Xue!" Song shouted, instantly tensing under Ren's fingers.

"I'm okay. I swear. I'm used to this kind of thing." He worked his fingers into the muscles, loosening up Song's knee once again.

"I don't want you used to this kind of thing. You should have told me."

"I'm fine."

Song fell silent, and Ren turned his head slightly to catch a glimpse of Song's expression from the corner of his eye. He seemed…sad and hurt.

"What?"

Song's expression crumpled even more. "Why didn't I realize you were hurt? I'm your laoshi. I should have seen it. You saw it in me, and I thought I hid it well."

Ren smiled and tried not to think about the fact that he

very much wanted to lean in and kiss the adorable pout right off Song's lips. "It's probably because I always look awkward and move like I'm hurt. You're used to seeing that."

"You are not awkward!" Song's eyes widened and the muscles in his jaw tightened like he was clenching his teeth. It was as if he were preparing to jump into battle even though Ren still had a good hold on his knee.

Laughter bubbled up from Ren and he shook his head. "I am so awkward, and you can't deny it. I'm like a stork who doesn't know how to manage his limbs."

"You're a swan," Song argued, which only wrung more laughter out of Ren.

"Song laoshi, you're drunk or dehydrated. I am no swan."

Song crossed his arms over his chest and dropped his chin, sinking back into his previous pout. "You are *my* swan."

Ren quickly ripped his eyes away from Song, keeping his head down and praying that the wig he was still wearing fell forward enough to block his face. Song did not need to see the blush that was already burning its way across his cheeks.

His swan. Fuck, he wished that were true. He wished he were that beautiful, just for Song.

But he wasn't a swan. And he wasn't Song's.

"If it helps," Ren started slowly when he could speak in an even tone. "I think the worst of the pulled muscles came while you were in Hong Kong. That fight scene, when it was done, I thought I was going to lie in the field with the dead."

"I'm sorry, didi. I'm sorry I wasn't here."

"Nothing for you to apologize for."

"I should have been here. So I could at least do this for you."

Ren bit his tongue. There was no point in arguing.

He squeezed some more ointment onto his fingers and continued to work his way up and around Song's knee. Soft moans eased past Song's lips and Ren closed his eyes, letting himself get lost in the feel of his warm skin and strong muscles.

It was only when a strong hand clamped on his wrist that Ren's eyes popped open to meet Song's wide ones. His lips were parted on a ragged breath.

"I think I'm good now, didi," Song said roughly.

Ren lowered his eyes to find that his hands had worked their way up his leg, with his left hand pressed to the hot skin of Song's inner thigh.

How the fuck had that happened?

And why wasn't he releasing Song? He needed to move his hands. He needed to get up and run as far as he could. Space was the only thing that would get air into his lungs and his brain working.

Why wasn't he moving?

Why wasn't Song moving?

Song was trapped. He had Song trapped between his body and the back of the couch. He couldn't move, and Ren's hands were wandering.

"Fuck! I'm so sorry!" Ren cried out, humiliation burning across his face. He tried to jerk his hands away, but only one moved. The one Song held remained trapped on his inner thigh.

"Ren, look at me."

He couldn't. He couldn't face him.

"I'm so sorry," he repeated, giving another tug on his hand to free himself, but Song held tight.

"Ren." Song's voice was hypnotic. Low and deep, a gentle caress across his fractured nerves. Against his will, he felt himself turning his head and lifting his gaze to meet perfect dark eyes. He was falling into those eyes, leaning closer. Song's other hand came up and the tips of his fingers barely grazed his jaw. "It's okay, Ah-Xue." Song's thumb lifted and brushed the corner of his mouth.

Trembling rolled throughout Ren's entire body, and he

squeezed his eyes shut. If he moved just a centimeter to his left, he could kiss the pad of Song's thumb. Such a tiny move, but he knew if he did, it wouldn't stop with his thumb. He'd have to kiss each one of Song's fingers before moving down his wrist to the soft part on the inside of his elbow, and then up to his lips. If he began kissing Song, he'd have to kiss all of him. There was no stopping it.

So, he wasn't allowed to start.

"I have to go," Ren choked out. Both hands suddenly released him and Ren nearly sobbed at the loss of contact. He cleared his throat and opened his eyes, forcing a smile. "I mean, get up. I have to get up."

Very carefully, he slid out from under Song's leg and rose to his feet. He refused to look Song in the eye as inane babble poured from his mouth. "I just need to wash my hands. Then I'll get you ice and dinner. You need food. I'll make something for us to eat."

"Ah-Xue..." Song whispered, but Ren didn't stick around to hear him.

He practically ran to the tiny bathroom at the back of the trailer and shut himself inside. He needed a moment to himself. Away from Song's dark eyes and perfect mouth. It was the only way he was going to be able to pull himself together.

Gripping the sink with both hands, Ren stared at his reflection in the mirror and nearly jumped. His face was flushed, and his pupils were blown so wide. How close had he come to cracking?

Thoughts of kissing Song were growing more intense. He wanted this man more than he wanted food and air.

At first, he'd thought this was about character bleed, but now he was having doubts. These tangled feelings didn't swamp him while they were working. The worst of them came when the rest of the world fell away and they were chatting over dinner in his room or simply hanging out in their trailers.

He didn't want Tian Xiuying. He wanted Song Wei Li.

Maybe he needed to talk to him about it.

He needed to put some space between them, but if Song didn't understand why, it would hurt his feelings. He would understand, right? This wasn't going to destroy their friendship.

Ren squeezed his eyes shut and swallowed a pitiful whimper.

God, please don't let me lose Song.

16

HIS COSTAR IS GOING TO DEVOUR HIM

SONG WEI LI

Song: Did you ever worry about it being character bleed?

He stared at the text for several seconds, gripping the phone between both hands tight enough that his knuckles were turning white.

Yesterday, Ren had given him a massage that had left him hard and panting. If Ren's fingers had inched any higher, the man would have been left with zero doubt of his attraction, and Song did not want to scare him away.

While things were a little rough after Ren left his hiding place in the bathroom, they'd found their rhythm again and acted as if nothing had happened.

His ankle and knee were better. Filming was normal.

But Song was growing more frustrated with each passing day. When he closed his eyes, he could still see the way Ren had looked at him. He'd thought his costar was going to devour him and Song had welcomed it.

This couldn't be character bleed. Ren had to have feelings *for him*.

He'd started thinking about confronting him. Just coming completely clean. Laying everything on the line.

And then he remembered what Zhu Fang had told him about texting *before* he did anything stupid.

Confessing could be a huge, stupid mistake.

So, he texted Zhu Fang first.

Sitting on the edge of his bed, Song lowered his head and tapped the edge of the phone on his forehead. What were the chances that Zhu Fang wasn't incredibly busy with his own life? He probably didn't have any time or interest in dealing with Song's shit.

He needed to figure this out on his own.

His phone pinged.

Jerking his head up, he tapped on the screen to read Zhu Fang's text.

Zhu: What the hell have you done now?

Song: NOTHING! Yet…

Song: Weeks ago, Ren lost his temper. Insane jealousy, but then he blamed all his feelings on character bleed.

Song: How do we know if any of this is real?

Zhu: Imagine a quality he has that is nothing like the character he's playing. What is it?

Song: Shy

Song: Awkward

Song: Insecure

Zhu: All right, lover boy. That's enough. How do you feel about those qualities? Annoyed?

Song: They're perfect. They're adorable. They're him!

Zhu: Idiot. That's not character bleed.

Song hesitated. He hadn't really thought he'd been confusing things when it came to Ren An Xue. The man who dominated his every thought and feeling was not Zhao Gang. Yes, the character was interesting and attractive in his own ways, but he wasn't the man who cooked lunch for him and teased him in the morning when he was grouchy. Zhao Gang was never insecure or awkward, but Ah-Xue was, and he was precious.

But what about Ren?

Was he only attracted to the standoffish man who grunted more than spoke in complete sentences and fixed all his problems with a sword?

Or did he enjoy the fact that Song liked to sing silly things to him? Did he mind that Song laughed too loud or that he couldn't cook to save his soul? Did he hate that Song was messy and forgetful?

Song: I don't know if he really cares for me…or just my character.

Song: I was thinking of confronting him. Telling him how I feel.

Zhu: Don't do it!!!!!!

Song: I'm dying here! I need to know!

Zhu: What if it blows up in your face? What if he doesn't feel anything for you?

Zhu: What if he's a fucking homophobe?

Song: Ren is NOT a homophobe!

He refused to believe that about Ren. He couldn't be. Not the way he spoke about the original book for *Legend of the Lost Night* with such love and reverence. He wasn't disgusted or put off by the idea of Zhao and Tian being in love. No. Not Ren.

Zhu: Fine, but you've still got two months of filming. This could get fucking awkward.

Song: It's fucking awkward now!

Zhu: Wait! Let me send Zi to you.

Song: What?!?!?!

Song's brain might have exploded in his head. Did Zhu Fang just offer to send in his boyfriend Guo Zi to help? He couldn't have read that right.

Zhu: Zi starts filming at Hengdian in a few days. He can pop over to your set. Talk some sense into you. Maybe feel your boy out.

Song: I do not want him anywhere near MY BOY!

White-hot jealousy shot through Song. It was bad enough he was snarling at Liu every chance he got, he did not want to worry about hot idol Guo Zi turning Ren's head. It didn't matter if Guo Zi was happily in love with Zhu Fang. Song was beyond rational thought.

Song frowned at his phone, waiting for a new text message from Zhu. His insane friend did have a point. Confessing everything to Ren meant that things could become a hundred times more awkward and painful for the next two months if Ren didn't feel anything for him.

No, longer than two months. Even after the filming was done, they would have months of interviews and appearances together to promote the show.

But what if Ren did feel something for him? What if there was something there? Confessing meant they could have some time together before they were ripped apart by their careers and the rest of the world.

Wasn't a little time together better than no time at all?

His phone vibrated and pinged in his hand. He looked down to find that Zhu was calling him rather than texting.

Sighing, Song answered the call and immediately put it on speakerphone.

"You're an idiot," Zhu Fang said the second the call connected.

"And you've got shitty advice," Song snapped.

"He usually does," a voice he didn't recognize replied.

Song jerked, nearly dropping the phone. *Who the hell was that?*

"Thanks, gege. Despite my shitty advice, I still managed to land you," Zhu countered. A purr of smug pleasure filled his voice.

"It's a good thing you're cute."

Was...was that Guo Zi?

"Song, in case you haven't figured it out, I conferenced in Guo Zi for this call so he could agree with me," Zhu filled in as if reading his mind.

There was a long, suffering sigh that filled the line, and then Guo Zi spoke again. "I'm sorry we haven't gotten the chance to meet properly, Song Wei Li. I will be in your area soon, and we can meet for coffee if you would like to chat." The voice was smooth and surprisingly proper compared to Zhu Fang's manner. Just from the sound alone, the two people seemed like complete opposites. "I will stay away from Ren An Xue if it would make you more comfortable."

Okay, maybe that was a little more like Zhu Fang.

"Sorry. I'm…touchy when it comes to didi right now."

Zhu Fang snorted, but he thought he heard a hum of agreement behind it.

"Don't worry. I get it. Zhu Fang was just like that," Guo Zi confirmed.

"Hush! Don't tell lies!" Zhu gasped.

"He says that I shouldn't confront Ren," Song stated, trying to keep them from going down a separate rabbit hole of insanity.

"Don't!" Guo Zi immediately replied. "You don't want to rush him or scare him. You've got work to do and that probably has him stressed already."

"Flirt with him. Tempt him!" Zhu Fang suggested.

Guo Zi snorted. "Your flirting style is like getting hit with a sledgehammer. Song, be subtle. Also, be careful, but make sure he understands that you're open. See if you can get him to come to you."

"I don't know. I—" He stopped when there was a knock at the door, his body freezing up for a second.

"Song?" Zhu Fang prodded.

"Shit. I think he's at the door," Song whispered, jumping to his feet.

"Don't hang up! Don't hang up!" Zhu Fang demanded in a harsh, excited voice.

"Fine. But don't talk." Song hurried across the room and opened the door to find Ren standing on the other side. His hair was damp from a shower and he was dressed in his usual T-shirt and shorts.

God, he looked beautiful.

They'd grabbed takeout on the way to their rooms, and then Song had left Ren's early with the excuse that he wanted to do a little reading.

Lies. Lies. Lies.

It was getting harder and harder to sit next to Ren without reaching over and touching him. He needed some distance to clear his head. Which, unfortunately, had led to texting Zhu Fang.

"Hey!" Song said with forced cheerfulness.

"Hey! Sorry, are you on a call? I thought I heard you talking. I didn't mean to disturb you. I can come back," Ren replied, wincing and retreating a step toward his own room.

"No! I mean, yes, I'm on a call, but they can wait a minute. What's up?" Song retreated into his room and waved at Ren to follow with his empty hand.

Ren entered slowly, hanging near the door. "Oh, I made you lunch. Since I won't be on the set tomorrow, I wanted to make sure you had something to eat. I think I should be back in time to make dinner." He held up a dark-blue box between both hands.

"He made you lunch!" Zhu Fang roared from Song's hand. Song flinched and Ren's eyes widened so much they looked like they were going to roll from his head.

Song jerked the phone up to his face. "Shut up! You promised to stay quiet!"

"He made you lunch? He cooks for you?" Zhu Fang continued, ignoring him completely. "Hit the video button! I want to see him! Hit the button!"

"No!"

"I can't believe he cooks for you! Gege, you never cooked for me!"

"You were too annoying. Of course I didn't cook for you," Guo Zi immediately grumbled.

Song sneaked a glance up to Ren to find that his eyes had somehow gotten wider.

"Who is that?" Ren whispered in a shaky voice.

"Zhu Fang and Guo Zi," Song answered, realizing he was beaten.

Ren gasped, slapping a hand over his mouth. He staggered back a step and looked as though he was about to sink to the floor. *Shit. Shit. Shit.*

Song hurried to Ren's side, snatched up the box with his lunch, and placed it on the counter. He then grabbed Ren's elbow and ushered Ren over to the bed to sit down. It wasn't ideal, but it was better than just letting him collapse to the floor.

The entire time, Zhu Fang was chanting like a two-year-old, "Hit the button, Song. Hit it! Hit it! Hit it!"

"Fang Fang[1], my hair is a mess," Guo Zi interjected.

"You're always beautiful, gege. Hit the button, Song!"

Song turned his attention to a shell-shocked Ren. Guo Zi and Zhu Fang were a pair of the most popular actors in their world right now. It had to be a little overwhelming to be in their focus. Song would have been if he hadn't already been blindsided by Zhu Fang once before.

"What do you think? I won't, if you don't want me to," Song inquired.

"Please, Ren!" Zhu Fang immediately pleaded.

Ren flushed and ran a hand through his damp hair. "Oh. I-I guess it's okay. I—"

"You're beautiful," Song reassured him, moving to sit next to him on the bed. Ren snorted and bumped him with his elbow.

Taking a deep breath, Song tapped a button, switching the call over to video. Zhu Fang's grinning face immediately filled the screen. A second later, it was cut in half and Guo Zi's handsome but more subdued face filled the available space.

"Song! You're right! He is cute!" Zhu Fang declared.

"Behave, Fang Fang," Guo Zi chastised. "Hi, Ren An Xue. I'm Guo Zi, and that lunatic is Zhu Fang. It's nice to meet you and Song."

Ren lifted a hand and gave a tiny wave. "Hi," he said softly. "It's an honor to meet you both."

"Do you really cook for Song?" Zhu Fang asked. "It's clear Song got the better costar."

"If I don't cook for him, he doesn't eat," Ren answered.

Zhu lifted a finger and tapped his lips, lifting one eyebrow in thought. "Is that the trick, huh?"

"Still would have let you starve," Guo Zi murmured, his delivery amazingly dry.

"Gege! How could you!"

Guo Zi rolled his eyes. "Hang up, Fang Fang. You've had your fun."

"Wait! Wait! Ren, are you coming to the concert next week?" Zhu Fang demanded. He leaned closer to the camera as if he were trying to stare Ren down.

"I-I wish I could, but the filming. I can't get away," Ren stammered. His shoulders slumped, and Song couldn't stop himself from lightly placing his hand on Ren's back in support.

Zhu Fang pouted, his bottom lip sticking out. "No!"

"Behave," Guo Zi admonished. "I'm sure you can get your assistant or even Song's to record some of it for Ren. You know how hectic filming can get."

With a heavy sigh, Zhu Fang nodded. "Yeah, yeah. I get it. We'll have to meet in person another time. You just look out for my duet partner in the meantime."

Ren perked up and nodded. "Yes. Of course!"

Guo Zi smiled. "We should let you and Song go. I'll be filming in Hengdian soon. If you would like, we could meet for dinner one night. We can swap stories about filming a BL."

"Yes," Ren gasped. "That would be great! Thank you!"

"Wonderful. I'll get Song's info off Zhu Fang. I'll be in contact."

They said good-bye, and Song quickly ended the call before anything else terrifying could come out of Zhu Fang's mouth.

That wasn't a total disaster, right?

17

IS THIS MORE THAN FRIENDSHIP?
REN AN XUE

The second the call ended, Ren collapsed.

He fell forward, pressing his chest to his thighs and covering his face with his hands.

What the hell was that?

Had he really just talked to Zhu Fang and Guo Zi? *Frozen River* was *the* mega-hit BL TV series, even a year later. Nothing touched it. There had been a handful of other shows that had come out since and they'd enjoyed some very solid popularity, but nothing had the staying power and buzz as *Frozen River*.

Not only that, both Guo Zi and Zhu Fang were *the* mega CP[1] of the BL world. When they were supporting the show, appearing in interviews together, people lost their minds. There were endless amounts of fanfiction, memes, videos, and social media posts about them.

But…all of that was over…

They weren't supposed to be in public together or have any kind of contact. That was the rule.

And yet, they were both on the same phone conversation. They were still clearly in contact with each other to this day.

How…?

Song's hand slowly moved up his spine in a gentle caress that kicked off a wave of tingles washing through his body and scattering his thoughts. Part of him screamed to run, while another demanded that he lean into that touch. He split the difference and didn't move.

"Didi? Are you okay?"

Sucking in a deep breath, Ren dropped his hands from his face. "Yeah, I…" he started and then blinked, still trying to pull together a coherent thought. "Kind of feel like I just survived a typhoon."

Song chuckled and continued to rub his back in the most wonderful way. "Yeah, meeting Zhu Fang for the first time was kind of like that. He's definitely a force of nature. Sorry you got sucked into that."

Ren pushed into a sitting position again and smiled. "No, it's good. He seems fun, and a little crazy. I didn't know you were also acquainted with Guo Zi."

"I'm not." Song stopped and winced. "Or rather, I wasn't. That was my first conversation with him. I was texting with Zhu Fang, and he decided that he needed to call in Guo Zi to support him because I didn't believe him."

Turning his head to gaze at Song, Ren let his eyes skim over the man's handsome face. He was staring down at the phone still clamped in his left hand. The clenched muscles in his jaw made him appear anxious and unsure—two things Ren rarely ever saw on his face, but they were showing up with more frequency recently. Ren didn't know the cause. However, he was beginning to fear that it might be him.

Had Song reached out to talk to Zhu Fang because he didn't feel like he could talk to Ren?

Ren stomped on that bit of jealousy before it could bloom. If Song needed help with something, Ren was glad he had someone he could talk to, even if it couldn't be him.

"I forgot to ask. Did you ever get that selfie with Zhu

Fang?" Ren inquired, hoping to put a smile on Song's lips again.

His friend's eyes lightened. "I did, actually."

Ren gasped and gave him a shove, rocking him to the side a bit. "And you didn't say anything? What kind of friend are you? Show me now!"

Song grinned and he pulled his hand away to start scrolling through the photos on his phone. Ren immediately missed the pressure of his hand on his spine, but when Song rocked back, his body inched closer so that their shoulders and arms were touching. If Ren spread his legs apart another inch, their legs would be touching as well.

He fought the temptation.

"Here," Song murmured. He leaned even closer as he held out his phone so that they were touching from shoulder to knee. Ren couldn't even see the image for a second. He was just washed in the heat of Song's body, the sweet scent of his soap from his shower earlier in the evening.

Blinking, he finally brought the picture into focus. It was a damn good picture. Song was beautiful as always, his adorable smirk and luscious obsidian eyes seducing him without even trying. He couldn't tear his gaze away for a couple of seconds to notice Zhu Fang there, but he did at last.

Yes, Zhu Fang was sexy as well. They actually had matching expressions, and it wasn't hard to see why the man was ranked as one of the sexiest men in all of China. Hell, all of Asia.

But all Ren could see was the fact that Zhu Fang had his arm wrapped around Song, pulling him in far too close. Zhu Fang's chin was touching Song's hair. His chest had to be touching Song's shoulder. *Why did he have to be so close?*

"You don't like it?" Song asked. There was a note of hurt in his voice that jerked Ren from his dark thoughts. "I thought it was a good picture."

"What? No! It's a great picture! You look wonderful!" Ren quickly argued.

He snorted. "It's written all over your face. You don't like it."

"No, that's not it. I like it. I swear. It's just…"

"What?" Song pressed when Ren's voice faded off.

"It's just that Zhu Fang is hanging all over you. Why does he have to be so close?"

"What?" Song gasped, the pitch of his voice spiking. "It's a selfie. You have to be close."

"But his arm is *on* you," Ren mumbled. He knew he sounded like a petulant five-year-old, but he couldn't stop himself. "He probably fell in love with you the second he met you. Could you imagine if you were both in a show together? All of China would implode."

He could feel Song's eyes watching him, and his face burned. Yeah, he'd said way too much. He needed to get out of there.

"I'll get going so you can return back to your reading," he murmured. He started to rise, but Song's hand clamped down on his arm, holding him in place.

"Don't. Didi. You don't have to worry about Zhu Fang." Song's words came out haltingly, as if he were trying not to reveal too much. "I…I wish I could show you the picture he showed me while I was in Hong Kong."

Ren frowned and nibbled on the inside of his mouth, trying to follow what Song was saying. What did that have to do with his insanity?

"It was a picture of him and Guo Zi together. In Paris."

Ren's frown deepened. "Was it from their promotional tour?" he asked, though that didn't make any sense. The promotion of a Chinese wuxia drama wouldn't have reached that far, even if it had been insanely popular. Maybe a product sponsorship like Louis Vuitton or Givenchy.

"No. They were there on vacation not long ago. Together."

Ren opened his mouth to essentially brush off what Song said, but then the true weight of his words slammed down on his head.

Zhu Fang and Guo Zi were together.
Together.
A couple.

Nearly two years after the filming of their show, they were together.

Ren's heart raced and he was suddenly light-headed. Together. They were together. How? How did they do this? What…

His brain couldn't even complete a thought any longer. It kept repeating "together" as if it were the answer to all his problems. Those little cells sparked and stretched, reaching for images of Song, but shied away again.

If they were together…

"Oh," he finally managed after what felt like an eternity. He could feel Song staring at him as if he were waiting for something more, but Ren couldn't. There was nothing that made sense in his head.

Images he'd seen from *Frozen River* as well as social media pictures of Zhu Fang and Guo Zi flashed through his brain. All those smiles and shared laughs, had they been real? It wasn't just fan service and promotional clips. Were they really in love?

"Didi?"

"Sorry." Ren cleared his head and forced a smile. "Just surprised."

Song grinned at him, seeming to relax. "I was too. Are you…okay…with it?"

"What? Yes! Of course! I mean, it doesn't matter if I am or not. That's their business, not mine. But yes, I'm good with it. Happy for them." Ren suddenly clenched his teeth together to stop his babbling.

"Okay. Good. I thought you would be," Song said and dropped his eyes to his phone again. "I…yeah. You won't… tell anyone, right?"

"No, I won't share their secret. I promise." He knew how dangerous it was for Guo Zi and Zhu Fang. If their real relationship status was leaked, it would mean disaster for them, their family, their careers. Possibly even their lives. He felt honored that Song had even trusted him with this.

"Thank you."

Ren nodded and then suddenly pushed to his feet. He needed to get out of there. He needed to think. This…this was such a big thing.

"I should get going. Let you read. I need to finish preparing for tomorrow," Ren announced. He flashed Song a weak smile, hoping to smooth over his awkwardness.

Song grinned. "Sure. Good luck with your audition, didi."

"Thank you." He took a deep breath, feeling some of his balance return. "Don't forget to eat while I'm gone, Song laoshi."

The look in Song's eyes softened, and Ren's heart fluttered in answer. "I don't know what I'd do without my didi. Come back to me quickly."

"Always," Ren whispered roughly. He escaped Song's room before it became any harder to leave.

When he was in his own room, Ren curled up on his bed with his pillow hugged to his chest while his mind swirled with chaotic thoughts.

Zhu Fang and Guo Zi were together.

A couple.

Dating.

Lovers.

They'd met on the set of a BL drama, and now they were

dating. Even if they had to keep it hidden from the world, they were together.

And Song told him.

Ren rolled over and curled into a tighter ball as his traitorous brain conjured up every moment he'd spent with Song in the past two months. He remembered every touch, every laugh, every lingering look that set his soul on fire.

Could Song care about him...*like that?*

Was this more than friendship?

Could he one day reach out, pull Song in close, kiss his lips, and drink in the taste of him? Could he hold him at night, press his ear to his chest, and fall asleep to the beat of his lover's heart?

Could Song love him?

Ren squeezed his eyes shut. Was Song even gay? Or bi? When he'd first met the man, he would have snorted and said definitely not.

But now, after two months of seeing Song nearly every day, of spending countless hours together, he wasn't so sure. Was he just seeing what he wanted to see? Reading more into all their interactions because his heart so desperately wanted it to be true.

Or was what Song felt simply character bleed?

A bitter sound broke from Ren's throat and he rolled over onto his other side, facing the wall.

Character bleed.

Wasn't that a lovely excuse? He'd managed to cling to that for all of two weeks out of pure desperation. Character bleed meant he had at least a sliver of hope of returning to a normal life. Character bleed meant his heart wasn't going to splinter into a million tiny shards.

But if he was stupid enough to fall in love with Song Wei Li, how the hell was going to return to a normal life? How was he going to move on?

Twenty-four hours away from Hengdian and Song Wei Li

was going to be a good thing. Ren could put all his protective walls back in place. He could figure out how to be normal again.

Because, right now, if he saw Song, he was going to kiss him.

Fuck the consequences.

18

HE WANTS YOU, DIDI, AND HE CAN'T HAVE YOU
SONG WEI LI

Both the crew and other actors were avoiding him.

Not that he blamed them at all.

It was bad enough that Song had to suffer through filming all the previous day without Ren, but no, it had to get infinitely worse, as if the universe was determined to play a cruel joke on him after he felt like they'd inched forward while talking about Zhu Fang and Guo Zi.

Ren was supposed to return last evening, but Song had received a late message that Ren was delayed and wouldn't be returning to Hengdian until that morning. Fine. That sucked, but he could understand it. Ren had been invited out to dinner with the director and producers he'd been auditioning for. That was usually a good sign.

Then he'd awoken to a text from Ren stating that another actor was sick and he was being sent over to film with the other team today. They wouldn't be working together at all.

The soonest he'd be able to set eyes on Ren was *after* they were done with work.

This was bullshit.

Almost forty-eight hours apart.

So, yes, maybe he was something of a grumpy pain in the ass today.

And yes, he'd overheard more than one person complain about his attitude and how Ren needed to come back to the set to manage Song. He didn't give a shit. He was happy to let Ren *manage* him.

The only good thing about the day was that Sun Jing had shifted his scenes to battle sequences rather than the light banter he was supposed to be enjoying with Ren. The constant physical activity burned off the frustrated energy. The muscle strain and sore body helped him forget how much his heart was missing Ren.

God, it felt worse because Ren wasn't even that far away.

His brain kept frantically searching for a way to sneak to the other set, except he was down in the city setting while Ren was supposed to be up in the bamboo forest.

So close. So close and he couldn't touch him. Couldn't hear his laugh. Couldn't see his shining smile.

Then Ren's bright laughter drifted between the trailers.

Song stopped, his ears straining. Had he really heard his didi? His mind had to be playing tricks on him. It was too late in the day for his lunch break. Could Ren be done? Song was only on a break because of an equipment malfunction. They were estimating that it was going to take at least an hour to get everything set up again. He'd planned to relax in some air conditioning while he waited.

There was a burble of laughter followed by another, deeper voice. Song's feet were moving before he could form the thought in his head. That laugh sounded so much like Ren's. He was probably losing his mind, but he had to check. He had to be sure it wasn't him.

As he turned a corner, his heart attempted to leap from his chest. Ren was standing next to one of the trailers and beside him was Chen Junjie. The attractive actor had his hand resting on the trailer near Ren's shoulder and was leaning way too fucking close. This man was born to make trouble for them.

Oh, Song knew that smile, too. Chen was oozing charm, and Ren was smiling so sweetly at him.

No.

Hell, no.

Fuck, no.

There was no way he was letting Chen sink his claws into Ren. No one was allowed to have Ren but him.

With a snarl, Song stomped over to Ren. His didi spotted him, his eyes widening and mouth opening to likely greet him, but Song didn't give him a chance. He grabbed Ren by the wrist and pulled him away from Chen. There was nothing he could say to Chen, but the man did get a parting death glare that he was fully prepared to follow up on after he dealt with Ren.

"Hey! What the fuck!" Ren shouted in surprise. "Song laoshi? What—"

Song ignored him, his fingers tightening on Ren's wrist so his costar couldn't escape.

Luckily, his own trailer wasn't far away. He ripped open the door and climbed inside, pulling Ren with him. It was only when they were standing in the middle of the cool darkness that Song felt secure enough to release the man. He paced a few steps away, his damn robes, flaring out and brushing against everything. He lifted his hands to shove them into his hair, except he was wearing his stupid wig.

"Song! What the hell! What's wrong?" Ren snapped.

Whirling around, Song rushed to Ren. "What are you doing here? I thought you were filming on the other side of the lot today."

Ren jerked, his expression twisting up. "We just finished. I was heading to my trailer to change when I ran into Chen."

"You need to stay away from him," Song growled.

Ren made a choking noise and blinked at him. "What?"

"Stay away from him. Chen wants you." Song tried to grind those last three words to dust between his teeth. No one was allowed to have Ren.

"You've lost your mind. He does not!"

"He does!"

"Chen is not interested in me. He wants you."

Song shook his head. He couldn't believe they were even having this argument. "After he met you that one day—"

"You mean the day I acted like a lunatic, and he was hanging all over *you*," Ren interrupted.

"Yes! He texted me after we had dinner and said he regretted giving up the role because he wanted to work with you. He wants *you*."

An ugly laugh tripped from Ren's lips and he shook his head. "Even if he hadn't given up the role, we would never have worked together. He was signed on to play Zhao Gang. He would have been playing opposite you."

Song shook his head. "That was just a bullshit rumor. Chen was always supposed to play Tian Xiuying. They were in the middle of casting Zhao Gang when he had to drop out. Chen was the one who put my name in for Tian. He contacted me directly about the role. You were chosen after I signed on because they thought we'd look good together."

Ren took another step backward, his mouth hanging open. "I...I thought..."

"He wants you, didi, and he can't have you."

Song could feel himself unraveling. Time apart seemed to make him more unstable instead of putting him on an even keel. He needed Ren. At the very least, he had to finally remove all the doubt. He had to know once and for all if Ren could ever care about him, if there was a real shot for them.

Yes, losing Ren would be the worst misery, but he couldn't continue to hang in this limbo. He was losing his mind and on the verge of destroying his career and friendships with rampant jealousy.

"Song…"

He shook his head, squeezing his eyes shut against the sudden burning there. A lump formed in the back of his throat, and he struggled to swallow. His chest had become a cavernous hole that was consuming the entire world. He had to find a way out of this darkness and the only light he had was Ren.

"I've fought off both Liu and Chen. I've snapped at Zhu Fang and Guo Zi even though they are happily together. I'm losing my mind. I'll fight the entire world to keep you to myself, but it's like you don't even see me." Song slowly lifted his eyes and his voice trembled. "When are you going to finally see me?"

Ren blinked and tears streaked down his pale cheeks. Song stood frozen as Ren took two steps, closing the distance between them. The silence of the trailer was deafening. There was just the brush of their costumes and each ragged breath that rattled from their chests.

Terror gnawed away at Song's soul. His entire world hung by a strand, waiting for Ren to snap it. How would he go on when Ren left him? Would he even try?

A shaking hand rose and cupped Song's cheek, causing the air to catch in his lungs.

"Ah-Xue…"

"Song. My Song," Ren whispered, and more tears fell. "I see you. You're the only one I have ever seen."

Ren leaned forward, bringing their lips within a millimeter of each other. Their breaths danced between them. Song sucked in the air, dragging that tiny bit of Ren into his lungs. He tilted his head up and their lips brushed so slightly, but an electric current sparked between them. Everything tingled and the world turned fuzzy.

Song wasn't sure which of them moved first; he was

already drowning. The kiss was as light as a butterfly landing on a rose petal. Hesitant, as if they were each expecting the other to suddenly jerk away. But then there was another and another. More pressure. A sigh. The sweet tug of flesh and heat. The tiniest sweep of Ren's tongue along his bottom lip.

More. He needed more.

Song took a half step closer and placed his hand on Ren's chest, sliding it up to grip the side of his sweat-damp neck. The softest moan left Ren's throat, and he angled his head to deepen the kiss.

Knocking on the door of the trailer exploded through the room.

They jumped apart, a good two feet suddenly appearing between them as if by magic.

"Song! You're needed on the set!" one of the assistants shouted through the door.

Song couldn't tear his eyes away from Ren. His mouth bobbed open and closed a couple of times before he could find his voice. "Be-be there in a minute!"

There was no other sound. They just stood there, staring at each other. Ren's beautiful brown eyes were wide and looked so very lost. His face was flushed, and each breath was a rough explosion from his parted lips.

"Ren—"

"I've got to go! Take the costume back!" Ren shouted and darted for the door. Song lunged for him, trying to grab his arm to stop his escape. They couldn't end it like this. They needed to talk. They needed to do a lot of talking.

And then Song wanted to do a hell of a lot more kissing.

But talking first.

Song missed Ren and nearly fell on his face. The taller man could move fast when he wanted to.

Swearing, Song got his feet beneath him and rushed out after him, but Ren was already hurrying toward his own trailer, and Song was expected on the fucking set.

Later.

He only had a few more hours of work, and they would talk in Ren's room. Song had gotten a taste of his sweet didi. He had nowhere else to run. Nowhere to hide. Song was coming for him now.

19

DO YOU THINK I'D LET YOU RUN FROM ME AGAIN?

REN AN XUE

Ren didn't have a clear thought in his head until he reached his room.

He changed out of his costume, chatted with members of the cast and crew, and caught a ride to the rooms all while his mind screamed.

He'd kissed Song.

He'd fucking kissed Song.

How could he have kissed the man?

Very easily, actually.

When Song had looked up at him with that lost expression, believing Ren didn't see him, how could he not have kissed him? In the span of two months, Song had become his entire world. The sun rose and set with Song's smile. The spinning of the globe was powered by his laughter. And each contented sigh was the wind that stirred Ren's hair.

Compared to Song, all the Lius and Chens of the world faded away, becoming little more than white noise in a gray world. Song was music and color.

But that didn't mean kiss him, right?

Ren shut the door to his room and pressed his spine to it. His mind replayed every second of that kiss, falling into the softness, the heat, the taste, as if it were happening all over again. He barely even noticed that he was sliding to the floor until his butt hit the faux wood.

Song had kissed him back.

He'd always imagined that Song would shove him away, shout, punch him. Maybe he wouldn't hurt him. That wasn't Song's style, and his laoshi did care about him.

Song could have gently pushed him away and said that he wasn't attracted to him. That he didn't think of him in that way. That he wasn't gay.

It could still happen.

Song might have been caught up in the moment. He was probably feeling a little possessive after they'd spent so much time apart and had been pissed that Ren had chatted with Chen rather than coming to find him first. It made sense. *Sort of.*

After Song had some time to think about it, he would come to the realization that he wasn't really physically attracted to Ren. That they needed to forget about what happened and move on like they always had. They would never do that again.

How could he move on?

Now that he'd kissed Song once, he wanted more. He wanted to hold him tight and explore every inch of his hard body with his fingers. Then follow it up with his mouth.

How was he supposed to pretend that he didn't want Song with every fiber of his being?

He couldn't. Not yet.

But he knew Song. He'd want to talk this out. He'd want to make sure Ren understood that this could never happen again, and Ren couldn't take that. Not yet. He wasn't prepared for it.

Space and time. That was what he needed. He needed some space and time to himself to forget about the feel of

Song, to forget about the taste of him. To forget that this man was essential to his existence.

Shoving to his feet, Ren stumbled toward the bathroom, stripped off his sweaty clothes, and stepped into the cool spray. He scrubbed off the salt and dirt that clung to him. He washed away the last of the makeup and wig glue, easing the burn on his scalp.

But he couldn't wash away his memories of Song.

How could he have been so stupid?

This side of him wasn't supposed to exist. It wasn't allowed to exist in China. He was supposed to work hard, be manly, marry a woman, father a child, and live for his country.

But they considered him weak. They considered him less. It didn't matter how hard he worked or how much joy he brought to the world. It didn't matter how much money he accumulated or the donations he made to charity. He could give and give and give, and none of it would matter because he loved a man.

And he did love Song.

Ren leaned against the shower wall and closed his eyes. Tears slid along his face with the water. He loved Song. There was no changing it. No avoiding it. No lying about it.

He loved everything about Song. He loved his playfulness and tender caring. He loved his silliness, his beautiful voice, and his dedication to his work.

He even loved his questionable traits like his moodiness, his poor eating habits, and his absent-mindedness.

What was he supposed to do?

Forget.

He had to forget and move on.

He had to bury all these feelings and desires deep down where they would never see the sun again.

If he tried to act on them or cling to them, they would destroy everything he'd been working for over the last several years. All the sacrifices he'd made would be for nothing. All the hours he'd put in and the pain he'd suffered would have been wasted.

Clenching his teeth, Ren wiped the water and tears from his face. He slapped off the spray and grabbed a towel. What he needed to do was go for a walk and clear his head. It would help him to pack all of these emotions and dreams away. When he could feel nothing at all, he'd be able to face Song and apologize. They could move on as if nothing had happened.

His heart screamed and his soul felt like it was being shredded, but that was life now. He wasn't allowed to have what everyone else had, but the trade-off was that he might get to keep doing what he enjoyed.

Ren blindly pulled on clothes. A dead weight had settled on his chest, making it difficult to breathe as it crushed everything within him. He didn't want to move. He didn't want to turn his life into a series of moments where he was simply going through the motions, but what choice did he have?

He reached for his phone, picking it up from where he'd tossed it onto the bed, only to have Song's name flash across the screen. He dropped it as though it had exploded into flames.

Song was calling.

He couldn't talk to him yet. He was a fucking mess. He was still attempting to pull himself together.

But if he didn't answer, Song would know something was wrong. He'd be upset.

With trembling fingers, he snatched up the phone and answered the call.

"Hey," Ren answered, trying to sound like everything was normal, but the wobble in his voice gave him away.

"Hey! Where are you?"

Ren's brows snapped together. Not what he'd been expecting at all. "In my room," he replied and then reconsidered. If he was in his room, he was trapped. He needed to escape and meet with Song when he was ready. When he'd found the right words to say and all his feelings were neatly packed away. "But I was thinking of running out to get some things for dinner."

"I can go with you."

"Nah. That's okay. You've got to be exhausted." Ren hurried and grabbed his wallet while he was talking, his escape plan forming in his brain. "I'll get some food, cook, and bring it over to you a little later. You just shower and nap."

He slipped his feet into a pair of slides, snagged his room key, jerked open his door, and screamed.

Song was standing outside his room, a wicked smirk on his lips.

Holding out his phone, he tapped the End Call button while his eyes never left Ren's face. "Do you honestly think I don't know you by now, didi?"

Ren couldn't think. His heart was racing and his stomach was twisting into hundreds of tiny, tight knots. Song was here. He'd caught him.

For every step he took backward, Song took a step forward until he could close the door, sealing them away from the world.

"Did you think I'd let you run from me again?"

"Song laoshi, I—"

The beautiful man held up a finger, his dark eyes narrowing. "If you dare apologize for what happened today, I will lose my temper."

Ren immediately bit his tongue to keep those very words inside. His entire body was trembling, and he felt so very exposed standing there. He wanted to hide and prepare, build up new protective walls around his heart so this moment wouldn't hurt quite so bad.

"What I would like is for us to sit down and talk. We need to face this, didi."

With his phone clutched tightly in front of him with both hands, Ren looked at it because he couldn't hold Song's unwavering stare any longer. "I don't think I can, Song laoshi."

"Please, Ren. The past month has been the sweetest torture, but I can't go on like this. We need to talk." When Ren lifted his gaze to Song, it was to find a tender smile on his lips. "And I'm hoping after we are done talking, we can try some more kissing."

Ren's phone clattered to the floor from his suddenly dead fingers.

What?

"Shit! Is it broken?"

Song's gasp freed him from that mental scream, and they both jumped for Ren's phone at the same time. Their fingers bumped, but Song retreated first as Ren picked up his phone to find that, thankfully, his screen had not cracked.

A sigh of relief tripped from his lips, but it was short-lived. Song's long fingers slid around his wrist and lightly gripped him. He raised his eyes to Song to find a mix of fear and hope swirling in those black depths.

"Thirty minutes, didi. That's all I'm asking. We both turn off our phones for thirty minutes. No directors, managers, assistants, or social media. Nothing. Just us talking with no interruptions or distractions. Please."

Song didn't need to beg. He'd do anything for this man, even though he was absolutely terrified.

"Okay."

Ren rose and turned off his phone. At the same time, Song moved away from him, settling on one of the stools at the bar. Ren sat on the edge of the bed and placed his phone on the nightstand.

The silence stretched for several seconds.

"Ren," Song started, and Ren couldn't stop his flinch. Song so very rarely used his name, and it didn't feel like it was a good thing. Song saw it and sighed. "Didi," he whispered, and it was an immediate balm on his nerves. "I like you. A lot." He broke off again with a wild laugh. He shoved his hand through his hair and shook his head. "God, I sound so ridiculous. This shouldn't be so hard, but I sound like we're still in school."

"It's okay. I really have no idea where this is going."

Song's wide eyes snapped to him. "Are you serious?"

"Yes."

He chuckled while Ren continued to twist his fingers together in a sweaty knot. "I thought I was so fucking obvious."

"No, definitely not."

Song pushed off the stool and slowly crossed the room to kneel in front of Ren. He covered Ren's hands in both of his and held them. "Ren An Xue, I think I'm falling in love with you."

For one glorious second, Ren's heart soared. Song loved him. Song—

"No," Ren murmured brokenly as he crashed back down to earth. "It's character bleed. You don't—"

"This isn't character bleed," Song argued sharply. "I said Ren An Xue. *My didi.* Zhao Gang is nice, but he's not the man who worries about me and takes care of me. Zhao Gang is not the type of person who worries about whether I'm laughing and happy. But my didi does. My Ren does hundreds of sweet, kind things all day for complete strangers just because that's the person he is." Song lifted one of his hands and cupped Ren's cheek. His thumb smoothed away a tear Ren hadn't even realized had slipped free. "My Ren has the biggest heart and the sweetest smile. How could I not fall hopelessly in love with him? How could I not be insanely possessive and jealous of everyone who dares to get near him?"

Ren closed his eyes and turned his face into Song's hand, letting his lips brush against the heel and palm. His wonderful warmth sank into him while the lingering scent of soap and sweat tickled his nose. His Song laoshi had come straight from the set to him. He'd come to him.

"Song," he whispered. Anything else he might have wanted to say was locked behind the lump in his throat.

"If you don't feel anything for me, if you don't think you'll ever feel anything for me, please say it now. I swear I will never bother you again. I won't touch you. I will never speak of this."

Ren's soul cried out at those words. How could he not want everything Song could give him? How could he go on without Song's touch?

"I just...I just need to know." Song's sweet voice trembled.

"I love you," Ren whimpered as fresh tears slid free. His eyes fluttered open and he stared, lost in Song's. "I love you so much. I've tried so hard to stop, but I can't. I can't stop loving you."

"Don't! Don't ever stop!"

Song pulled him in and crushed their lips together in a hard, demanding kiss that Ren immediately yielded to. He wrapped his arms around Song, his fingers twisting in his shirt, trying to pull him even closer. They kissed again and again, teeth tugging and tongues tangling. Ren was drowning in the heat and taste of Song. The world exploded, and everything he knew was Song.

They shifted, trying to get closer. Ren didn't know if he'd thrown Song off balance or what, but they were suddenly crashing to the floor. They separated, rolling onto their backs, their cries of pain mixed with laughter.

Ren tipped his head to Song, who was laughing and staring at the ceiling. "Look at what you did!"

"Me? This was all your fault!"

"Idiot."

Song turned his head toward him and grinned. "Only for you." He pushed up and crawled over, bracing his hands on either side of Ren's head. "You've turned me into a babbling, reckless, possessive, jealous, insane idiot."

"Don't forget sexy. You're also a sexy idiot," Ren teased.

Bending his elbows, Song lowered himself, taking Ren's lips in a slow, deep kiss. A moan lifted from Ren's throat as he immediately opened his mouth to Song's wandering tongue. The kiss stretched on and on, building the heat and desire in Ren's chest to the point of overflowing. It bubbled and surged through every part of his body.

Ren reached up, sliding his hands across Song's chest, feeling the hard muscles that jumped at his touch. He wrapped one hand around Song's neck, tightening, pulling him closer. Needing more contact.

Song broke off the kiss on a gasp. He stared down at Ren for a second, panting as though he'd just run a marathon. He smiled broadly. "Slow. We should…we should probably…go slow."

A laugh jumped from Ren and he nodded. His body cried foul, but at least one brain cell was still working and it agreed with Song. For now.

"Yes. Slow."

Song shifted to sit next to his hip, while Ren remained stretched out on the floor. A hand came to rest over Ren's pounding heart and Song's smile became a little sweeter, a little more tender.

Ren turned his head toward Song and narrowed his eyes. "One thing…" he started and then stopped.

"I'm sure there's more than one thing," Song replied. "But what are you thinking?"

"You're not gay," Ren blurted out, which earned him a look from Song. Ren rolled his eyes. "I mean…I was sure that you weren't. But…"

Song's smile turned wicked, and he waggled his eyebrows as he leaned close enough to bump his nose against Ren's. "Amazing actor, right?"

A new ache throbbed in Ren's chest, and he blinked back a fresh swell of tears. "The best," he whispered roughly.

"No, didi. Don't." Song turned Ren's head and kissed away the tear that slipped from the corner of his eyes and across his temple. "No more tears. Other than a bit of loneliness, I've had a very good life." He brushed a kiss across Ren's cheek and another to the corner of his mouth. "And right now, I have my Ah-Xue." He straightened and lifted one eyebrow at him. "Besides, you're…"

"Bi," Ren instantly answered. "But I've tried very hard not to be."

"I know, didi. I know." Song twisted and lay on the floor, resting his head on Ren's chest.

Smiling to himself, Ren *at last* ran his fingers through Song's soft hair. How long had he waited to do this? It felt like a lifetime, but it was so very worth the wait. He closed his eyes and listened to Song breathing, soaked in the feeling of Song's fingers running up and down his arm. For long minutes, they just existed together.

A muffled giggle rose from Song, and Ren opened his eyes. He turned his head to see a grin spreading across Song's slightly puffy lips.

"What?"

"Why are we lying on the floor, Ah-Xue?"

Ren closed his eyes again and sighed. "No idea."

They still didn't move. Minutes ticked by and they lay on the hard floor, holding on to this moment for as long as they could.

Because when they moved, they'd have to figure out what came next.

20

DO I HAVE A BOYFRIEND NOW?
SONG WEI LI

Being this happy had to be illegal.

He'd lived a good life with wonderful friends, achievements, and awards. Every day, he was able to get up and pursue two different careers that he loved. He made enough money to live comfortably and travel where he wanted.

But right now, he was lying on a cold, hard floor in the middle of a tiny temporary apartment and he couldn't remember a time when he'd been happier.

Of course, the source of all this happiness was currently lying under his head, his fingers slowly threading through his hair in the most relaxing caress.

Ren An Xue loved him.

He hadn't thought it was possible. Hadn't thought he'd ever find this. And not with the flustered and nervous man who'd rushed into that first table reading, looking overwhelmed by the world.

If they could stay like this forever…

A low, gurgling growl rose from Song's stomach and he curled around it, trying to hide the sound, but it was too late. Ren's stomach bounced under his head with laughter. His sweet love opened his wide brown eyes and smiled at him.

"I think that's the sign that it's time to get up," Ren announced.

"No! Not yet. Just a few more minutes," Song argued. He clutched Ren's arm. Moving felt dangerous. If they moved, this moment would be broken, and the outside world would sneak in. Everything still felt so fragile. He wanted to protect it for as long as possible.

"Song laoshi, did you eat at all today?"

He winced and closed his eyes. That was not a happy tone.

"Song..." Ren prodded when he didn't immediately respond.

"No. I wasn't hungry. I was pissed."

"Because I returned late?"

"Because you were assigned to the other team after returning late." He turned his face into Ren's stomach and said in a muffled voice, "I was looking forward to seeing you."

With a groan, Ren shoved into a sitting position and Song reluctantly joined him. He turned so that he was facing Ren with their right hips pressed together. He wrapped his arms around Ren, causing the man's eyes to widen. Yes, when they were alone together, this was something they'd get used to—touching each other. Holding each other. Kissing...

Song leaned forward and captured Ren's mouth in a sweet kiss. He tried to take it deeper, but Ren pulled away.

"Don't think you can distract me. You need to eat," Ren warned. The most wonderful flush was spreading across his face, proving he wasn't entirely unaffected by the kiss.

"I bet I can distract you." He tried to kiss Ren again, but the man dodged him and then gave him another dark, warning look. Okay, now he was pressing his luck.

"I'm serious, Song Wei Li. You need to take better care of yourself. I won't always be ar—"

Song pressed his fingers to Ren's lips to stop those horrible words. "Don't. Don't say that. I'm afraid."

Ren watched him closely as he caught Song's hand in his and pulled it away from his mouth. "What are you afraid of?"

"This. It's so beautiful." Song's voice shook as he moved his hand to cup Ren's cheek. "So perfect. Like you, I never thought there was anyone out there for me. I never thought I'd get to have a moment like this. But it feels so fragile. I'm afraid if we move, if we let the outside world in, it will break and I'll lose you."

Ren took his hand in both of his and held it while he turned to press a kiss to the palm. When he pulled Song's hand to his lap, Ren was smiling. "You're right. It is fragile, because it's new, but it will get stronger as time goes by because you are not the type of person to back down from a fight. And neither am I. The more the world tests us, the stronger we will become."

The world's goofiest grin spread across his lips, and Song sighed. Yeah, he didn't fucking care how sappy and schmoopy he looked. "I love you."

A matching grin lifted the corners of Ren's mouth. "I love you, too. Let's get something to eat and talk more."

"Do you really need to go out and get ingredients?"

Ren cringed before lowering his head to rest on Song's shoulder. "No, I think I've got some stuff here."

"So, you were running?"

"Maybe."

"Didi?"

Ren sighed heavily, his warm breath rushing past his neck. "I was sure you were coming over to tell me that you weren't attracted to me. That we were just friends and that was all it would ever be. That the kiss was a giant mistake and you'd appreciate it if I didn't accost you like that again."

Song's arms wrapped around Ren, holding him tightly against him. "Oh, didi, your imagination is a scary place. How could you think that? I am never letting you go."

"Except when I cook for you."

A low snort left him. "Maybe, but even then, I'm still keeping you in my line of sight."

With some groaning at sore muscles and aching backs from lying on the floor, they helped each other to their feet. Song was so very tempted to pull Ren into his arms, but food did sound good, and he didn't want to irritate Ren with his neediness. It was just that after living on the edge of a cliff for so long, it felt good to finally step into relative safety. And that safety was Ren.

Ren snatched up his phone and powered it on as he crossed toward the kitchen. Song swallowed a sigh as he grabbed his phone from the bar and did the same. As he slid onto the seat, he sang, "What are you making for dinner, Ah-Xue?"

The tall man with the puppy eyes smiled at him as he pulled open the door to the fridge. "I noticed that you like to switch between didi and Ah-Xue."

"Do you mind?"

"No," he said as he pulled vegetables out. "I was just wondering why."

Song shrugged. "I've never given it much thought. It's more of a feeling."

"What are you feeling?"

"When you're didi, you remind me of a sweet bunny or a puppy. I want to gather you close and protect you."

Ren tipped his head and moaned. "These fucking eyes—"

"Are perfect," Song finished. "But they aren't even your best feature."

Ren stopped short, his mouth falling open. "What? Really?"

"It's your heart. You have a beautiful heart." Ren directed bright eyes at him, looking as if he were going to crumble. But Song didn't want to get too serious. "Though based on the pictures I've seen of you online, your abs are apparently your next best feature."

"Song laoshi!"

"And your pants aren't nearly tight enough, but I suspect that you have an amazing ass as well."

Ren choked on a laugh, and a green bell pepper tumbled out of his arms to roll across the floor.

Song jumped to his feet and scrambled into the kitchen to grab the escaped vegetable. Ren dropped the rest into the sink to be washed, and Song added the pepper to the mix.

"Asshole," Ren muttered, but it was said with tenderness.

Song moved close to brush a kiss along his cheek when a *ping* jumped from Ren's phone. Song glanced at it on the counter and frowned.

"It looks like you've got a new voice mail. You want me to finish washing those while you check it?"

Ren glared at his phone for a second before taking a deep breath and nodding. It was a little reassuring to see that Ren wasn't exactly rushing to let the outside world into their bubble, but they couldn't hide here forever.

Song took his place at the sink while Ren dried his hand and snatched up his phone. He stood, listening to the message, and then quickly moved out of the kitchen. Song watched the tension in his shoulders tighten and his back become ramrod straight. This was not a good message.

Had he not gotten the last role he auditioned for? Was there something in the latest BTS video that his manager didn't like? It couldn't possibly be anything related to this job —Ren was doing amazing.

When the message was over, Ren didn't call the person as Song expected. Instead, he shoved one hand through his hair and tossed his phone onto the bed. He stood there, glowering at the wall. Song could feel him gathering himself together.

"Bad news?" Song asked, breaking the extended silence.

"Not really. Just more of the same old news I've been hearing for a few years," Ren murmured. He turned and strolled into the kitchen. His mood was more subdued, almost melancholy.

"Will you tell me about it?"

Ren stood in the kitchen entrance watching him. To his surprise, a slow half smile formed on his lips. "Yeah. It was my mom. She called to ask when I would be done with my latest bit of nonsense so I could return home to help with a rush of wedding orders."

Song could only stare at him. Though he understood every individual word Ren said, those statements didn't make sense to him. "I'm sorry, what?"

Ren's smile grew wider. "My family has run a florist shop for the past four generations. I was expected to take over when my parents decided to retire."

"Ah, and you decided to be an actor."

"Model, actually." He gave a smirk before taking some of the washed vegetables over to a cutting board. "I was scouted when I was making a floral delivery to an agency." Song turned to watch him in front of the cutting board as he sliced up peppers. "Modeling seemed more interesting than making deliveries and trying to figure out how to make floral arrangements. I like flowers, but not so much that I want to spend my life around them. Besides, other than you, everything else I've tried to care for has died."

"I'm more cactus than delicate orchid." Song smiled. His heart raced and skipped to hear Ren talking about his life prior to acting. When they'd shared personal stories in the past, it had always been in relation to their work.

"Since the modeling thing was going well, I decided to study acting and performing while I was at the university. My parents were never happy about it. Thought it was a waste of time and money. Even after I started landing acting jobs and making a living at it, they kept saying I was wasting my time. They make it sound like it's all going to fall apart any second, or that what I'm doing isn't a real job."

"That's fucking ridiculous. What do you have to do to prove that you're successful?" Song snapped.

"I honestly don't know," Ren admitted with a small sigh. "Even if *Legend* becomes huge like *Frozen River*, that's not going to be enough because it's BL."

Song's blood ran cold. Not that he was overly surprised. There were too few parents in China that were understanding and supportive of the LGBT community. Ren's parents sounded more like the norm.

"Then I guess they wouldn't be too excited to hear that you've got a boyfriend," Song said softly.

Ren had been in the middle of slicing a pepper and set the knife down. He looked over his shoulder at Song, the widest, most amazing smile lighting up his face. "Do I? Do I have a boyfriend now?"

"Fuck yes, you do." Song groaned and crossed the kitchen, wrapping his arms tightly around Ren. "Do you think I go about telling every sexy, amazing, talented man I meet that I love him? You're mine. There is no escaping."

Ren kissed him, never losing that brilliant smile. The kiss led to another and another until Song's stomach grumbled in complaint. Ren sent him to his seat while he worked on their meal.

"If you're worried about my family causing problems for us, don't. We're not close. Haven't been for a long time." Ren paused and shrugged as he worked. "We haven't been close since I realized they didn't care what I wanted for my life. I guess I'm not a good, filial son. When my career takes off, I'll do what I can to support them, but I'm not giving up what makes me happy." Ren glanced over his shoulder and smiled again. "And right now, that's you and acting."

"I want you happy, didi, and I don't want to cause you trouble."

"I'm sure there will be plenty of trouble in the future, but it won't be from my parents." Ren plated the food as it finished cooking, the delicious scent already filling the air. "What about your family? Would they be all that excited to learn you've got a boyfriend?"

Song jumped up and grabbed a couple of bottles of water out of the fridge, bringing them over to the bar. "It's just my mom and me. She's always been supportive of my career, but then she was an actress as well. Mostly stage rather than TV and movies. She's retired, but she'll still take on a project here and there when something interests her." Song eased onto his seat when Ren sat on his. With chopsticks in hand, he immediately started putting pieces of meat on Ren's plate.

"Stop it. Feed yourself. You haven't eaten," Ren chastised while placing some food on Song's plate.

"As for having a boyfriend, I don't think she'd be all that shocked. It's not like I told her I was gay. I think she might suspect. I've never had a girlfriend, and I never showed any interest in girls while growing up." He stopped talking long enough to shove some food into his mouth and hum happily to himself. Ren was a fabulous cook.

"And the boyfriend?"

Song grinned at him. "I think she'd like you. How could she not like someone who takes such good care of her son? Someone who doesn't tolerate his nonsense?"

"Your nonsense is part of your charm," Ren murmured.

Song could only smile. This was nice. This was what people lived for. Someone to share a meal with and pleasant conversation.

"Ah-Xue." He sighed.

Ren lifted an eyebrow and smiled as well. "Song laoshi."

When they were finished, Song took over the cleanup despite Ren's protests. He was pleasantly surprised to see that Ren remained at the bar, watching him work, as if he didn't want to be farther from him than necessary.

"I think we timed this poorly," Ren stated while Song was drying the last dish.

"What do you mean?"

"You leave tomorrow."

Song could only stare at him in confusion. Why did Ren think he was leaving? There was no way he was leaving Hengdian when he just—

Holy shit, I'm leaving tomorrow!

Ren's cackle filled the room as he fell back in his seat.

"No!" Song howled. "I can't leave now!"

How could this be happening?

"I can't...I can't believe...you forgot!" Ren gasped between his wild giggles. "Biggest concert of your life! A concert with Zhu Fang and *you forgot!*"

Song put the bowl in his hand on the counter and left the kitchen. He moved around the bar and grabbed Ren, pulling him into his arms. His long, lanky body was still shaking with laughter, but those strong arms quickly wrapped about his shoulders while Ren snuggled his face against Song's.

"You have been the only thing I can think about recently," Song mumbled into Ren's shoulder. "I just got you. We just got *this*. I don't want to leave." His grip on Ren tightened as he spoke, as if he were afraid the man was going to disappear.

"I'll be here waiting for you. This isn't going to end because you're gone for a couple of days." Ren brushed his lips across the shell of Song's ear, sending the most wonderful shiver of pleasure through his body. "After this, I don't have any plans to leave town again. We have almost two full months of seeing each other every day."

And every night, it would be them alone.

"Still not happy about it." Song pouted.

"Don't be ungrateful. You're going to have a wonderful time. This is great for your career. It's going to be fantastic support for building the fan base of *Legend*. You'll get to spend some time with your new friend."

Song lifted his head and glared at the owner of his heart.

"Why must Ren laoshi speak so much sense when I want to stay here?"

Ren surprised him by placing a small kiss to his cheek. "Because you know I'm right."

"What about you? What will you do? Will you be okay?"

Ren's smile shifted a little and his eyes darted away. "Actually…I do have plans for that night during the concert."

"What?" Song's fingers twisted in Ren's shirt, locking the man in place so he couldn't possibly escape. "What are you doing? You're not going to dinner with Liu, are you?"

Ren snickered and shook his head. "Of course not!"

"Then what?"

"I received an invite from Guo Zi," Ren replied, his voice bubbling over with excitement. "He's here in Hengdian for the next couple of weeks, filming. Apparently, Zhu Fang's assistant is going to be filming the concert and uploading the videos to a shared cloud drive. Guo Zi invited me over to where he's staying to watch the videos as they are uploaded." Ren's eyes softened and his smile grew sad. "It's not the same as being there, but I'll be able to watch it almost as it's happening."

Tipping his head up, Song stole a kiss, his heart aching for Ren and maybe some for Guo Zi. They both wanted to be there, but work was keeping them apart. He also liked the idea of Ren becoming friends with Guo Zi. Song didn't know what the road held for them, but having someone Ren could turn to for advice was going to be critical.

"That sounds like an excellent plan," Song said. "But the next one, you're there."

"Definitely."

Leaving Ren's room that night was one of the hardest things Song had ever done. But he'd completely forgotten about the concert, and he wasn't prepared for tomorrow's departure. He needed to pack and start working through his planned playlist. He had one day of rehearsal before the concert the next night. The next two days were going to be so busy, he wasn't going to be able to sneak chats with Ren.

Of course, Ren was going to be busy with shooting while he was gone as well.

But when Song got back, he was going to devote all his spare time to his didi.

21

COME HOME TO ME
REN AN XUE

He was going to hang out with Guo Zi.

Yeah, not intimidated at all.

Except the guy was insanely popular and incredibly talented.

Okay, he might have been good-looking too, but he really didn't compare to Song. No one compared to his Song when he smiled.

But Guo Zi's popularity could be felt in just Ren's approach to the hotel he was using. A bodyguard/driver had been sent to pick him up and escort him past the fans who were camped outside the building with their Guo Zi signs and flowers for the actor. Some of them even had little dolls of his character from *Frozen River*.

Was it too much to hope that he would see a tenth of this popularity when *Legend* was released?

Song definitely would. Everyone loved the gruff and grumpy man who fiercely protected his soft heart. It didn't hurt that Song was also gorgeous.

But Zhao Gang? He spent so much of the show as a bad guy who was pursuing Tian Xiuying. Would they rather see Zhao Gang hanged than catch their hero?

Luckily, those thoughts were shoved to the back of his mind when he knocked on the door to Guo Zi's suite. The actor greeted him with a surprisingly wide grin and waved for him to enter. He was wearing a pair of baggy shorts and a T-shirt with Zhu Fang on it. His gray-toned hair was cut short and styled in a kind of wavy bedhead mess that made him look even younger and more adorable.

Ren quickly shed his shoes and offered the chocolate tarts he'd brought as a thank-you for having him.

A surprised laugh bubbled up from Guo Zi. "I like where your mind is." He motioned for Ren to follow him to the small kitchen where a mad array of junk food was already out. "I hope you're not currently on a diet, because I don't have anything remotely healthy here." He paused and turned shy eyes up at him. When Guo Zi finally spoke, his voice was softer. "It's been nearly two months since Fang Fang and I have seen each other in person. I thought I'd be able to make it to this concert, but filming…"

Ren's stomach sank. He reached back to lightly grab the counter to steady himself. *They haven't seen each other in two months?* Panic and fear ripped through Ren and wrapped around his heart. The low-level melancholy that kicked in following Song's departure threatened to become full-blown depression.

How long would they go between seeing each other after they finished filming?

Would they just drift apart?

"Anyway, I thought you'd be able to commiserate with me. Junk food felt like the best option for our pity party," Guo Zi continued.

"Yeah, definitely," Ren breathed.

"How about a drink? I've got water, tea, beer—"

"Beer, please." Ren had not come here with the intention of drinking, but now it was almost necessary.

Guo Zi snagged two bottles and led the way into the small

living room. The space was sparsely decorated like his own place, but Guo Zi's rooms were bigger, with a dedicated sitting area. He glimpsed an unmade bed through an open door and another door led to a tidy bathroom.

A laptop was set up on the coffee table showing a single folder with a couple of videos. As they sat, Guo Zi tapped on the first video. "Fang's assistant popped out briefly and recorded a view of the audience. The place is already packed."

The video started to play on the large-screen TV on the wall, showing a slow pan of the crowded venue. Fans filled nearly every available seat, and more were still hurrying down the aisles. Many were holding light-up signs with Zhu Fang's name on it, but there were several that also had signs with Song's name. Pride and pure joy swelled in Ren's heart, pushing out the worry. Yes, he missed Song, but he wanted this for him. He wanted his boyfriend to absolutely revel in this moment.

"Looks like it's going to be a great night for them," Ren murmured when the video ended.

"Oh, yeah. I wish I was there."

"Me too."

Ren glanced up to find Guo Zi watching him, a crooked grin on his face. "Do you mind if I ask how things are going with you and Song Wei Li?"

Ren ripped his gaze away and stared at the table for a second. "The filming has been good. Hectic but good. Song is great to work with. He's taught me a lot and has so many fantastic ideas about how to do a scene. I've been very lucky to have him as a costar for this show."

"Uh-huh."

Glimpsing Guo Zi out of the corner of his eye, he found the man's smile had grown even wider, and his eyes were practically laughing at him.

"And…we…might be dating now," Ren admitted in an even softer voice.

Guo Zi thrust both hands into the air, "Yes!" He fell back into the couch cackling loudly. "We knew it!"

"What?"

"Fang Fang texted me a few times yesterday, reporting that Song was completely different in the rehearsal. Happy, energetic, giggling constantly over the smallest things. Totally different from the somewhat reserved, worried man we'd both spoken to."

Ren swallowed and bit down on the inside of his mouth to keep from grinning like a fucking lunatic. "Well, he'd probably be excited about the concert."

"Or…he's excited about finally getting his hands on the man who's completely possessed his heart and brain for the past two months," Guo Zi teased. "I'm so happy for you and Song.

Burning crept across Ren's cheeks and was stretching to the tips of his ears. "Thank you."

Guo Zi cocked his head to the side, his smile sliding away. "Unless you're not happy…"

Ren immediately straightened, his eyes going wide. "No! I'm happy. Stupidly happy!" He winced at that shout and quickly lowered his voice closer to a whisper. "It's just…I've never dated a guy. I have no idea what I'm doing. At all. And then throw in that we've only two months left of filming. What happens after that? Will we ever see each other? What if someone discovers us?"

Guo Zi's eyes widened as well and he lunged forward, grabbing both of Ren's arms. "Stop! You can't go into this worrying about all of that. How long have you even been together?"

"Three days. Sort of. It kind of feels like only a day, though." Ren launched into the insanity of their first kiss, which had led to

Ren running like a coward and Song cornering him in his own room. Guo Zi released him and turned on the couch to face him, one bent knee on the cushion between them and a broad smile on his pink lips. And yeah, Ren might have lingered on how they lay on the floor, just being together, before he made them dinner.

His new friend snorted. "You cooking is going to be the bane of my existence. That's all I hear from Fang. When am I going to cook for him? I barely cook for myself."

"Sorry," Ren murmured, but Guo Zi waved him off.

"He loves to complain and start trouble." Guo Zi placed his elbow on the back of the couch and leaned his head into his hand. "Right now, you need to enjoy the time you've got together. Steal all the time you can. Hide from the fans as long as possible. No one is expecting you to be out making appearances and signing autographs. Let this be your time."

"And when we're out of our time?"

The man's smile wavered and slipped into something sadder. "By then, you've hopefully turned this new relationship into something you're willing to fight for, because it will be a fight. You're going to go months without seeing each other. Your time together is going to largely be video calls and text messages. You're going to struggle to coordinate when you're both available. You're going to be jealous of everyone who gets to see him, touch him, hear his voice." Guo Zi paused and shook his head. "But then he's going to smile at you, and you'll know it's all worth it because he doesn't smile at anyone else like that."

"And what if we're caught?"

Guo Zi shivered and turned his gaze to the computer screen, his face becoming a pained scowl. "You pray it doesn't happen, but that thought alone will keep you up a lot of nights. If you're caught, especially after the promotional period is over, you have to face the likelihood that you're going to be blacklisted. Both of you. You'll lose your careers. Your families will be hurt. Your lives could even be in danger. So, you're always careful." He stared at Ren. "Always be careful. Second and third guess every decision. Weigh the risks. Plan everything out. Coordinate your social media so there's no question that you're nowhere near each other."

He glanced at the screen again and shivered. "We were nearly caught a couple of times. Fang tried to end it both times to protect me. I wouldn't let him." A small smirk played on his lips. "That man has no idea that I can and always will be more stubborn than him."

"Good. I can be stubborn too."

Guo Zi chuckled, losing some of his earlier tension. "Good! That will help. Probably more than anything else."

"Look! Another video was posted," Ren nearly shouted, pointing at the screen.

His friend bounced a little on the couch, turning his body to reach the laptop. He tapped on it and the TV instantly filled with the stage. Everything was dark, but they could hear the fans screaming and chanting both Song's and Fang's names.

And then it all exploded in lights and music. The two singers walked out together from different sides of the stage to meet in the center. Ren's eyes burned with tears and he had to fight the urge to climb to his feet so he could move closer to the TV.

His Song looked stunning. He was dressed in blue and black, making him appear slim and fierce. His now shoulder-length hair was pulled back, but his long bangs hung down, partially obscuring his eyes to give him a roguish air. Ren wanted to be there. He wanted to be standing in that crowd, screaming his head off with all the other fans.

As they reached the center of the stage, they launched straight into a duet.

"Ha! Liar! I knew you'd start with that song!" Guo Zi shouted at the TV as he jumped to his feet. He turned to Ren, the biggest, sappiest grin on his face. "He always kicks a show off with one of three songs, and I knew it was going to be this one."

Ren could only laugh and turn his eyes to Song. Yes, Zhu Fang was amazing, but he couldn't look away from his man. So beautiful. So seductive. So brilliantly talented. He wanted the entire world to see how great Song was.

The video ended at the same time as the song and Ren shouted, jumping to his feet while Guo Zi flopped back on the couch.

"Sorry about that. His assistant is filming with two different phones. She's stopping between songs and uploading the video of each song. That way we can sort of watch the concert as it happens, but there are going to be lags."

Ren dropped down and took a long drink of his beer. "No, don't apologize. Thank you so much for having me over. If it wasn't for you, I'd probably be curled up in bed, trolling the Internet for any videos people might have posted of the concert."

Guo Zi's smile became a bit shy as he stared at the computer. "And thank you…for your friendship. There's really no one I can talk to about what I have with Fang. I mean, there's a small group of people who know and support us. They help us where they can, but only Yuan Teng Fei and Shen Ruo Xuan are going through the same things, but it's hard to catch them since they've both been swamped with work the past several months. Well, we're all busy, but it's nice…to have a support system."

A bubble of giddy laughter rose up in Ren's chest, and he fought to shove it aside. He never imagined that Guo Zi would see him as a real friend, but he agreed. They would need each other.

"You know, I'm happy to listen anytime Zhu Fang does something to drive you crazy."

Guo Zi tossed his head back and chortled. "Oh, my God! I'd be texting and calling you all the time."

Their conversation was cut off by another video appearing in the folder.

The rest of the evening passed quickly with videos and relaxed conversation. Zhu Fang and Song took turns singing and then teamed up for some duets. Ren ate way too much horrible junk food and laughed too loudly at Guo Zi's stories of Fang's antics on the set of *Frozen River*.

For the last song of the night, Song took the stage alone and the world stopped. His beautiful voice lifted in an exquisite song Ren had never heard before. But what knocked the air out of his lungs was the giant video screen behind Song. It was a montage of clips from *Legend of the Lost Night*. He was up there on that massive display with Song. And he looked good. Really good.

The entire concert venue was deathly quiet. It seemed like every fan had stopped breathing as they all drank in those first scenes from the show that wouldn't release for several months. Despite the shoestring budget and the fact that they were only half done with filming, everything appeared incredibly lush. The scenes had an epic feel to them. And Song…Song was just incredible, both his appearance on the show trailer and his beautiful voice adding depth to the scenes.

As the last notes of the song faded away and the title screen came up for *Legend*, the entire venue exploded in cheers. Fans were chanting the name of the show, sending a wave of goose bumps down his arms.

It was only when Ren dropped his face to his hands that he even realized they were shaking and his cheeks were wet with tears. A slender arm wrapped around his shoulders and gently squeezed.

"Holy shit," Guo Zi whispered. "That was gorgeous. I can't wait to see it. You and Song are going to hit so fucking big with this."

And for the first time since they'd arrived in Hengdian,

Ren began to believe that they just might have something huge on their hands.

But even with that hope taking root in his chest, his heart was longing for one thing: Song Wei Li. He wanted him right there in his arms. He wanted to hold Song and tell him how amazing his performance was. He wanted to ask a million questions and hear all his thoughts about how the concert went. He wanted to be bathed in the man's excitement and joy.

Right now, there was one thing he could do.

Ren grabbed his phone and opened his messenger to the last text he'd sent Song. With quick fingers, he typed out the only thing that needed to be said:

I love you so much. You were amazing! Now come home to me.

22

DIDI, THAT'S A GOOD THING
SONG WEI LI

How could it be possible that the first time he saw his new boyfriend after returning from a massively successful concert, he couldn't kiss him in greeting?

That was evil. Just fucking evil.

Also, he was ready to sing about Ren's perfection after the text he'd received from the man.

I love you so much. You were amazing! Now come home to me.

Fucking perfect.

But that was where all the perfection ended. It was nearly three in the morning when he shuffled to his room. Everything in him cried out to skip going to his bed and bang on Ren's door, demanding the man let him in so he could at least feel his strong arms around him.

Unfortunately, Ren had an early call time and Song was not going to disturb his sleep, knowing the poor guy was expected in the makeup chair before six a.m.

Song didn't have to report until ten, giving him a chance to catch up on sleep.

So here he was, prowling the set like a wild animal, back in his Tian Xiuying garb, desperate to get his hands on either Zhao Gang or Ren An Xue.

Through the crowd, he finally spotted Ren. His costar towered over most of the other people, and it didn't hurt that he was in his white hanfu. Ren needed to shoot some scenes that would go with the first few episodes of the series. Then he was in wardrobe after the lunch break for a new outfit.

When he caught sight of Ren, his feet just stopped. He was glowing in the late-morning sun, his fan creating enough of a breeze to stir the heavy hair of his wig. His expression was serious as he listened to what one of the assistant directors was telling him. Such focus and dedication. Every time he pulled on his costume, Ren gave everything to his role.

"You might want to turn down the heat of that look," a familiar voice next to him drawled. Song's head whipped around to see a smirking Hua Jun Bai standing next to him.

How the fuck had he not noticed the man?

Dressed in a white hanfu of diaphanous layers, Hua Jun Bai looked more menacing ghost than god. His face was heavily made up so that he was even paler, as if the guy hadn't stepped out in the sun in a lifetime.

They'd worked together on several costume dramas in the past, and he was incredibly talented but more than a little nosy. His character appeared halfway through the series and would accompany them on their journey from here on out, alternating between driving Zhao Gang and Tian Xiuying crazy.

It seemed like he'd decided to start with Song in real life.

"What? I don't know what you're talking about," Song argued.

Hua Jun Bai snorted and leaned in closer so he could lower his voice. "I can hear your brain calculating how soon you can viably pull that man into the shadows." His smirk widened into a wicked grin that stretched rose-pink lips. "Planning to accost him right here on the set?"

"You're insane," Song snapped. He reached out and poked Hua in the shoulder. "I haven't seen you in months. At least begin with something normal like 'How are you?' or 'It's good to see you.' Crazy bastard."

Hua cackled. "It's good to see you. Since when did you turn into such a grump?"

"Shut up. I'm not a grump." But he was because he wanted to see Ren. *Alone.* "Have you started shooting yet?"

Hua continued to smile his annoying smile. "Yesterday. That's when I ran into Ma Daiyu, and she informed me of all the nauseating cuteness that's been happening on the set."

"It's nothing," Song groaned, dropping his head back. "We're friends. He's a fantastic actor, dedicated to his work."

"I—"

"There's our superstar!" Sun Jing's voice rang out. "The man who is already putting *Legend* at the top of all the hashtag lists on Weibo[1]!"

Song looked up to see that nearly every eyeball on the set was turned toward him. People clapped loudly and congratulated him on the excellent concert. He smiled and nodded, but his eyes automatically sought out Ren.

The second their gazes met, Song could feel himself going up in flames. Ren's face was half-hidden behind his fan, but his eyes were burning him up. At least he wasn't the only one hoping to get a moment alone.

"Yeah, just friends," Hua muttered under his breath before walking away.

Screw Hua. He'd worry about him later.

Right now, Song had to do the impossible: walk through this sea of people, smiling and laughing, while pretending that he wasn't screaming on the inside to rush to Ren.

After more congratulatory comments than he could recall, Song finally reached Ren, who was still standing next to Sun.

"Congratulations on the concert last night," Ren said with a modest smile and sweet voice, while his eyes continued to eat him alive.

"Thank you," Song replied with a bow of his head. "Were you able to see any of it?"

Ren lowered his eyes at last and Song felt like he could draw in a full breath at long last. "I did. I watched with a friend."

Oh, that's right! Guo Zi.

That was something else he was dying to ask Ren about, but only after he got to taste his boyfriend's lips.

"He totally ditched us!" Ma Daiyu complained as she bounced up to their little trio, a wide grin on her gamine face.

Ren smiled patiently as he closed his fan. He tapped her lightly on the top of the head. "I never promised I'd join your watch party. A friend is in town, and I watched with him so we could also spend the time catching up."

"I heard you were spotted with Guo Zi's bodyguard," she teased in a light voice.

Song's eyes snapped up to Ren's face and to the man's credit, he didn't outwardly react to Ma's comment.

"Do you know Guo Zi?" Sun gasped.

Song inwardly winced. He could guess at the calculations the director was making in his head in terms of marketing. It wasn't enough that Song was associated with Zhu Fang. No, he would want to have his other star linked to *Frozen River's* other powerhouse.

"You shouldn't listen to such ridiculous Internet rumors," Ren sighed, his tone more Zhao Gang's disdain than his sweet Ren, but it was a perfect dodge.

Sun Jing made an exasperated sound and waved his hands at them. "At least I've got my little family back together, and Hua Jun Bai is here. We can complete the last half of this drama without any more interruption."

With that pronouncement, Ren and Ma were herded into place for a scene while the makeup jiejies descended on him for touch-ups to his wig and adjustments to his robes. As soon as Ren was finished with his scene, Song was pretty sure he would be starting his first scene with Hua in a pub.

And that was it.

That was his loving, impassioned first greeting with Ren.

His soul howled, but his mind tsked and reminded the rest of him that at least he got to see him in person. Later that day, they would be able to have some time away from the rest of the world. They'd hold each other without watchful eyes, and they'd talk without so many ears listening.

To his shock, Ren suddenly turned toward him, cutting through half a dozen people to walk to his side. A very determined expression darkened his face, as if daring anyone to get in his way. Song's heart hammered and his mouth went dry. He wouldn't…wouldn't dare kiss him in front of all these people.

A beautiful smile broke across Ren's face when they were standing barely a foot apart and he grabbed one of Song's hands. His long fingers squeezed so tightly for a second, and his smile wavered for the blink of an eye.

"Song, could you hold this for me?" Ren asked, and Song could only stare at him. His brain stopped working and his breath was caught in his chest. Ren pressed his red, battery-powered fan into his hand and then turned back to where he was supposed to be shooting.

Song wanted to giggle. The man had passed at least six people—*including his own assistant*—who would have happily held it for him, only to place that fan in Song's hand.

He felt it in that touch, in that smile.

I love you.

Somehow, Song managed to pull his head out of the clouds and focus on his work after that incredibly brief encounter. Ren gave the impression of being a professional, but every time he was between takes, his eyes automatically sought out Song.

And every look, every smirk, set Song on fire.

When the afternoon break was called, Song practically sprinted off the set, his footsteps dogged by Hua's loud laughter. He didn't care. He didn't care what Hua or anyone on the set thought of his quick departure. He needed to find Ren.

But where was he? He wasn't needed for the scene that Song had completed with Hua. He would have gotten out of his white hanfu, but they wouldn't have shifted to his new outfit for the afternoon shots yet. Not when he needed to relax and eat lunch.

Trailer!

He had to be in his trailer.

When he reached Ren's trailer, he just barely remembered to knock rather than simply ripping the door open. Dating or not, he could respect Ren's privacy. Give the man a tiny bit of space. For two more seconds at least.

"Come in!" Ren called out.

Song stepped inside the dark coolness, and his heart sank at the sight of Ren's assistant sitting at the table, typing away on a tablet while Ren stood behind the counter, cutting up some fruit.

"Oh. Hey," Song started and cleared his throat in hopes of ridding it of the bitter disappointment. He should have known Ren would be working in his free time, and not simply waiting around for Song to show up. "Sorry to bother you. Didn't know you were in a meeting. I can catch you later."

"Don't move an inch, Song laoshi," Ren ordered, pointing the knife at him as he began to back out of the trailer. "I bet you haven't eaten in a day. Stay."

The assistant made some excuse that required her to beat a hasty retreat out of the trailer while Ren set aside his knife. Song didn't hear a word of what she said. Her voice was noise in his ears that was drowned out by the pounding of his heart. As she left, he stepped fully into the trailer. His brain just barely recalled the need to lock the door behind her.

And then he was alone with Ren.

The air became electrified as they stood frozen, staring at each other.

"I missed you," Song breathed.

"I missed you, too."

It was the tiny break in Ren's voice that snapped the last of Song's control. He lunged across the distance, but Ren was moving too, meeting him halfway so that they collided in the center of the trailer. The first touch of Ren's lips against his own dragged an almost pained groan from Song's throat. He sank into that blissful heat, clutching Ren to him as tightly as possible. Fingers dug into hard muscle and Song was lost in the perfection that was Ren An Xue.

Teeth bit into Song's lower lip and he whimpered, but the flash of pain was erased with a slow swipe of Ren's tongue before it slid into his mouth. The slick touch of Ren was heaven, and every hungry sound that rose from Ren was the sweetest.

Song let his hands explore, running up Ren's muscular back and then down again to dig into the hard globes of his ass. He pulled him in tighter, molding their bodies together. Ren broke off the kiss and gasped for air as he tipped his head up toward the ceiling. His boyfriend was dressed in a T-shirt and thin basketball shorts, which allowed him to feel exactly how excited he was to be in Song's arms.

Of course, he was still stuck in part of his costume. The wardrobe jiejies had managed to pull the first two layers off him as he cut across the studio lot, but they'd been unable to keep up with him. He was still wearing too many clothes—anything that kept him from being skin to skin with Ren was too much.

Holding Ren trapped, Song thrust his hips forward, rubbing his hard dick against Ren's through their clothes. The cry of pleasure wrung out of Ren sent a shiver along Song's spine.

Oh God, I can't wait to get Ren naked in bed.

The thought had barely passed through Song's brain when Ren was shoving out of his arms and turning to face the counter. He stood with his back to Song, his stomach pressed tightly to the cabinets while his shoulders were hunched up to his ears as he gulped in great swallows of oxygen.

Cold air swamped Song, and he could only stand there, dazed.

What the fuck happened?

"I'm so sorry, Song laoshi," Ren said, his sweet voice trembling.

"Sorry? For what?" Song carefully walked over to Ren, moving slowly so as not to spook him. "Talk to me, please."

"It's embarrassing. I...I just got too excited. I need a minute...to calm down."

Song placed a hand on the middle of Ren's back and tried to peer around his arm to see his face, but Ren shifted so that he was still hidden.

What the hell did that mean? How was too excited a bad thing?

"I don't understand, didi. Why are you embarrassed?"

Ren moaned softly. "Please don't make me say it."

It was like getting hit in the head with a brick. Song nearly laughed in his relief, but he caught himself. That would have made things a hundred times worse.

"Ah-Xue, do you mean that you're embarrassed because I made you hard?"

Ren didn't answer, but his entire body seemed to tense up even more.

"Didi, that's a good thing," he cooed. "I'd be worried if you didn't have any kind of reaction to me." Song grabbed Ren's bicep and tried to turn Ren to face him, but the man refused to budge. "Look at me, please. Did you honestly not feel that I'm as turned-on as you?"

That got Ren to turn just a bit toward him so that Song could see those enormous lost puppy eyes that threatened to drown him every fucking time. "I thought...maybe...but then I realized you could feel…"

Song's brain decided to finally stage a war against his libido. His body screamed to pin this man to the nearest wall, drop to his knees, and suck all thought out through his dick. But his brain was craftier. It posed a scary question that Song could not escape.

"Are you a virgin?" Song whispered.

"No!" Ren practically shouted while lurching away from him. "No! Of course not!"

That was a little too defensive.

"So, you've been with a man…" Song pressed before Ren could escape more than a couple of steps.

That stopped Ren and those lost eyes returned to his face. "No." He flinched and swallowed hard. "You have."

Song wasn't entirely sure if it was a statement or a question. It didn't matter. The answer was yes, but the few times he'd been with other men didn't even come close to comparing to what he already had with Ren.

He closed the distance between them and threaded his fingers through Ren's.

Those eyes snapped up to his face in surprise, and Song just knew he was hopelessly in love with this man. The trust and need that wrapped him up tight were stealing away all his personal concerns and desires. His every drive was becoming about Ren and his happiness. Whatever Ren needed or desired, Song's sole purpose was to make it happen.

And right now, Ren needed to regain his confidence.

"I don't know what I'm doing. I don't want to disappoint you," Ren choked out.

Song tightened his fingers in Ren's and cupped his cheek with his free hand. "Ah-Xue, you could never disappoint me. The only thing that will hurt me is if you force yourself to do something you're not comfortable with."

Ren closed his eyes and turned his head to brush the sweetest kiss across Song's palm. "I just need slow."

"That's fine. We'll go as slow as you need." Ren's eyes flicked down and regarded him with doubt. Song smiled. "I'm serious. All I need is to see you and know that you're happy. That's enough for me."

Ren snorted and tugged on the hand holding his, pulling him in closer. "I don't need quite *that* slow." Their chests bumped and Song held perfectly still, letting Ren come to him. Those perfect lips brushed against his, stoking the fire that never quite went out. Song wanted to dive into another deep, drugging kiss, but he held himself back to sweet, slow kisses.

"Did I tell you that I missed you?" Song murmured into Ren's mouth.

He could feel Ren smiling as he said, "I think you did."

"Dinner and talking tonight?"

Ren sighed and Song understood his discomfort, but it probably was a good idea if they both shared a little about their past and expectations.

"Will there be more kissing as well?" Ren asked in a grumbly tone.

"If that's what my Ah-Xue wants."

"It is."

"Then yes."

Anything Ren An Xue wanted, Song would do for him.

And when Ren was ready for Song to truly seduce him, Song would be more than ready to take this man apart in bed.

23

IT WAS BAD, SONG LAOSHI. SO FUCKING BAD

REN AN XUE

Was it wrong that he was ready to get out of this "talking" phase of their relationship?

No, that sounded wrong and bad. He didn't mean it like that.

He was ready for a break from the heavy and horribly embarrassing conversations where he felt like an awkward idiot while wondering why someone as beautiful, funny, and amazing as Song was with him in the first place.

All in all, he loved talking to Song. He loved all their random conversations about things that interested them or even weird, idle chitchat about nothing at all. He even loved their serious conversations about work and life.

It was the more revealing things that left Ren feeling far too vulnerable that he was eager to just avoid for the time being.

But that wasn't right. He couldn't keep worrying about what Song thought about him. Song said he loved him.

Him.

Not Zhao Gang.

Not some happy, perfect version of him.

The real him. And that meant all his eccentricities, awkwardness, and annoying habits.

He couldn't keep worrying about hiding all that stuff because he was afraid of losing Song. If they were going to have anything at all, Song needed to know everything he could about him. They needed to support each other, and Song couldn't do that if Ren kept pushing him away and hiding shit.

No. He was facing this head on. Yes, it would be embarrassing and awkward and he'd want the floor to swallow him whole, but he'd survive and Song would reward him with kisses.

"What was that sigh for?" Song asked as they entered the elevator to go up to their rooms.

Ren smiled at him. "Just glad to have the day over."

Okay, maybe he was also glad to have Song all to himself, but they weren't alone in the elevator. The two women who worked as part of the crew might have had their eyes locked on their phones, but Ren knew they'd notice if he so much as brushed his arm against Song's.

Now that they were dating, he was so much more aware of other people. It felt like they were always watching. Their phones were always pointed at them, recording every little thing he said or did. He was avoiding all social media. He wasn't ready for that yet, but he knew he was living on borrowed time. He was still making daily posts, but he wasn't reading the comments or scrolling like he used to.

A couple of floors before theirs, the elevator stopped and both women wished them a good-night as they exited. As soon as the doors closed, Ren slumped on the wall and sighed. Just one step closer to having no one around to watch them.

"Bao Shi grabbed some takeout for us and dropped it off in my room about fifteen minutes ago. Let me snag it and I'll be over," Song announced.

"Nope."

Song jerked, his brow furrowing. "What?"

"You said we had to talk, so we're eating and talking in your room this time."

"Why?"

"Because it feels like we're always having serious talks in my room. It's filling up my space with negative energy. We need to start sharing some of these talks with your room, too."

Song cackled and bumped into him as the doors slid open. He stepped out and then turned to wait for Ren to join him. He glanced around to find they were alone in the hall before he leaned in and whispered, "We've also kissed in your room. That's got to count for something, right?"

"Yes, and if you play your cards right, there will be kissing in your room, too."

Song hummed a happy tune as he led the way down the hall. "I like that idea, but you have to give me five minutes to clean up."

"No."

His boyfriend stopped and stared at him for a second. "Come on. Five minutes."

"No." Ren stepped closer so that his chest was pressed against Song's arm and he dipped his head so that his lips were inches from Song's ear. "I want to know everything about you. Beautiful and messy. I don't want us hiding anything. I want to love all of you."

"Fuck, Ah-Xue," Song exhaled in a soft moan. He turned his head and Ren just barely managed to keep himself from stealing a kiss right there in the hallway. As it was, they were already standing far too close together.

"Let me in, Song laoshi," Ren murmured as he retreated a step to put some breathing space between them.

"You're going to be the death of me," Song muttered, but he led the way the last dozen or so feet to his door and unlocked it. He stepped back and waved Ren inside.

The small temporary apartment was messy, but not

disgustingly so. Song hurried past him, snatching up dirty clothes strewn all about the room. He tossed them into the closet on the floor and shut the door. He grabbed the blanket and quickly pulled it up the bed to cover the twisted sheets, then hurried into the kitchen, snatching up old bottles, cups, and cans along the way.

"Song laoshi." Ren laughed. "You don't have to clean for me."

"Of course I do. Your place is always neat and tidy. You shouldn't have to sit in my mess."

Ren crossed to the kitchen and wrapped his arms around Song's waist and pressed a kiss to the side of his neck, which proved very effective in stopping the man cold. "I've seen your trailer. I know exactly how messy you are."

"Still…" Song murmured, sounding like he was almost pouting, though he did tip his head farther to the side to give Ren better access. "What if you decide you want someone who will take better care of you? Someone who isn't messy."

Bending his head, Ren pressed slow kisses onto Song's warm skin, loving the goose bumps that were breaking out across his arms. It was one of the things he adored about Song. His boyfriend made no effort to hide his responses to him.

"I'm not looking for someone to take care of me," Ren whispered, letting his hot breath curl against his now damp skin. "I want someone to love me exactly as I am."

Song turned in his arms and reached up, threading his fingers in his hair to hold his head captive. "No one will love you as much as I do," he said fiercely before taking Ren's mouth in an almost bruising kiss. Ren opened to his thrusting tongue, losing himself to the wonder of Song's relentless hunger.

But as quickly as the kiss started, Song was pushing him away again.

"Ah-Xue!" he cried. "You distracted me! We're supposed to be eating and talking!"

Ren laughed and pulled Song into a tight hug. "I wasn't trying to distract you. I couldn't help myself."

Song pushed him and kept pushing until he was in the main room. "Go sit. I'll pull the food together."

Still chuckling, Ren did as he was told. He truly wasn't trying to distract Song; it had just sort of worked out that way. But he'd behave himself now. Dropping to the floor by the small table, his shoulders resting against the bed, he took a moment to gaze about the room.

His boyfriend had brought far more items with him from home. There were a couple of pictures on his nightstand that appeared to be of Song and his mother. Two stacks of well-worn paperbacks were pressed to the far wall as well as a handful of magazines.

But what really interested him was the pair of beaten and weathered notebooks under the table. He wanted to know what was in them. Were they notes Song made about his scenes? Journals? Or maybe song lyrics? His boyfriend had written a few of the songs on his first album. How many other songs had he written?

As much as he was dying to know, he wouldn't peek without Song's permission. He might want to know everything he could about his laoshi, but he wasn't going to invade his privacy. He wanted Song to invite him in.

Song entered carrying several bowls filled with food, arranging it all carefully on the table. He rushed to the kitchen again. "Beer or water?"

"Water, please," Ren answered.

Song quickly returned with two bottles of water. To Ren's surprise, he didn't sit on the opposite side of the table but settled beside him so that their legs were touching. The same as when they sat together at the breakfast bar in Ren's room.

It was only then that it occurred to him that he should

have sat at the bar. Ren giggled and shook his head. "Sorry. I just realized what I did. We should have sat at the bar."

"Nope, I like this better." Song wiggled so that he brushed along Ren from knee to shoulder. "It's closer."

It was also a good thing that Ren was right-handed. With Song so close, his left hand was pretty useless unless he wanted to constantly elbow Song.

They talked about random things, Song mostly telling him stories about the concert, though they were largely of Zhu Fang's antics. Ren soaked in every word, loving the excitement in Song's voice.

Ren told him about hanging out with Guo Zi and the man's shouting at the TV during certain songs, which had been more than a little surprising considering his overall reserved demeanor.

But, in the end, they finished with their meal too quickly and Ren was left picking at the scraps on his plate to stall a bit longer.

"Do you want to go first or me?" Song finally asked.

Ren gave up the ghost and put his chopsticks down on his plate. Oh, the coward in him very much wanted Song to go first, but he was the one who was all tangled up in knots.

He leaned back against the bed and tipped his head so that it was resting on Song's shoulder. It might be easier to talk like this, with Song pressed to him, because he didn't have to look him in the eye.

"I had a girlfriend once. Just once," Ren admitted on a sigh. "While I was in college."

"Not before?"

Ren shuddered. "No, I was so awkward and dorky. And this"—he paused and drew a circle in the air around his face with his index finger—"didn't kick in until I was in my late teens. Girls didn't pay much attention to me. That was fine. I wasn't paying much attention to them either."

"But in college?"

"There was this one girl. We started out as friends. We shared some introductory classes and she liked to borrow my notes. After a couple of months, we were hanging out more and we sort of fell into dating."

"Ah-Xue," Song began, sounding very hesitant. "Not to sound like an ass, but did you actually like this girl?"

He chuckled and snuggled a tiny bit closer. "I'm not telling this very well. Yes, I did like her. She was nice and funny. She didn't seem to mind my awkwardness."

"She was your first?"

Ren bit his lower lip at the grumble that entered Song's tone as if he hated the idea that anyone had been with him at all. Yes, Song's possessiveness and jealousy might just push all the right and wrong buttons in him. It probably wasn't sane or healthy, but he loved that Song wanted Ren all to himself.

"And only," he admitted, ripping his mind toward the uncomfortable topic. He squeezed his eyes shut and groaned. "It was bad, Song laoshi. So fucking bad."

Song huffed a soft laugh. "How bad could it have been? I can attest that you are a very good kisser."

"Thank you," he muttered.

"Did you not know where things went?"

Ren jolted upright and shoved Song's shoulder. "Oh my God, Song Wei Li!"

"What?" Song snapped, his voice jumping in pitch. "You're giving me nothing here. Save me from my imagination!"

Dropping his head against the mattress, Ren moaned and shut his eyes. It was easier if he couldn't see Song. "It was horrible. I was nervous and so was she. It was all fumbling and awkward. I...I couldn't stay hard," he finished in a whisper. He sighed and shook his head. "She kept apologizing and I told her it wasn't her, but that seemed to make it all worse. God, after too fucking long, we just stopped. I couldn't get out of there fast enough. We broke up the next day because we were both too embarrassed to even look at each other."

"Oh, didi," Song said so very gently that Ren had to moan again.

"Please don't pity me, Song laoshi. I can't take it if you pity me."

"It's not pity, didi. I hurt for you. I wouldn't wish that first experience on anyone."

Ren snorted. "Yes, well, it worked to cure me of the temptation of dating for a very long time. By the time I started acting and knew that marriage and dating were pretty much impossible, I'd lost all interest in it."

Next to him, Song shifted and fingers drifted through Ren's hair, pushing it back from his forehead. "And yet, here you are with me."

Turning his head, Ren opened his eyes and smiled at the face that had stolen his heart away. "Only because you've put me under a spell. You're all I think about."

"I am sorry, didi."

Ren narrowed his eyes on Song's ridiculously wide grin. "Then why don't you look all that sorry or sad for me?"

Song winced and pressed his face into Ren's shoulder. "Don't hate me."

"It's not likely to happen."

He slowly lifted his face to meet Ren's gaze. "I hate that you suffered, but it means that you still get to have all those firsts. You get to have them with me. They're all going to be mine. I don't want to share you, Ah-Xue. I want all those wonderful first moments to be mine alone."

Okay, so maybe that made his heart melt into a puddle in the middle of his chest. Maybe he was embarrassed about his lack of experience, but if it meant that he could make so many memories with Song, it was worth it.

"Will I be your first in anything?"

Song's eyes darted away for a second before returning, his smile wilting. "You're my first love."

Ren leaned in and captured his mouth in a sweet kiss. "That's the best first."

When he pulled away, Song was still smiling, but the sadness hadn't been completely chased away from his eyes. But it was better if they got this out of the way so Ren could work on removing the last of his worries.

"Tell me," Ren ordered in a firm but gentle voice.

Song turned so that he was sitting with his shoulders against the mattress and his head tipped up as he stared at the ceiling. "You've got more experience with women than me."

"I wouldn't expect you to have any."

Song shrugged. "I'd thought I'd try. I guess I was hoping that I was at least bi or that I could fake it. I don't know. It was one of the darker periods in my life. Anyway, it didn't get much further than some kissing, and I knew I wasn't into it."

The pause stretched, and Ren chewed on the inside of his lip. He didn't want to rush Song, but he knew there was more to the story.

"Hey, if you don't feel comfortable talking—" Ren started.

A ragged laugh escaped Song, and he shook his head. "No, that's not it. I guess I'm worried that you're going to think I'm some slut, though I'd never thought that about myself. Until…"

Ren shoved away from the bed and turned so that he could glare in Song's face. "I am not going to look down on you for your experiences. I have no right to judge you for how you've lived your life. The only thing that matters to me is your happiness."

The shadow of a smile returned to his lips and he rolled his eyes. "God, didi, I really don't deserve you." He sucked in a cleansing breath and released it. He stared right into Ren's eyes and admitted, "I've been with three men in the past. It was all secret hookups. Two of them were complete strangers and they didn't know who I was. We used protection, I swear. One…one was another actor I was on a show with."

Ren froze. It took him everything not to immediately demand if that one person was Chen Junjie. He would not ask. He would not be that psycho boyfriend who—

More laughter exploded from Song and he rocked into Ren, bumping his knees. "Oh my God, it wasn't Chen!"

Heat burned Ren's cheeks, and he had to pull his eyes away. "Did a shitty job of hiding that thought, didn't I?"

"Didi, your eyes will always be the best tell for me. They give you away all the time." Song leaned forward and pressed a kiss to his jaw. "It wasn't Chen. It wasn't anyone we are currently working with. I don't think you've ever worked with him in the past. I'd tell you to ease your mind, but we respect each other's need for privacy."

Some of the tension that had knotted in Ren's stomach uncoiled, and he could breathe a little easier. Yes, his own curiosity demanded he get the name, but if this person was going to protect Song's secret, he could definitely respect Song's protection of the stranger.

"I understand and respect that."

Song carefully grabbed Ren's chin and turned his head so that their eyes met again. "The important thing is that it was just sex. I didn't feel anything for those people. What I've experienced with you has already been a million times better than those three very brief moments in my life. And I never thought anything could be this amazing."

Song leaned in and pressed their lips together in an impossibly slow, seductive kiss that tore down any defenses Ren might have wanted to put up. It was wrong how quickly he was losing himself to this man. Song was becoming his everything with each beat of his heart.

"Sorry," Song murmured against his lips.

Ren immediately pulled back and smiled. "Sure, I'd love to be your first in everything too, but there is one really good thing that comes out of this."

"What?"

"At least one of us knows what he's doing."

Song's grin grew into something wicked and dirty, sending fire licking through every part of Ren's body. He leaned in closer, brushing his lips lightly across the corner of Ren's mouth. "Does that mean you trust me to take care of you?"

"Yes. Until..." Ren drawled out.

His boyfriend retreated, lifting his eyebrows in question. "Until what?"

"I learn all your secrets and take very good care of you." Ren closed the distance between them in a heartbeat, stealing kiss after kiss from Song's sweet lips.

No more talking. They were so very done talking. Ren needed action. He needed kiss after kiss, getting completely lost in the heat and taste of Song. He opened his mouth and let Song's tongue tangle with his own. One hand gripped the back of his head, moving him exactly how Song wanted him, while the other slid up his chest.

This was ecstasy. When songwriters and poets extolled the bliss of kissing, this was what they were talking about. He'd never thought such perfection could be found in a little thing like this, but Ren didn't want it to ever stop.

The only problem was that they weren't close enough. They may have been seated next to each other on the floor, but their long legs were getting in the way. Ren needed to be closer. He wanted to feel more of Song, to be pressed down by the weight of him. He needed *more*.

"Bed," he whispered against Song's lips. "Please. Bed."

Song smiled and moved his kisses along his throat. "What happened to slow?"

"We...we can still go slow," Ren panted as Song edged closer to his ear. It was so difficult to think when Song kissed him there. His entire body tightened and a moan became lodged in his throat. His trembling fingers slid to Song's waist and plucked at the hem of his T-shirt. He bit his lower lip and slipped his hand under the fabric, at last touching Song's wonderfully hot, smooth skin.

Song froze as a delicious groan of pleasure drifted out of him. "Yes. Bed. Promise me you'll stop me if you're uncomfortable."

"Yes. Promise," Ren exhaled. He would have been willing to promise anything at that moment just so long as they could continue. He couldn't imagine ever wanting to stop Song, but his brain had quit working several kisses ago. He had to trust that his body would figure out what was too much before it was too late.

They separated and Ren instantly missed the heat of Song. Planting his hands on the mattress behind him, he lifted himself onto the bed but stopped to watch Song grab the back of his shirt and rip it off his body.

This was not the first time he'd seen Song Wei Li shirtless, but it was the first time seeing it while they were alone. It was the first time seeing him shirtless while Song looked at him like he wanted to fuck his brains out. The first time Ren could give in to the temptation and run his hands over every inch of him.

What little blood was left in his brain rushed to his groin, leaving him painfully hard and throbbing in time with his racing heart. He didn't care if Song could see his erection pressing against the front of his pants. There was no room left for fear or embarrassment.

"Slide up," Song directed in a low, rough voice that sent the best shivers through Ren's body.

He nodded and planted his hands, pushing so that he was in the middle of the narrow single bed. Song climbed on after him, placing his knees on either side of Ren's thighs, trapping him. When Ren started to lie down, Song caught his shirt and pulled it up. Ren automatically lifted his arms, allowing Song to remove it.

A long hiss escaped him as their bare chests came into

contact. He was scalded and loved it. Their lips came together in another endless kiss that followed Ren to the pillow. The wonderful scent of Song instantly enveloped him.

Wrapping his arms around Song, Ren rolled them onto their sides, their legs tangling together so that nearly every inch of their bodies was touching. Ren moaned and thrust his hips forward, seeking more friction as his dick brushed alongside Song's hard cock. His boyfriend cried out and gripped his hip tightly with one hand. Song ground into him, sending wave after wave of pleasure through him.

Oh God, he did that.

He made Song hard and needy.

Ren was utterly intoxicated with a panting, desperate Song.

He wanted more. So much more.

His skin was too hot and tight. There were too many clothes, but some part of his brain was still hesitant about shedding the last bits that separated them.

"Ah-Xue," Song whimpered against his lips. Song wanted more too. Ren could hear it in his name, but his sweet boyfriend was trying so hard to be considerate. To not push and ask for more before Ren was ready. Just that was enough to make him brave.

"Please. Song."

"What do you want? Anything you want. You only have to tell me."

Ren blinked open eyes he hadn't realized he'd shut and found himself staring into bottomless black eyes of hunger. Song Wei Li made him brave.

"I need...I need to come. Please, Song, help me," Ren begged. Any other words were trapped in his throat. He was afraid to ask for anything else because when he started to think about how Song would make that happen, panic ate away at all the pleasure coursing through his veins.

Judging by the way his smile spread across his lips, Ren

thought Song might have read his mix of panic and desperation.

Song's hand moved slowly from his hip to brush across his cock through his jeans. Ren swore loudly, his hips punching forward of their own accord as his body demanded more. His fingers shook as they skimmed along Song's shoulder and across his pecs. Song's heart hammered under his touch and his stomach muscles clenched, but he hesitated.

Song's nimble fingers were unbuttoning his pants and lowering his zipper. He should do the same, right? Everything that Song did to him, he should be returning. And he wanted to. He wanted to make Song as happy as he felt, but his nerves were stealing away his bravery.

A low chuckle jerked Ren from his racing thoughts and he groaned when Song lightly bit his jaw.

"Stop thinking so hard, Ah-Xue," Song teased.

"But—"

"You don't have to do anything you're not ready for."

Ren wanted to argue, to say something, but Song's fingers slid inside of his underwear, brushing the side of his dick so that all higher functions shut down. There was a brief touch of cold air and then Song gripped him, stroking strong and slow.

"Oh fuck, Ah-Xue," Song moaned against his throat. "You're beautiful." He licked up to his earlobe and exhaled while he continued to jerk him. "One of these days, I'm going to drop to my knees and suck this dick. You're going to fuck my mouth and lose your mind."

Ren clenched his teeth, thrusting his hips in time with the movements of Song's hand. His entire body was winding tighter and tighter. All he could do was cling to Song and try to fight the pressure of his building orgasm. He wanted to come but not yet. He didn't want this to end, but the images flickering through his brain were burning away at his restraint.

"And when you're ready," Song continued, his voice

becoming a dark drug, "you're going to push inside me and fuck me with this perfect cock."

A gasp ripped from Ren's throat as his orgasm exploded through him. He cried out Song's name, coming so damn hard the world went white along the edges. Song growled and stroked him through it, his hot breath caressing his neck.

The moment he had nothing left, Song released him and shoved up to his knees while Ren flopped onto his back. Every inch of his body was loose and utterly sated. Not a coherent thought existed in his brain. He could only watch as Song muttered a rough, "Can't wait," and straddled Ren's hips.

With frantic hands, he opened his own pants and pulled out a very lovely dick. He swiped his hand through the mess coating Ren's stomach and used Ren's cum as a lubricant as he quickly jerked himself.

There was nothing sexier, more erotic in all the world than Song Wei Li. His head tipped up, mouth open, muscles straining and glistening with sweat as he lost himself to the exquisite pleasure of the moment. It didn't take more than a few strokes, and he was moaning, hot cum splattering across Ren's chest.

Ren smiled. He was never going to forget this. It was perfect.

Song collapsed on him, not caring about the mess. They wrapped their arms around each other, both still panting as if they'd run a marathon.

"I love your idea of slow." Song sighed, snuggling his face into the crook of his neck.

Ren laughed and tightened his arms. "I couldn't help myself. I can't get enough of you."

Song lifted his face so that he could meet Ren's gaze. "But I was serious about what I said. We move at your pace. You don't have to do anything you're not comfortable with. Just because I suck your dick, it doesn't mean that I expect you to reciprocate."

"But—"

Song stopped his argument with a short kiss. When he ended it, he gave Ren another warning look. "I'm serious."

"But—" Song tried to kiss him. Ren jerked, hitting his head against the wall. They definitely needed a bigger bed. Song winced and rubbed the spot on Ren's head even though it didn't actually hurt.

"Song," Ren started. "It's not fair if I'm not returning...everything."

Song smirked at him and shook his head. "Ah-Xue, do you really think I'd fall for a selfish lover? There is no one who is more considerate or giving than you. When you're ready, I'm sure you'll do all kinds of things to drive me crazy in bed. But nothing will hurt me more than knowing you forced yourself to do something you weren't ready for."

Ren could only nod. The lump that had grown in his throat wouldn't let him speak. Song smiled gently and kissed him over and over again.

He hadn't thought it possible, but Ren was falling even deeper in love with this amazing man.

24

SOME THINGS...TAKEN OUT OF CONTEXT...
SONG WEI LI

Song was trying not to look like he was sailing on a cloud when he hit the set the next day.

But when everyone was commenting on what a surprisingly good mood he was in, there was no denying it. He was doing a miserable job of hiding how happy he was.

Even Hua Jun Bai gave him some side-eye as he strolled out of hair and makeup to catch his ride to the set.

Fuck it. Who cares?

He was in love with the greatest man on the planet, and he was loved in return. He'd just had the best night of his life, and now he got to work with the guy before they went back to their private bubble away from the world.

Last night, they'd cleaned up separately in his shower. He'd wanted to join Ren, but the damn thing was so small, it was a lucky thing Ren could fit his tall frame in there alone. Afterward, they'd wrapped around each other in the bed and fallen asleep while talking.

Ren had slipped away a few hours prior to dawn to get some real sleep in a bed he could stretch out in. Song had been reluctant to let him go, but he understood. They both had to put in a long day. Besides, it gave him the chance to roll over, press his face into the pillow where Ren had slept, and breathe in his scent.

His sheets might be filthy, but he was loath to change them. They smelled like sex and Ren An Xue. Perfection.

The only thing that could possibly put a damper on his good mood was this unexpected meeting with Sun Jing. He couldn't even begin to guess what the director wanted. As far as he knew, they were still on schedule and he had great chemistry with his costar.

Okay, so maybe his chemistry was better than great and probably way better than Sun wanted, but so long as they gave the performance he needed, what did it matter?

After getting the basic layers of his hanfu on, he wandered over to Sun's trailer while the wardrobe jiejies took the rest of his costume to the set where they'd be shooting. Ren was still in hair and makeup. He wished they could get it done at the same time, but they'd been warned against showing up and leaving at the same time since there were always fans right there to get pictures and video. Everyone was concerned it would stir too much talk too early if they were constantly seen together.

Just the idea made Song want to roll his eyes. In his opinion, he didn't see enough of Ren, but he understood. They had to try to control some of the talk.

He knocked on the door to the temporary office and one of the assistants immediately opened it, welcoming Song inside.

One step in and Song froze. It was an explosion of papers on every surface. Stacks teetered in random places and created a narrow aisle that led to a table with even more insanity of papers and old paper cups that had once held coffee or tea. How in the world was this show even being made if this was the brain of their director?

Oh, that's right. They also had an amazing producer and four talented assistant directors. *Thank God.*

"Why does everyone look like that when they come in here?" Sun cried.

"Because I'm afraid if I sneeze, we'll lose an entire day of shooting to the mess I make," Song shouted at him.

Sun stared for a second and nodded. "Don't sneeze."

Song groaned. "What did you want, my fearless director?"

Sun made an exasperated noise and then surprised Song by shooing away the two assistants that were somehow tucked in the empty corners of the trailer. Sun wanted a private word, which meant this was not going to be a good conversation.

Had someone seen something?

Did Sun know that he and Ren had become more than friends?

Panic tightened Song's chest and his heart sped up. How could anyone know? They just laughed and joked while they were on the set. All their interactions were harmless fun. No one knew besides Guo Zi and Zhu Fang. That was it.

Everything was fine.

"Sit down, Song," Sun instructed, waving to the lone empty chair next to the overloaded desk. "Want something to drink. I've got some tea—"

"How bad is it?" Song demanded.

"What?"

"You've got some horrible news to tell me, and you're stalling. Is it the censors? Are they giving you problems already?"

"What? Yes, of course they are." Sun sighed and dropped into his own chair. "Considering what we're shooting, of course they're giving us grief, but I've got people dealing with them. We keep moving forward. Everyone is going to love this story. Even more than *Frozen River*. Let the censors try to stop us."

Song smirked and eased into the chair. He loved Sun's determination and stubbornness. When this man had a vision, he refused to let anything stand in his way. Chen Junjie might have suggested him for the role, but it had been Sun Jing who'd really swayed him to take it.

"What's the problem?"

Sun lifted his eyes to Song, a pained look filling his face. "Song, you know I love you. You have been doing an amazing job as Tian Xiuying. I think this is going to be a great new step up in your career."

Song glared at the director. "Cut the crap, Sun. We've known each other for too long. I'm not one of those actors whose ass you have to kiss."

"I need you and Ren to cut the cuteness on the set."

Song jerked, his mouth falling open. He couldn't speak for several seconds, but there was no mistaking the burn of embarrassment in his cheeks, stretching up to the tips of his ears.

Sun dropped his face into his hands and moaned. "That came out wrong."

"No...I don't think it did," Song managed, still trying to get his lungs to completely fill with air.

Every director wanted to build a close, warm, almost familial atmosphere on a set. Particularly when they were filming day after day for four months. It made spending incredibly long, hot days more bearable when you liked the other people you were trapped with.

Song thought they'd achieved that. Both he and Ren joked together, but they also tried to include the other actors, such as Ma Daiyu and Hua Jun Bai.

But if Sun was asking him and Ren—*the romantic leads*—to stop...

Sun lifted his head from his hands and pinned Song with pleading eyes. The man looked like he was blushing as badly as Song felt he was. "You and Ren together in a scene, you're pure magic. It's amazing. Beautiful. The world is going to eat it up. And I don't want you to think that I don't love that you've both become such good friends."

"But…" Song prodded when Sun paused for too long.

"Some things…taken out of context…might be construed that you and Ren are significantly more than friends."

"What?" Song gasped.

Fuck. Someone saw something. When? Where?

Sun sighed heavily and picked up his tablet. He tapped it a couple of times before handing it over to Song. "Watch this. It'll be easier than me trying to explain. Just watch it from the point of view of a fan who desperately wants to ship you and Ren. And then the point of view of the censors."

Song accepted the tablet and found that a video had been queued up. He tapped play and within the first ten seconds, his stomach dropped. It was a clip from the behind-the-scenes camera of him and Ren. They were talking and laughing together, but then Song cackled and latched on to Ren's arm, leaning his entire body into him until he was practically hanging on Ren.

The video changed to another scene. They were talking, but this time Ren flipped up his fan and leaned close. Song remembered that day. Ren had gotten close to whisper about a heat rash he was developing on the inside of his thigh. He was embarrassed, but from a fan's point of view, it looked as if Ren had leaned in to kiss him.

The video clips went on and on. From his own perspective, every last one of them was innocent. They never did anything horrible in the view of others, but they were constantly touching, leaning, grabbing, and poking.

Twenty minutes of video.

And Song had a feeling this was just the tip of the iceberg. They'd been like this for a solid two months. How much video was out there like this? Or had it only recently gotten worse?

Song covered his face with his free hand as he handed the tablet to Sun.

"Please don't panic on me," Sun pleaded softly.

"Sun, I am so sorry. This…this is bad. I thought we were being careful. It's-it's not how it appears. I—"

"Song Wei Li, look at me."

Reluctantly, Song lifted his head and met Sun's worried but determined gaze. "The reality of things—I don't give a shit, and that's all I'm going to say about that." Song's heart skipped and stuttered for a second as what Sun was saying sank in. He knew, or at least suspected, about him and Ren and didn't care. Sun continued to hold his gaze, unwavering for another couple of seconds before nodding with a small grunt as if to say they understood each other. "My only concern is the perception of things from the point of view of the censors. If talk heats up too much, they will shut us down. The BTS cameras we control, I can edit what goes out. Right now, we don't have a lot of workable material of you and Ren together, and I need more."

"Okay. We can do that," Song agreed, his voice low and tight.

"I don't want to kill the fun you're having, so my best advice is to keep a foot of space between you two at all times. Always have something in your hands."

Song nodded. He got it. If both of his hands were occupied, he couldn't make a grab for Ren.

"Unfortunately, we don't have control of *all* the cameras," Sun complained and flopped back in his chair, the metal springs groaning under the shift in his weight. "Nowadays everyone has a fucking camera on their phone, and they're constantly sneaking videos. I've got people specifically running interference, but we can't catch them all." He offered Song a lopsided smile. "We've been lucky so far. Only a few snippets have been uploaded to Weibo, but they haven't been as popular as what we've been putting up."

"But if Ren and I keep supplying them with new material, we'll be in trouble. I understand."

He did understand, just like every other actor. His career

lived and died by the love of his fans. And too many of those fans were more interested in his real-life moments—good and bad—than they were in his acting and singing performances. He'd escaped suffering any kind of scandal so far, and he wasn't interested in creating one with Ren.

Oh fuck. Ren!

He was so new to acting. He was still trying to make a name for himself. He did not need to get his name dragged through the mud already. Song refused to be the reason his career was destroyed before it had a chance to take off.

"Song, don't panic on me, okay? I think we've caught this early enough," Sun reassured him.

Song managed a jerky nod, still trying to pull his brain back from the edge of panic. It was okay. Their secret was safe.

"Okay. Thanks. I'll-I'll talk to Ren. We'll be more careful."

His friend heaved an enormous sigh of relief and lunged forward to drop his head on the desk. "Thank you. Thank you. Thank you," he repeated over and over again, earning a weak chuckle from Song. "I had no idea how I was going to tell him without him completely freaking out."

"Oh, I'm pretty sure he's still going to freak out," Song admitted in a wobbly voice. He was still freaking out on the inside. Ren was definitely going to panic. This was his first big drama production. He was terrified of fucking up.

Sun lifted his head, another pained look twisting up his features. "Can you tell him so he doesn't?"

"No, we both know how self-conscious he is. He's going to blame himself and worry that he put the show in danger. He's going to be sure that you're pissed at him."

"What?" Sun squawked. "Why would he think that?"

"Because that's what I'm going to tell him."

A strangled noise escaped Sun and he snatched up a stack of papers. He attempted to smack Song on the head with them, but Song dodged, which only sent a different stack of papers spilling to the floor. Sun swore and Song cackled, which helped to put them both on more normal footing.

"Pain in the ass," Sun muttered, dropping back in his chair and setting the papers aside. "You are not to tell him that I'm angry. I'm not angry. Just worried."

"I know. I know. I'll talk to Ren when we have lunch today. I'm his laoshi. It's my job."

Sun narrowed his eyes on Song and stared at him for a second as if he had a few interesting things to say about how Song was taking his role of laoshi, but the kind director kept those thoughts to himself.

"But," Song continued, delivering his own warning glare, "you know things are going to be awkward for a while. We're going to be self-conscious until we get our balance again."

Sun made a dismissive noise and wave his hand at him. "Yeah, yeah. I expect that. But you're going to be shooting with Hua Bai Jun almost nonstop for the next two weeks. That man is enough of a troublemaker on his own. He'll provide plenty of distraction."

Song could not argue with that.

With a sigh, Song pushed to his feet to leave. This was not the best way to start what would be a long day of shooting, but it was better to know the truth sooner rather than wait until it was too late to fix things. He just had to figure out how best to break this news to Ren without him panicking.

The director laid both of his arms on his desk and leaned forward. He offered Song a look that managed to be both happy and a touch sad.

"All jokes aside, I've never seen you so happy, Song. We've known each other for a few years now, and you've always been the carefree guy who laughs easily, but this is different. It's like you're happy all the way down to your soul, and I'm glad for you. You deserve this kind of happiness in your life."

Song smiled at his director friend, his throat tightening

with too many emotions. "I am happy, and no matter how long it lasts, I'm grateful that I found this."

With a final smirk, Song left the office and stepped into the blistering Hengdian sun. Summer was still in full swing, and they were going to melt yet again. Stopping outside the trailer, Song tilted his head up to the sun and closed his eyes, soaking in its brightness and letting it beat back the dark places of his mind.

Yes, too much of their world was against their love, but he was not going to let this stop them. It wasn't going to crush them. Didi was going to panic, but Song would hold him and provide solutions. If necessary, they would call Zhu Fang or Guo Zi. They would get the reassurances they needed to keep moving forward.

There would be stumbles and roadblocks, but this was love, and he would fight for it with his very last breath.

25

WE'VE GOT A PROBLEM
REN AN XUE

Ren groaned.

He rolled over to his stomach and pressed his face into his pillow. It was too early. His alarm hadn't even gone off yet. Why was he awake?

Today was his late day, right? Night shoots. Yes. That meant sleeping in.

But he hadn't slept.

Yesterday had been the lunch talk from hell.

Ren groaned again and pulled his blanket up over his head, trying to shove away the memory of that afternoon, which was only succeeding in waking him up more when he needed to sleep.

Oh, Song had been the sweetest person ever, but it didn't change the fact that they'd fucked up. They'd thought they were being so very careful and sly, but what Song told him about the videos proved to be the exact opposite.

Fuck. Ren should have just leaned over and kissed Song, removing all doubt about his sexuality while sending the remains of his career up in flames.

It was nice to know that Sun Jing wasn't pissed at them,

but it didn't matter because Ren was too pissed at himself over the matter.

Of course, to make it all worse, they had to go back out there and pretend that everything was fine while remembering not to stare too long. Don't touch. Don't laugh too hard. Don't do anything that could possibly be construed as anything more than friendship.

Yeah, that was utterly impossible.

Thank God for Hua Bai Jun. He'd taken one look at them, figured something weird was up, and managed to fill all the awkward silences for the rest of the day. They fucking owed that man something big.

A loud knocking on his door echoed through the room, and Ren jerked upright, his head leaping into his throat. Was that what had woken him in the first place?

"Didi? Wake up, didi!" Song called through the door.

Ren ripped off the blanket and jumped to his feet. He hurried across the room, rubbing one eye with the heel of his palm. What was going on? There was no way he'd overslept through his alarm. His assistant would have come to fetch him before Song.

Pulling open the door, he faced a Song with bedhead and wide, worried eyes. He appeared as if he'd just jumped from bed as well.

"What's wrong?" Ren asked, his voice still rough with sleep.

"We've got a problem," Song announced as he pushed his way into Ren's room. It was only then that he noticed Song's assistant, Mo Bao Shi, was trailing right behind him.

"What's wrong?" Ren repeated, after shutting the door. He paused at his closet and snagged the first T-shirt he saw. He quickly pulled it on and passed a hand through his hair, trying to pull himself together.

"I'm assuming that you haven't been on Weibo since yesterday," Song started with a wince.

"No. I just woke up. What happened?" If Song didn't spit it out soon, Ren was going to shake it out of the man. He wasn't conscious enough for guessing games.

"Someone posted a video of you and Song on Weibo late last night and the Internet has exploded," Mo blurted out.

"What?" Ren gasped, lurching backward. *Someone had a video of them together? When? Where?*

Song swore and smacked Mo hard on the chest as he crossed to Ren. He grabbed him by the shoulders to keep him upright. "Breathe. It's okay. It's not what you're thinking," Song quickly said. "You remember that first day after the concert when you asked me to hold your fan?"

It took far too long to get his brain cells working, but after a moment, Ren recalled the day and nodded. "Yes. I remember."

"It was a video of that."

"What? Wait…what?" Ren's sleep-deprived brain completely locked up.

That didn't make any sense. According to what Song had told him yesterday at lunch, there were videos out there that were far worse and more incriminating than that. Sure, he'd held Song's hand, but it couldn't have been for more than a second before he gave him the fan. How…how was that video a problem? It wasn't like his dick had been hanging out. He'd been under fourteen fucking layers of robes.

Song pulled out his phone and turned it toward Ren as he played the video in question. He watched it from beginning to end. The entire thing was *thirty* seconds. He held Song's hand for *two seconds* and then walked away.

Ren handed the phone back to Song and went to get his own off the charger. Only when he flipped it over did he discover that he'd apparently forgotten to take it out of silent mode. He'd missed five calls from his manager and a dozen from his assistant. *Shit.*

He'd call them both in a minute. He opened Weibo to find

that he'd been tagged hundreds of times. There were tons of hashtags and thousands of posts and comments. It was like the world was coming apart, and it was fucking messy.

Song was right there, guiding him onto a stool, before cupping his face so that he had to lift his eyes to meet Song.

"It's not all bad," Song said firmly.

Behind Ren, Mo Bao Shi snorted and Song threw him a dirty look.

"You've got to stop sugarcoating it," Mo replied.

That was the truth. Ren couldn't understand what was happening, how that video could be a problem. He shifted in his chair to face Song's assistant and braced himself for the hard facts.

"What's going on? What's wrong with that video?"

To his surprise, the gruff Mo actually winced, his eyes darting to Song for a second, then moving back to Ren.

"Okay, Song's not wrong. It's not all bad. About half the fans think you're dating and feel what happened in the video is fucking adorable. You've been shipped hard, and that's good for the TV show," Mo admitted.

"Fine. What's the bad?"

Mo sighed and stared at the ground. "Some of the fans are pissed that you walked past your own assistant and treated Song like he was your bitch. Some are demanding that you fire your assistant. And a lot are pissed at you for what you did to Song. Unfortunately, Song has a bigger following than you, so the tide of opinion is against you. Song needs to get his ass in gear and defend you to start deflecting his shit."

Ren whipped around to Song's worried gaze. He opened his mouth, but he couldn't even speak. He'd never meant any of that. It had been a joke. No, it has been a selfish moment. He hadn't seen Song in forty-eight hours, and he'd wanted *one second of just them* while they were stuck in a crowd of people.

"Didi, I know," Song said. "I know." Song leaned around

Ren and glared at Mo. "All right, you've done your damage. Give me a moment alone."

"Ten minutes is all you get. Then you need to get ready for the meeting. Both of you," Mo warned as he walked out of the room.

"Meeting?" Ren demanded, looking from Mo to Song.

"A meeting has been called with my manager, your manager, and the producer. We've got to figure out some damage control. It'll be fine," Song reassured him.

The sound of the door closing behind Mo stole away the last of Ren's tight control of his panic. "How is this going to be fine? I never meant for this to happen. I have *never* thought of you as-as my bitch. It was a joke. I wanted to see you, touch you," Ren confessed, his voice cracking at the end.

Song cupped Ren's cheeks in both hands and stared deep into his eyes. "I know, Ah-Xue. I know. I *loved* it. I thought it was the most perfect moment. I thought you were brilliant."

"But the fans…"

A heavy sigh slipped from Song and he shook his head. "We never know what's going to set them off. It can be the smallest, strangest thing. Just like this. We gotta talk it out and come up with something to smooth over the moment. I swear, we'll get through this together."

Ren nodded, his eyes too wide and his mind swirling.

"Didi, look at me," Song said sternly, snapping Ren out of his dark thoughts. "Together. We will do this *together*. I love you, and they are not going to break us."

And like that, Ren could suddenly draw air into his lungs. Some of the tension cracked in his chest. Song believed in them. Song loved him. He knew he hadn't meant anything by that little silliness. It was going to be okay.

"I love you, Song laoshi," he murmured. "We've got this together."

Song's smile was brilliant. He leaned in and grabbed Ren's mouth in a hard, breath-stealing kiss that ended too quickly.

"Get dressed. Cars are being sent. We have to leave separately, but you'll be right behind me. When we're in the meeting, follow my lead. I've got an idea. And call your assistant. I'm sure she's a mess about this too."

Oh, fuck! Wu Dong Mei!

As Song escaped back to his room, Ren shot off a message to his manager, stating that he was aware of the chaos and getting ready for the meeting. The rest of the time was spent talking down his poor assistant. He didn't even get a shower. He pulled on clothes, brushed his teeth, threw on deodorant, and snagged a ball cap because there was nothing he could do about his hair at this moment.

Poor Wu Dong Mei alternated between apologizing and crying, not giving Ren much of a chance to reassure her that what had happened in the video was *not* a reflection on how he felt about her or her work. He refused to fire her and definitely wouldn't accept her resignation. As it was, he was pretty sure he had to give her a raise or a bonus of some sort for dealing with this insanity.

God, he was such an ass.

How did he not know Wu Dong Mei was worried about this? He needed to get Song off his mind and remember there was an entire world outside of this one man.

Except he didn't care about anything else. There was just Song's smile and his laugh. The rest faded away.

He needed to do better.

Unfortunately, his first thought was disappointment at missing the opportunity to see Song get into his car with Mo Bao Shi. When he reached the ground floor, Song's car was pulling away and his own was arriving with a tear-streaked and sniffling Wu Dong Mei in the back seat already.

When they reached the office where the meeting was being held, Wu Dong Mei had at least stopped crying and mopped up her tears. Since both Song and he were expected at the set for filming, there were no fans waiting to snap pictures of them. *Thank God for that small miracle.*

His manager, Zhou Yuying, was waiting for him outside the meeting room with a stern and somewhat exhausted look. He immediately bowed to her, apologizing for creating this chaos and reassuring her that this incident was not a reflection on Wu Dong Mei's work.

Zhou Yuying sighed, her expression immediately softening. It might have helped that he tipped his head to the side, flashing his enormous puppy eyes. Oh, he was not above using them for his own evil purposes if it meant keeping Zhou from yelling at him.

"Save it for Song and his manager," she muttered. "If we're lucky, we can convince him to help you out of this mess for the good of the picture."

Ren immediately lowered his head to hide his smile, but he didn't miss Wu Dong Mei's sudden throat clearing as if she were choking on a laugh. He glanced over to find her eyes wide and biting her lips. He winked at her prior to following Zhou Yuying into the meeting room. Wu Dong Mei knew as well as him that Song wouldn't mind helping him. His lovely assistant was with him all day on the set and had to know that he and Song were close friends.

Wait…did she suspect they were more?

Yes, he definitely needed to give her a raise after this.

Ren followed his manager into the meeting room where the producer, Song Wei Li, and Song's manager were already waiting. He kept his head bowed and walked to the far side of the table, opposite Song. Before anyone could speak, he bowed low and offered up a sincere apology to Song and his manager. He'd barely finished speaking when Song launched to his feet, reaching across the table for Ren.

"Please stop, Ren An Xue. This is ridiculous. It's a misunderstanding," Song argued.

"Be that as it may, my careless actions have created trouble for you and the production team. I don't want to do anything that would jeopardize everyone's hard work."

"Of course not, Ren An Xue," Yang Lan Fen murmured. At least he thought that was her name. She was one of the two or three producers on *Legend*, but he hadn't spoken to her more than once or twice in the past several months. "No one believes you did this intentionally. Please sit and we can discuss this."

Ren straightened and reluctantly lifted his eyes to find Yang Lan Fen sympathetic and Song's manager looking somewhat irritated. Song was clearly pissed, but he didn't think it was with him. He was likely angry at the situation, his manager, and just about anyone who'd hurt his didi. And that idea made his heart warm.

Only when Ren sat did Song drop into his own chair in a huff. "The fact of the matter is, that whole thing is technically my fault, and didi is covering for me."

"Song laoshi!" Ren gasped.

"I made a bet with Ren An Xue and lost. I don't even remember what it was over. Something stupid, I'm sure," he said with a distracted wave of his hand. Ren could only stare at him with his mouth hanging open over the bald-faced lie he was delivering with such ease. But then, Song was a skilled actor. Of course he could lie through his teeth. "Anyway, I always pay up on my bets. I had to carry didi's things for that day. No big deal."

"Are you kidding me?" Song's manager snapped. Ren thought he heard Yang Lan Fen mutter something similar under her breath as she rubbed her brow with one hand.

"What? It was totally harmless. It's not like didi dared me to streak across the set," Song deflected with ease, which just squeezed more horror out of Song's manager and Yang Lan Fen.

Ren sneaked a peek at Zhou Yuying beside him to see a dangerously speculative look on her face as she watched Song.

"Except for the fact that whoever caught you with the filming didn't get the whole story, making Ren An Xue appear quite bad," Yang Lan Fen filled in.

"That's why I think Ren and I should shoot a video explaining what really happened." Song leaned forward, placing both hands on the table, all his attention on Yang Lan Fen. "We can shoot it on set in our costumes. Just make it into the silly story it is. We can even toss in a few fan questions. I'll apologize to didi and his assistant for dragging them into this mess. We'll be cute. The shippers will be happy. My fans will see Ren and me getting along, so they'll fall in love with him. It'll be fine."

Zhou Yuying's eyes widened and her face relaxed. Yeah, she was happy. Her only concern had been how to get Song in his corner to help save his career before it went up in flames. If Song was going to apologize to him in a video, he was safe and she was happy.

Yang Lan Fen stared at Song in silence for several seconds, then sighed heavily. "Fine. I think that should do it, but I want a dozen videos like that from you and Ren over the next month. We need more fan service to keep them happy."

"Six," Song immediately shot back.

"Eight, and that's my final offer. I also want details on this so-called bet. Something better than 'I don't remember,'" Yang Lan Fen countered, pointing one pale finger tipped with a dark-red fingernail at him.

Holy shit! She saw straight through Song's bullshit and didn't even bat an eyelash at it.

Song shamelessly grinned at her. "Done!"

"You and Ren are going straight to makeup from here. You're shooting the first video now. I want this chaos nipped as soon as possible," she added.

Song moaned, and Ren nearly joined him. "We have night shoots. We're not due in makeup until after the lunch break," Song complained in a near whine.

"Now, Song. This is punishment for both of you for this chaos." Yang Lan Fen pushed to her feet and they all rose with her. "Thank you, everyone, for meeting today. I'll leave Song and Ren to clean up their mess." She walked by, but as she passed Ren, she paused and patted him on the shoulder. "Watch out for Song. He's a demon in disguise."

"Yang Lan Fen!" Song gasped extravagantly. "How could you say that! You love me!"

Yang Lan Fen gave Song a little smile and then left the room.

Ren was in a sort of daze as he followed everyone else out, his mind still a blur with what had happened. After all the panic, chaos, tears, and frantic phone calls, their punishment was that they had to shoot a bunch of videos for social media? Did Yang Lan Fen forget they'd already agreed to do videos?

Oh, my fucking God! She did, and Song made their punishment into existing work!

Yang Lan Fen was right. Song just might be a demon in disguise.

There wasn't time to give any of it thought. Song latched on to his arm the second they were in the hall and convinced everyone that it made the most sense for them to show up in makeup at the same time. They needed to put up a unified front and prove to everyone that they were still close friends.

It was like getting caught up in a whirlwind. He didn't know what was happening or which way he was going to be blown next. He could only go with it and pray he didn't get smashed against the rocks.

When they were safely tucked in the minivan with Wu Dong Mei and Mo Bao Shi and on the way to makeup, Song's expression turned serious and he tightly gripped Ren's hand in both of his.

"Are you okay?" Song asked.

"Yeah, but I think Yang Lan Fen is right; you are a demon in disguise."

Mo Bao Shi barked out a loud laugh, and Song kicked the passenger seat he was in and turned his attention back to Ren. "Nah. I've just had to deal with bullshit like this. You have to give fans something juicier to distract them. Us being cute on video and talking about a secret bet will be plenty of distraction. It'll all work out."

"I'm okay. I'm sorry that Wu Dong Mei was hurt in all this."

Song immediately turned in his seat and flashed his sweetest, most dazzling smile at Wu Dong Mei, who immediately blushed. This woman had spent more than a month at Ren's side, had plenty of time to be around Song, and yet she still looked starstruck.

And okay, maybe Ren felt a little jealousy rise and threaten to choke him as Song profusely apologized to Wu Dong Mei until she was giggling and acting as if the man had hung the moon in the sky for her alone.

Yet before Ren could get too peevish, Song squeezed his hand, reminding him that it was his hand he was holding so tightly. He was the one Song kissed and teased. He was the one that guarded Song's heart in his own chest.

And it was his ass Song was working so hard to save.

Yes, Song Wei Li was pure chaos. He might also be a demon.

But Ren loved everything about him and wouldn't change a damn thing.

26

HIS REN-SHAPED PILLOW
SONG WEI LI

Song now knew what hell was.

He knew what it looked like, smelled like, and felt like.

It was Hengdian in the late July heat, Ren An Xue's soft cologne wafting to him on the breeze created by his fan, while the man sat just inches away from him. *And he couldn't touch him!*

His hand *ached* to feel Ren's hand, knee, arm, *something* under it.

His entire body was twitchy and restless.

For the entire car ride over to makeup, he'd held Ren's hand tightly in his own while blocking it from view of the driver with his leg. He didn't give a shit if Bao Shi glanced over and saw their clasped hands. His assistant had been his friend since they were teenagers, long before Song started acting. He knew all of Song's secrets and didn't care who he was attracted to. Bao Shi only wanted Song's happiness.

While he was relieved Yang Lan Fen had let them off the hook relatively easily after the mess that had been created, he wished she could have put off this video shoot until later in the afternoon. Ren looked as though he was running on pure nervous energy and needed to go back to sleep.

Song had wanted to return to their rooms and curl up in

bed with Ren, where he'd hold his boyfriend as he fell asleep. He'd whisper a hundred reassurances in his ear, letting his words sink in and wash away the last of his fears.

This entire ordeal was so incredibly insane, and the timing couldn't have been worse. Just yesterday, they'd had an awkward talk about being more cautious on the set and trying not to touch each other. And now there was this.

Yes, he might be contemplating a fuck-it-all attitude that would have him wrapping his arms around his costar, who was putting on a brave face but clearly needed a hug.

And yes, this probably meant he needed to call Zhu Fang to talk him out of doing something incredibly stupid.

He knew it was stupid, too. Hugging, snuggling, and kissing Ren right now would be caught by at least half a dozen phones. It would destroy his career. It would destroy Ren's. It would totally tank this production.

They could wait.

Ren was strong. Ren was amazing. Ren was smart.

They could wait until they had a free hidden moment away from the world, then they would hold each other and everything would be okay.

"Everything okay?" Ren asked, pulling Song from his thoughts.

He jolted up from his slouch and flashed his companion his most brilliant smile. "Perfect."

Ren snorted, which turned into a high-pitched laugh. "You are such a liar. You look like you're half-asleep over there."

Song lifted a hand to rub his eye, but stopped himself at the last second, remembering the makeup that was perfectly in place on his face that didn't need to be smeared or wiped away. "I had trouble falling asleep last night. I was supposed to have another five hours with my pillow when Bao Shi woke me up."

Ren's stare became all soft and sweet, as if he knew Song's

trouble sleeping had been because he'd not had his Ren-shaped pillow to hold. Not that sleeping together in those narrow beds was easy. Song had started to contemplate evil things like finding a way to bring his bed over to Ren's room and positioning them so they could sleep together more comfortably. Or at least dragging his mattress over so they could arrange the mattresses on the floor.

But he was sure someone would eventually notice that Ren's room had two beds and Song's had none.

Not subtle.

"Well, this video shouldn't take long, and then you can take a nap in the trailer until it's time for us to shoot," Ren suggested.

Song perked up, careful to not look at Ren. This was something he'd not thought of. Sleeping in his trailer.

Sleeping in his trailer *with Ren*.

The bed in his trailer was bigger than the bed in his room. It would fit both their long frames.

Sleeping could lead to other things.

But he'd have to find a way to keep Ren quiet. His lover made the best sounds in all the world, but they were not soft, quiet sounds. They were already in hot water. He could not add to their problems.

No. A plan was starting to form.

They just had to complete this video first.

"Okay!" Song announced with a loud clap of his hands. "Are we ready to do this thing?"

The makeup and wardrobe jiejies were making their final passes, dabbing away sweat that was already forming and smoothing out loose strands from their long, black wigs. While Ren was supposed to be shooting in his black hanfu today, he'd requested to be put in his white one as it made him look less evil and more angelic. And right now, this man needed to be seen as a sweet, innocent angel.

Song was in the blue-and-gray hanfu that he'd be shooting

in later. He'd received several warnings from the wardrobe team not to fuck it up or they'd have his balls. He believed them.

"We're not livestreaming this, right?" Ren inquired.

Song shook his head. "Yang Lan Fen and Sun don't trust me not to say something stupid. They want to be able to edit it later."

Which also explained why one of the director's assistants was handling the simple video shoot and why anyone who wasn't absolutely necessary was being chased away so rogue videos couldn't be taken. It didn't hurt that they were seated at a table inside one of the buildings, eliminating the chances of someone randomly passing by and catching them.

"Whenever you're ready," the assistant director called out with his smartphone pointed at them.

Song glanced over at Ren, one corner of his mouth tilting up in a smile that had Ren rolling his eyes, but his fingers still relaxed around the fan he was holding.

"Hi, I'm Song Wei Li and I'm on the set of *Legend of the Lost Night*, where I will be playing the part of Tian Xiuying," Song kicked off with a practiced ease.

"Hi, I'm Ren An Xue, and I'm playing the part of Zhao Gang in *Legend*," Ren added a bit stiffly.

"We had some free time today before we jump into shooting some new scenes, and we thought we'd answer a few questions from our fans." Song reached down and picked up the small stack of cards that had been placed on the otherwise empty table. He made a show of reading a couple and flipping through them, but he already knew all the questions.

"What characteristic do you think your costar shares with his role?" Song read off. They wanted to kick off with a random question prior to getting into the heart of the matter.

"Are you going first or me?" Ren inquired.

"I can go. It's easy. I think Ren An Xue is a very caring,

considerate person, which is also a characteristic of Zhao Gang."

Surprised laughter jumped from Ren and he rocked into Song, their shoulders briefly bumping only to have him rock back the other way. "Zhao Gang spends a lot of time killing people for being a caring, considerate person."

"Yes, but he's very caring and considerate when it comes to Tian Xiuying. That's what matters."

As if on cue, Ren flicked out his fan, half hiding his face as he said, "But only for his Ah-Ying." That honeyed tone always did the most wonderful things to Song's brain and other parts of his body, but he managed to keep in control. *Barely.*

Song smirked and shook his head as if he were accustomed to Ren's flirting. "What's my similarity?"

"Other than the fact that you're grumpy for the morning shoots just like Ah-Ying's always grumpy toward poor Zhao Gang?"

Song mock gasped and poked a finger at his costar. "I don't like mornings!"

"But seriously, I think one big similarity is that Tian Xiuying is a teacher and protector at heart, and so is Song Wei Li. This is my first wuxia drama, and Song laoshi has been very diligent about helping me learn how these shows are done and that I'm comfortable on the set. I am very grateful for my laoshi."

Song looked away and briefly covered his face against the real blush he could feel forming. His didi was always so fucking sweet, it melted all his common sense, but he held on. They could not fuck up this video and get into more trouble.

"Then I guess everyone wants to know why your laoshi was carrying your fan," Song said with a heavy sigh.

Ren snapped his folding fan closed and narrowed his eyes Song, while clearly fighting a smile. "Yes, which got me into trouble."

Song grinned and stared straight at the camera. "I lost a

bet," he admitted. He made a show of appearing embarrassed and amused, rubbing his finger across his bottom lip before continuing. "Ren An Xue is a very hard worker. He's always one of the first actors in makeup and one of the last to leave each day. He always knows his lines, and he has significantly more than me. One day, the heat was very bad. It was getting to both of us, and Ren was struggling with a particular line. I bet him that the next person to mess up had to carry the other person's fan that day."

Ren leaned closer, bumping their shoulders again. "And...?"

Song sighed long and loud, dropping his head back as if he'd suffered the worst fate. "Ren An Xue delivered this beautiful, elegant speech flawlessly, and I screwed up. I had one sentence. *One!* And I messed it up."

Ren laughed and Song gave a groaning chuckle. It wasn't quite a lie. That had happened. More than once, actually, but they'd never bet on it. The explanation made Ren look sweet and perfect, and Song like a troublemaker who got what he deserved.

"So, he had to carry my fan," Ren chimed in.

"Except you made me do it only that one time," Song complained. "I lost. You should have taken advantage of that."

Ren shook his head, his eyes immediately softening to something sweet and loving. "It was hot and we were both tired. I couldn't do that to you."

They might have stared into each other's eyes for too long. And it might have taken Song way too long to remember that he had his hand resting on Ren's arm. But he told himself that someone could edit it out if they wanted. Or maybe it would help with the shippers. Who knows?

They breezed through three more questions with the same light and teasing banter. There were a few more small bumps and touches. Song told himself that it merely made them appear to be good friends rather than lovers. No one would watch this video and know that Ren An Xue was the owner of his heart. No one would realize that Song had tasted Ren's lips or that he'd memorized the exact tenor of Ren's moans.

When the video ended, the assistant director was hurrying away, shouting at them that the video would be online within the hour. The costume jiejies descended like a cloud of mayflies, plucking away the layers of their hanfus, while others carefully removed their wigs.

"Nap," Ren wailed as soon as he was free. "I just want a nap."

"Are you returning to the apartments?" Song asked in a low voice.

"There's no point since I'm already here. I can crash in my trailer for a few hours. I've got some earplugs if I need them," Ren said easily.

"I was wondering if you'd run some lines with me first. I'm worried about tonight's shoot."

Ren stopped walking toward the trailers and stared at him as if he'd lost his mind. Yeah, Song knew what he was thinking. Ren was the one with all the fucking lines tonight. Most of the shoot was going to be fighting and wire work. Very little talking.

Song could see the exact moment Ren's tired brain caught up, as his eyes widened and his mouth snapped shut. "Running lines" meant they had an excuse to be in the same trailer for a few hours.

"Sure. I'd be happy to run lines with you. Let me grab my script and a snack. I'll be right over."

Song's heart did the happiest flip and then went off to skip around his other organs while he managed to give Ren an appreciative smile. Okay, Ren wasn't fooled. His boyfriend rolled his eyes and snorted.

The important thing was that they weren't touching. Song wasn't hanging on him. There was *nothing* for the BTS cameras to catch and post on social media. They were behaving.

But that shit was ending the second he got Ren alone in his trailer.

In Song's defense, he didn't attack Ren the second the man locked the door behind him, but it was a close thing when he saw that Ren had brought him another shiny red apple along with his script.

"How are you holding up?" Song inquired as Ren put the script and apple on the table.

Ren offered up a weak, lopsided smile as all the fake layers started to peel away. "I've been better. I could use a hug."

Fuck self-control.

Song was wrapped around Ren before the man could finish speaking. Ren dropped his head into the hollow of his neck, his hot breath fanning along his skin, while strong arms threatened to crack his ribs. He didn't care. He was holding his didi after way too long.

He scolded himself yet again for not insisting they sleep together last night. Though that would have been a disaster since Bao Shi had come pounding on his door at an ungodly hour. He'd left only because Ren was still feeling uneasy after Sun had cautioned them to be more careful. Instead of allowing Ren to pull away, Song should have held him tighter, reassured him more.

"Tell me we haven't fucked things up," Ren whispered in his ear.

Reluctantly, Song released his tight hold on his lover. He grabbed his hand and led him to the bed he'd just cleared of random clothes and papers. They sat together on the edge, with Song turned to face him.

"Let's be logical about it. Sun caught shit prior to it getting out. What has already leaked hasn't raised too many questions to put us in danger. We look like we've become friends, which the censors are fine with. And the shippers who want us to be a couple have enough fodder to keep them happy."

"Sun?"

Song shrugged. "If he suspects something, he honestly doesn't care. He said that he's happy that I'm happy." Song squeezed the hand he was still holding. "And you do make me happy. Very, very happy."

Ren's smile was small and tentative, while worry lingered in his eyes. "I'm happy too, but I don't want to damage your career."

"You're not. My career and yours are fine. We're being more careful on the set. The little video gremlins aren't going to get anything else on us. Right?"

His lover drew in a deep breath through his nose, held it, and slowly released it through his parted lips. As the air flowed out of him, some of the tension eased from his stiff shoulders and he slumped a bit more. "Yes. You're right."

"And this nonsense with the fan video? It's taken care of. The new video will be out in an hour. You were fucking adorable and flirty. That stuff with the fan, hiding like you're shy. Everyone is going to fall in love with you, while I continue to look like the lovable dork that I am."

"You don't think it was too much? I wasn't too flirty?"

Song lifted a hand and lightly dragged his fingers along Ren's jaw. The man naturally drew closer, his lips parting on a delicious catch. It was like Song had him hypnotized and that power was sending all the blood racing to his dick. Would there ever be a moment when he didn't want Ren with all of his being?

"You were the perfect mix of Zhao Gang flirty and Ah-Xue sweetness," Song murmured.

"I try to save all my Ah-Xue flirting for you."

"Smart," Song purred as he leaned in the last bit to nibble at Ren's bottom lip. On the next press, the kiss deepened, Song's tongue slipping inside of Ren's mouth to taste. Song tried to keep it light and gentle, but Ren moaned and pulled Song closer.

Ren took control of the kiss, eating at Song's mouth like a starved man. Song relaxed, letting Ren take whatever the hell he wanted. God, nothing pushed his buttons like being overpowered. Yes, he enjoyed being the one in control and turning Ren inside out with pleasure.

But he also loved being the one pushed down and left utterly powerless. It was as if his overactive brain finally shut off and there was only the cleansing wash of pleasure pouring through him.

It also didn't help that it had been…

Oh, come on! It couldn't have been less than forty-eight hours since he'd gotten into Ren's pants!

Math was lying to him.

No. He refused to believe it More time had to have passed since he'd kissed him, touched him, felt his body tremble as he came in his hand.

The kiss went on and on, but Ren didn't lift his hands to run them over his body. He didn't shove Song's clothes out of the way. The kiss was hungry, desperate, and practically begging Song for more, but his sweet Ah-Xue wasn't ready to take the reins. He was asking for Song to take them back to the edge the only way he could.

Song was so happy to oblige. He'd steer this crazy ship as long as Ren needed him to.

"Ah-Xue," Song panted against Ren's lips. "Can I touch you?"

"Please," Ren whispered in a trembling voice. He broke off the kiss and ripped his T-shirt over his head, tossing it to the floor.

Oh, hell yes. He loved this enthusiasm. Song jumped to his feet and shimmied out of his sneakers while lifting his shirt over his head. Ren's hand hesitated on the waistband of his basketball shorts, which were already doing nothing to hide his hard-on.

"You can take them off, or I'm going to steal them from you," Song teased with a waggle of his eyebrows.

To his shock, Ren stood and shoved his shorts and underwear to his feet. In just a couple of quick movements, the tall, sexy man was completely naked and smirking at him as if daring him to come up with a new challenge. Song wanted to, but his brain was completely locked up on all the beauty.

This was the first time he'd seen Ren without clothes, and he wanted to bask in all those hard muscles and soft skin. He might have seen some pictures on the Internet, but Ren's abs in person were a thing of splendor. He ached to run his tongue over every bump and divot, to explore every inch of him.

"Fuck, Ah-Xue. You're beautiful," Song murmured as he moved his mouth along Ren's shoulder, licking and kissing his way to Ren's pec.

"I bet you say that to all the naked boys in your trailer," Ren groaned.

Song lightly bit Ren's nipple, earning a soft yelp. They both winced at the noise, their eyes snapping to each other. Quiet. They needed to be quiet.

"Lie down and be quiet, Ah-Xue," Song scolded. He quickly turned and closed the door leading to the rest of the trailer. The main entrance was locked against surprise visitors, but this would give them an added sense of security. He then snatched up a backpack he kept next to his bed and dug around until he found a tiny bottle of lube.

When he turned to the bed, it was to find that Ren had scooted to the far side and pulled a thin sheet across the lower half of his body. Song's heart lurched in his chest to see Ren's pale skin on his dark sheets, his nearly black hair spread on his pillows. *This.* He wanted this. He wanted this for the rest of his life. Whenever he climbed into his bed, he wanted to see Ren lying there, waiting for him.

"What's wrong?" Ren asked. He leaned up on his elbow as if he were preparing to climb out of the bed.

"I was just thinking that my bed has never looked so inviting in all of my life."

Ren dropped onto the pillow, a smile growing on his damp and puffy lips. "Come here, smooth talker."

With a smirk, Song slipped under the blanket while Ren turned on his side to face Song. Their skin touched in so many wonderful places, snatching Song's breath away. The heat of Ren contrasted the cool air that filled the trailer. The room was dimly lit, with only a bit of light filtering in around the blinds over the one window in the room, but it was enough to give Song a clear view of his lover's face as he reacted to just the feel of their bodies rubbing together.

That response was enough to give him a very wonderful idea.

Kissing Ren deeply, he pushed his lover onto his back and crawled between his thighs. He thrust, rubbing his hard cock against Ren's to wring another harsh gasp from him. With his hands planted on either side of Ren's head, Song slowly moved his hips as he kissed Ren again and again. When Ren started thrusting with him, Song lifted up.

"Want to try something new?" He shifted his weight to one hand and held up the little bottle of lube.

Ren's eyes widened and he swallowed hard. "Umm…Song laoshi…I—"

Song swore softly and kissed Ren hard. "No. Not that. Something else that doesn't involve penetration."

Ren sighed so heavily, he seemed to melt into the mattress. Both hands came up and covered his face. "Song, I—fuck, sorry," Ren babbled.

Moving his weight to his knees, Song gently grabbed one of Ren's hands and pulled them from his flushed face. "Ah-

"Xue, in case I didn't make it obvious the other night, I'm a bottom. Not to scare you further, but I'm a 'pin me down and fuck me hard' bottom. When it comes to penetration, it's more you penetrating me. If you want to try it, though, I'll be happy—"

Ren slapped a trembling, sweaty palm over his mouth, stopping his words. "Fuck, Song!" He squeezed his eyes shut and sucked in a few ragged breaths. "If you keep talking, I'm going to come."

It was only when Ren called attention to it that Song noticed Ren's cock did feel harder. Slick pre-cum was teasing along the side of his dick. That was lovely to discover. He could drive Ren crazy with just his words. Ren also liked the idea of fucking Song. *Oh yes, this was going to work out very nicely.*

"Then let me help," Song murmured. He snapped open the plastic cap on the lube and squeezed some into his hand. He wrapped his hand around both their cocks, liberally spreading the gel so that they were both coated.

Ren's mouth opened on a moan and Song quickly covered it with his own, swallowing down the sound. He removed his hand and pressed both into the mattress while thrusting his hips forward. The smooth slide of their dicks together, nestled between their hot bodies, was shorting out what little thought he had left in his brain.

Song placed a series of nibbling kisses along Ren's jaw to his neck. "You're in control. As fast or as slow as you want," he panted in his ear.

At last, those magnificent hands spread across his back, holding him trapped as they dug into muscles. Song loved those hands. Ren had beautifully large hands with long, elegant fingers. He was not above having many, many dirty fantasies about those hands and all the wonderful things they could do to him.

And right now, those hands were working their way along his spine to grab both globes of his ass as Ren rocked up into him, thrusting deliciously. Song kept his face buried in Ren's neck while his fingers twisted in the sheets. His orgasm was burning away at his control, demanding to be let loose, but he didn't want this to end yet. He wanted to hang on so he could fly off the edge of the world with Ren.

But with every thrust, the most desperate whine slipped from his lips to be muffled against Ren's sweaty skin. Those hands were kneading his ass, spreading his cheeks. Closer and closer those fingers were creeping to his hole, teasing him until he was balanced on the thinnest strand.

"Ren, please," he begged, though he wasn't quite sure what he was pleading for.

A finger brushed so lightly across his entrance and his control snapped. His orgasm exploded through him. He clenched his jaw, holding in his cries of pleasure as best he could while coming hard on Ren's stomach.

Ren stiffened for a heartbeat under him and then thrust even harder, his fingers pressing so deep into his ass he was going to be feeling it for the rest of the day. Ren swore softly as he came, adding to the mess Song had already created.

When it was over, Song could only lie on top of Ren, panting and limp. Holy shit, that was amazing. Every part of his body tingled and his brain was useless mush. Ren's hands had loosened their hold, but he was now running them up and down his body as if he couldn't stop touching Song. If that became Ren's newest addiction, Song was just fine with that.

Ren started to shake with giggles and Song summoned up enough energy to push up on his elbow so he could look into his lover's face.

"What's so funny?"

"I was thinking that when you agreed to be my laoshi, this wasn't what I was expecting you to teach me."

A loud bark of laughter escaped Song as he flopped onto his back, kicking the sheets to their feet. "No, I really doubt this is what Sun Jing had in mind when he asked me to be your laoshi." He turned his head on the pillow to smile at the sweaty, flushed man with the shining dark eyes. "Any regrets?"

Ren frowned and stared up at the ceiling as if he were seriously considering his answer. It was enough to make Song's heart painfully stutter in his chest.

"Ren An Xue!"

The beautiful man chuckled and rolled onto his side, pulling Song close. "No. Not a sing—" he started and then stopped, a strange smile forming on his lips. "No. One."

"What?"

"Do you remember that day I massaged your knee?"

Song snorted. "Trust me, that is not a day I will ever forget."

"I regret not kissing you that day."

Song sighed softly. Yeah, he'd had a feeling Ren had been close to kissing him that afternoon in his trailer. "No regrets. The important thing is that you did kiss me, and that we keep kissing for the rest of our lives."

Ren bumped his nose against Song's, their lips brushing in a teasing almost kiss. "Not a problem. There's no one else I ever want to kiss."

27

HUA NEEDS TO STIR THE POT
REN AN XUE

The video worked.

Sort of. Mostly.

Within a few hours of the Q&A video being released, most of the haters had settled, or at least were drowned out by the Song superfans who enjoyed crowing about the cheeky adorableness of their idol.

Ren's fan base significantly expanded as well, judging by the new followers he'd gained on his social media pages, and they were also celebrating his shy adorableness.

And then there were the growing number of shippers who just loved anything that had Song and Ren together.

Of course, the furor shifted thanks to another couple of *innocent* BTS videos that popped up, and one video that tried to make things look less than innocent. Ren might have lain in bed with Song wrapped around him as he snickered at that one. The creator had taken the time to slow down and circle in red anytime they touched each other. Half of them were in relation to a scene they were filming or Ren simply helping Song back to his feet. As if Ren was supposed to stand over the man as he sat on the ground, not offering him a hand. Like that wouldn't have sent the fans into a new frothing tizzy.

"You're damned if you do, and you're damned if you don't. It's better to give them as little fodder as possible," Song had murmured on a yawn before drifting off to sleep, his arm draped across Ren's waist.

Ren had pressed a kiss to the top of Song's head, smiling to himself. The two of them crammed together in a tiny bed was the world's best scandal fodder, but it was also a slice of heaven.

A week had passed in relative quiet. An advertising campaign for sunglasses had launched with Song as their new lead spokesman, and Ren had new pictures hit for a cosmetics company. The fans had a crap-ton of new glossy photos to drool over, and they still had more than a month of filming to complete for *Legend of the Lost Night*. Ren was clinging to this peaceful period with both hands.

"Has he gained weight?"

Ren jerked around to see Hua Jun Bai watching Song with narrowed eyes as he ran through a scene with the assistant director.

"No, he's not gained weight," Ren said, trying hard not to snap or sound peevish.

The one consistent way they'd found to stop touching each other and otherwise appearing too close on the set was to simply not stand anywhere near each other if they weren't filming a scene. It had cut down on their side chats between scenes, but Ren found that he still stood close by, watching his lover. It was enough to see him.

"Are you sure?" Hua continued to prod. "He just seems fuller in the face." He waved at his own rounded cheeks as he spoke.

Ren bit on the inside of his mouth. He generally enjoyed trading barbs with Hua, but the man was trying to drag him into a revealing conversation about Song, and he was not going to be sucked in. He was smarter than that.

Despite Hua's need to constantly stir the pot, Ren did

enjoy working with the man. He was a god of understatement, delivering some of his best lines with a brittle dryness and a cold, smug expression. He was also a master at getting under Zhao Gang's skin. They spent nearly half of the TV show sniping at each other, forcing Tian Xiuying to separate them again and again when weapons were drawn.

But it was clear that Hua was so good at his role because it was somewhat similar to his own personality. The man loved needling Ren and Song until they both snapped. The moment either of them started shouting at him, Hua was practically prostrate with belly laughs.

"I heard you've been cooking him lunch nearly every day," Hua continued.

"Song Wei Li is my laoshi. He's taught me a lot since I took on this role. The least I can do is make lunch for him," Ren recited, giving the same response he'd given to a few other nosy people who thought it was amusing that Song still followed Ren to his trailer every time the midday break was called.

Hua tilted his head so that his face was in Ren's direct line of sight, the long black hair of his wig spilling over his shoulder in an inky cascade. His smirk said it all. *Exactly what was your laoshi teaching you?*

"Don't you have a scene coming up you should be practicing for?" Ren sniped, earning several loud guffaws. God, he shouldn't have opened his mouth. Now Hua knew without a doubt that he was driving Ren crazy, and that would only make him worse.

But to his surprise, Hua didn't continue that line of poking and prodding. He straightened and took a step closer to Ren. "You know, this isn't my first wuxia drama with Song. We were in this romantic thing called *Snow Blossoms*...or *Falling Snow*... no! *Blossoms Falling in Snow*. We didn't have a lot of scenes together since he was the hero and I was on the side of the villain."

"Big shock," Ren mumbled under his breath.

Hua wasn't put off. The man even snorted and bumped Ren with his shoulder. "It's always surprising the difference in the characters he plays and his own personality. On the *Blossoms* set he was always running around, laughing and playing jokes on people. He took his work seriously, but he was also the guy putting smiles on everyone's faces."

"He's definitely been the bright spot on this set," Ren murmured.

His costar hummed softly in disagreement. "Not as much as I was expecting."

Ren glanced over at Hua, lifting one eyebrow. "Really?"

Hua's smile grew wider. "It seems like the majority of his focus has been on one person in particular."

Ren scoffed. And there it was. Constantly prodding and picking, trying to get details about whether he and Song were actually…what? Did Hua think they were too close? Did he think they were more than friends?

Did it matter to him?

The idea of anyone discovering the truth quickened his heart and left a cold sweat breaking out across his skin despite the blistering hot temperatures. That kind of gossip could sink both his and Song's careers.

It felt as though a lot of the speculation about them had stopped on the set in the past week after the stupid fan video went viral, starting a kerfuffle on Weibo. Ma Daiyu and some of their other costars had dropped all their teasing.

Ren pulled on the mantle of irritated Zhao Gang and sighed heavily at Hua. "I can't believe you've gotten sucked into the BL nonsense just because that's what we're filming. I thought someone with your experience would know better."

Oh, Hua's grin turned so very fucking evil. Ren was in trouble.

"Would you like to run an experiment with me?" Hua asked.

No. No, he very much would not.

But Hua didn't give him a chance to argue. He tilted his head toward Ren and smiled. "Have you noticed that even while preparing for his scene, Song's eyes keep coming back to you?"

Ren bit his tongue. He had noticed that. Song had been watching him very closely, particularly since Hua had started chatting with him.

A burst of unexpected laughter erupted from Hua, and the man grabbed his arm as he leaned to his right, bumping into Ren. Hua's hand felt uncomfortably warm on his bare skin. Ren had stripped out of his hanfu as he waited for his next scene and was wearing a white V-neck T-shirt and loose black shorts. God, he couldn't remember the last time someone touched him like this. Was Hua the first? Was that why it felt so wrong?

"Look at that scowl," Hua chuckled softly. "I think he intends to break my hand."

Ren sneaked a glance over at Song to find that he was in fact sending the dirtiest scowl in Hua's direction while one of the makeup jiejies fixed his wig.

With a roll of his eyes, Ren pulled his arm free of Hua's grip. He shook his head without gazing at Song, but he trusted his lover would understand that Hua was being an ass.

"Stop. He's just protective," Ren muttered.

"I think the word you're searching for is *possessive*," Hua snickered. "Song has always been that touchy, feely guy. He grabs people and leans on them the second he begins feeling comfortable. I've been on this set for nearly a month, and the only person he touches is *you*. And the only person who's allowed to touch you and keep all their fingers intact is *him*."

The idea warmed something in Ren's heart for a moment. He liked the idea of Song belonging to only him. And yes, maybe it was a little unhealthy, but he also liked the idea of

Song being possessive over him. He wanted to belong to only Song.

But this...this digging around and taunting Song, Ren wasn't in the mood for it, and he couldn't understand Hua's reasoning for it.

Reaching into his pocket, he pulled out his ever-present folding fan and flicked it open with a hard snap. Hua's eyes widened and the man actually retreated a step as if Ren had suddenly pulled a knife on him.

He turned to face Hua, his gaze quickly sweeping the immediate area to check that no one was particularly close to them and there weren't any phones pointed in their direction. There was one woman who appeared to be watching them. Her phone wasn't aimed at them, but that could change in a heartbeat.

With a stiff smile, Ren lifted the fan, waving it to create a breeze while at the same time blocking the view of his lips. He'd seen enough videos where people were trying to read their lips in order to understand what Song and Ren were talking about. Most of the time, they'd be disappointed to discover it was about pulled muscles, sweaty costumes, and what to have for dinner.

But this, he didn't want anyone to uncover.

"What are you getting at?" Ren demanded in a low voice while trying to maintain a friendly expression. "Are you gathering bits to use for blackmail later? Do you hate me or Song that much that you want to destroy our careers?"

To Hua's credit, he looked genuinely horrified by Ren's accusations. He rocked back a step, his eyes wide and mouth falling open. For a second, the man seemed incapable of speech. He leaned forward, his voice a low, harsh whisper. Ren shifted the fan so that it no longer blocked his face and he waved it at Hua, so that his mouth was now obscured. Ren's smile was wide and friendly as if he were happily sharing a breeze with his costar.

"Absolutely not! Has someone done that to you? Have they threatened you or Song?"

For a heartbeat, Ren forgot to wave his fan. He stood frozen under the force of that near snarl. Hua Jun Bai appeared ready to rip someone apart at the mere thought that some homophobe might threaten him or Song. With all his teasing, Ren had never in a million years expected this man to be one of his possible defenders.

"What? No. But I thought…" Ren stammered. He was thoroughly confused. "You keep hinting…"

Hua made a disgusted noise, but Ren wasn't sure if he was disgusted with Ren or himself. They turned toward the scene that was getting ready to film and Hua sighed. He leaned close and dropped his voice. "Please wave and smile at your boyfriend. He's about to come over here and break my fucking neck."

Shit!

Ren looked at Song to find that he was glaring at Hua, seeming ready to throttle him within an inch of his life. They both smiled broadly and waved at him. It still took another second or two before Song relaxed and returned his attention to the scene.

"Fuck," Ren moaned, dropping his head back and squeezing his eyes shut. His heart was racing in a mix of fear, anger, panic, and the rush of relief.

"Sorry," Hua muttered next to him, snapping Ren's head up. "We don't know each other well yet. Everyone knows I'm a troublemaker, but I shouldn't have picked on this topic."

Ren shook his head. "No, it's okay. I'm just…sensitive."

That was a fucking understatement.

He was overprotective of Song and his career. And then, there was a part of him that constantly lived a state of terror of being discovered. The only time those feelings weren't threatening to overwhelm him was in the evening when they were in his room or Song's. The door was locked, the curtains were pulled, and for a few hours, the rest of the world simply didn't exist. There was just Song and their happiness. Nothing else mattered.

Hua huffed. "Yeah, well. If you're happy, that's all that matters. Song seems like he's happy." Hua paused and directed another smile at Song even though the actor wasn't looking in their direction any longer. "At least he does when he's not plotting my death."

Ren chuckled softly and shook his head. Yeah, he had a feeling that he and Song were going to have a very long talk about Hua tonight when they were finally alone. And even afterward, he wouldn't be surprised if Song had a few curt words for their costar.

"Hey, if anyone gives you shit, you tell me, okay. I've got your back. And if you were to ever need, like, an alibi, I can try to give you a hand," Hua offered.

Ren barely caught the loud bark of laughter that tried to erupt from his throat. He slapped his free hand over his mouth while his shoulders shook. Hua stared at him as though he'd lost his mind.

He leaned close and whispered in his ear, "If I ever need an alibi, I'm not sure stating I was with a different guy is going to be of much help."

Hua made a choking noise and covered his mouth. His eyes watered with barely withheld laughter. They both probably looked like lunatics, but Ren didn't care. This was one of the best laughs he'd had in a while, and it was definitely nice that he could laugh with someone who wasn't Song.

"Good point," Hua said, clearing his throat. "We need to get you some more female friends. I'm sure Ma Daiyu would be happy to help."

"I think my manager would appreciate it if I didn't have my name linked to anyone too much, male or female." He sighed. "I have a feeling she'd appreciate it if I wasn't friends with a troublemaker like you."

"Oh, I can guarantee she'd hate us being friends," Hua snickered.

"But I'm glad we are," Ren murmured. Hua smiled and nodded, as they sank into a comfortable, companionable silence.

Ren watched Song running through his scene with a practiced, professional ease. Something in his chest felt lighter, easier, that hadn't been there a minute ago. He fanned himself, letting the rest of the world drift away.

He was right.

Song managed to hold it all together until they met in Ren's room for dinner. Ren was still washing the vegetables when Song turned off the water, wrapped him up in a tight hug, and demanded to know what the hell he'd been talking about with Hua. That was considerable restraint on Song's part since all three of them had scenes together the rest of the afternoon. Close to five hours had passed, and Song had held it together.

That night, his lover might have cursed and ranted.

He might have threatened to break Hua's various body parts.

He might have conceded that Hua was a pretty good guy when Ren finally kissed him into submission.

And, of course, the next morning, they woke to half a dozen new videos speculating on what Ren An Xue and Hua Jun Bai were intensely chatting about while Song Wei Li jealously glared at them.

Some accused Ren of cheating on poor Song with Hua right in front of him.

Some accused Hua of trying to break up Song and Ren.

Some accused Song of being too jealous and possessive of poor Ren.

No one was even remotely close to the truth.

Naturally, Sun Jing pulled them aside the second they hit the set that morning, informing them to forget his earlier instructions. Go back to being cute.

Damned if you do...

28

AH-XUE, YOUR LAOPO IS ROASTING!
SONG WEI LI

Laopo[1]*?*

Seriously? He was laopo?

The legions of fans had decided that *he* was laopo?

What. The. Fuck.

For some bizarre reason that was beyond his understanding, the number of videos appearing on Weibo, WeChat[2], Douyin[3], and all the other places were multiplying at a faster rate. The speculation was ramping up. The conversations and banter were largely positive.

And insanely enough, the fans and shippers had decided that he was laopo. Ren was the sweet, tender one. He should be laopo.

Song had to stop scrolling through social media. He also had to get Ren to stop scrolling, because every time he found something amusing or irritating, he immediately showed Song, which got him scrolling all over again.

This was not healthy.

But neither was being buried under a blanket inside of a building while the heat of the day was still clinging to the world, leaving him feeling like a steamed bun.

The shooting schedule for the day was winding down, and

they were on the last few shots before they finally got to leave. Song was tired and ready to be done.

He shouldn't be complaining too loudly since he had the easy part of the scene. His job was to lie still, looking unconscious and injured while Zhao Gang took care of him and played a healing song on his flute.

The only problem was the goddamn blanket. The upper half of his body was still in the robe, while the lower half had been reduced to shorts to keep him from baking.

While Ren and Sun discussed the blocking and movements for the scene, Song was being tended to by the jiejies and assistant director, making sure his costume, hair, and makeup were all in place. He wanted to lift the blanket and get some cooler air to his legs, but if he moved, the crew would have to get him situated all over again.

"Are you okay, Song laoshi? Are you planning to just nap through this scene?" Ren teased as he drifted over while the director talked to the people handling the lights and cameras. He kneeled next to the bed, a wide grin playing on his beautiful face. Zhao Gang was in an exquisite set of blue-and-cream robes while his xiaoguan[4] was an intricate silver crown, making him look like a chilly prince or a young godling descended from the heavens.

"Don't mock me, didi. I'm baking in here," Song grumbled.

Smirking, Ren grabbed the edge of the blanket and pulled it up a bit while he bent his head as if peeking under the blanket. "How many layers are you wearing under there?"

"Too many. And I so hope someone got you on the BTS camera sneaking a peek under my blanket."

Ren blushed and rapidly lowered the blanket. His eyes were wide when they met Song's, as if he'd suddenly realized exactly how bad that was going to appear if someone caught that on video.

"I tried to convince them to put the cool air vent under the blanket, but they said the breeze would poof up the blanket too much," Song continued, hoping to distract Ren from his horror. "My next suggestion was to let me be naked from the waist down. Guess how that suggestion went over?"

As he'd expected, Ren blushed for an entirely new reason and shook his head. "You are shameless, Song laoshi."

"All right, all right! Places. We're ready," the director's assistant shouted.

With a final smirk, Ren stood and started to move to his beginning mark. He paused and patted the blanket in place from where he'd disturbed it. He even took Song's right hand and placed it on top of the blanket after smoothing out his long sleeve.

The hair-and-makeup crew instantly flocked over to Ren, getting the last bit of hair in place while patting away a few drops of sweat from his neck and brow. The assistant director moved in behind Ren, grabbed Song's right hand, and placed it under the blanket.

Ren glared at the man's back as he retreated. Ren then walked over and placed Song's hand outside of the blanket and situated his sleeve.

"Song, I know it's hot, but keep your hand under the blanket," the assistant director chided as he returned to move Song's hand again.

Song gasped at the injustice of being blamed when he and Ren were the ones who kept moving his damn hand for the shot.

"Song's hand needs to be out of the blanket," Ren grumped at the poor guy.

"In the last shot before this one, Song's hand was under the blanket."

"Then we're going to need to edit it, aren't we?" Ren said in the most snappish tone Song had heard him use. "My direction is to cross to the bed, take Tian's hand, and check his pulse." Ren did exactly as he described, sitting on the edge of the bed. But instead of grabbing his hand, Ren picked up the blanket. "Do we think the censors are going to be a fan of me sticking my hand under the blanket and digging around for Song?" Which he proceeded to do.

Song yelped and darted under the blanket, away from Ren's long fingers while earning snickers from the rest of the crew.

Ren ignored him completely as he snatched his hand and placed it gently on the blanket. "It seems more natural to pick up his limp hand from on top of the blanket."

"True, but you could do it with less reaching," the assistant director suggested.

"Yes, but it still feels invasive. On top of the blanket feels like a safer move to me."

As they continued to argue over the placement of his hand, Song was dying under the hot blanket. He wanted this scene to be done so he could stand in front of the cool air vent. If he didn't have to deliver one tiny line, they could have used a dummy for this scene.

"Ah-Xue, your laopo is roasting!" Song cried out.

There was a heartbeat of absolute silence before the entire set erupted in laughter. It took Song an extra second to realize that he'd said *laopo* when he'd meant to say *laoshi*.

Fuck.

With his luck, that had definitely been caught on camera, and now the nickname was going to stick.

Whatever. Staring up at that perfect face with eyes shining in amusement, Song was proud to be this amazing man's laopo.

"I'm sorry, Song laoshi," Ren managed to wheeze as he tried to catch his breath. He leaned down so that his face was only a few inches above, that wonderful smile for him alone. "I promise I have something that will distract you from the heat."

Ren retreated to his spot, and the assistant director left his hand outside of the goddamn blanket.

Song wanted to demand to know what the hell kind of surprise Ren could possibly have that would take his mind off sweating buckets under this stupid blanket.

But places were called, and cameras were rolling.

Song closed his eyes and tried to shove away all random thoughts. This was supposed to be the scene directly after their mad escape from the prince's army that forced them to jump from a waterfall. Tian Xiuying was severely injured, and Zhao Gang was his worried and attentive nursemaid.

Unconscious and hurt was easy to play. Don't move. No facial expressions. Pretend to be fucking sleeping.

The majority of the scene would have a musical soundtrack playing over it, so the assistant director was barking out commands as Ren crossed the room and sat on the edge of the bed. His long, elegant fingers lovingly picked up his hand and turned it over with such care, as if he were afraid his Ah-Ying would shatter at his touch. Two fingers were placed to his pulse and Song had to fight the flinch at Ren's cold touch. How were his fingers cold? Had he handled a cold drink before the start of the scene? Ren couldn't possibly be nervous. This was such a basic, easy scene.

Even with his eyes closed, Song could imagine Ren's pale, handsome face filled with worry. His pink lips slightly downturned, his dark eyebrows sharply angled. And those enormous puppy eyes overflowing with concern. The audience would be melting over this man in this scene. Screw the poor injured Tian Xiuying.

When directed to cross to the table, Ren carefully placed Song's hand on the blanket, but there was an extra little caress across his palm, as if Ren wasn't quite ready to stop touching him. That tiny touch made his heart skip, and he almost smiled.

Idiot! You're unconscious! Play dead!

There was a scrape of Ren's feet moving across the floor to the table, and then he was crossing back. He sat on the very edge of the bed. This was supposed to be where Ren played his magical healing flute song that would help to mend all of Tian Xiuying's wounds and return him to consciousness.

The assistant director had said they had a rough recording of the song that they'd play to help Ren time the head motions and finger movements.

But what he heard was not a recording.

The song was a bit wobbly to start, but it was crisp and clear. And it was coming from right next to him.

Song's heart sped up as he realized Ren was actually playing the flute. He was playing the song. It wasn't a recording.

He'd heard that little sneak tell Sun Jing that he hadn't played the flute since he was a kid. He was a stinky liar.

Unless he'd studied up and relearned how to play just for this scene.

He had. That was the sort of thing Ren would do. This man put his all into everything he did. To become Zhao Gang, Ren learned how to use a fan in combat, wire work, became an expert with a folding fan, and relearned to play the flute for this scene.

Song was in awe of him.

Well, that and frustrated. He wanted to open his eyes and watch Ren playing, but he was supposed to be an unconscious, suffering patient. He couldn't open his eyes.

But with his eyes closed, he could focus on each lilting, dancing note as it passed over him. It was a light, delicate song. So very serene, painting pictures in his mind of rolling green hills dotted with delicate white blossoms in the spring and winding, glittering streams in the golden sun. It was a sense of peace that reached down to his soul.

All the more because Ren was creating those notes.

After several minutes, the song faded away, and Ren's hand returned to his wrist.

"Ah-Ying?" Zhao called softly.

Oh, fuck! Right! Acting!

Song's eyes slowly fluttered open and he was greeted with the sight of Ren's large, chestnut-brown eyes watching him so closely, filled with concern and love. So much love.

"Ah-Ying?" he repeated.

And Song's mind went blank. He had a line here. One freaking line. But it was gone. There was just nothing there.

Song groaned loudly, and Ren's composure cracked into a crooked grin.

"Line!" Song shouted, and the assistant director yelled cut.

"You had one line!" Ren laughed.

Song launched himself into a sitting position and briefly wrapped Ren in an almost tackling hug. "It's your fault! You completely made me forget my line with your playing! You said you couldn't play!"

"You weren't the only one who was surprised," the assistant director admitted as he walked over to them. He narrowed his eyes on Ren as he shoved a hand through his sweaty dark hair. "I was told that you couldn't play a note. I was not expecting you to break out with the actual song in that scene!"

Ren pointed the elegant bamboo flute at the assistant director. "That is not true at all. I never claimed that. I stated that I hadn't played since I was young. When I heard that they had the song that would play in this scene written, I got a copy of the sheet music. I've been practicing for three months. The song isn't all that complex."

It was on the tip of Song's tongue to demand to know when he'd practiced, but he bit back the words. Nothing good would come of revealing that they spent nearly all their free time together. Ren must have been practicing early in the mornings. Their days were spent on the set or on other promotional obligations, and they spent all their evenings together.

"I can't believe you didn't tell me," Song murmured.

Ren smiled at him in his special way that turned all of Song's organs to utter mush. "I wanted to surprise you."

Song opened his mouth and then promptly shut it. A hundred thousand things came to mind that he wanted to say to this man, but they were surrounded by people, and phone cameras were pointed at him. They didn't have a scrap of privacy, and what he wanted to say to Ren belonged only to his ears.

"I know," Ren whispered.

"Well, I'm sorry to say, we have to do it all over, because someone couldn't remember his line," the assistant director declared after clearing his throat. "You know, we'll still have to dub in the soundtrack recording. You don't have to play if you don't want to."

Ren tipped his head up to the assistant director and grinned. "I know, but I practiced for too long not to play. Besides, I'm sure this will make a nice bonus clip for Weibo and WeChat."

The assistant director laughed and nodded. "Yes, it will." The man turned around and lifted his hands into the air. "All right, places. Let's run this again."

Ren placed his hand over Song's, the motion blocked by his own hip from the view of everyone but the makeup artist fixing Song's hair. "You remember your line now?"

"Yes, didi. I got my memory back," Song replied, trying to infuse all his love and devotion into those words.

They returned to their starting places and the scene played over, with Ren's gentle touch, his beautiful playing, and Song remembering his damn line.

But in his mind, Song kept repeating to himself that he had to find a way to keep this man at his side for the rest of his life. There was no way he'd ever meet another person who was so perfect for him. There was no one more amazing in his eyes, and he had to find a way to tell Ren that there was no one else. There never would be.

And he just might have an interesting idea of how he could do that…

29

HOW TO SEDUCE SONG
REN AN XUE

REN PACED.

Unfortunately, his room didn't offer a lot of space for good pacing. It was just a couple of steps before he was turning and wandering back the way he'd come.

Not that he noticed.

His brain was a mess of tangled thoughts. Today, they'd had the first of the farewells. There was some cake, flowers, and photographs. Three actors who had been part of the main crew and on the set since the very beginning filmed their last scenes.

The sight of those giant, colorful bouquets made Ren's stomach sink and a cold sweat break out across his skin. His eyes had immediately darted over to Song to find the same tense smile on his lips.

It was the end of July. They had less than one month left of filming. From here on out, there would be more actor departures as they finished their final scenes until at last, they were all gathered for a photo and no more.

And then what?

Well, technically, Ren knew exactly what came next.

His schedule was largely planned out for the next six

months. He was slated to fly to Beijing, where he'd begin filming his next romantic comedy for a week. He had three commercials to film, an easy dozen photo shoots, two fashion shows, and a scattering of other appearances. And that was all before he started making appearances on TV and web shows with Song to promote *Legend of the Lost Night*.

He imagined Song's schedule was going to be even worse since he was a bigger star.

When were they ever going to see each other? In a month, would they have only text messages, brief phone calls, and the occasional video chat late at night when they were supposed to be sleeping?

What they had right now was a luxury. Each day they were together on the set, filming scenes and laughing. Each night, they shared a meal, talked about random things, and held each other until one of them fell asleep.

That was the other thing that was chewing on his brain.

Sex.

Things had sort of stalled in the past week following their stolen fun in Song's trailer. Part of it was due to their intense schedule, which left them both bone-tired at the end of the day. They were lucky to be preparing a meal and curling up together. A couple of times, Song had drifted off almost the second his head hit the pillow, his arm draped across Ren.

But Ren wasn't an idiot. Song was waiting for him. He was unwilling to push things faster than Ren was comfortable with.

Except they didn't have time for Ren to be fucking shy and nervous.

When were they going to have a better chance than now to enjoy each other's company?

Song also hadn't hidden the fact that he was waiting for Ren to show more initiative. To take control.

And he wanted to do that. He craved Song's beautiful body. He wanted to be the one who made this amazing man tremble beneath him, to wring all those addictive sounds from his throat.

He just didn't know what he was doing. Everything in him immediately locked up with worry whenever he tried to take control, and the same anxiety that gripped him during his first horrible sexual encounter came rushing back.

What if he couldn't get hard?

Fuck. What if he couldn't get Song hard?

That certainly hadn't been a problem so far, but Song had always been the one initiating things.

How was he supposed to seduce Song and take control of their fun in bed?

Damn. He probably should have been watching porn for research.

But the idea of trying to do some of the things he'd seen in those videos made his stomach twist into a knot. It wasn't like he was watching the strange and kinky stuff. No whips and collars and tying down. Hell, most people would probably call him vanilla and boring.

What if Song didn't like vanilla and boring?

Were they doomed because Ren wasn't adventurous enough? Was he going to sink this relationship because sex with him was too boring?

A knock on his door had Ren nearly jumping out of his skin.

It was Song. They'd finished filming at different times today. It was one of the rare days they'd not eaten dinner together. Ren had made something small for himself, even though he'd not had much of an appetite, while Mo Bao Shi had promised to have something waiting for Song in his trailer when they took a break in the evening.

Shoving a smile on his lips that he was sure appeared normal, Ren opened the door to Song's smiling face. But that smile shifted into a sigh, and Song shook his head after taking one look at Ren.

"Oh, didi," Song murmured.

"What?" Ren asked, as he stepped out of the way to allow Song into the room.

"Your acting is so much better than this," Song declared as he strolled past him, pausing only to kick off his slides. He smirked over his shoulder as Ren closed the door behind him. "Or I've just gotten that good at reading you. That was your 'worried but trying to hide it' smile."

"*Ugh*, Song laoshi." Ren shuffled into the kitchen and grabbed Song a beer. "Do you have to know me that well?"

"It comes in handy when you're trying to hide things from me," Song teased. "But I have a feeling our minds are in the same place."

Ren almost snorted. He doubted that. When it came to sex, Song was the epitome of confidence.

"The farewells today took me by surprise," Song admitted when Ren handed him the beer.

Ren flinched.

Fuck. Yep. That had been on his mind until his brain had swirled back around the whole "how to seduce Song" question that had been plaguing him for close to a month.

Song didn't miss his reaction. He lowered his beer after a quick sip and placed the bottle on the table. "That wasn't on your mind?"

Instead of sitting on the bed, Ren slid onto one of the stools at the breakfast bar, which that alone brought a lifted brow to Song's worried expression. If they weren't eating a meal, their nights were usually spent sitting or lying on the bed as they talked or watched TV.

But right now, that bed was a harsh reminder of his failures.

"No, that's been on my mind today. I'd been focused on remembering all my lines for the forest confrontation scene. I'd forgotten that it was Li Ming Tao's last day of filming. When they brought the flowers out, it was like a slap to the face." Ren scrubbed a hand over his eyes and across his face as if trying to rub away that slap. "There's going to be more of those until we're down to the last day."

"Why doesn't it feel like that's what's bothering you?" Song strolled over and gripped the bar on either side of Ren so that he was trapped. "What else is on that busy mind of yours?"

For a full second, Ren considered lying. He thought about making some silly joke and brushing off the topic. He could distract Song with something else, blame it on yet another social media post or other nonsense to deflect his attention.

But no matter how uncomfortable the topic, how embarrassed he felt, it didn't change the fact that if he avoided it, nothing was going to change.

Time was ticking away. Why was he wasting it?

"I was thinking…about…sex," Ren haltingly forced out.

A myriad of strange and unreadable emotions flashed across Song's face before it finally settled on concern. "Thinking about sex should not be a stressful endeavor. Why do you find sex stressful?"

Ren opened his mouth, but no words left him. He was locked up, trying to come up with a way to voice his fears without unloading all these unwanted emotions on Song, or worse convince Song that he wasn't worth all this insanity.

"Spit it out, Ah-Xue. Don't you dare sugarcoat shit with me. If you can't talk to me, we've got way bigger problems than sex."

"I don't know what I'm doing," Ren blurted, and it was like a dam inside of him broke. All the words came spilling out and he couldn't stop the flood. "What if I'm too vanilla and boring for you? I know that you want me to jump in and take control, but I don't know what to do. I don't know how to seduce you or what you like. And what if I do something you don't like? We've been dating a month and I feel like I should know these things, but every time we start kissing and touching, it's like my brain shorts and I can't think of anything other than how badly I want to come. And then I think about what a shitty lover I am because I should be thinking about how to please you. I don't—"

Song cut off the torrent with a kiss. He broke it off only to kiss Ren again, softer and slower. That kiss led to another and another, until all the tension seemed to flow from Ren's body. His arms naturally wrapped around Song, pulling him in between his legs so their bodies were pressed flush.

When Song ended the kiss, he dipped his head to nibble on Ren's neck. "Oh, didi. You should know that when it comes to you, I'm easy. You smile at me, and I'm seduced. When you walk across the set in the morning sun, I'm seduced. When you're irritated with me and give me that glare, I'm so very seduced."

"Song laoshi, I'm being serious," Ren grumbled.

Song lifted his face and met Ren's eyes. "Yes, that glare. So seduced," he said with a sigh that left Ren fighting a smile. "But I'm being serious, too. I've been attracted to you since the very first day you stumbled into that table reading, flustered and nervous. I took one look at you and was completely lost."

Ren snorted. "Did not. You looked at me and thought I was an idiot."

"I gazed up at you, and my first thought was that you were beautiful." Song's hands shifted to Ren's back, his fingers massaging muscles that were trying to tense up. "Didn't you think it was weird that I practically ran out of that meeting when it was over? Everything out of my mouth made me sound like a fucking idiot. I didn't want you to hate me before we even started shooting."

Ren could only stare at him. Had he really thought that? It had never crossed Ren's mind. Song had been so cool, calm, and collected. He was the star actor at ease with the world around him. Ren had been the bumbling newbie making a fool of himself.

"Ah-Xue, your problem has nothing to do with sex, and everything to do with this." Song reached up and tapped a finger on his forehead. "You're thinking way too much."

"But—"

Song silenced him with a quick kiss. "There are no buts to this. Close your eyes and think about when we've been together. Has there been a time when I wasn't turned-on and hard?"

A shudder ran through Ren as he clearly remembered the press of Song's dick against his own. No, that wasn't a problem.

"And did it seem like I had any trouble coming?"

"No," Ren whispered, trying to ignore the fact that his own dick was getting hard at those memories. The sounds of Song's cries were echoing through his brain, and his lips tingled with the phantom of past kisses. "But I don't know what you like. Or how to initiate things."

"I like you kissing me. I like your mouth on any part of my body." Song paused and pressed a kiss to the corner of Ren's mouth. "I love the idea that you are comfortable walking up to me and touching me anytime you want because you know that I belong to you and only you."

"But what if I do something you don't like?"

"Then I tell you." Song suddenly pulled away and pinned Ren with a dark glare. "Have I done anything you don't like and you not told me?"

"No! No!" He gasped, jolting so that he was now sitting up straight.

"Then why would I hide that from you?"

Okay, that made some of the fear slide out of his chest.

Song's grin returned, a little cheekier than before. "Though I doubt you could do anything that I wouldn't like."

Ren's smile returned. This man was such a perfect dream. How could he not fall hopelessly for him?

"But yes, if you really want the secret to making me lose my mind," Song started and paused. Oh, that evil look in his eyes was magical. It always succeeded in turning Ren's brain to utter mush. Song leaned in, his voice a rough whisper. "Tell me what to do."

"Like what?" Ren gasped.

"Anything."

"Kiss me," Ren commanded.

The words had barely left his lips when Song's crashed into his. The kiss was deep and hungry, sparking a fire that was quickly burning Ren up. His tongue snaked into Ren's mouth, tangled and withdrawing again. Ren threaded his fingers through Song's hair and tightened, holding his head captive as he chased after that tongue. A soft whimper lifted from Song, and it was like wine.

Ren pulled Song's head back and moaned, "My neck. Lick my neck."

Song opened his mouth across Ren's Adam's apple, licking it before placing a series of wet, openmouthed kisses up to his ear. "More. What else? Please."

That note of desperation made Ren bolder, more confident. "Get undressed."

Song retreated a step, his eyes blown wide and his puffy lips parted as if he couldn't believe Ren had said that. But he didn't get the chance to steal the words away. Song ripped his shirt off over his head. He tossed it aside and unbuttoned his shorts with fumbling fingers. He shoved both them and his underwear down.

He stood in the center of the room, his cock hard and his body trembling under Ren's naked appraisal. But Song was right. Every little command seemed to turn the man on. He was hungry for Ren, and Ren was drunk on this taste of power. He wanted to make Song feel so damn good, and if this did it, he was more than happy to play this role.

Shoving to his feet, Ren slowly closed the distance between them. He extended one hand and let his fingertips barely graze Song's chest, sliding up and across his shoulder as Ren walked behind him. When he was standing behind him, Ren wrapped his arms around Song, pulling their bodies together. Song panted and leaned into him, his ass rubbing against the hard-on in Ren's pants.

Ren pressed his face into Song's soft hair, breathing in the scent of his shampoo. "Is this what you wanted? You want me to make you mine?"

"Yes, Ah-Xue. Please. Anything you want. Just so long as I'm yours," Song panted. His hands moved back and brushed Ren's thighs but stopped short of grabbing him. Because Ren hadn't told him to.

Smiling, Ren dipped his head and bit the spot where Song's neck met his shoulder, earning a beautiful howl of pleasure, while his hands pressed to Song's chest. They ran down across tight stomach muscles, into the hollows of his slender hips, to brush over that wonderful cock.

Ren licked the tender spot. "Don't you know? You're mine already. No one is allowed to touch you like this. Every inch of you belongs to me."

A shivering sigh left Song as though a great wave of relief swept through him.

"Undress me, Ah-Wei," Ren whispered.

Song instantly turned, grabbing at Ren's shirt and lifting it over his head. The shirt fell away and Song's fingers hooked in the waistband of his pants. Song pressed hot kiss after kiss to Ren's chest, working his way across his stomach as he lowered Ren's pants. He teasingly skipped over Ren's straining dick to kiss along his hip.

Ren placed a shaking hand on Song's shoulder as he carefully stepped out of his pants, but his knees still felt like they were going to give out when Song looked up from where he kneeled and licked his lips.

"Suck it," Ren ordered in a rough voice.

A slow, evil grin spread across Song's lips and his eyes narrowed. "Suck what?"

Ren returned the smile and wrapped his fist around the base of his cock. Did he really think he wasn't going to say it? They'd come this far, right? He brushed the head against Song's perfect lips. "Suck it, Ah-Wei. Suck my dick."

That beautiful mouth opened, and Song slowly pulled him into amazing wet heat. They both moaned as Song took more and more of him with each stroke. Nothing in this world had ever felt so wonderful. Hands came up and tightly gripped his hips, fingers digging into tight muscles.

The world was spinning. His orgasm was trying to break free, but Ren clamped on it. Not yet. This was too perfect. He stared at Song's lips stretched around his dick, taking him so deep that he could touch the back of his throat. Song tipped his head slightly to watch him with those dark, fathomless eyes of hunger and need.

He wanted inside of him. He wanted Song bent over and filled with him, begging for it hard and deep.

But he needed this first.

Ren gave one shallow thrust, and Song groaned.

"Are you going to swallow for me?" Ren asked, no longer caring about shyness or embarrassment. He was so fucking close, and his dick so perfectly filled Song's mouth.

Song groaned, the vibrations from that long sound massaging his cock as his lover nodded. Ren thrust carefully, trying not to choke Song. The suction and wet heat were making his toes curl. His orgasm was demanding to be set free, and Ren didn't want to wait another second.

On a cry of sharp pleasure, he came, losing himself completely to the electric ecstasy sweeping through every nerve ending. The entire time Song licked and sucked, taking everything he had.

The moment his brain clicked on, Ren slipped free of Song's mouth. He tangled his fingers in Song's hair and pulled him up to his feet, shoving his tongue past his lover's swollen lips. Song moaned and thrust against him as Ren invaded his mouth, tasting himself.

"Oh God, Ah-Xue. I'm so close," Song whimpered. He thrust again, his body seeking the friction he needed to finally tip over the edge.

"Bed," Ren growled. He pulled Song those last steps over to the bed and pushed him onto the mattress. Ren crawled between his thighs, his eyes locked on to that hard cock leaking little clear drops of pre-cum.

"Fuck, Ah-Xue. Touch me and I'll come," Song pleaded.

He wanted to do a hell of a lot more than touch him. He might not have ever sucked a dick before, but right now everything in him was crying out to just feel Song on his tongue. To taste him, if only for a second.

Leaning his head down, Ren licked a stripe up that straining, trembling cock. Song swore loud enough that others on their floor likely heard him, but Ren couldn't bring himself to care. His tongue swirled the head, lapping up that taste of saltiness, and he wanted more. He took more of his dick into his mouth and Song cried out. Fingers grabbed his hair tight enough to cause pain. Song gave three shallow thrusts, the last one rubbing against the roof of Ren's mouth, and then he exploded.

Ren choked on the unexpected load of cum and pulled off, but he quickly gripped Song's dick and finished him with several fast, hard strokes, coating his stomach in white stripes.

"Ah-Xue," Song whispered and pulled him on top of him for a series of languid kisses that wrapped Ren up in a warm blanket of love.

When Song ended the series of kisses, he looked up at Ren

with sleepy eyes and a crooked smile. "Don't you dare doubt yourself again."

"That was okay?"

Song huffed a soft laugh. "My brain barely works now. If it gets any better, it's probably going to kill me."

Ren pulled him in even closer, wrapping his arms around him so that Song's head rested on his chest. "I just want my Ah-Wei happy."

A sound left Song as though he was purring. "I like that, too."

"I figure Song laoshi is good for everyday wear, but I could use Ah-Wei when I'm holding you in my arms."

"Perfect."

Ren closed his eyes, sinking into the feel of Song's heart beating against his body. He didn't know how much longer he was going to have this. And once the filming ended, would they ever have another chance to share a moment like this?

He didn't want to think about their dwindling time as he clung to the feeling of gratefulness that surrounded his heart. He was grateful for every second he had with Song Wei Li. He was grateful for the gift of feeling comfortable in his own skin —something Ren had known too little of before he met Song.

His lover gave him that.

Song Wei Li liked everything about him.

No, Song Wei Li celebrated everything that made Ren who he was.

He needed to fight for his Ah-Wei. There was no fucking way he was letting him go.

He just had to figure out how he was going to keep his Ah-Wei and not give up everything he'd worked so hard for.

30

REN LEAVING EARLY?
SONG WEI LI

Song sat on the edge of his bed and stared at the black box in his hand.

Was this too much?

Not enough?

Did this put pressure on Ren? It wasn't a big deal, but it somehow felt like a very big deal.

He'd never given a gift to a boyfriend before. Of course, he'd never had a boyfriend to give a gift to.

It wasn't as though he'd been searching for a gift for Ren. He'd been randomly scrolling on social media on his phone and had seen an interesting bracelet that was little more than a thin red string, which sparked him to seek other variations of that.

He thought maybe they could get similar bracelets that could be easily hidden under the cuffs of their shirts or overlooked with a mix of other bracelets or a watch. Something that might be missed by fans, but they'd know they were both wearing something similar.

He was well aware of the fact that Ren couldn't wear anything he gave him on a regular basis. For the most part, they were both walking advertisements when they were in public. Fans took apart every article of clothing for close examination. They'd definitely notice something if they were both wearing it. But maybe it could be occasionally hidden or worn when they were traveling. Or even if it was just something that was worn while they were home alone, a reminder of what they had.

And that was what it came down to.

Song didn't want to be forgotten. When the miles separated them, he wanted something to remind Ren that he still existed, of the time they spent together. He wanted his Ah-Xue to look at it and know that his Ah-Wei was thinking of him too.

Because when the day came, Ren wouldn't want to forget about what they had, right?

No. Absolutely not.

He could do this. Ren was going to like it.

Song stood, shoved the box into the pocket of his shorts, and pushed his feet into a pair of slides. He snatched up his phone and room key before crossing the hall to Ren's. He lifted his hand to knock, but the muffled sound of his lover shouting halted him at the last second.

Ren shouting?

In the months they'd known each other, he'd heard Ren lose his temper only once, and that was when they'd gotten into an argument over Chen Junjie.

"I don't give a damn what they want! You call them and fix this!" Ren's voice reached through the door. Song took a step back, debating whether to return to his room or knock. Ren needed his privacy, but he was afraid that his lover needed his support more than he needed privacy.

"Then cancel the contract," Ren snapped after a lengthy silence. "I won't do the part. They knew when they approached me what the shoot schedule for *Legend* was, and they agreed to the terms. They're breaking the deal. If they can't respect me and my time, I won't work with them. Fix this, Zhou-jie. I'm not budging on this."

Song stood paralyzed in the hall. It felt as if someone had doused him with cold water. What the hell was going on? He knew that Ren was scheduled to start filming on another show as soon as he was done filming *Legend*. Were they trying to move his schedule around? Were they trying to steal him away sooner?

It wasn't unheard of. Shooting schedules moved all the time. It was just expected that an actor would be flexible and simply be ready to go at a moment's notice.

Song's indecision was overridden when he heard the crash of breaking glass from inside Ren's room. He lurched forward and banged on the door.

"Didi! Are you all right? Didi, let me in!" he called.

The door ripped open a second later, revealing a shirtless Ren with glassy eyes and a flushed face. The man somehow managed to look lost and pissed all at the same time.

"Song?"

"I heard shouting and something break. Are you okay?"

"No, I'm not," Ren snarled, to his shock. Song had honestly expected him to deny anything was wrong and try to hide it from him. It could only mean that he was truly rattled by what had happened.

Song snagged both of Ren's wrists and pulled, turning his hands over to check for injuries.

"No, not physically. I feel like I'm going to be sick, though." Ren stepped back, forcing Song to release him as he entered the room while he shut the door behind him.

"What's going on? What broke?"

"Fuck." Ren sighed and lurched toward the kitchen. "I was so distracted and angry. I grabbed a glass bottle of juice and tried to put it on the counter, but I missed and hit the edge. It fell and smashed on the floor. It's a fucking mess. I need to clean it—"

Song seized him as he tried to enter the kitchen and steered him instead to the stools at the breakfast bar. "You need to sit, calm down, and tell me what's going on. I'll clean."

For about a heartbeat, it looked as if Ren was going to argue with him, but the man flopped onto the stool after a moment's hesitation. He propped his elbows on the bar and dropped his forehead into his hands.

Song moved into the kitchen to find red juice quickly spreading across the tile floor mixed with chunks of glass. He carefully stepped around it to the small closet that held the cleaning implements. He grabbed the mop and started sopping up the juice.

"What happened? Was that your manager you were talking to?"

"Yes." Ren's voice had become soft and dull, as if all the angry life had been drained out of him. "She called to say that the producer of the next show I'm supposed to work on wants me on set a week earlier than we previously agreed. Apparently, Zhou Yuying has already talked to Sun Jing and Yang Lan Fan about rearranging some of the shooting schedule so I can leave early."

Song stopped mopping and leaned his weight on it just to remain upright when it felt like the world was going dark.

Ren leaving early?

No. No. No. No.

They still had twenty-six days left.

If Ren left a full week early, that meant they would have only nineteen days.

No! That wasn't enough time.

"I refused to do it. I told her there's no fucking way I'm leaving early. They are disrespecting me and my schedule. They're disrespecting the producer and entire crew of *Legend*. I'd rather not do the fucking show than leave early." Ren lifted enormous tear-filled brown eyes to Song. "I can't leave you early."

Song leaned the mop on the stove and stepped over the mess that remained to round the counter. Ren was on his feet by the time Song reached him, pulling him tightly into his arms.

"I can't leave before you," Ren whispered into his neck. "I have to stay here until the very last moment just so I know we spent as much time as possible together."

"It's okay. It's okay," Song repeated while trying to get a handle on his own rising panic. "We have time. Your manager will fix this."

"What if she can't? I don't want to get a reputation for being difficult to work with. No one will hire me."

Song huffed out a ragged laugh and pressed kisses to Ren's bare shoulder. "Didi, people are going to be fighting to hire you the moment they see your Zhao Gang. This little thing will be forgotten in an instant."

"But what if it's not? What if…"

Pulling back so he could look Ren in the eyes, Song lifted a hand to wipe a tear that had slipped free and slid down his lover's pale cheek. Those large eyes had been his weakness since the very first day, but it had taken him weeks to realize it was because they reflected Ren's beautiful, pure heart. How could he not love that?

"Let's play worst-case scenario. It can't be fixed and you're locked in a contract. You have to leave early," Song said in as firm a voice as he could muster. "We would still have almost three weeks. We make the most of that time, and then we plan. This does not end with filming."

Ren gave a shaky nod, but he didn't appear convinced.

"Say it," Song demanded. "Say it's not going to end when filming finishes."

Ren grabbed him and pulled him in so that their foreheads

were pressed together. "This doesn't end with filming. I swear. I love you, Song Wei Li. I will never stop loving you."

"I love you, too," Song replied. His voice ragged and breathless as he dragged Ren those last few inches for a desperate kiss. He didn't want to lose that final week, but they both needed to remember that this wasn't over just because *Legend* stopped filming. This was love. Forever. He was not letting Ren An Xue go.

After a few moments, Song felt strong enough to release his tight hold on the man and settle him on the stool. He could feel Ren's eyes on him as he returned to the kitchen and finished cleaning up the mess. When the mop was put away, he got them both some water and ushered Ren over to the bed for some cuddles.

But when Ren sat, he looked utterly drained. There were dark circles under his eyes, and his entire body was slumped as if he didn't have the energy to remain upright another second.

"Would you rather I leave so you can get some actual sleep?"

His lover released a soundless laugh that made his body sort of jerk. "I'd rather you never leave my sight again."

Somehow those words reminded him of the box in his pocket. How had he forgotten about that? Would that bring a smile to his lips? Or would it simply stress Ren out more because it was a reminder that they'd be separated too soon?

Song dropped his hand to the pocket, one finger touching the corner of the box as he weighed his options. He only wanted Ren to feel better. Maybe he should save it for later.

"What's wrong? What's in your pocket?" Ren asked.

Shit! He'd taken too long to think.

"Oh…ummm…I got you something. Just a little thing—"

"What?" Ren gasped. His eyes went wide, and it was like watching new life flow into his nearly limp body. "What is it?"

The corner of Song's mouth tilted up. He'd never expected to see such a reaction from Ren. Both of them received gifts and tokens from fans all the time. There were also things they got from companies they signed with to be representatives. Ren always showed reserved but respectful gratitude.

But this was pure giddy excitement.

"It's something small. I wasn't sure if I should give it to you. I've never gotten a boyfriend a gift before," Song said, intentionally drawing out the moment.

Ren thrust out both hands and made a grabbing motion. "Give it. You got it for me. You have to give it over. You can't tease me like this, Song laoshi!"

He didn't know how it was possible, but Ren was making him both ridiculously excited and nervous at the same time. His heart was racing and his palms were sweating.

"Okay, but make room on the bed for me too."

Ren shifted over while Song pulled the flat black box out of his pocket and sat. Ren surprised him by turning so that one of his long legs was behind Song while his other was tossed across his lap, completely wrapping him up. Yes, this was perfect.

With a tremble in his hand, he gave Ren the box.

His lover's eyes flashed up to his face for a second and then down to the box as he lifted the lid. Resting inside on a pad of white cotton were two bracelets—one with a red leather cord and the other black. In the center of the cord was a silver device almost like a tiny watch. The one on the red cord had an ocean wave inscribed on it while the black one was a mountain peak.

"They're beautiful," Ren whispered, picking up the red cord bracelet.

"It's more than a bracelet. You can add an app to your phone and sync it."

Ren's eyes jumped to his face. "What?"

"One for you and one for me. With just a touch on yours, you can make the one I wear light up or vibrate. A private coded message that only we know. A light or pulse message that means I love you or I miss you." Song punctuated each message with a slow kiss. "No matter where we are in the world, we can send that message."

"And the wave and mountain?"

"Because our love is as endless as the ocean and as eternal as the mountains."

"I love it. I love it so much!" Ren wrapped his arms around him, kissing him several times.

"Not too cheesy?" Song asked between kisses.

Ren tossed his head and laughed. "Fuck, it is so cheesy, but it is also absolutely perfect. I love your cheese."

They unwrapped enough to put the bracelets on each other and get them synced to the new apps on their phones. The rest of the night was spent cuddled in bed, sending vibrations back and forth. Song always knew before the vibrations hit his wrist, though, because Ren would start giggling uncontrollably.

Yes, he knew that tomorrow when they left for the set, they'd both have to remove their bracelets. There was no point in taking them when they'd only have to remove them for the shoot. It was also safer for now if people didn't notice them both wearing them while they were together.

But when they returned to the privacy of their rooms, they would go on. The hiding sucked. Pretending Ren An Xue wasn't his entire world sucked.

But it helped to know that there was a red corded bracelet[1] in Ren's possession that marked him as Song Wei Li's and no one could ever steal that from him.

He just had to figure out how to bring Ren even deeper into his life.

31

THE DOUBLE DATE
REN AN XUE

Ren walked beside Song as they headed to the next shoot location, a nice breeze winding through the trees to stir their long wigs. They'd both shed their robes so they could better enjoy the wind that was helping to take the worst of the edge off the heat. It was still morning, but the air was growing stifling already and promised to get worse as the day wore on. Sweat was trickling down the back of his neck and gathering in his light T-shirt.

Beside him, Song was humming a random melody, seeming lost in his own little world. Ren didn't recognize the tune. He wasn't sure if it was something he'd simply never heard before or if Song was making it up as they strolled along. Didn't matter. He enjoyed the sound of Song's voice.

Hua Jun Bai was a couple of steps behind him, chatting with his assistant. His voice was also a soothing bit of white noise. They'd entered their fourth month of shooting, and everything about it had become a comfortable routine. He looked forward to seeing the familiar faces each day of both his fellow actors and the members of the crew. Hengdian felt like a second home.

Except in a matter of weeks, he'd be leaving his home.

Yes, his manager had straightened his schedule out and he wasn't leaving early, but the clock was still ticking away. The time he had left with Song here was growing short, and they had yet to tackle the biggest question of all: what was next for them?

How in the world were they supposed to continue dating if they couldn't see each other?

What were holidays and birthdays like?

What did a date even look like for them?

It felt like it was the one subject they were trying to avoid every night when they were closed away from the world in either his room or Song's. It didn't take a genius to figure out why. Neither one of them had an answer that was good.

Maybe it was time to get on a call with Zhu Fang or Guo Zi. Ask them how they'd managed for so long. At the very least, find out what their idea of normal was.

A long, heavy sigh left his lips, and to his surprise, Song turned his head and lifted a questioning eyebrow at him. Ren could only smile. He'd been sure Song wasn't paying the tiniest bit of attention to him—but then, his lover always seemed to know what he was thinking or feeling.

Ren opened his mouth to reassure him that everything was fine when a flash on the screen of the phone in his hand caught his attention.

"Oh!" He quickly showed the display to Song. His eyes also widened at the name.

Guo Zi.

"Hey! Everything okay?" Ren asked the second he answered the call.

Guo Zi's pleasant laughter filled the line. "I know I promised to call when Fang drove me crazy, but this isn't one of those. Everything is good. How's filming? You're almost done, right?"

"Good. Busy. About three more weeks. They're putting the finishing touches on the sets for the studio scenes we're scheduled to do," Ren replied.

"That's good. Those days are always better."

Ren hummed. "Air conditioning."

Guo Zi chuckled. "Exactly!" He cleared his throat and started again. "Anyway, I know I can't keep you. I was wondering if you've got dinner plans for tonight."

"No. Well, just my usual," Ren murmured, assuming Guo Zi could guess that his usual plans were dinner with Song in his room. "Are you here? I thought you finished filming weeks ago."

"Oh, no. I'm back in Shanghai. Fang and I have a rare night together and we were interested in a sort of dinner double date. What time are you done tonight? The four of us could jump on a video call and pretend we're in a restaurant like normal people having dinner together."

"Umm...I think the shoot will be done before six. This is a brilliant idea. I'd love to." Ren paused to glance over at Song, who was staring straight ahead as they walked, but there was a new tension in his shoulders that convinced Ren that the man was hanging on to every word that he could hear. "We're walking to the next location at the moment, but he's right here with me. You want to pitch your idea to him?"

Guo Zi's laugh was a little lower and maybe a touch evil. "Surrounded, aren't you?"

"Completely." Ren sighed. Most of the time it didn't bother him too much, but there was a tingle of irritation that pricked along his skin whenever he took a call or was responding to texts that others were always trying to sneak a step closer to get a peek at his private business.

"Give Song the phone. I'll fill him in."

Ren nudged Song, who grinned broadly at him. "He wants to talk to you."

Song accepted the phone and warmly greeted Guo Zi. Ren listened to the other half of the conversation, marveling at how Song always managed to be friendly while at the same time not say anything that would give away what Guo Zi was suggesting.

A minute later, Song ended the call and handed the phone to Ren with a smile. Nothing else. Everyone around them who'd been hanging on their half of the call was now dying to know what the plans were, who had called. But Song gave nothing away.

There was just that smile, and then he went back to singing his song.

Ren's heart bounced and he fought his own laugh. They were having dinner with Zhu Fang and Guo Zi.

WHILE THE IDEA OF A DINNER DATE SOUNDED BRILLIANT, REN managed to spend the rest of the day in a state of low-key panic.

What was he supposed to cook? It wasn't like he had hours to properly prepare a meal worthy of their first date. There was no time to properly marinate any meat. He had no tare or base ready for ramen or a soup. That took hours to prepare.

At lunchtime, Song proved that he knew exactly where Ren's mind was at and suggested they simply order something from a restaurant.

Ren might have lost his temper. He might have shouted questions about Song's sanity and threatened to never cook for him again.

Sadly, their own lunch was little more than salads as Ren spent most of it texting with his assistant, providing her with a ridiculously long shopping list. He didn't know what she'd be able to find, and he needed to have as many alternatives on hand on the chance that he had to improvise.

He gave Song one job: dessert.

Ren didn't care what it was or how he procured it. Dessert was the least of his concerns.

When the shooting day was over, Ren raced through offloading his costume and wig, catching the first ride back to the residence while chatting with his assistant about what she'd managed to get.

Turned out, she got a lot of food. Pretty much everything on his list. At least he and Song were going to be eating some very good meals for a while.

Unfortunately, he was short on time.

When Song arrived, he was finishing up the Thai green curry with chicken and sweet potatoes, minced chicken in lettuce, and pork and shrimp dumplings.

His lover sucked in a deep breath, taking in all the delicious smells, and wrapped his arms tightly around Ren's waist from behind. "Oh God, please don't ever leave me," he moaned between Ren's shoulder blades.

"Song laoshi, you're being ridiculous."

"I'm not. The smell is creeping down the hall and I saw people sticking their heads out, wondering if you're starting a restaurant. They would *pay* you to cook for them." Song pressed a kiss to the side of Ren's neck, sending a shiver along his spine. "I only have to sell my body to get access to your cooking."

"I think I'm getting the better end of the deal."

"That's debatable, but if you're happy, that's all that matters to me." Song released him and smirked.

"Did you bring your laptop and dessert?"

Song held up the backpack that had been slung over one shoulder and unzipped it. He pulled out a box and handed it over to Ren, who burst into laughter. Dessert was an exquisite collection of macarons arranged in a rainbow.

"Love it?" Song asked, practically bouncing on the balls of his feet.

"I do. It's perfect." He leaned forward and snapped a quick kiss before placing the box on the counter. "Why don't you set up the laptop? It's almost time. I need to change shirts; then I can begin plating everything."

Ren hurried to his closet, grabbed the black collared shirt he'd mentally selected earlier, and darted into the bathroom. It took only a few minutes to change and freshen up his cologne. He frowned at his hair as he ran his fingers through it. There wasn't much he could do there without washing it and starting from scratch. He wished he could look his very best for his date.

Song had shown up in a beautiful deep-purple button-down shirt and nice jeans. His bangs perfectly framed his handsome face. His hair had grown so long during filming that he'd taken to pinning chunks of it back in the evening, as if he couldn't completely shed Tian Xiuying's influence with his elegant topknot.

Ren might not have Zhao Gang's grace and poise, but he could at least make sure his man was taken care of.

When he left the bathroom, Song was sitting on the floor with the laptop on the table in front of him. He glanced over his shoulder, and a slow smile spread across his face.

"Ah-Xue, I don't think it's a good idea to seduce me before dinner. Zhu and Guo will be pissed if we stand them up," Song teased.

"Then I promise to hold off and seduce you *after* dinner."

Song pumped his fist into the air and turned to the laptop with a goofy grin on his face.

Sure, he'd spent a few years as a successful model. He knew he was attractive. He'd gone through all the training, knew exactly how to hold his body or tilt his head to maximize his attractiveness from various angles. But none of that meant anything when Song looked up at him. It was as though Song was staring straight past his face, eyes, and abs to gaze straight into his soul. That was what Song loved, and it left Ren breathless.

Later.
Food first.
Sexy time after.

While Ren was plating all their food, making sure it was as artfully arranged, he heard Fang's voice fill the room followed by Song's laugh.

"Ren An Xue, are you making my life hell? Did you cook?" Guo Zi suddenly called out.

Ren grabbed the small salads he'd tossed together, moved into the main room, and kneeled next to Song. The laptop had been pushed the farthest edge of the table so they could both be picked up on the camera. The screen was filled with comfortable and casual Zhu Fang and Guo Zi.

"I told him that we could order out, but those words nearly cost me my life," Song said.

"This felt special. It was our first meal together with others on a sort of date. I thought it was only appropriate that I cook," Ren added.

Zhu Fang elbowed Guo Zi. "See? Special."

"You could have cooked," Guo Zi pointed out.

"The last time I tried that, the fire department had to be called." Zhu Fang turned his attention to the screen. "They even dressed up. Both are so handsome and pretty."

Guo Zi narrowed his eyes at his boyfriend. "Are you saying that you're going to leave me and join them in a threesome?"

Song, unfortunately, had been taking a drink of water, which ended up sprayed across the laptop. Ren was lost to giggles as he alternated between patting Song on the back and wiping off the computer screen.

That was pretty much the entire dinner. Zhu Fang ooohed

over the food Ren made and tormented poor Guo Zi. Not that Guo Zi needed anyone's pity. He was more than capable of putting Zhu Fang in his place with a couple of sharp comments. It was a small miracle that none of them managed to choke to death over all the laughing they were doing.

Zhu Fang entertained them with crazy stories of things that happened while filming *Frozen River*. Many embarrassed Guo Zi, but he managed to get his digs in. Song added a few of his own stories, though Ren was grateful they were a mix of embarrassing stories for the both of them. He was also ridiculously pleased that Song bragged over the fact that he'd relearned to play the flute for one small scene.

It was only after dinner was completed and they were lingering over beers that they managed to shift to somewhat serious conversation.

"Do you mind if I ask how long you've been dating?" Ren inquired.

He was not expecting to see both Guo Zi and Zhu Fang look at each other with wide, dumbfounded eyes.

"Wow. Is it really that hard of a question?" Song added.

"Well," Zhu Fang started and then paused. He shoved the black baseball cap he'd been wearing off and rubbed his hair. His face was framed with a pair of black-rimmed glasses that made him appear both older and more serious. *Lies. All of it lies.* "Things didn't go all that smoothly for us."

"And why is that?" Guo Zi prompted.

Zhu Fang leaned toward the camera and grinned. "Because I'm a giant idiot." When he settled against the cushions, Guo Zi draped an arm across his chest and rested his head on Zhu Fang's shoulder, a bliss-filled smile spreading across his pink lips. "But cumulatively, it's probably been around a year. Definitely less than two. There are days it feels like it's been forever, though."

"And others when it feels like five minutes," Guo Zi finished.

"I'm guessing it's hard to find time to be together like this," Ren murmured.

The mood of the evening crashed with that comment, and Ren wished he hadn't said that. He had been enjoying the laughter and silly stories. He loved the camaraderie they'd fallen into so quickly. But when he looked at Guo Zi and Zhu Fang, he wanted them to also be his future with Song. He needed to know what to expect and how to prepare for it.

"It is," Guo Zi admitted on a sigh. Zhu Fang turned his head and pressed a kiss to the top of his boyfriend's head. It was the first time all evening they'd seen him quiet and serious. "We're lucky if we have two nights like this in an entire month, and just having this takes a lot of planning."

"We try to video chat every night," Zhu Fang said. "But with concerts, and sometimes we're on different sides of the globe, it can't be done."

"But there are texts and lots of pictures being sent back and forth." Guo Zi giggled. "Fang Fang takes the worst pictures. Even with the best phone, everything is out of focus or cut off."

Zhu Fang snorted. "Yeah, because I can never stop to take the picture. I have to keep moving or the fans will catch me."

"Treasure the time you can find together," Guo Zi murmured.

"Song mentioned that you went on vacation together to Paris."

Both immediately lit up. Zhu Fang pulled out his phone and started showing off various pictures of Guo Zi or him in places around the French capital. Yes, some of them were a little out of focus, but they looked like they had a great time and were able to be out in public together.

"It was shorter than either of us would have liked," Guo Zi admitted. "I was there for work for the first couple of days. Zhu Fang arrived after my assistant flew home. We had about three days there together, and then I flew home first. He followed a day later."

Zhu Fang leaned forward to stare directly into the camera. "But if you want to vacation together, go to a small town in America. Rent a house. That's our next plan. A beach house in America. No one is going to recognize us. We can hang out in restaurants or go shopping and sightseeing."

"Paris was great, but it was crowded with people from all over the world. Even wearing masks, you get paranoid about being recognized."

A hand inched over and covered Ren's. He smiled at Song as he threaded their fingers together and lifted their joined hands to his lips. "We'll be okay."

A lump formed in his throat and Ren nodded. They would. They would find a way to make it all work. Song's smile was worth it. His love, joy, and support were worth it.

"We suggest combining your schedules so you can more easily see when you have openings," Guo Zi suggested.

"You'll also more easily remember why your partner isn't replying to your texts. He's not *ignoring you*." Zhu Fang pressed his forehead against Guo Zi's, smashing their noses together. "He just had a late rehearsal and fell asleep on the couch the second he got to the hotel."

"I'm sorry, Fang Fang. I missed you," Guo Zi murmured, softly kissing him.

"It's okay, gege," Zhu Fang whispered. The man looked like he was melting into a pool of goo right before their eyes.

Song made a sound that was somewhere between clearing his throat and covering a laugh. "Well, I think we're going to call it a night. We'll have to arrange another dinner."

Both of the men on the computer grinned at them, still cuddled together.

"Yes. Maybe Song could cook next time and Ren can take it easy," Guo Zi teased.

"Or we can try to get together when we happen to all be in Shanghai at the same time," Zhu Fang suggested.

Ren nearly laughed at the idea, but he couldn't deny the appeal. It did sound like a lovely dream. The four of them sitting in Guo Zi's or Zhu Fang's apartment as they shared a meal and too much laughter.

The call ended, and they both rose to clean up the plates. Ren washed and Song dried without needing to be asked. His lover put things away and wiped down counters. They didn't say a word, but Ren couldn't escape the warm, comfortable feeling that grew in his chest.

Yes, there was a part of him that wanted this all the time, but the realist in him was quick to point out that he didn't even have this when he'd been single. Too often, he was traveling from one location to the other either for photo shoots, filming shows, or other projects. He kept a tiny, barren apartment—not because he couldn't afford more, but because he was never there.

And in truth, he loved his life. It was crazy, hectic, and utterly unpredictable, but he was meeting interesting people, doing new things, and making good money that would support him and his parents.

It was only that he'd never expected to find someone like Song.

A hand slid slowly up his spine and wrapped around the back of his neck, massaging tense muscles. Song pressed a kiss to the bottom of his jaw, and Ren sighed as tension automatically flowed out of his body.

"Are you worried?" Song whispered.

Ren smirked at him. "Would you believe me if I said I wasn't?"

"Not even for a second."

Ren turned, leaning against the sink. He spread his legs and pulled his lover between them, just needing to hold him. Neither of them knew what was going to happen when they left Hengdian in a few weeks and returned to their normal lives.

But Ren was starting to feel like he needed to answer one important question: Would he be willing to give it all up for Song?

32

YOU'LL DESTROY HIS CAREER
SONG WEI LI

THERE WAS ONE GOOD THING ABOUT SHOOTING THIS SCENE—at least he wasn't hot.

Song and Ren stood several yards away from the rocky shore of a murky lake. The cool water was lapping at their waists and swirling the bottom half of their robes around their legs. Water was soaked into their top half already and weighed down their wigs.

But at least they weren't hot.

This was essentially their last scene shot in an outdoor location. Tomorrow and for the next two weeks, they'd be on a sound stage with pre-built scenery and a shit-ton of green screens. The part where they would be chased to the edge of the waterfall and "jump" would be shot on the sound stage. Today, they just needed to get the section of the scene where they waded out of the water and collapsed on the shore.

They were currently waiting for the last of the cameras to be set up for the series of shots. He glanced over at Ren to see the man flash him a sickly, uneven smile.

Everything within Song demanded that he make a joke or a quip that would even out the smile and bring actual joy to

Ren's wide eyes, but he shoved aside the urge. He knew that his lover was getting into the proper mindset for the scene that was supposed to end very tragically.

It didn't help Ren to try to make him happy. His costar was trying to dredge up every shred of pain and fear that squatted in his heart.

Song ached for him, but he kept his mouth shut. He wasn't going to do anything that would force them to shoot this scene more than necessary.

"Ready?" Sun shouted from the shore.

"Hurry it up! I'm starting to dry!" Song called to him. He had no desire to dunk himself yet again in this filthy water.

One of the assistant directors counted down and Ren's hand clamped on to Song's right forearm.

"Action!"

Together, Song and Ren began trudging out of the water, leaning heavily on each other and stumbling over the hidden rocks on the lake floor. That part at least didn't demand much acting on their part. More than once they both fell face-first into the water, but they were always there to catch each other.

They moved slowly, panting heavily as if they had outrun an army and nearly jumped to their deaths. The freaking swim in these long, water-sodden robes wouldn't have been an easy task either. Song was inwardly grateful that Sun hadn't demanded a swimming shot because it was likely one or both of them would have drowned.

As they reached the shore, all but their feet out of the water, Song collapsed first. He rolled onto his back, his wet bangs plastered to his temples while water slipped along his face to glisten in the bright afternoon sunlight. His breathing was ragged, and it wasn't all acting. The walk through the water hadn't been easy.

Zhao Gang dropped to the ground right next to him on his stomach. Tian Xiuying tipped his head to the side to gaze at his companion, a half smile on his lips. Zhao Gang was exhausted, but so very beautiful in his sodden black robes and sleek wet hair. Even tired to his very soul, the man looked powerful, as if he could still push to his feet and take on the entire army alone.

After a couple of seconds, Zhao Gang lifted his head and stared at Tian Xiuying. Their eyes met and held. A wide grin spread on Zhao Gang's mouth and Song suddenly remembered what Ren had said that night on the rooftop. This was the perfect scene for their first kiss.

He understood it now.

It was more than the months they'd spent together running and fighting. It was more than the betrayal they'd both suffered and the lies they'd told each other.

This moment was where they realized they trusted each other completely. Zhao Gang fell in love with his soul mate much earlier, but this was when Tian Xiuying gazed at his soul mate and realized that he loved this man with all of his being. They'd just jumped off a waterfall, willing to die together rather than risk being separated.

They'd escaped and Tian Xiuying was beginning to hope that they could have a life together.

Tian Xiuying poured all his love for Zhao Gang into that look, inwardly praying his soul mate could understand what he felt when he had no words.

The smile that brightened Zhao Gang's face made Tian's breath catch. He saw. He understood.

"All right, Tian. Now."

Sun's soft direction was a knife to Song's heart. He didn't want to do this part. Not to his Ren. But there was no choice.

Tian's eyes fluttered shut, and his entire body went limp as if he'd passed out.

"Ah-Ying?" Zhao Gang demanded, gently at first.

Tian didn't move.

Song fought every instinct to open his eyes as he listened to Ren shove upright and scramble across the rocks. Fingers were pressed to a pulse point. A shaking hand cupped his cheek. Zhao Gang was shouting his name. Each time the sound grew more fractured and desperate until it was Ren's soul screaming his name in between sobs.

Ren's cries were shredding Song's heart. His throat tightened and burned. A tear slipped from the corner of Song's eye, and he prayed that the camera wouldn't pick it up because he couldn't make Ren do this again.

Where the fuck was Sun? Why wasn't he ending this torture? He had his shot!

"Cut! Cut! We got it! Perfect!" Sun was suddenly bellowing.

Song's eyes snapped open and his heart stopped to see the pure anguish twisting up Ren's handsome face. Tears streamed down his flushed cheeks, and his black hair was clinging to him like poisonous tentacles.

Song reached for him, grabbing at his arms to pull him into a tight hug. He needed to bring his lover back from this emotional nightmare, to reassure him that everything was just fine. He could let all these ugly emotions go.

But two members of the crew were already hoisting Ren to his feet and moving him several feet away from Song. Ren didn't get far before he collapsed to his knees, his broken sobs echoing across the frighteningly silent set.

Song was trying to shove to his own feet to go after him, but other hands were gripping him and moving him in the opposite direction.

"What the fuck?" he snarled. He twisted in the strong arms, trying to break free, but they kept moving him farther up the bank.

"Don't."

Song looked up to find that it was Hua Jun Bai holding his arm in a death grip, his expression frighteningly serious.

As he was about to demand what he was doing, Hua turned his attention to Sun. "You're done with him?"

"Yeah, go!" Sun immediately shouted, waving his arm at them.

"No!" Song roared. He tried to dig in his heels, but they were off the rocks and passing through grass. The wet soles of his stupid shoes were sliding, keeping him from getting any traction. "Didi needs me! I have to go back! Let me fucking go! Didi!"

"Stop it! You'll destroy his career," Hua snarled in a low voice.

That at least stomped on the panic that was trying to control Song's every action and got him to stop fighting Hua. Song blinked and glanced around at the scores of crew members watching him while Hua quickly escorted him to a waiting golf cart that would take him to his trailer.

"Wait! I can't leave," Song argued, but he didn't try to physically fight him.

"Yes. Ren arranged all of this. I'm to take you to your trailer. Ma Daiyu and Ren's assistant are taking care of him. They will talk him down and get him to his trailer, I promise. Ren arranged everything," Hua explained in a calm, soothing tone.

Song's brain swirled with fragmented thoughts, while his stomach churned. His head ached and he felt like he was going to be sick. Yes, away from all these people and their cameras was best. But Ren...

"You're sure?" he whispered.

"I am. Ma and that assistant already have him in hand. Sun's hovering, too. The assistant director is getting rid of people. He'll be okay."

With a nod, Song climbed onto one of the open seats at the back of the cart while Hua took the other one. The second they were in place, the driver had them bumbling along the dirt road toward signs of civilization, putting more distance between them and the staring crowd.

"I don't understand. You said Ren arranged this…" Song started, trying to get his brain to move past the painful memory of Ren's broken heart and painful sobs.

Hua shrugged his extremely broad shoulders, a weak smile lifting one corner of his mouth. "He knew what would happen with that scene. He'd lose it, and you'd immediately try to comfort him." Hua leaned closer and dropped his voice, though Song doubted the driver could hear him over the cart moving onto gravel. "You'd hold him and kiss away all his tears. Ren wouldn't be able to stop you. And no matter how well-meaning, you'd both destroy your careers in a fucking heartbeat. Even if it wasn't captured on a BTS camera, the story would get out."

"Fuck." Song sighed heavily. He flopped against the hard seat and scrubbed a hand over his face. Hua was right. It had been the only thing in his mind. His body had been operating purely on instinct and it had screamed for Ren.

His soul mate.

"Ren talked to me yesterday," Hua continued, his expression softening. "Asked me to get you out of there the second the scene was over to protect you both. He asked Ma to be on the set today so she could help him."

Song could only shake his head. He thought he'd spotted Ma Daiyu out in the crowd waiting for the scene to start, but he'd convinced himself that he was mistaken. Ma had finished her scene earlier in the day. She had no reason to travel to this location when she was done until tomorrow.

But she did it for Ren.

"I was there when he shot that 'Tian Xiuying's dying scene.' You were out of town for it." Hua gave a dismissive wave of his hand. "He was amazing with that scene, but yeah, he has a lot of trouble coming back down after some of those heavier emotions. Ma was there to help him. I'd say he's in danger of burning himself out that way, but I have a feeling a lot of that heaviness is tied to one person in particular. He won't have the same problem when he moves to other projects."

Song grunted. There was nothing he could say. Hua was probably right.

"I've looked over the script. You've got two scenes like this. No…shit. That alternate ending. Three scenes. I know I'm on set for at least two of them. Do you want me to hang out?"

It was on the tip of his tongue to say that it wasn't necessary, but he'd been thinking only of himself. Two of those scenes Hua was talking about were Zhao Gang "death" scenes where it was Tian Xiuying doing the desperate screaming. Song had done a couple of similar scenes in other shows and hadn't had trouble reining in his emotions.

But that was before Ren.

Even if he could handle himself, there was no telling how such scenes would impact Ren. He was just as liable to go running up to Song to comfort him, destroying all of today's careful planning.

"Yeah, if you don't mind. I'd appreciate it if you could keep an eye on Ren for me on those days," Song replied in a low, ragged voice.

"No problem."

When they reached Song's trailer, he fully expected Hua to wave good-bye and mosey on to his own so he could finish changing into his own street clothes. Right now, he was down to a T-shirt, hanfu pants, and costume shoes from his scene earlier in the day. But Hua followed him straight into his trailer.

"I'm okay. I'm thinking clearly. I don't need a babysitter," Song muttered as he pulled off his still sodden robes.

"The baby doesn't get to dismiss the sitter," Hua declared as he plopped on the couch, his hands neatly folded on his stomach. "I was hired by Ren, and he asked me to stick with you until you're at the residence."

Song narrowed his eyes on the man. "And you're doing all this out of the kindness of your heart?"

"Of course." Hua paused, his smile growing. "Plus, lunch." Song groaned loudly and Hua laughed. Asshole. Ren could talk anyone into anything with the promise of a free meal.

"Go shower! You smell like dead fish. I'm not going anywhere."

Song flipped the man off, which earned him more laughter as he stomped to the small bedroom. He stripped out of his wet clothes and wig and wrapped a towel around his waist so he could slip into the bathroom. He'd text Bao Shi later to take his costume and wig to wardrobe. God only knew if they could save any of it after it had soaked in that lake.

The brief hot shower managed to clear his head and fill it with dark thoughts. Yes, the scene of Tian Xiuying's near death brought up a lot of false, ugly emotions, but it was the real-life scene afterward that was still destroying Song nearly half an hour later.

They'd been separated for "their own good."

Something as simple as holding Ren, comforting him, would have destroyed their careers. The world wasn't allowed to see them for what they truly were—two men deeply in love with each other.

And what about after this TV shoot was over?

What if one of them were in an accident or sick and had to be rushed to the hospital? It wasn't like Song would be allowed to see him. He'd never have any rights over how his lover was treated. Was he going to be stuck on the outside, sending in trusted emissaries to gather intelligence and convey his feelings until they could steal a secret second?

This was bullshit.

Fucking bullshit.

But what was the alternative? Saying good-bye to Ren An Xue forever?

It might be the best thing when it came to their careers, but what was the point if the idea of never seeing his Ah-Xue left him wanting to die?

33

CAN I HAVE YOU?
REN AN XUE

HE WAS A FUCKING MESS. AGAIN.

He wasn't entirely sure how Ma Daiyu and Wu Dong Mei managed to get him to his trailer. There might have been others involved. He wasn't positive.

The first clear thought in his head didn't appear until he saw Hua Jun Bai's text that Song was in his trailer and okay.

Good. Song was okay.

Everything was going to be okay.

Yes, there were probably stories already circulating that he was a complete basket case. Just another temperamental actor who couldn't pull his shit together.

But he could accept it. It was better than being labeled other things in this world. This label meant that he could keep his job. That his life wasn't going to be threatened. That the lives of his parents weren't going to be the focus of cyber violence and harassment.

After fumbling through a shower and getting dressed, he handed his filthy clothes and wig off to his assistant to take to wardrobe. Sitting alone on the floor of his trailer, he dug through the backpack he'd brought with him, his fingers desperately searching for the red-corded bracelet Song had given him.

The second he slipped it over his hand and tightened it, he felt like he could breathe again.

He blinked away tears so he could stare at the single ocean wave curl, loving that Song had given him something so very precious. Biting his lower lip, he pressed the button and sent the coded message of three short pulses.

I love you.

He waited, telling himself that Song probably wasn't in his room yet. He'd probably left his bracelet there for safekeeping. It was too soon to expect a reply.

Only a few seconds passed when his own bracelet vibrated three times as well. His brain wanted to tell him that he'd imagined it, but the little wave flashed as well. *Song!*

I love you.

Ren choked on a sob as he lifted his wrist to his lips and pressed a kiss to the bracelet. Song had heard him and answered.

Immediately after, there was another long pulse.

I miss you.

Ren sent the same thing back before grabbing his bag and anything else he needed. Hua was supposed to be escorting Song to the apartments. That was where Song would be waiting for him.

He needed to find Song, to hold him and tell him that he loved him.

The trip to the residences was short, but it was plenty of time for a sense of doom to sink into Ren's bones.

Why were they doing this?

What kind of happy ending could they possibly reach in this world?

They would never be able to go on a date like everyone else. They couldn't live together. They couldn't get married.

This time next year, they wouldn't be able to be seen together, period.

Well, they could have that if they left their home.

Yes, China had more than its fair share of problems, but it was still his home, the only home he'd ever known. It was where countless generations of his family had lived and died. It was where he'd built a successful career and a good life.

How good would that life seem when he left Hengdian and never saw Song Wei Li again?

As it was now, the road ahead of them was filled with disasters waiting to happen. If they weren't constantly cautious, constantly on guard, someone meaning them ill or even innocent could destroy everything.

But despite knowing all of this and trying to be fucking rational, Ren could feel his steps speeding up as he got off the elevator on their floor. He was nearly running down the hall, his body flying to Song. He lifted his fist to pound on his lover's door, but it was already standing wide open.

Song sat on the bed, his black-banded bracelet clenched in his fist and his long, damp hair hanging around his face.

"Ah-Wei," Ren breathed as he crossed the threshold. He slammed the door shut behind him and collided with Song in the next step in the center of the room.

Their mouths came together in a rush of violent kisses and grabbing hands. The blackness that had tainted his thoughts was shoved out, and Ren was wrapped in the sweetness that was Song Wei Li. There wasn't room for doubts and fears when he held Song.

"Are you okay? I wanted to—" Song managed to get out before Ren consumed his mouth, the words getting lost to a low, deep moan.

He knew what Song wanted to say. He knew Song. The man would have been right there the second the scene ended, holding him, kissing him, soothing away all of his pain, and Ren would have welcomed it with open arms.

But they couldn't allow it. They had to remain vigilant and prepared at all times.

Ren slid his lips down Song's throat, licking straining muscles and nipping at the tender lobe of his ear. "I know. I'm okay. I have you. I'm okay."

Song's fingers tugged at the hem of Ren's shirt, slipping under it to glide up his spine, igniting a rush of flames along his skin everywhere he touched.

Grabbing Song's ass with both hands, Ren pulled him in tight, hitching him a little higher so that their dicks rubbed together through their clothes. A needy sound was pulled from Song, and Ren's control wavered.

"Want you," Ren bit out as he kissed his way to Song's mouth. "Can I have you?"

There might have been a growling yes in between the sudden flurry of clothes being flung off and the crash of naked skin against naked skin. They stumbled over to the bed and fell awkwardly onto the mattress, Ren's elbow banging into the wall.

Song twisted around to his stomach, grabbing for the bottle of lube he kept hidden in his bag. Until now, they'd only used it for jerking each other off, but Ren was determined to slide inside his partner's tight body.

Ren lifted and took a second to just marvel at the beauty of Song's elegant body. Wide shoulders and a strong, muscular back tapered into a slender waist and the rounded globes of a perfect ass. Ren lowered his head and pressed openmouthed kisses into the dip, working his way to one cheek and then the other.

"Oh God, Ah-Xue," Song moaned. Ren looked up to see Song had his forehead pressed into his pillow while his trembling hand held out the tube toward him. "Please hurry."

Ren snatched the bottle from him and squeezed some of the clear gel onto his fingers. He made quick work of stretching his partner.

Yes, there might have been some incredibly embarrassing online searches that talked about the importance of this part.

Song's cries of pleasure plucked at his self-control and Ren found himself thrusting at Song's rumpled sheets for some relief, moving in time with Song's hips as he fucked himself on Ren's fingers.

The tightness. The insane heat. He'd never felt anything like it. And there was no way he was going to last inside of this man.

"Enough. That's enough. I need you," Song panted.

Ren had no interest in arguing. He picked up the lube again and smeared it on his dick. Inching closer on the bed, he brushed the head of his dick against Song's stretched and greedy hole. A whimper left Song and he pushed backward, trying to force Ren inside of his body. Ren was happy to give him exactly what they both needed.

He pushed inside, getting the thick head just past the tight ring of muscles before stopping.

Oh, God! This...fuck...

Ren clenched his teeth and held perfectly still while trying to get a stronger grip on himself. When he was sure he wasn't going to lose it in the next second, he pushed forward, sliding deeper and deeper into Song. Nothing...nothing had ever felt like this. The slick, hot tightness was scrambling his brain. He could barely breathe.

"Fuck. Ah-Xue. Fuck," Song chanted, his voice muffled as his face remained pressed into the pillow.

When he was fully seated inside of Song, Ren stretched out on top of him and grabbed both of Song's wrists, pinning them to the bed. "Is this what you wanted, Song Wei Li? To be stuffed with my cock?" Ren whispered in a harsh voice, directly in Song's ear.

"Yes! God, yes!" Song cried out. He shifted his hips, trying to get Ren to move, to fuck him, but he was thoroughly pressed to the mattress. "Since that...that first day..."

"I'll fuck you hard, Ah-Wei, but you're not allowed to come."

"What?"

Ren bit down hard on the junction between Song's neck and shoulder, earning a sharp, needy cry of pleasure and pain. "Don't come. I have plans for you. Don't…you…dare… come." He punctuated each sentence with a short thrust.

"Okay. Okay. But hurry. I'm so close."

With his fingers still wrapped tight on Song's wrists, he lifted, taking Song's hands with him to pin them to Song's lower back. He wanted to go slow, to savor every long glide. To memorize the feel of Song's body closing around him and gripping him so fucking tightly, but it all just felt too good. Every thrust of his hips, the sound of their bodies slapping together, each muffled cry of exquisite pleasure from Song was sending sparks throughout his entire nervous system.

His orgasm became a fire racing through dry kindling, consuming him in a brilliant flash. Ren clenched his teeth to hold in the shout as he emptied himself into Song's welcoming body. He poured all his love and need into his lover, wanting this moment scorched into his brain.

He'd barely finished coming when he withdrew and roughly flipped Song over. That beautiful cock was flushed dark red and so fucking hard. Ren gripped the base and swallowed him, touching the back of his throat with the semi-soft head. Song yelled and gripped his hair tightly with one hand as he began thrusting into Ren's mouth. It was only a few seconds before Song was coming down his throat, and Ren greedily swallowed everything this time. No choking. No mess. He wanted every part of Song.

Only when Song was lying completely still and Ren had licked his dick clean did he allow Song to slip from his swollen lips. He stretched out and collapsed on top of the man, their sweaty skin sliding and sticking together.

Thought was slow to return to his blood-starved brain, but it was accompanied by shock and horror.

What had he just done?

"Song, I'm so sorry," Ren whispered brokenly.

Song huffed a breathy laugh. "I have no idea what you're apologizing for. That was…fuck…my body still won't work."

"I didn't wear a condom. I knew I should, but I…I'm sorry, I was selfish…"

Turning onto his side, Song wrapped his arms around Ren, pulling him in even closer while snuggling his face into Ren's neck. "No, it's my fault. I even felt a condom in my bag but didn't grab it. I wanted to feel you. Wanted some part of you left inside of me. I'm negative. I get tested annually. The last one came back negative just before I left for Hengdian. I should have asked you, but I was afraid you'd say no."

Ren felt a lopsided smile form on his lips as he raised his head enough to look into Song's wide eyes. "So, what you're saying is that we're both fucking idiots?"

"Pretty much." Song's answering smile was warm and brilliant, reaching straight down to the cold spots in Ren's soul. "I knew after today I wouldn't want to be with anyone else. You're it for me, Ren An Xue."

"What if we're caught? What if someone figures out that we're dating? Everything we've both worked so hard to build will be ruined. We'll be blacklisted." Ren hated that he was giving voice to all the fears that had been eating away at his sanity for the past few days, but they just came tumbling out.

"What is the alternative? That we go on lying about who we are, even in the secret of our own homes. That we never have another moment like this. What's the point of building that life if when I get home, I can't even look myself in the mirror? I don't want to live a life where I can't one day hold you in my arms again. I am willing to take on the risk and live for the little moments, because for me, it's enough." He paused and his expression softened. "But I know I can't speak for you, and if you decide that it's not enough, I won't judge you. It'll hurt, but I will let you go, Ren An Xue. You've got more to lose than me. My mother will stand by me. She's been saying 'fuck the world' for a really long time. If you're outed, you will very likely lose the support of your family."

Funny enough, his parents had never factored into his thoughts. Song was right. His parents would cut all ties with him if he was linked to such a horrible scandal. But that idea didn't hurt as badly as it should have. He'd been distancing himself from his parents for years.

But his friends?

His work?

Except he'd still have Guo Zi and Zhu Fang. He had a good feeling he'd keep Hua Jun Bai and even Ma Daiyu if shit hit the fan.

He loved acting.

But those wide, dark eyes staring up at him; the tentative, worried smile? He loved them more.

"I'm scared, but I can't let you go," Ren admitted.

"Me too. But you know what? You're fucking amazing. What you arranged today was brilliant—I hadn't even thought of that." Song's expression warmed until he became a small glowing sun in Ren's arms. "You totally covered our asses today. Saved us from a mistake. My Ren laoshi taught me how I need to handle things if we're going to survive. *You* gave me hope for our future."

"I did?" Ren said around a catch in his throat.

"You're perfect! You saw exactly what our weaknesses were and took steps to counter them. It was stunning! I've never been so proud of my didi." Song leaned forward and bumped the tip of his nose against Ren's. "I've already asked Hua to hang out on the day I have to shoot your 'death' scenes as a just in case."

Ren tipped his head back and laughed, his arms naturally tightening on Song. "Oh my God, we are going to owe Hua so fucking huge. We are never going to get out of his debt."

Song sighed and pressed a kiss to Ren's throat. "Probably not, but he is generally tolerable."

"You think we'll make it?"

"I'm not saying it'll be easy or that we won't get incredibly frustrated, but yeah, I think we will. I love you too much, didi, to not at least try."

"I love you, Song Wei Li. I love you with everything that I am. I want to try."

They pulled each other close, skin sticking together, legs tangled, and Song's head pressed to Ren's heart. Ren had no idea what was going to happen when they separated at the end of filming, but he knew he'd never be able to face himself, he'd never know another moment of happiness if he didn't at least try to hang on to the love he'd found with Song.

34

LAST DAY...
SONG WEI LI

LAST DAY OF FILMING.
 Last day.
 Last...

Since Song woke up that morning, it had been like a boulder was sitting on his chest. He couldn't suck enough air into his lungs.

The sun had already started to peek over the horizon when Ren had left his room and moved to his own bed for a few hours of sleep. Song doubted either of them got much of that during the night, though. They'd lain, crammed in his too-small bed, a jumble of limbs and terrified thoughts.

For the past two weeks, Song had endlessly repeated words of encouragement and confidence to help buoy them both, but now that they were staring down at the final day, he was a vast black hole of fear.

Every instinct screamed to grab ahold of Ren and run. He didn't know where to run or even how far. It was just run. Keep running until there were no more eyes. No more cameras. No more anything else besides Ren's smiling face.

What made it all the more painful was trying to fake the same giddy and weary excitement as everyone else in the cast and crew. Four months at the height of summer was a long and exhausting schedule. Several people on the set fainted from the heat. There were the natural delays and breakdowns that turned long days into even longer days. People missed their families and their homes.

Song wanted another four months.

No, years. He wanted to remain for years at Hengdian with Ren, shooting movies and TV shows, while the rest of the world simply faded away.

The day's shoot itself was a blur. Sun Jing had arranged for some relatively simple scenes to close things out. Nothing that required him or Ren to truly exert themselves, as if Sun had already guessed that they wouldn't be able to put forth their best performances under the circumstances.

When Sun called "Cut!" for the last time, a great cheer echoed through the sound stage. Song clenched his teeth and clapped with everyone else, forcing a tight, close-lipped smile while blinking rapidly against the sting of tears. He traded a tense look with Ren, but they weren't given a chance for a final hug.

It was probably for the best. Song wasn't sure if he'd be able to let go once he got Ren in his arms.

Massive bouquets of colorful flowers were brought out and one was handed to him, Ren, the director, and the producers. He was placed next to Ren for a quick photo, and then it was an endless round of hugs, more crew photos, actor photos, official photos, and selfies.

Song hated that he was going through the motions. He stapled that damn smile to his lips and refused to allow it to slip. He thanked everyone who had worked beside him every day and signed autographs. But his eyes still drifted toward Ren.

As the minutes ticked by, he noticed that the distance separating them on the sound stage grew larger and larger, as if they were purposefully being drawn apart.

By the time the final blessing over the production was said and the cake was cut, most of the actors and crew were between him and Ren. He caught his lover's gaze and found the same pained expression on his face.

"Just keep smiling. It's almost over," Hua whispered suddenly in his ear as he slung an arm across his shoulders.

"I'm dying," Song bit out while still grinning ear to ear.

"Ten more minutes, and then we'll make our escape to wardrobe," Hua suggested.

Song was about to agree to it, but a new development had Song changing his mind. "Bao Shi is here. He can go to wardrobe with me. You run interference for Ren."

The arm resting on his shoulders tensed. "What's up?"

"Liu. I don't trust him near Ren."

The man in question had been done on this shoot for nearly a week, but he happened to show up in time for the closing celebration. Figured. One last attempt to get his hands on Ren, but Song was not going to let that happen. Not while Ren was feeling at his most vulnerable.

Oh, and he'd had his supposed rain check fulfilled with Ren. It just so happened that Song, Hua, and Ma crashed that lunch as well. Seeing the disappointment fill Liu's face had been the sweetest thing in all the world.

Hua groaned in his ear. "Little fucking snake. Got it. Do you mind if I cause a scene since I'm not getting paid for this?"

Song choked on his first laugh in over twenty-four hours. "No. Go ahead. Try not to embarrass Ren."

Hua shot him a parting look that said he wasn't making any promises, and then he sauntered through the crowd. Song lingered and took a few more selfies with the crew before shouts and loud laughter exploded from the other side of the room. Liu was bellowing something, maybe threats at Hua, who appeared to be professing his innocence.

Hua Jun Bai was a madman, and Song was really starting

to love him for it. Well, so long as he wasn't the target of his insanity.

Ren caught his eye from across the room and his lips tipped up in a knowing smirk and maybe some gratitude. Song bowed his head to his lover, acknowledging all the emotions they couldn't express in front of the world.

But that was it.

He couldn't cross the room and wrap his arms around the man. He couldn't share in the laughter more than he already was. It was better if they got into the practice now of keeping a distance while in the public eye.

He turned and found Bao Shi standing a short distance away, an expectant expression on his face. Yeah, he was ready to go. Song quietly slipped out of the crowd and escaped the building, his assistant closely shadowing him. His costume and wig were handed over a final time, and he changed into his own clothes.

The ride back to the residence was a quiet one. Song glanced through his various social media accounts to find a handful of new pictures from their last day. The buzz was positive. There were haters, of course, going out of their way to call him names or Ren names or just generally disparaging the production, but he'd gotten better at filtering them out. There was no pleasing everyone.

He did note that there were a few people who'd remarked on the fact that there were almost no pictures of him and Ren together. It was okay. Song and the marketing team had a short video compiled of all the main actors from the show. It included Song and Ren together.

Plus, in three weeks, he and Ren would begin a brief whirlwind media tour. There were interviews and variety shows they would be appearing on. There was also one massive photo shoot he found himself looking forward to. *Frozen River's* Zhu Fang and Guo Zi had done a beautiful glossy photo shoot and spread in the same magazine with an airy, ethereal vibe. He was hoping for the same thing with Ren.

They would see each other.
They would see each other.

It was something he kept repeating in his mind.

When he was finally alone in his room, he collapsed onto the bed and scrubbed both hands across his face. He needed to shower and pack his bags. He needed to review his schedule again. He was immediately flying out tomorrow morning for…a photo shoot? No, a commercial shoot in Beijing. Ren was going to Shanghai to begin filming that romantic comedy he'd agreed to do.

Completely opposite directions.

But it meant both their evenings were likely to be free. They'd be able to have a video chat tomorrow night.

And they would have tonight.

Several hours passed before Ren knocked on his door. Song quickly ushered him in and for the first few minutes, they stood just past the threshold, hugging each other. Ren looked utterly drained, as if only willpower was keeping him upright.

"Have you eaten?" Song murmured against his throat.

"A bit at the farewell dinner. You weren't there," Ren observed, but he didn't sound surprised by it. Song had mentioned last night that he was thinking about not attending. There was a limit to how much fake smiling and pretending he could do in a single day. Hanging out at that party, drinking, and trying not to spend every second of it staring at Ren sounded like hell. There was going to be plenty of that in his future. There was no point in diving straight into it now.

"I wasn't up for it. I texted Sun."

Ren huffed a laugh that almost sounded bitter. "Yeah, he asked me to check up on you."

Song snorted. "Such as a nosy asshole."

"Have you eaten?"

"That dumpling from yesterday's lunch." It was the last thing Ren had made for him. He'd managed to choke it down after he stopped sniffling over it. Ren was going to cook for him again. Fuck, he was going to learn to cook without telling Ren so he could surprise him one day with a special meal. Yes, that was an excellent plan.

Assuming he didn't catch himself and his apartment on fire.

Ren loosened his death grip on Song and frowned at him. "We're going to have to send each other pictures of our food. I can't spend every second we're apart worrying about whether you're eating."

Surprised laughter jumped from Song and he smiled at his lover. "It's like you don't trust me."

"I don't!" Ren grabbed Song's hand and pulled him over to the bed. They sat with their shoulders pressed to the wall. "I saw how you ate *before* I started cooking for you. It was pure garbage when you did remember to eat. I've already got Bao Shi's contact info. If I think you're lying to me about your eating habits, I'll just contact him."

Song lurched upright on a gasp. "What? You expect him to tattle on me?"

"I know he will. If you won't listen to him, at least we know you're going to listen to your Ren laoshi," his sweet lover replied with a very smug smile.

Song's heart skipped. He was right. Ren was so fucking right. He would listen to his Ren and do whatever he said because he was completely and utterly lost over the man.

"I can't believe you convinced my assistant to gang up on me," Song muttered as he fell back to his previous position, his head leaning against Ren's.

"Actually, Bao Shi was the one to volunteer his info. In case I ever needed something, and I couldn't reach you directly. I also gave him mine." Ren shifted, reaching into the pocket of his jeans. He pulled out a folded slip of paper and held it out to Song. "I've got a little gift for you."

Song took the paper and opened it up to find several names and matching contact information for them. The names at the top were for Ren's manager and assistant, but his parents' information was also on there.

"What's this?"

"It's one of the things that's been bothering me the past several weeks," Ren admitted. His eyes darted away from Song and then bounced into full, wide puppy mode. "What if something happens to me? A car accident or something on a shoot. Or even something small like the flu or food poisoning. If you hear about it through social media, you're going to lose it. And it's going to be worse if I'm not in a position to take your call and tell you myself that everything is okay. This way, you can contact my assistant or my manager to get the truth. If you get really stuck, you can call my parents. I've already told my manager and assistant that you're at the top of my emergency contact list now. This way, I know you won't have to worry about me."

Song tried to blink them away, but it was too late. Tears slipped free to run down his cheeks and land on the paper. This...this was the sweetest, most thoughtful thing he'd ever been given. Private contact information was sacred in their line of work, and Ren had just handed Song the keys to his world.

"Ah-Xue," he whispered in a rough voice.

Ren's strong arms wrapped tightly around him and soft lips brushed his temple. "You are my everything. I want you to be able to reach me at all times."

Song nodded and cleared his throat. With the heel of his palm, he brushed away the last of the tears. "I'll get you all the same info. I don't want you to ever worry. And if you can reach Bao Shi, you're generally covered. That bastard always knows everything."

"I'm glad you've got such a good friend."

"What about you? Do you have anyone you can lean on?"

Ren's smile was crooked, but it was at least there on his lips. "Guo Zi and I have been texting more. He's helping to keep me sane. Wu Dong Mei and I have gotten closer. I haven't actually told her anything, but she seems to understand without needing details. It's…nice."

That was good. Song might have already confessed way more to Bao Shi than the man ever wanted to hear, but they'd been friends for years. If anyone understood Song, it was his oldest friend.

"Did your manager think it was weird that you've added me to your emergency contacts?"

Ren winced. "Maybe a little, but I told her that you've taken the role of my laoshi very seriously and demand to know that I'm well."

Song chuckled softly and pressed a kiss to the tip of Ren's nose. "I don't know whether that makes me sound dedicated or like a psychopath."

"I don't care what she thinks. If she doesn't like it, she can cancel our contract and I'll find a manager who will listen to me."

That was his stubborn, fierce Ren.

They fell into a long silence that was finally broken when Song bumped his shoulder against Ren's, drawing the man's sad gaze up to his face.

"You fly out first thing tomorrow?"

Ren grunted. "To Shanghai. You?"

Song nodded once. "Beijing. Commercial shoot." A smirk lifted one corner of his mouth. "You want to fool around until we're both broken and hobbling onto our respective planes tomorrow?"

Ren's loud laughter filled the room for only a second before Song was tackled to the mattress. For the rest of the night, they kissed, laughed, and fucked. Neither of them could move a muscle when they were done.

They didn't part until the very last minute when they were both forced to rush in packing their things so they could make their rides to the airport. Song's ass was so damn sore and it felt like every inch of his torso was covered in bruises and bite marks. Ren wasn't much better.

Song had no regrets, and as he caught a glimpse of Ren's parting smile as he climbed into his car, he was sure Ren didn't have any either.

Three weeks from now, they'd meet up for interviews and TV appearances.

In the meantime, Song's bracelet vibrated.

I love you.

35

PURE, UNDILUTED HELL
REN AN XUE

Ren scrolled through the messages on his phone, the frown on his lips growing deeper. There was still no response to the texts he'd sent to Song last night. He'd checked their shared schedule last night after sending them, and the only thing that Song had written down for his day was a photo shoot and a meeting with his manager. He didn't think something like that would run late.

Unless his manager had decided that the meeting needed to include other things such as dinner and drinks or dinner and drinks with producers. Or companies wanting to use Song as a brand ambassador.

Ren had been sucked into plenty of those meetings in the past weeks that were just supposed to be a quick hour but had morphed into this never-ending monster of drinks and shaking hands and listening to one sales pitch after another while getting complimented on his looks or popularity.

He was trying to be understanding, but it was getting hard.

Responses to his messages seemed to be growing more delayed.

More than a month had passed since they finished filming *Legend of the Lost Night,* and they were both constantly on the run. Ren had finished filming the romantic comedy in five short days, and he had to admit that it was more fun than he'd been anticipating. There was none of the weight that came with working as the lead of a wuxia. None of the heavy costumes or flowery, complicated lines. He'd been the goofy friend to the romantic lead. He hadn't expected to have his own smaller romantic subplot, but even that had been light and fun.

He'd even begun to rethink his stance on leaving romantic comedies behind. They could be a refreshing break from the heavier shows, especially if they were well written. He just needed to pressure his manager into getting him a full script and synopsis before he agreed to audition for anything.

Sadly, his mind was still cringing from the scripted kiss. His costar was pretty and nice, but when the time came, his mind had been full of all the kisses he'd shared with Song and how this was *not* Song.

Yeah, he definitely needed to get a handle on that or he was going to have a very short, very limited acting career.

But even after the filming was done, there were modeling gigs, interviews, and commercials. They managed to keep up with each other for a bit. Even enjoyed a few sexy video chats.

Then came the four days of intense interviews and variety shows for *Legend* where they'd actually gotten to see each other.

Hell.

Pure, undiluted hell.

It had been like walking a starving man past a buffet and not letting him have a single nibble.

Everything took place in Shanghai, where Song was living, which was convenient for him. Ren had even fanaticized about possibly seeing Song's apartment one evening after all the chaos, but he had been pretty much under lockdown every second he was in Shanghai. He was shuttled—*separately from Song*—to every interview and performance. From the moment they were on a set or appeared for an interview, they were surrounded by people. They couldn't so much as share a look without it being photographed or recorded by a few dozen people.

At one point, they were sitting next to each other and texting because they couldn't risk anyone overhearing their silliness.

He couldn't complain too much. It had been heaven to just see Song in the flesh. To see his smile and the twinkle in his eyes as he laughed.

But to not touch Song? To not be able to hug Song and breathe his scent into his lungs?

A nightmare.

By the third and final day, there were more random brushes. They bumped knees while answering interview questions. Song would laugh wildly and rock into Ren, leaning almost the full weight of his body on Ren before straightening. It was heaven.

It was hell.

The car stopped and the opening door jerked Ren from his thoughts. He looked up to see Wu Dong Mei staring expectantly, though her gaze also seemed more than a little worried about him as well.

"Ready to go?"

It was on the tip of his tongue to ask where they were when it suddenly came to him that he was heading into another photo shoot. This one for…shoes? Yeah, shoes.

"Just a sec," he replied, forcing a smile he didn't feel.

Ren: Sorry I missed you. Heading into ad shoot.
Ren: Phone off until lunch.
Ren: Love you.

REN'S SONG

S*ong:* S*orry!* S*orry!* S*orry!* A*ll my fault!* P*roducer stopped by "unannounced" during meeting. Turned into dinner and drinks. Crashed the second I got home.*

Song: *Are you free tonight for a video chat? I got something to show you!!!*

Song: *Love you*

Ren silently swore and seriously considered throwing his phone into the wall when he turned it on. He'd just missed Song.

The ad shoot had taken twice as long as it should have because the photographer was being a prima donna. He didn't like the wardrobe that had been selected for Ren. And he didn't like how his hair had been styled.

Ren had wanted to shake the man and remind him that they were supposed to be focusing on the fucking sneakers on his feet, but that wasn't his place. His job was to do what the photographer said and be pretty or sexy or coy or whatever the fuck he needed to be.

As it was, lunch had become anything he could shove into his mouth while running to the car and racing to his next appointment. Even then, he was still nearly an hour late for the interview, and his stomach was upset from rushing lunch.

Ren: *Running late. Shoot ran stupidly long.*

Ren: *Will text after interview when I get time to look at schedule*

S*ong:* T*omorrow night might be better.* T*rying to get out of late audition but might not be able to.*

Song: *Just caught your latest web interview. You look exhausted, didi. Are you sleeping?*

Ren could only sigh when he saw the new texts from Song. He'd been so flustered over his late arrival to the interview that he'd forgotten to turn his phone on until he reached home. He'd missed Song…*again*.

It turned out that he did have an opening tonight for a chat, but tomorrow night was bad. Right now he was stretched out on his couch, staring at his phone, with no clue as to what he should even send his boyfriend.

They were going to miss each other yet again.

And no, he wasn't sleeping. But he didn't want to tell Song that because he would only worry.

Ren rubbed his burning eyes. He didn't know if it was from unshed tears or pure exhaustion. Probably both. It had been a long time since he'd last had an entire day off work. Some days were lighter, but he couldn't remember the last time he'd been able to sleep in. To simply lie around his place and read a book. Or even blow the entire day playing video games.

He needed to schedule some time off. But even if he did that, it wasn't like he'd be able to run off and hang out with Song. He hadn't seen his own parents in eight months, and his mother's demands for him to visit were growing more strident and caustic. If he didn't make an appearance soon, she would be convinced that he was shaming all his ancestors with his failure to be a good, filial son.

A snort escaped him at the thought. Just wait until she found out that he had a boyfriend. That would be a good one for the ancestors to swallow.

Ren closed the message window for Song and opened the one for Guo Zi. They chatted here and there, exchanging random messages and pictures every couple of days. From what it sounded like, his and Zhu Fang's schedules weren't any better.

Ren: *Tell me it gets easier. Even if you have to lie to me.*
Guo: *You home? Wanna chat?*

Ren blinked at the message that appeared within less than a minute of his own. A bitter laugh rose up. He couldn't remember the last time he'd gotten a message from Song that quickly. Not that he was blaming Song. Just their fucked-up schedules.

Ren: Sure. Why not?

Yeah, he probably looked like shit, but he was comfortable with Guo Zi. They'd seen each other at their most relaxed. He'd listened to his friend practically shouting at the world because he'd not gotten to see his boyfriend in a month. If anyone understood, it was Guo Zi.

A video call rang through and Ren answered it. The screen was instantly filled with Guo Zi's handsome, smiling face and very kind eyes. His hair was now dark brown, though. He was pretty sure the last time he'd seen it, the color had been blue.

"You look like shit," Guo Zi immediately announced.

A loud laugh jumped from Ren and he shook his head. "Nice to see you too, gege." He paused and lifted an eyebrow. "Is it safe?"

"Yeah, you're good. Let it out."

"*Fuck!* It's been the worst fucking month. I have barely stopped moving. I don't even know where I'm going or what I'm doing until someone reminds me. We are constantly missing each other on text. And I can't fucking sleep because my arms are fucking empty!" Ren screamed at the top of his lungs.

"Yep, that all sounds normal," someone who was *not* Guo Zi stated. It wasn't even Zhu Fang.

Guo Zi's eyes snapped up to glare just past the phone at the speaker.

Ren's heart was lodged in his throat as he mentally replayed everything out of his mouth. Did he say anything potentially incriminating? Pronouns? Names?

"Who's that? You said it was safe," Ren rasped.

Guo Zi dropped his eyes back to Ren, his expression full of sympathy. "You are, I swear. It's all good. You're safe." He glared at his unknown companion. "He said he wasn't going to speak so I didn't have to introduce him, but he just screwed himself over, didn't he? Get your ass over here."

There was some shuffling and Guo Zi turned his phone so that the screen could easily fit a second person.

And it wasn't just any person.

Ren instantly recognized the stunningly handsome and severe face of Yuan Teng Fei, star of *Path of the Poison* and yet another man who'd fallen in love with his male costar.

"Shit," Ren breathed.

Yuan Teng Fei's lips twitched into a sardonic smirk. "I get that reaction a lot."

Guo Zi elbowed him and muttered, "Asshole," then turned his attention to Ren. "Ren An Xue, this is Yuan Teng Fei. We've both signed on to costar in this detective drama and the producers took us out to dinner—"

"Mostly to kiss my ass," Yuan Teng Fei interjected.

Guo Zi snickered. "It's the truth. I've been wanting to do a contemporary drama like this. Signing me was easy. It was convincing this one that he needed to take a chance on acting with me."

Yuan Teng Fei rolled his eyes.

"Didn't you know each other before today?" Ren asked.

"Oh, yeah. He let his manager use his so-called hesitance as a bargaining tool to get more money out of them," Guo Zi replied.

"True. But this kid's got plenty of talent. I've got no problem working with him."

Guo Zi made a scoffing noise and bumped Yuan Teng Fei. "Whatever, Lao Fei. You've got what? Three years on me? Don't give me any of this kid bullshit."

A real smile finally formed on Ren's lips. It was good talking to Guo Zi. The man always had a way of lifting his spirits. At the very least, he felt less alone in all of this insanity.

"Look, I'll let you go, gege. I didn't mean to disturb your

night—"

"No! Ren, no! We were just catching up. Lao Fei and I don't talk as often as you and I do. But I wanted to give you the chance to meet him and to have another person tell you that it gets better."

"It doesn't," Yuan Teng Fei immediately corrected him.

Ren sucked in a harsh breath. It was as if Yuan Teng Fei had punched him hard in the gut. Guo Zi screeched, but Yuan Teng Fei was unmoved as he stole the phone from his friend so that the camera was pointed only at him.

"Guo Zi said that you're a month out of filming?"

Ren nodded. He couldn't have spoken if his life depended on it. Despair was threatening to swamp him completely.

"It gets worse. You are going to go months without being able to steal time to hold each other. You're going to question why you're putting yourself through this. You're going to wonder why you're taking these risks. Everything you're feeling and thinking, he's going through, too. He's miserable just like you. And if you're thinking of caving after one little month, you're not really in love. Or at least, you don't deserve Song Wei Li."

"I'm not caving!" Ren snapped.

"Are you going to fight for him? For both of you?"

"Yes!"

"What if he has doubts? Are you still going to fight?"

"Yes, I'm not letting him fucking go!" Ren shouted at the screen. He stared at Yuan Teng Fei's smug grin as he struggled to catch his breath. It was as though he'd just collapsed on the couch after running a marathon. "Asshole. You really are an asshole."

Guo Zi's cackle echoed in the background.

"True, but at least you're done with your pity party." Some of the smugness left Yuan Teng Fei's expression. A look of sympathy filled his eyes. "I do get it. The beginning always feels like the worst since you got accustomed to seeing him every day, but it does get easier. You fall into your old rhythm. You start to remember what it was like to go through your day without him there. That's the real scary part; when you feel like you don't need them anymore. When you begin to wonder if you can move on without them."

"No," Ren whispered. He shook his head, his heart pounding hard in his chest for a new reason. "No. That won't happen. Can't. I won't ever let go of Song."

"Good," Yuan Teng Fei said, but the sadness lingered in his eyes as if he didn't completely believe Ren.

The image on the screen blurred for a second before Guo Zi's determined gaze filled it again. "Any better?" he asked.

Ren took a deep breath and released it, quickly assessing his mental state. "Yeah." He huffed a soft laugh. "Yeah, I'm better. Thanks. This helped a lot."

"I'm glad. Also, tell Song that Guo Zi said to get his head out of his ass and work on matching up his schedule with yours."

They chatted for a few minutes longer about a lot of nothing. Yuan Teng Fei didn't say much beyond some snarky comments that made Guo Zi roll his eyes. The man had a reputation for being incredibly cold and standoffish, but it clearly didn't bother Guo Zi in the slightest. It had to be nice going into a project already knowing someone and being comfortable with them.

When the call was over, Ren shifted over to the messages from Song. He stared at them for a second, his thumb rubbing lightly over Song's words when he finally decided what to say.

Ren: I am exhausted, and I miss you so very much. I don't know what I'm doing most days. I just go where they tell me to, and I smile when they tell me to. The only thing I know every second of my day is that I love you.

After sending the text, he lay there smiling at it for a bit. He didn't want Song to worry over him, but he also knew they weren't going to make it if they were constantly hiding how they truly felt from each other. Song had to be tired and lonely as well. Ren wanted Song to know that he wasn't the only one who felt like shit.

But even in all of that, he was still loved with all of Ren's heart.

Pushing up from the couch, Ren walked into the bedroom and dug out the red-banded bracelet from where he kept it hidden in the nightstand drawer. His schedule had been so frantic recently that he hadn't wanted to risk wearing it out in public.

He slipped it onto his left wrist, tightened it, and sent their three-pulse coded message.

I love you.

Ren shoved his phone into his pocket and turned to head into the kitchen. He couldn't remember the last time he'd eaten and he needed to grab something before falling asleep.

Three pulses.

Ren's entire body jerked and he lifted the bracelet to see the light flash on the wave curl.

Three pulses.

I love you.

Grabbing his phone, he tapped the screen to find that Song hadn't replied to his texts yet. Hadn't even read them. He must be somewhere that he couldn't look at his phone, wasn't free to respond.

But he was wearing his bracelet.

In the middle of whatever crowd or business meeting he was in, Song had received his message of love and sent his own back.

Ren's knees gave out and he found himself sitting on the floor of his bedroom, crying on the bracelet pressed to his lips. Song was tugging on the red thread that tied them together, reminding Ren that they were still together. Neither distance nor time would separate them.

Three pulses. *I love you.*

36

DRUNK WITH ZHU FANG
SONG WEI LI

Song glared at the TV. A basketball game was on, and he should be finding it incredibly exciting. The score had been close the entire game, and they were down to the last two minutes of the second half, but he couldn't scrape together enough energy to care.

Ren was in Tokyo.

He was supposed to be in Shanghai with him for their first secret meeting since they left Hengdian two months ago.

But he was in Japan.

Song had no one to blame but himself.

A huge opportunity had arisen for Ren. This gaming company not only wanted Ren to do voiceover work, but they wanted his sexy face to be the image for the lead character. It meant that he needed to go to Japan *now*.

Ren had begged, pleaded, and argued for them to push it just a few days. Song had witnessed a few of those desperate calls to his manager.

But the gaming company couldn't budge. If Ren couldn't do this now, they had to find someone else.

Ren had been on the cusp of walking away from the deal

when Song urged him to go. It was the right thing for Ren's career. It was the kind of thing the supportive boyfriend would do.

He was glad for Ren's success. He was proud of his sexy, sweet boyfriend.

But he was also disgustingly depressed, missing Ren An Xue more than he could put into words.

Things had gotten better for a while. Their schedules fell into a quieter routine and they were managing to video chat at least four nights a week, and they were catching each other on text more.

They'd just had their hopes up about actually seeing each other. It had been two months since he'd held his Ah-Xue in his arms, felt his lips against his own, smelled his shampoo and body wash.

It wasn't about sex either.

Though sex with Ren was so fucking amazing.

He'd be happy to simply hold him all night, listening to his steady breathing as he slept. Song had never thought he'd enjoy sleeping with another person. He loved his space and hated to feel trapped. But when he slept with Ren, he never felt trapped. Not once when they were wrapped in each other in that tiny bed did he long to be somewhere else with more room.

Now he was stuck in that big, cold bed of his alone.

Maybe he should have flown to Tokyo.

Except tomorrow evening he was expected at a charity gala, and that was followed closely the next morning with a photo shoot and an audition for a new wuxia drama.

A non-BL wuxia drama.

After shooting *Legend of the Lost Night* with Ren, he didn't think he could do another BL-based drama. At least, not as one of the romantic leads.

Maybe they'd let him be one of the villains. Those things

always had more than one. He was certainly feeling angry and bitter enough. He'd make an excellent villain.

Song's phone vibrated on the table and he shifted his glare to it. It wasn't Ren. His lover was either on a plane or on his way to the hotel. It was too early for him to call.

Unless there was a problem…

Song lunged for the phone before it could stop ringing to discover it was Zhu Fang.

He hesitated but answered it. If he didn't answer, the man would just keep calling until he drove Song crazy.

"Hey—"

"What floor are you on?" Zhu Fang demanded, not even letting him finish his greeting.

"What?"

"Your doorman won't let me up unless I can prove that we're besties," Zhu Fang replied. "What floor are you on?"

"Seven," Song answered without thinking. In the next heartbeat, the rest of his friend's words registered in his brain. "Wait! Are you here?"

"Of course, I'm fucking here! The calvary has been called in to add alcohol to your pity party." Zhu Fang said something else, but the words were muffled. He must have been talking to the doorman who protected the building from people who very much did *not* live there.

"On my way up! Put some pants on," Zhu Fang ordered and hung up the phone.

Oh, God. Song couldn't decide if this was a good thing or a very, very bad idea.

It was definitely too late to run now.

And who had called in the calvary to save his sorry ass?

Ren.

He should have known. The moment Ren had canceled on their secret night, he'd probably reached out to Guo Zi for advice. Song had been chatting with the happy—*and crazy*—couple here and there when time allowed. He'd been relieved to hear that Ren was finding nice support from them. He'd just never expected to be on the receiving end of that support at a time like this.

Shoving to his feet, Ren took a quick look around his apartment. It was a little untidy, but he doubted Zhu Fang would even notice. He shuffled to the door and peered down the hall just as his friend stepped off the elevator. The man was dressed in the typical disguise of actors: baseball hat pulled low, mask, glasses, and baggy clothes. Anything to disguise their most recognizable features. When it came to Zhu Fang, Song figured it was a toss-up between his smile and his eyes.

In one arm, he carried a large brown paper bag while a backpack was slung over the opposite shoulder. Was that an overnight bag? Song nearly whimpered. Probably. If the other bag held as much alcohol as Song feared, Zhu Fang was getting no farther than Song's couch. Unless it was to simply fall on his floor.

As soon as he spotted Song, he waved his free arm wildly in the air as if Song would have trouble spotting the only man in his hallway. At least he wasn't shouting.

"Get your ass in here," Song muttered.

"Oh, come on! Don't be like that. You know you need some cheering up," Zhu Fang said the second he was inside Song's apartment. He kicked off his shoes and slipped into a pair of guest slippers while Song took the too-large bag of alcohol from him. Zhu Fang stripped off the oversized jacket, hat, glasses, and mask, leaving them all near the door.

Song peeked inside the bag and groaned. "What the hell! How many people did you invite over?"

"It's just us. Gege has an early morning tomorrow, or he'd be here too. I tried to wrangle Yuan Teng Fei and his boyfriend too, but scheduling conflict. Besides, I didn't know what you liked to drink."

"Beer would have been fine."

Zhu Fang made a dismissive noise as he followed Song into the living room. "Beer takes too long and way too many to get properly shitfaced. I've got whiskey, vodka, sake—"

"Whiskey will do just fine. What's your poison?"

"Whiskey on the rocks, if you don't mind." Zhu Fang wandered over to the sliding glass doors that led to his small patio overlooking the city. He was in a somewhat quiet neighborhood, allowing him to escape much of the city noise while still having a great view of the skyline at night.

Song went into the kitchen, pulled the whiskey out of the bag, and grabbed a pair of tumblers for them both. After adding ice and some healthy splashes of alcohol, he carried the drinks out to see Zhu Fang staring out the window but standing away enough so that he wouldn't be visible if someone should be looking toward his balcony.

"As far as I know, the fans haven't found me yet. Or if they have, they've learned it's a waste of time to try to stalk me here. I'm never home," Song stated as he handed over Zhu's glass.

"That's good. I've been thinking about moving. I used to be able to sneak in and out of the underground garage, but a few fans have managed to even get into the garage. It's gotten too crazy. Gege can't risk coming over anymore." Zhu's bottom lip protruded in a pitiful pout for a moment, and then he tossed back the entire drink.

Shit. He wasn't the only one in need of a pity party.

"I'm assuming Ren called you," Song said as he dropped onto the far end of his charcoal gray couch.

"Yep. Well, he tried to call gege first, but he's trapped in rehearsals for the next week. He got me next," Zhu explained as he moseyed to the kitchen. He returned a second later with his free hand wrapped around the whiskey bottle. He claimed the other end of the couch and refilled his glass. "He feels bad about missing your date for work. Seriously, he's a mess."

Song sucked down half his drink and groaned, sinking lower on the couch. "I don't want him to feel bad. I know he didn't do this on purpose. I *told* him to take the job."

Zhu stared at the amber liquid in his glass and frowned. "He's afraid of this one-time thing becoming more." He paused and sighed. "He's right, though. It's a slippery slope. Once you make work more important than the time you schedule together, where do you draw the line?"

Song hated to admit that the same thought had crossed his mind. When did they say enough was enough? That their time was sacrosanct?

"I don't want to be the reason that he doesn't achieve everything he desires with his career."

"And what about your career?"

Song shrugged. "Mine is already in a good place. I've got a solid résumé, and I can afford to be picky. I can take more time off than he can. He's still in the early phase, building up his experience."

Zhu snorted. "And we both know all that shit is going to change after *Legend* is released. Are you going to draw the line then? When you're both incredibly hot commodities and companies are willing to pay any price to get their hands on you?"

Fuck.

Song finished the rest of the whiskey in his glass and slid it down the coffee table toward Zhu. "I thought you were supposed to be cheering me up. If that was your plan, you are failing miserably."

"My friend, we are not nearly drunk enough to hit cheerful. We're still in the mopey 'life sucks and I miss my boyfriend' phase." Zhu refilled Song's glass and might have topped off his own again.

"You're not trying to get me drunk enough to sing sappy sad love songs with you, right?"

Zhu Fang's eyes grew so wide, his face lighting up with what looked to be the most brilliant, evil idea. "We can video it and post it on WeChat! People went crazy at our concert. This will be like part two: the drunk afterparty."

"No! Absolutely not!"

Zhu Fang slid down the couch and laid his head on Song's shoulder. "Please, Song Wei Li. People will love it."

"No! Fuck, no! My manager would kill me."

Maybe. She did really love his concert with Zhu Fang and she'd been poking at him to establish a better relationship with Zhu Fang. Song was not about to admit to her that he was already damn good friends with the man. He didn't want to leverage their friendship for his career.

Zhu Fang giggled. "I could record us singing, but I can't post anything."

"What?"

Straightening on the sofa, Zhu Fang held up his phone and waved it back and forth. "I promised gege that I would log out of all my social media accounts before I reached your place. No chance of drunk posting because I can *never* remember any of my passwords."

Song dropped his head on the couch and breathed a heavy sigh of relief. Thank God one of them managed to use their brain for good.

"But I still think we should sing a duet when we get really wasted. It'll be fun."

"No recording anything."

Zhu Fang grinned at him and lifted his glass to his lips. "No promises."

Many, many drinks later...

They went through the entire bottle of whiskey and started on the vodka.

Many horribly sung songs were videoed.

Song fell off the couch.

Zhu fell while laughing and trying to help Song onto the couch again.

There were drunk calls to Guo Zi until he blocked his boyfriend.

Song might have shown off his bracelet to Zhu and sent many gibberish messages to Ren until he called. Ren hung up on him a short time later, but Song was pretty sure he'd been laughing at the time.

It was around three in the morning when they began to sober up. Zhu Fang was stretched out on the couch, cuddling a half-empty bottle of water. Song was seated on the floor with his back to the couch, nursing his own bottle of water.

"Well, I'd say this disaster was a success," Zhu declared.

Song chuckled. "Thanks. This was a much better night than I'd been expecting."

"Do you and Ren have a day planned yet when you'll be able to see each other? Something to look forward to?"

A groan escaped Song as he rolled onto his hands and knees. He crawled over to a little side table and pulled a sheaf of papers from the drawer. When he was seated in front of Zhu, he started flipping through the paper calendar, searching for the day highlighted in yellow and circled in red ink.

"Late November. About three weeks away."

Zhu grunted and snatched the crumpled, worn pages from Song's hands. "Seriously? Paper? You don't have all this on your phone?"

"Of course, I do! I just like paper, too."

The man grunted. The scrape and crinkle of papers being flipped back and forth sounded from behind Song's head as he took another sip of water. He'd spent countless hours studying those pages, trying to find ways to move things around a tiny bit so they could see each other sooner.

"Wait a minute. What about this day in a week? You've got an early morning photo shoot that would probably be done before noon. He's got the day off. Why aren't you at least meeting up for lunch or dinner? Something!"

Song twisted and squinted at the paper, his heart racing. How was it possible that Zhu saw something that they'd both missed? When he saw the day Zhu was pointing to, he sighed heavily. Yeah, he'd spent way too much time trying to make something out of that day. At best, they were guaranteed a long video chat.

"Oh, he's got an event the previous night that will stretch late, and then the day after his free day he's got an early commercial shoot. He's lucky to be sleeping in his own bed that night."

Zhu's eyes narrowed on him and he continued to stare at Song as if he were speaking a foreign language. "You live in Shanghai full-time?"

Song nodded.

"And where the fuck does Ren live full-time?"

"Just outside of Beijing."

"Idiot!" Zhu shouted. He lurched upright and slapped Song on the top of the head with the stack of papers.

"What?"

"Moron! Idiot! This is why you can never see each other!" He ranted, continuing to hit Song on the top of the head with each sentence. "One of you has to move!"

"What?"

Zhu tossed the battered papers into Song's lap and leaned close enough that their noses were nearly touching. "This will never work if you have so little chance of seeing each other. One of you has to move to the other's city." Zhu rolled his eyes in disgust as if he couldn't believe they'd overlooked something so simple.

The truth was, Song had considered it, but he'd been afraid to bring it up to Ren. They were still so new to each other and moving was a big deal.

"Why are you in Shanghai?" Zhu suddenly asked.

"Work and to be close to my mom. She has a place just outside the city."

"And Ren? Why's he in Beijing?"

"I think it's mostly because Beijing is where he finished school. He's comfortable with the city. His family doesn't live there."

Zhu sighed and flopped back down on the couch. "It's settled. Ren moves to Shanghai." Song turned to see him staring at the ceiling and then give a nod. "That really does work best since me and gege live here too. Yuan Teng Fei splits his time between here and Wuhan—family. Shen Ruo Xuan is here, but he also works in Taipei a lot."

The impressive list rattled around in Song's brain, sparking what felt like a very insane idea. He knew a lot of his fellow actors lived in Shanghai. There were just as many up in Beijing, but he'd never given it any real thought until Zhu began naming them all. Particularly when he listed those who were in a similar situation as himself.

Song turned to face Zhu, his heart hammering faster and faster. He poked at the man's shoulder. "Hey. Hey!"

Zhu batted Song's hand away and cracked open an eye. "What? Ow, quit it. What?"

"Why aren't we living in the same building?" Song asked.

"Huh? What? You and me?"

"No!"

"Oh, you and Ren? You can't. That would totally throw up too many red flags. People would figure out you were both living in the same building eventually. Rumors would start. It would totally break the no-fraternizing post-promo rule."

"No, all of us," Song corrected. His words sped up as the idea solidified in his brain. "You, me, Guo Zi, Ren, Yuan Teng

Fei, his boyfriend, Shen Ruo Xuan. Hua Jun Bai is a solid, trustworthy ally. We could drag him in. I'm sure between all of us, we know a few other trustworthy people in the industry. We all get apartments in the same building. We watch out for each other, but it also creates the perfect cover. No one has any definitive proof that anything is happening."

It would create a safe zone for all of them.

It would allow him to be practically living with Ren.

Yes, neither one of them was home all that much, but it significantly increased their chances of seeing each other when they were free.

"But…" Zhu croaked, his voice immediately dying off. "Fuck!" he suddenly snarled and jerked on the sofa, shifting to pull his phone from his pocket.

"Who are you calling?"

He swore and showed Song his phone. "Gege still has my number blocked from earlier."

Song placed his hand on the phone and lowered it from where it was nearly pressed to his face. "It's almost four in the morning. He'd kick your ass before he bothered to listen to you."

"Yeah, but this sounds like a really, really good idea, and we're both too drunk to figure out why it won't work. Why didn't we think of this earlier?" Zhu Fang's voice was nearly a desperate whine.

Song got it. He wanted this to work too. His intoxicated and sleep-deprived brain said it should work, but Zhu was right to be skeptical. There had to be a good reason why it shouldn't.

Zhu pointed at him. "Get a pen. Find a pen and write this down. We can't forget this. We will talk about this again when we're sober."

Crawling back to the drawer where he stored the calendar, Song located a pen and scratched out a note about friends living together in a single building in Shanghai. He prayed that was enough to trigger his memory.

When he looked at Zhu Fang, his friend's mouth was partially hanging open and soft snores were lifting from him.

At least they'd figured out one thing: Either he or Ren needed to move.

37

GIVE ME SOME EYE CANDY
REN AN XUE

Ren was stupidly giddy.

He shouldn't be this happy. Especially over what amounted to a phone call.

But after the failure of their first meeting, Ren was grateful for the fact that they were able to lock in this video chat.

Today was a rare day off. He probably should have attempted to see his parents, but travel would have eaten up most of the day and it would have meant being unable to do more than exchange a handful of texts with Song.

Instead, he'd gotten up, worked out, eaten breakfast, and called his mother. After a tense thirty minutes listening to how he was wasting his time and how he looked silly in that long wig—she'd seen his picture plastered on a *freaking billboard*—Ren managed to escape with his good mood still roughly intact.

It seemed like Song might be as excited for their call. Ren had woken to a text from his boyfriend and then received another when he was leaving for his photo shoot. Another arrived just a few minutes ago to report that he was on his way home and would be free after a quick shower.

He stopped in front of the mirror for what felt like the

fiftieth time to check the way his hair was laying. Not bad. Casual but still appearing like he put forth some effort. Definitely not hanging down to block his eyes. He might hate that so much of his success was thanks to being born with these eyes, but right now, he was not above using these eyes to enamor and seduce the sexiest man he knew.

Despite the cooler weather, he'd chosen a sleeveless T-shirt to show off the new definition he'd acquired in his biceps. His latest show had required two different shirtless scenes and he'd worked hard to get these muscles and six-pack. At the very least, he should be able to get a little appreciation from his boyfriend.

And, fuck yes, he was horny.

It had been way too long since he'd enjoyed anything remotely physical with Song. It might be another two weeks before they saw each other in person, but he was hoping he could get a taste of his lover today. Just enough to hold him over for two more weeks.

Ren's phone chimed a ring designated for Song alone. His phone was usually on silent, but he hadn't wanted to risk missing this call. He darted across the room, scooped up his phone, and crashed onto his mattress with a bounce. The second he answered the call, Song's beautiful face filled the screen.

"Didi." Song sighed as if seeing Ren was a balm for all the things that ailed him.

"Song laoshi," Ren replied, pushing past the sudden catch in his throat. His eyes ate up the man in front of him. His hair was shorter now and loosely slicked back after his shower. There was a slightly rosier tint to his face from the hot water, and his lovely dark eyes glowed with joy.

"You look amazing," Song murmured. "You are the most beautiful person I have ever met. I miss you so much."

A tingling burn brushed over his cheeks, but Ren didn't let himself glance away from the camera. Song was the only one who could praise him and leave him feeling embarrassed. But then, Song was praising more than his appearance. When Song stared at him, Ren felt like he was gazing straight into his soul.

"I've missed you, too, Ah-Wei. How was your day?" He stretched out on his bed, tucking one bent arm behind his head.

Song flashed him a half smile. "Not bad. The photo shoot went smoothly. Traffic was manageable. I wasn't mobbed. All things that allowed me to hurry home to you. What about you?"

Ren shrugged. "Quiet day at home. I kind of forgot what those were like. Have you eaten?"

That got the eye roll he'd been expecting. "Bao Shi stuffed some takeout in my fridge. I'll heat it up later. I'm not hungry right now for anything but my didi."

Ren was tempted to follow up on Song's comment about food. It was the one thing he'd tried to be diligent about since they'd left Hengdian. Song sent him regular snapshots of the food he was eating to prove that he was eating. Ren sent him some here and there so his laoshi didn't worry. During their first month apart, neither one of them had been great about eating.

But Song had provided him with the perfect opening for a little playfulness.

"You're not the only one who's hungry, Ah-Wei. Why did you get dressed after your shower? You should have given me some more eye candy to enjoy," Ren teased.

Song's eyes widened briefly and a slow, wicked spread across his full, peach-tinted lips. "You want to see more of me, didi? I think that can be arranged. Where are you? You look comfortable."

"Stretched out in my bed, waiting for my show."

The screen briefly flashed to the ceiling of Song's room and the speaker was filled with the sound of rustling fabric.

When Song filled the screen again, it included his shirtless chest. The muscles appeared more defined.

"Ah-Wei, I want to touch you. No, kiss you." Ren sighed.

The background blurred for a second as Song lay on his own bed. They'd had a few bedtime conversations, and Ren felt like he knew those dark-navy sheets very well. His Song was particular about his thread count and loved his silky, smooth sheets. Ren was dying to stretch out on those sheets with his lover, to experience them firsthand.

"Exactly where do you want to kiss me, Ah-Xue?"

"I'd start on the corner of your mouth, then your Adam's apple. I'd lick across your collarbone. And down. I'd keep moving down. I'd lick and suck on your left nipple until it was hard on my tongue."

Song whimpered, squeezing his eyes shut tight and gritting his teeth as if he were trying to hold in a moan.

"I miss your skin, Ah-Wei. You have the best, softest skin. I want to kiss and suck every inch of you. I want to taste all of you."

"Didi, you need to lose some clothes so I've got some eye candy too," Song gritted out. "I need help remembering what it feels like when you're pressed against me."

Ren barely held back a silly giggle as he set his phone aside long enough to sit up and rip off his shirt. He tossed it aside and lifted his hips to shove his shorts and underwear to the bottom of the bed.

"Naked!" he declared as soon as he picked up the phone again. "What about you? You can't feel me if you're still wearing clothes, Song laoshi."

Song narrowed his eyes at him for a second. "We're really doing this already? My didi is starved."

"Starved doesn't begin to cover it. If I was there, I would have attacked you the second you stepped past the threshold. I would have pinned you to the door, pulled down your pants, and sucked your cock until you were screaming my name."

"Oh God, yes. That. I want that," Song groaned. At the edge of the screen, Ren could see Song's arm moving as if he'd started stroking himself.

"When I come to town, I might need to suck you a few times. I've only done it twice, and I need the practice. Will you let me practice on you, Ah-Wei?"

As he spoke, Ren's hand slid along his stomach and wrapped around the base of his cock. He loved the idea of his words driving his boyfriend to the edge of orgasm. Song's face was beautifully flushed, and his lips were wet as he licked and sucked them.

"Whatever you want, Ah-Xue. All of me belongs to you," Song panted.

"Do you want me inside of you again?" he whispered. Song's voice crested into a loud moan, sending a spike of pleasure into Ren's dick.

"Yes. I want to feel you inside me so bad. Please. I need that."

"Toys!" Ren suddenly shouted as the idea struck him.

Song seemed to jump. "What?"

"Toys. Do you have any toys?" Part of Ren couldn't believe he was even asking this question. Was he willing to go down this road with his boyfriend? It was just a few months ago that he'd been afraid to even touch Song's dick. Now he was practically begging to watch Song insert sexy things into his body.

"Are you serious?" Song choked out. His eyes were wide and his face appeared red for an entirely new reason.

"Don't you dare get shy on me, Ah-Wei. I've been inside of you. I've swallowed your cum," Ren purred.

"Not shy, didi," Song admitted and cleared his throat. "I'm wishing I did. Just thinking about you telling me what to do with a toy has me on edge."

Ren grinned at his lover, his hand speeding up on his own dick. Wonderful tingles of pleasure were kissing along nerve endings and leaving him lightheaded. He needed to come so fucking bad, but he wanted to hold off. He wanted to hear Song lose his control first. "I'd tell you to get something by the time I arrive in town, but there's no point. I don't want anything else coming between us. I want all of you. I want to fuck you in every room of your apartment, on every surface. For the hours we're together, I want to be permanently attached to your body."

"Yes. Fuck, yes. So close," Song cried out.

"Move the phone, Ah-Wei. I want to see it. I need to see you come," Ren demanded.

The camera grew shaky as Song stretched out his arm, giving him a long view up his body. His fist shuttled quickly along his red, glistening dick. He paused just long enough to gather up the pre-cum and use it as a lubricant to ease the glide of his hand.

Song lasted only a few more strokes and he was coming, shooting thick ropes of white cum across his stomach. But it was his harsh shout of pleasure that tipped Ren over the edge. He followed Song, calling out his lover's name. The world went black, all his muscles tensing and straining as ecstasy exploded like fireworks throughout his body.

"You…you kill me, didi," Song panted when Ren's brain started working again.

"Why do you say that?" Ren murmured, not caring that the goofiest smile was plastered on his lips.

"Because you are the sexiest thing. From your looks to everything out of your mouth. It's like you were designed for the sole purpose of destroying me."

Just like Song was designed to wrap tightly around his heart and never let go.

"I promise that every time I take you apart, I will be right there in the next second to put you back together."

Song huffed out a laugh. "That's good, because I don't feel like I can move anytime soon."

Ren hummed softly to himself, his eyes falling shut. "I wish I was there, Song laoshi." He could almost feel Song's body pressed to his, their skin sticking together, their breathing falling into a steady rhythm.

"Don't hate me, Ren," Song started and paused. He flashed his own big, dark eyes at Ren, giving him a taste of his own medicine.

"Impossible. Why?"

"I think I like the post-sex cuddling as much as I like the sex," Song admitted. "I like listening to your heartbeat under my ear."

Ren relaxed again. "I like running my fingers through your hair as you talk about weird things."

"Weird things? When have I ever talked about anything weird?" Song gasped.

A choked laugh escaped Ren, and he opened his eyes to stare at his lover's faux-indignant expression. He could clearly see Song fighting a smile. He knew very well that he loved to bring up the strangest topics just to get a reaction out of Ren. And Ren always knew exactly what he was doing.

"The logistics of raising guinea pigs," Ren reminded him.

"They're cute and they make that fun sound."

"Whether an apple orchard would be haunted if we used people's ashes to grow them rather than creating cemeteries."

"That's ecologically responsible. But also, if you made a pie out of those apples, would the pie be haunted?"

Ren cackled and Song quickly joined him. Ren loved how Song's mind worked.

They fell into a lot of silly, nonsensical conversations for the next hour. Ren knew he should get up and clean off, but he didn't want to move. He was comfortably stretched out on his bed, and his eyes were locked on his beautiful lover's face. What more could he ask for?

Well, he would prefer it if he was there, holding Song in

his arms, as they had their crazy conversations, but this would have to do until he got to Shanghai.

"I love you, Song laoshi," Ren announced suddenly.

Song's face broke into the sweetest, softest smile. His eyes grew shiny and he rapidly blinked. "I love you too, my Ren An Xue. Even when we're not together, I feel like I fall a little more in love with you each day."

"That's good, because you are so very stuck with me."

And one day, he was going to figure out a way for them to be together.

Even if it meant giving up the life he'd been working so hard to build for himself.

38

DON'T PANIC
SONG WEI LI

"Don't go on social media," Bao Shi announced the second Song opened the door for him.

Song dropped his head back and groaned as he stepped out of the way to allow his friend and assistant into the apartment. This was his first day off in *weeks*. When he woke up that morning, he'd been too tired to do more than text Bao Shi and beg him to bring over some food because his refrigerator was empty except for beer, condiments, and some noodles that were growing fuzz.

Legend of the Lost Night had started airing a week ago to rave reviews. People were losing their minds over it. The excitement in the air was palpable. His social media following and fan clubs were exploding. The same was happening for Ren and several of the other actors on the show.

The marketing division for the show was kindly giving him and Ren a couple of days off. *Ha!* Song knew better. They were going to work them into the ground over the next few weeks to keep the buzz going for the show. It was going to be endless interviews, talk shows, variety shows, web shows, commercial shoots, photo shoots, and whatever else they could think of.

The only thing that made all of that mildly tolerable was that Ren was going to be right at his side the entire time.

No, they wouldn't be able to touch.

And they wouldn't have a second for a private word.

But right now, Song would be happy with just sharing the same air as the man.

The last time they'd managed to sneak some private time had been in the middle of December—two months ago.

He'd wanted to spend the lunar new year with Ren, but they'd both agreed to be good sons and spend it with their respective families. Ren had texted almost constantly about the pain of being home, while Song attempted to lift his spirits with silly pictures and memes.

Song's mother might have suspected something, but she was kind enough not to ask too many questions. He was fairly certain she would accept him and Ren, but Song wasn't ready to head down that road.

Everything had been going well.

And now, Mo Bao Shi was warning him off social media.

Fuck.

He knew things had been going too good for too long. He'd even thought of an excellent way to approach Ren about moving to Shanghai. He'd floated it when they were able to meet up in November, but Ren had been hesitant, thinking it might look too suspicious if he moved too soon in relation to the release of *Legend*.

The man had a good point, but part of Song just didn't care. He needed his Ren closer to him.

"I don't want to know," Song mumbled as he shut the door behind Bao Shi.

"Good."

Song followed his friend and the heavenly scent of spices. It smelled like his friend had picked up his favorite stir-fry. This had to be really bad. "Does it also involve Ren?"

"I thought you didn't want to know," Bao Shi replied as he carried the food into the kitchen.

"I don't, but I figure it can't be too bad if my manager isn't blowing my phone up."

"Oh, she is, but I already talked to her and told her that I'd talk to you in person first."

Song's stomach complained as he bypassed the kitchen and walked straight into the living room for his cell phone. If Bao Shi was attempting to soften the blow, it had to be a fucking nightmare.

The first thing he noticed was a stack of missed texts.

Ren: Don't panic.

Ren: Don't issue any statements yet!

Ren: Working on something. Will call soon.

Zhu Fang: Don't be stupid. Keep your mouth shut!

Guo Zi: We got your back.

Hua: This has to be the snake. Going to crush the fucker!!!!

If anything, seeing all of that made him start to panic more. How was it that everyone was already reaching out to him?

This was why it was dangerous to sleep. These people couldn't post anything crazy at civil hours when he was awake and ready to tackle the world.

With a racing heart, Song popped over to WeChat. It wasn't hard to discover what had everyone in an uproar. A new video had been posted of him and Ren in an elevator together.

Yeah, okay, so they were both leaning their shoulders against the wall while facing each other. And yes, they were standing a bit close. And their expressions were more than a little intimate. Not great, but not horrible.

What the fuck...

The video panned in a slight blur to focus on a hotel check-in desk.

Someone had doctored the video to make it look like they were checking into a hotel together.

"What the fuck! This is fucking bullshit!" Song roared. He held out the phone toward Bao Shi who was standing on the other side of the room and shook it at him. "This is bullshit! This video of us was taken at Hengdian! We were in Hengdian, not some hotel! I don't think we've ever been booked in the same hotel together. We've never…" Song had started to say that he'd never even been in the same hotel as Ren, but then he remembered the time he'd taken Ren up to his hotel room just before they began filming *Legend*. Thank God no one had been around to catch video of that. Ren had been drunk and leaning heavily on him as they stumbled down the hall to his hotel room.

That would have been really bad, and no one would have believed that nothing had happened between them.

"We've never stayed in a hotel together," Song repeated. "This is a fucking fake."

"Yes, the last half of it is, but it's a pretty good fake. And most people don't care because the first half of that video is clearly real," Bao Shi pointed out. He crossed the room and flopped into one of Song's chairs. He pulled off his black baseball hat and ran his fingers through his black spiked hair. "Right now, everything is a giant mess. The CP shipper fans are over the moon thinking that you're a real-life couple. The show shippers are pretty happy as well. The solo fans—particularly the girlfriend fans—are pissed at both of you because you're ruining their fantasy of having either of you. The homophobes are also in an uproar."

"They hated *Legend* in the first place," Song snapped.

Bao Shi shrugged. "More fuel for the fire, I guess. Either way, everyone is fighting everyone. There is a small group out there stating that the video is obviously a fake, but too many people want it to be real, so they're being drowned out."

Song dropped onto the sofa and lowered his head into his

hands. "Do I want to know what the show producers and TV executives are saying?"

"From what your manager said, they are quiet. Not happy, but they aren't blaming you and Ren An Xue yet." He paused and snorted. "But you know that tune could change if the ratings for tonight's airing of the show drops or if the censors decide to stop the airing."

Song closed his eyes and wracked his brain for the exact memory of that day, but so many of them blurred together. It looked like it was at the end of a shooting day, probably after the first full month at Hengdian. But beyond that, it didn't stick out as anything special. They appeared exhausted and happy to be away from the world.

Whoever took the video had to be someone from the cast or crew. The elevators were tucked down a hall off the main entrance. Fans couldn't get that far into the building.

It was one thing to post the video of them in the elevator, but to add that fake part about the hotel was just malicious. Someone had set out to hurt them, and it left him feeling nauseated. Who could possibly hate them so much that they would do something like that?

Hua Jun Bai had mentioned "the snake." Could it really be Liu Haoyu? Yes, he had obvious designs on Ren and Song had thwarted him at every turn, but was that worthy of trying to destroy both their reputations and careers?

"Song?"

"This is bullshit," he muttered under his breath. He lifted his head and glared at Bao Shi. "I can't sit here and do nothing."

"Song—"

He shook his head and grabbed his phone, dialing Ren's number. His lover was supposed to have a light day of work. Song thought he might have a livestream or something, but he couldn't remember at that moment. If Ren was busy, he wouldn't answer.

"Hey, Song laoshi." Ren's sweet, gentle voice drifted into his ear after the second ring. It was like being wrapped in a hug, instantly easing some of the rage that had been building in his chest.

"This is fucking ridiculous," Song snarled.

"I know. The video is mostly a lie. I thought I was used to having my privacy invaded, but this feels worse because it was taken inside the residence hall at Hengdian. We had at least some small expectation of privacy inside the building."

Song paced to the sliding glass door and back, his anger rising. Every instinct within his body was beating against his brain, demanding that he do something to protect his lover. Ren was hurting, even if he was trying to mask it in his tone. And if didi was hurting, Song laoshi needed to fucking do something about it.

"Do you remember that day?" Song asked.

Ren huffed a bitter, breathy laugh. "Song, there were so many days in Hengdian that ended looking exactly like that. At best, I think that video might have been taken in July, after your concert, but I'm not one hundred percent sure. I watched it on my computer and found a brief reflection of the person who took the video in the doors as they closed. I've got a friend who's trying to clean up the image to see if we can figure out who took the original of us."

"Hua seems to think it's Liu Haoyu," Song grumbled. His fingers tightened on his cell phone until his knuckles ached.

Ren made a noise Song couldn't quite identify, but it certainly wasn't happy. "Yeah, he's the first person who crossed my mind, but I can't believe he's that big of an idiot. If we can prove it was him, does he think word won't get around our community that he stabbed fellow actors in the back? If it gets out that he can't be trusted, no one will want to work with him. No one."

"Yeah, well, I get the impression that he really wanted you, and I fucking cock-blocked him at every turn."

A low purring of happiness rippled through the phone and wrapped Song up like a tight hug. "Yes, my laoshi was very protective on the set. You didn't let anyone near me."

"Of course I didn't. You're mine, Ren An Xue. No one else is allowed near you. No one is allowed to hurt you," Song snapped, nearly shouting into the phone. "That's why I can't just stand by and do nothing right now when they are slandering you on the Internet. This is bullshit, and we all know it. I have to make some kind of statement, even if it's to say that I was the instigator. That I came on to you or that—"

"Song Wei Li, you have to promise me that you won't release any statement or post on social media yet." Ren's voice dipped low and hardened. It almost felt like Zhao Gang had ripped the phone from Ren's hands and started growling at the enemies of Tian Xiuying. It was a tone that Ren hadn't used in months, and it was like a splash of cold water across his face.

Song shuffled across the floor, pulling at his hair with his free hand. "We can't do nothing. It will only become more out of control as time passes."

"I'm not saying that we do nothing. My manager has contacted lawyers. We're looking into filing an official police report. Zhou Yuying has also talked to your manager and Yang Lan Fen about it. I think your manager is looking into it as well. I'm sure the production company already has a mob of lawyers. The police reports will keep the censors at bay, I think. For now, I'm saying wait to make a statement. I have a plan. Things are still coming together."

"But—"

"Song laoshi, do you remember the last time we had a video issue while we were in Hengdian? You made up the bet bullshit to protect me?"

He nearly growled at his didi. This feeling of helplessness was driving him crazy. He had to do something to protect his lover. "Yes, but that was a much smaller thing compared to this. We can't cook up some silly video explaining this away. You need to let me help."

"You will. I—" Ren suddenly broke off. His boyfriend continued talking, but the sound was greatly muffled as if he'd covered the phone with his hand as he spoke to someone else.

"Ren?"

"Sorry. I need to jump off here. Please, I'm begging you. Don't do anything yet. I'll have more instructions and information soon, I promise," Ren replied in a rush.

Before Song could reply, Ren ended the call.

Fuck.

He dropped the hand holding the phone to his side and turned to glare at Bao Shi. "Have you talked to him? Do you know what Ren's planning?"

"I got a text from him. He said he's got things under control. I am to keep an eye on you and make sure that you don't do anything stupid."

Song opened his mouth to shout at Bao Shi just because he needed to let some of this frustration out, but a knock at his door trapped the words in his throat. His heart skipped in his chest and he wasn't proud that his first thought was that it was Ren.

But that was impossible. Ren was in Beijing.

Right?

Song marched to the front door, his steps growing quicker. Who the hell could be at his place now? The only other people who had direct access to his building were his mother and his manager. His mom showing up in the middle of this scandal would not be good. She would have at least called first.

Besides, she knew better than to believe the rumors and talk.

Song ripped open the door and his mouth dropped.

"Hey, Song Wei Li," Yuan Teng Fei greeted with a half smile. "Ren sent me."

"I…what?" Song choked out. His brain decided to tap out and stop working. How the fuck had Ren gotten Yuan Teng Fei to show up on his doorstep?

The actor in question waved one of his hands at Song, motioning for the man to retreat into his apartment so he could enter. "Ren An Xue has a plan, but we need to get moving." Yuan Teng Fei's dark eyes swept down Song, taking in his rumpled clothes and then up to his messy hair. "And it looks like you need to at least take a shower first. Let's go. I don't want to tell Ren that I didn't get you ready in time."

Song backpedaled, allowing Yuan Teng Fei into his place.

Nothing made sense anymore, but one thing was becoming very clear. His beautiful, brilliant boyfriend had called in the big guns, and he was getting a sneaking feeling that Ren was going to take no prisoners when it came to protecting his Song laoshi.

39

OH MY GOD, I LOVE EVIL REN
REN AN XUE

"I've got to say, Ren," Zhou Yuying started as she glanced up from her phone, "you've got a much bigger evil streak than I ever would have guessed."

His manager was sitting in the chair opposite the couch, endlessly scrolling through the social media posts that were coming in on WeChat and Weibo regarding that stupid video.

"I figured that it's a good idea to hit hard now to show that I'm not going to be someone's target just because I am still relatively new to this industry," Ren murmured. He unbuttoned the cuffs on his stylish dark-red shirt and rolled up one sleeve above his elbow. He began on the other sleeve as he turned his attention to his assistant, who was working furiously on the laptop next to him. "Are we ready?"

"Yep. Everything looks great on our end. I'm ready to post this on your social media accounts and send it out to the fan clubs." She lifted her gaze to Zhou. "This is your last chance to say no."

"What do you think? Too harsh?" Ren asked. Nerves twisted in his stomach, but it was nothing compared to the rage that was bubbling over throughout the rest of him. This video was like the starter pistol to his master plan.

"Are you sure it's Liu who kicked off this shit show?" Zhou inquired.

"You saw the image I pulled from the video. That was totally him," Wu Dong Mei argued.

"Even if it wasn't him who created the fake add-on to the released video, it was clearly him who took the original video. Handing that over to anyone could not have been done with the best of intentions in mind. He was either looking to hurt Song, me, or both of us."

His manager offered up a regal nod of her head. "The lawyers approved the message. Fuck him up, Ren."

"Do it," Ren said with a smile.

His incredibly sweet and adorable assistant threw back her head and released the most evil cackle Ren had ever heard in his life as she slammed her index finger onto the enter key. It was as if she'd created this posting cascade. Emails flew out in the blink of an eye, and the video was uploaded. Ren sent out his own text to a group chat he'd created.

My video is live.

A couple of seconds later, the replies immediately started rolling in.

Ready!

Just finished up.

Oh my God, I love evil Ren.

Ready!

I swear to fuck, you have the world's slowest boyfriend.

Ren snickered at Yuan Teng Fei's text. He did not blame Song for dragging his feet. He would have too if Song had kept him in the dark. Ren hadn't wanted to, but it was hard to give details on something that had been constantly changing for the past several hours. With everyone's incredibly busy schedule, wrangling something of this magnitude had not been a small feat. Ren hadn't wanted to give Song hope of this if he couldn't pull it off.

And to pull it off, it had to be huge.

Wu Dong Mei squealed next to him. "The first post already has over fifty shares and counting. The hashtags TruthforRenandSong and BogusSongRenVideo are gaining ground over the HotelScandal hashtag."

Ren's video in response to the fake video was short and simple. He'd written the script and had it approved by his manager and their new lawyers before it was filmed by Wu Dong Mei. And yes, there were lines to read between for the fans.

Wu Dong Mei pulled up his video on the computer and he watched over her shoulder, double-checking that the playback was clean.

"Hello, everyone. Thanks for taking time out of your busy day to watch this. First, I want to thank everyone who has supported and shared kind words for Legend of the Lost Night. *I have been very excited to see how well loved the story and characters are. So many wonderful people worked very hard this past summer on it, and we are touched by your love.*

"Second, I want to address the horrible, fake video that has been floating around the Internet today. Yes, the first half of the video is true." Ren paused, his lips forming a tiny smirk. *"I have ridden in an elevator with Song Wei Li. While filming* Legend *in Hengdian, we were living in the same residence hall and occasionally we shared an elevator."* That smile disappeared and Ren's expression turned icy. *"But the rest of the video has been doctored with libelous intent. It is undeniably false. The video was released with the obvious purpose of harming myself and my costar.*

"I wish to state that I will not tolerate any attacks on myself, nor will I stand by and allow someone to attack those people whom I respect. We have already identified the person who took the original video, and steps are being taken. I have also shared this information with other people who I believe might need to protect themselves from this malicious person.

"Trust is a critical thing in this industry. We must be able to trust our fellow actors and the crew when we are working. And when that trust is broken, it's nearly impossible to regain it.

"Thank you again for all your love and support."

The video ended with a warm smile but a cold look in Ren's eyes.

That was just the warning shot.

"Yes! Ma Daiyu's video is up too!" Zhou shouted. "Shit. I had no idea she could be so scary."

"Good, though?" Ren asked. He'd given several people a rough script as well as a list of things *not* to say. They were not to name any names or attack anyone specifically, but the warning had to be clear. The person who took the video was known and they were on the shit list of a lot of actors in the community.

"Oh, yeah. She stuck to the script. Talked about how you and Song were always the model of decorum and the best of friends. Though I think she called the person who took the video a nutless sleezebag or something like that."

"Hua's video is also up!" Wu Dong Mei added.

Ren leaned over as she hit play on Hua Jun Bai's video. Ren blinked at it a couple of times, shocked to see him without long black hair. Every time he'd encountered Hua in Hengdian, the man had been on set in full costume. It was weird to see him in street clothes and a modern haircut. Was it also strange to be surprised that he was such a good-looking man?

And then Hua opened his mouth and reminded Ren exactly why he wanted to strangle him so often.

"*Are you shitting me?*" Hua started. He paused, leaned toward the camera, and offered up his sexiest skeptical smile. "*Did you really think you could float such an obviously fake video to convince the world that something was going on between Song Wei Li and Ren An Xue? Wow. Just...wow.*" He paused again and leaned back so that viewers could more clearly see his impressive chest stretching his black button-down shirt. Yeah, Hua was going for a lovely mix of condescension and sex appeal. He played the perfect asshole. Of course, most of the characters he played on screen were also assholes. People expected it from him.

"Look, I'll give you Song and Ren were convincing as Tian and Zhao, but as anything more than friends in real life? That's laughable. It only shows that you've got a pathetic, little…ax to grind, and now we all know it."

Wu Dong Mei giggled wildly and Ren groaned, dropping his face into his hand. *Good Lord.* This wasn't exactly the script, but then Hua wasn't naming names, so that was a plus.

"Slandering actors is never good. Lying and backstabbing are never acceptable. Hell, I can't believe I even have to say this, but hurting innocent people just because you don't like something is never good. And trust me, there are always consequences for actions like that." Hua dropped the playful, sexy smile and glared into the camera. "*I stand with Song Wei Li and Ren An Xue. They are innocent of these accusations. Please continue to support them with me.*"

Ren dropped against the couch and loudly sighed. "Okay, that ended strong at least."

"Guo Zi's video is up," Zhou Yuying announced. "God, that man is so hot and adorable. Oh, and he got a bunch of his friends to vouch for you and Song, too."

Ren grabbed his phone and dug up Guo Zi's social media account. The video was solid. Definitely less controversial and laden with less sexual innuendo than Hua's. It looked like he was on a break from rehearsal with the rest of his group. Guo Zi had a concert coming up in a couple of days, and it was all the more touching that he stopped on one of his few breaks to make this video.

It was even more touching that he'd pulled in the entire group to support Ren and Song.

"Oh! Oh! Oh! Zhu Fang's video is up."

Yeah, that had his nerves racing back with a vengeance. He'd been mildly worried about Hua Jun Bai. Zhu Fang was a total wild card. There was no telling what was going to come out of his mouth. It didn't help that Guo Zi was in Beijing and

Zhu Fang was currently filming in Hengdian. It was shocking he could even cram this video into his schedule.

"Hey, my lovelies! As everyone knows, I'm busy shooting at Hengdian for my newest drama, but I had to take a moment to comment on the ridiculous video that's going around about my close friend, Song Wei Li," Zhu Fang started.

Ren leaned closer to the computer screen. Where had Zhu Fang shot this video? The sound was strange, as if he were in a small, enclosed space.

"I thought I'd just clear up the question of where that elevator was located." Zhu Fang moved the camera farther away from his face so that they could see more of the background. *"This look familiar?"*

"Holy shit," Ren breathed.

There was soft ding and a mechanical noise. Zhu Fang began walking with the most devilish smirk on his lips as he revealed that he was in the same exact elevator where the video had been taken. At Hengdian.

That fucking evil genius.

Zhu Fang continued to go on about how he supported Song Wei Li and Ren An Xue while walking toward the front doors of the residence. He stepped outside, directed the camera at the fans who held signs with his name. From his surroundings, it was obvious he was in Hengdian.

It was the coffin nail they needed.

Proof that they were not in a hotel elevator running off to some secret assignation. No, they were just two actors exhausted after a long day of work.

No one needed to know the amount of flirting, kissing, cuddling, or sex that happened behind closed doors. But then, no one needed to know how much he loved Song Wei Li. The only person who needed to know that every second of every day was his Song laoshi.

Over the next hour, another dozen videos were posted by other actors that both Ren and Song had worked with over the years. Most of them Ren had personally contacted, but there were a few he hadn't talked to. They'd simply jumped on the bandwagon of support.

He asked Wu Dong Mei to make a list of every actor who'd posted a video in support of him and Song. Ren wanted to be able to send a personal message of thanks to each and every one of them. The outreach and warm support was overwhelming, and it was working to quell the negative chatter. So many actors were using their clout and their fan base for a positive cause. They were united for once instead of all the quiet backstabbing that so frequently happened.

Of course, it wasn't entirely altruistic. They could all see it. If they were united for this cause, these people could come to their rescue if they found themselves the focus of fake news that threatened their career.

"Ren?" His head snapped up to look at his manager who was smiling at him. "Yuan Teng Fei's video is now up too."

This was the one he'd been waiting on.

He pulled up Yuan Teng Fei's social media account, which was packed with millions of followers, and started the video. His heart gave a happy pitter-pat when he instantly recognized the background as Song's apartment. He'd visited it only twice, but Song had taken him on virtual tours as well. Ren had tried to memorize every inch of it so he could close his eyes and imagine Song in his own space.

Yuan Teng Fei's remarks were short and concise. He supported his friend, Song Wei Li, and denounced this attack on his character with an obviously fake video. He tossed out the casual remark that he was treating his friend to dinner to help him forget about this nonsense.

"But first, he does have something to say…"

The camera view shifted to reveal a dashing and sexy Song Wei Li, his expression sweet and somber.

"I just want to quickly say thank you to all who have defended and

supported me and Ren An Xue during this unfortunate attack. I will work to always be worthy of your love."

And that was it. He closed with a small smile and lifted his left hand to make a heart with his thumb and index finger.

Short and classy.

Perfect.

Song proved that he was above this chaos and nonsense. His friends did plenty to cover him, allowing Song to rise above it all.

The screen shifted to black and filled with Song's name as he called. Ren shoved to his feet and crossed to his bedroom so he could take the call in private.

"Are you okay?" he demanded when he answered and closed the door behind him.

Song's warm, amused voice wrapped around him. "I'm left wondering how I got so lucky as to get someone like you to love me."

"You know I will do anything to protect you," Ren murmured. He wished he was there. Every part of him longed to pull Song close and hold him until the last of these ugly thoughts faded into indistinct, foggy memories.

"I know, didi. I'm in awe of what you arranged. Thank you. Thank you so much."

"I think it's an important message as well to our friends that we've got their backs no matter what."

"And a good reminder that we aren't alone in this." He chuckled suddenly. "Yuan Teng Fei did just point out that we are expected at Shen Ruo Xuan's surprise birthday party in four months as payment for this favor."

Ren laughed. "Deal. Send me the date and location. I swear I'll be there with the best fucking gift."

"I love you, didi."

"I love you with all that I am, Song Wei Li. No one is ever coming between us."

"Never," Song whispered.

When the call ended, Ren pressed a kiss to the screen, wishing it was Song's lips, but it was okay. They'd meet up again soon enough. He was in love with the most amazing man, and nothing was going to keep them apart. They had friends to support them, and he and Song were more than happy to support their friends through the rough times.

40

FAMILY
SONG WEI LI

Song paced in the brightly lit space, each footstep crackling across the dirty floor and echoing off the newly sanded drywall. Wires hung out of openings like wild vines. The realtor said they were two weeks out from finishing the place. Two weeks from signing the final paperwork.

Two weeks from making one of the biggest bets of his life.

Quick footsteps echoed along the hall, and Song's heartbeat sped up. He could do this. It would work out.

He turned as a tall, lanky figure in jeans and a T-shirt appeared in the open doorway. The figure wore a red baseball cap, sunglasses, and a mask, but Song would recognize his lover anywhere.

Reaching up, he removed his own mask so Ren could see his smiling face. The tension in Ren's shoulders instantly disappeared as he pulled off his sunglasses and mask. He shoved the mask into his back pocket while hooking the arm of his glasses on the collar of his shirt.

"I was beginning to think you gave me the wrong address," Ren said with a wide grin. As Ren reached him, Song grabbed his hand and dragged him down the hall into what was going to be the bedroom. The moment they were tucked in some of the deepest shadows and away from the window, Song tugged Ren in close, capturing his wonderful mouth in a delicious kiss.

Ren moaned softly, lips parting instantly while his arms wrapped tightly around him. Since the launch of *Legend of the Lost Night* two months ago, they'd not been able to steal any time to be together. Today was their only day and even then, Ren was flying out late tonight to travel to Hong Kong while Song was preparing to return to Hengdian for a new project.

Their lives had been a good chaotic. There were a few more social media scandals, but nothing on the scale of the bogus hotel video and nothing that stuck for long. People were in love with *Legend*. They were in love with him and Ren.

But no one loved Ren An Xue as much as Song, and he wanted this to last forever.

Ren hummed softly and moved his lips to kiss the corner of Song's mouth. "I love this, but if we were going to have this kind of fun, we should have met at your place."

"But we are at my place."

His lover jerked backward, his eyes narrowing on Song in confusion before sweeping about to take in the nearly finished room. The bedroom needed a coat of paint, the final flooring to be laid, and the light fixtures to be added.

"Seriously? You bought this?"

Song threaded his fingers through Ren's and smiled, while his heart rate picked up. "I did. Let me give you the tour."

Hand in hand, Song took Ren slowly through each of the rooms. He was particularly pleased when Ren appreciated the larger-than-normal shower that would be able to easily fit both of them. He loved how Ren remarked on the abundance of light that poured into the place and how the space held an airy feel.

Ren ooohed over the kitchen with all of its counterspace.

Song might have spent a ridiculous amount of time imagining Ren in his kitchen while Song sat at the breakfast bar chatting with him. Just like in Hengdian.

When he'd completed his initial walkthrough with the realtor, the only question he asked himself was whether he could see Ren moving comfortably through this space. And room after room, the answer had been yes.

"Song laoshi, this place is amazing. I love it," Ren said as they moved into the living room.

Still holding Ren's hand, Song took a deep breath, reached into his pocket, and dropped to one knee. Ren's hand flinched in his while wide puppy eyes locked on his face.

"Holy shit," Ren exhaled.

Song pulled a box out of his pocket and lifted it up toward Ren. With a flick of his thumb, he knocked the lid off and revealed…a silver key ring with an attached medallion in the shape of a silver fan.

Ren rocked backward, his wonderful laughter filling the room.

Yeah, Song would have preferred it to be a different type of ring, but China didn't recognize the marriage of two men. Maybe one day he'd steal Ren off to another country where they could be married, but for now, this was a close second.

"Ren An Xue, I love you completely," Song stated, his voice trembling slightly. "I love everything about you, and I will never stop. You are my entire world. When I get my keys to this place, I want to put one of them on this key ring for you. I want you to view my home as your home. I want you to feel comfortable walking in that door whenever you want, whether I'm here or not. I want my home to be your home, always."

Ren plucked the silver key ring out of the box and lifted it to his lips. His bright eyes glistened with unshed tears and he nodded. "Yes. I love you, Ah-Wei. I want to be with you always."

Dropping the empty box on the floor, Song shoved to his feet and pulled the love of his life in for another sweet, hungry kiss.

When he pulled away, a couple of tears streaked Ren's face, but the most beautiful smile stretched across his lips.

Song held on to his smile as he launched into the hardest part of his pitch. The first half had been easy.

"You know," he began slowly, "it would be a lot more convenient for you to stop by our place if you were already living in Shanghai."

To his shock, Ren threw his head back and laughed. "And do you know how long I've been waiting for you to bring that up again?"

Song's eyebrows jumped toward his hairline and he stared at his boyfriend. "Really? You always talk about how comfortable it is to live in Beijing. How convenient it is."

"It's comfortable because it's familiar, but it's very inconvenient when it comes to you." Ren looked at the key ring in his hand, his thumb caressing the open folding fan. Song had chosen it to commemorate how they met with Ren playing the devilishly handsome and possessive Zhao Gang. "I've been waiting for you to say something for months, but I was starting to think that maybe you preferred having that breathing space between us. That you were afraid if we lived in the same city, you'd feel crowded by me."

Song grabbed Ren's side and pulled him in until their chests bumped. He pressed his nose against Ren's while saying through clenched teeth, "If I had my way, there would never be an inch of space between us. Of course I want you living in Shanghai." Song stepped back and growled. "I knew I should have said something just before we left Hengdian. I was afraid of rushing you."

Ren chuckled again. "I guess it's a good thing I've already begun searching for a place. Right now, I've got an opening in my schedule during the summer. I'm hoping to find a place and move in a few months."

Oh yes, thank you to whichever ancestor was watching out. This couldn't be more perfect.

"Well, I did hear that the place right next door to mine is still available," Song said in what was supposed to be a casual tone, but he was inwardly bouncing with way too much excitement.

Ren pulled completely free of Song, his mouth falling open. He just stared at him for a couple of seconds as if he'd completely lost his mind.

"I…what…no…" Ren stopped and started several times, as though he couldn't quite wrap his brain around what Song was suggesting. "But I couldn't…" He shook his head violently and took another step away from Song as if he were afraid his resistance would crumble at the smallest touch from his lover. "It would look too suspicious. I mean, it would be perfect. We could come and go between our places and no one would ever know."

That was what Song loved about the idea. *Privacy*.

No one would ever have to know which bed they fell asleep in each night. No one would know where they ate breakfast or lounged at the end of a long day.

No one would know but them.

Ren shook his head again. "Even if we both purchased our places under company names, people would find out eventually that we were living in the same building. We'd get blacklisted."

Song shrugged. "Maybe, but that's not the only thing you'd have to worry about. There are also the neighbors."

"Well, yeah—"

"Guo Zi and Zhu Fang have both bought places a floor below this one. I'm personally terrified about the idea of having Zhu Fang that close at hand. I'm just grateful that he travels as frequently as he does."

"What?" Ren choked out. "They're getting places here, too?"

Song nodded, hope rising in his chest. "Those apartments will be done next week, so they should be moved in before me. And then, Yuan Teng Fei has already bought a place two floors above me, because that asshole has to prove he's a top to everyone."

Ren snorted. "What about his boyfriend, Shen Ruo Xuan?"

"Signed the initial paperwork and submitted the down payment yesterday. Same floor as Yuan Teng Fei."

"Fuck," Ren whispered, the word even more muffled as he placed his hand over his mouth. He turned away from Song and took a few stumbling steps into the living room. His eyes were wide and dazed, as if he couldn't quite believe what he was hearing.

"That's not the worst of it."

"What do you mean?" Ren demanded, swinging back toward him and dropping his hand to his side.

"Hua Jun Bai managed to get a place on the same floor as Zhu Fang and Guo Zi. So, you'd be stuck with him as a neighbor too."

"I…I just can't believe…" Ren stammered.

Song walked over and took both of Ren's hands in his. "I know what I'm proposing is still dangerous. All of us will need to be careful and take precautions, but any accusations will be a lot harder to prove if we stick together." He squeezed Ren's hand and smiled at his lover. "You showed me that in February. We're stronger together. A united front."

"You are such an evil genius. I can't believe you've been working on this for…"

"Months," Song filled in. "And I can't take full credit. Remember that night I got drunk with Zhu Fang?"

Ren nodded. "You called me a few times talking gibberish."

Song rolled his eyes. "Yeah, well, I apparently managed to sober up enough to have one good idea. Zhu Fang and I have been quietly searching for a place since November. We needed to find somewhere that was nearing completion, but still had a lot of apartments available. And then Guo Zi is picky, so it had to meet his specifications. And then talking Yuan Teng Fei into anything is a headache. With everyone in one place, even if we can't spend time together because one of us is in another city, there's at least a chance that a friend is very close by." He paused and smiled at his lover. "But I couldn't bring the idea to you until I knew it was as safe as I could make it. I don't ever want to do anything to put your career, happiness, or life in danger. You are my everything, Ah-Xue. Everything I do from this day on, I want it to be another brick I lay in the foundation that is our life together. My only goal is protecting us."

"Okay."

Song's heart stopped, and he was almost afraid that he'd imagined the single word leaving Ren's lips. "Okay?" he repeated because his brain had locked up.

Ren's face broke into the most fantastic grin. "Okay. Who do I call? Who do I give money to? I'm in. You couldn't stop me from being your neighbor."

"I—really?"

Ren laughed, but it was soft and a little choked with emotion. He released Song's hands to cup his face with one and wrap the other around Song's waist, pulling him in as close as possible. "Song Wei Li, you're not just offering me a home. You're giving me an entire family."

"A loud, crazy, nosy family," Song pointed out.

"But also a loving, supportive, accepting, protective family. There is no greater gift in all the world."

Song smirked. "Except for your love."

"And your love." Ren bent his head a tiny bit, closing the last inches between them.

The kiss was the sweetest, most perfect kiss in all of Song's life. Ren An Xue was his home, his happiness, his heart. And no matter what happened from this day on, there was no one else who could ever compare to his didi. His Ah-Xue.

A FINAL NOTE

Thank you so much for going on this journey with Song Wei Li and Ren An Xue.

This was a passion project I never expected to write, but I'm so glad that I could share Song and Ren's story with you. If you've enjoyed it, please leave a quick rating.

If you are interested in reading how Zhu Fang and Guo Zi fell in love, I'm excited to announce that their story, *Falling Like Snow*, will be coming in early 2023. You can pre-order it now!

Sign up for my newsletter at gkoibooks.com/newletter so you don't miss it!

GLOSSARY

Translations:
 Ah- – another way of denoting familiarity that is added to a single-syllable name, such as Ah-Xue

 Didi – younger brother, often used as a term of familiarity. Not necessarily an endearment and not necessarily someone who is related. Can sometimes be added to a name such as Xue-di. But be wary of xiao didi (slang term for penis)

 Gege – older brother, denotes familiarity and not necessarily a family relation. Can sometimes be added to a name such as Li-ge

 Gong – refers to the dominant or top in a relationship

 Jiejie – older sister and a mark of familiarity. In this novel, it is used to refer to the group of women who care for the actors in the makeup and wardrobe departments. Can sometimes be added to a name, such as Zhou-jie

 Lao – roughly translates to "old," meant to denote familiarity or friendship when added to a person's name

 Laopo – wife

 Laoshi – teacher/mentor, term of respect

CULTURAL REFERENCES

BL – boys' love, similar to MM romance, gay romance, yaoi, danmei

Booting ceremony – most Chinese shows have a tradition of holding a special ceremony to open the first official day of filming. Incense is burned, prayers said, and lots of press pictures taken

BTS – behind the scenes. Asia, and particularly Chinese productions, put out a lot of behind-the-scenes videos showing the actors just being people between scenes. Some are released by the production studio, while many are sneaked by fans. Helps to build buzz and can be highly addictive

CP – couple in a BL

Danmei – a genre in Chinese literature that focuses on romantic love between two men, same as BL (boys' love) in Japanese fiction and gay romance in America

Douyin - Chinesee TikTok

Hanfu – historical style of clothing of the Han people that is typically characterized by a long, flowing robe. Common style of dress for wuxia dramas

Red string of fate/Red thread of marriage – a popular myth throughout Asia that speaks of an invisible red cord that ties a person to their one true love (soul mate). In some myths, the thread is tied to an ankle on each person. In other myths, the thread is tied to a man's thumb and a woman's little finger. In modern times, more frequently seen on each person's little finger

WeChat – Chinese social media similar to Snapchat

Weibo – Chinese social media that is sort of a mix of Twitter and Instagram

Wire work – when actors are hooked into harnesses and wires, allowing them to fly or do fantastic martial arts feats

Wuxia – type of Chinese drama about the martial arts world that includes elements of magic and/or mysticism such as characters who can fly and heal each other. Typically revolves heavily around sects, clans, and politics

Xiaoguan – (small guan) headwear that is worn around the topknot and typically held in place with a hairpin to help stabilize the topknot

CAST LIST

(Surname, Given name)

Chen Junjie – popular actor up for role in *Legend*, friend of Song's

Guo Zi – popular singer, dancer, lead actor of *Frozen River*, dating Zhu Fang

Hua Jun Bai – male costar, major troublemaker but friend

Li Ming Tao – actor on *Legend*

Liu Haoyu – male costar, troublemaker

Ma Daiyu – female costar of *Legend*

Mo Bao Shi – Song's childhood friend and assistant

Ren An Xue – lead actor of *Legend*, dating Song Wei Li

Shen Ruo Xuan – lead actor of *Path of the Poison*, dating Yuan Teng Fei

Song Wei Li – singer and lead actor of *Legend*, dating Ren An Xue

Sun Jing – director of *Legend of the Lost Night*

Wu Dong Mei – Ren's new assistant

Yang Lan Fen – producer for *Legend*

Yuan Teng Fei – lead actor of *Path of the Poison*, dating Shen Ruo Xuan

CAST LIST

Zhou Yuying – Ren's manager

Zhu Fang – popular singer, lead actor of *Frozen River*, dating Guo Zi

NOTES

1. Wow. He's Beautiful

1. Wuxia – type of Chinese drama about the martial arts world that includes elements of magic and/or mysticism such as characters who can fly and heal each other. Typically revolves heavily around sects, clans, and politics.
2. Wire work – when actors are hooked into harnesses and wires, allowing them to fly or do fantastic martial arts feats.
3. Danmei - a genre in Chinese literature that focuses on romantic love between two men, same as BL (boys' love) in Japanese fiction and gay romance in America.
4. Didi – younger brother, often used as a term of familiarity. Not necessarily an endearment and not necessarily someone who is related. Can sometimes be added to a name such as Xue-di, but be wary of xiao didi (a slang term for penis).

2. Song and Smart Are No Longer Acquainted

1. Lao – roughly translates to "old," meant to denote familiarity or friendship when added to a person's name.
2. Laoshi – teacher/mentor, term of respect.
3. BL – boys' love, similar to MM romance, gay romance, yaoi, danmei.
4. Hengdian – an enormous studio lot in the city of Dongyang, Zhejiang Province, where many movies and TV shows are filmed

3. Would You Prefer If I Called You Ah-Xue?

1. Ah- – another way of denoting familiarity that is added to a single-syllable name, such as Ah-Xue.
2. Jiejie – older sister and a mark of familiarity. In this novel, it is used to refer to the group of women who care for the actors in the makeup and wardrobe departments. Can sometimes be added to a name, such as Zhou-jie.
3. Hanfu – historical style of clothing of the Han people that is typically characterized by a long, flowing robe. The style of dress is common for wuxia dramas.

NOTES

5. You Whispered It Right in My Ear

1. Booting ceremony – most Chinese shows have a tradition of holding a special ceremony to open the first official day of filming. Incense is burned, prayers said, and lots of press pictures taken.

6. A God with the Face of a Very Wicked, Very Tempting Demon

1. Gong – refers to the dominant or top in a relationship. In Chinese, the bottom is the shou. If you've read Japanese BL, the equivalent is the seme while the uke is the bottom or shou.

8. All Ren's Giggles Belong to Him

1. BTS – behind the scenes. Asia, and particularly Chinese productions, put out a lot of behind-the-scenes videos showing the actors just being people between scenes. Some are released by the production studio, while many are sneaked by fans. Helps to build buzz and can be highly addictive.

10. Don't Get Attached

1. Laopo – wife.
2. Gege – older brother, denotes familiarity and not necessarily a family relation. Can sometimes be added to a name such as Li-ge. Used by Zhu Fang as a term of familiarity and an endearment for his boyfriend, Guo Zi.

16. His Costar Is Going to Devour Him

1. Note: As a random tidbit, one common way for forming an endearment for a person in Chinese culture is to double a person's name. In this case, Zhu Fang becomes Fang Fang for Guo Zi. One show that I'm a fan of has a character named Teng Mu Ran, but his close friend and future fake boyfriend likes to call him Teng Teng.

17. Is This More than Friendship?

1. CP – couple in a BL.

22. Didi, That's a Good Thing

1. Weibo – Chinese social media that is sort of a mix of Twitter and Instagram.

28. Ah-Xue, Your Laopo Is Roasting!

1. Laopo – wife.
2. WeChat – Chinese social media similar to Snapchat.
3. Douyin – Chinese TikTok
4. Xiaoguan – (small guan) headwear that is worn around the topknot and typically held in place with a hairpin to help stabilize the topknot.

30. Ren Leaving Early?

1. Red string of fate/Red thread of marriage – popular myth throughout Asia that tells of an invisible red cord that ties a person to their one true love (soul mate). In some myths, the thread is tied to an ankle on each person. In other myths, the thread is tied to a man's thumb and woman's little finger. In modern times, more frequently seen on each person's little finger.

Made in the USA
Columbia, SC
29 October 2022